The Wolf's Gold

By the same author in the *Empire* series

Wounds of Honour
Arrows of Fury
Fortress of Spears
The Leopard Sword

The Wolf's Gold

Empire: Volume Five

ANTHONY RICHES

HODDER &
STOUGHTON

First published in 2012 by Hodder & Stoughton
An Hachette UK company

1

A CIP catalogue record for this title
is available from the British Library

Hardback ISBN 978 1 444 71186 8
Trade Paperback ISBN 978 1 444 71187 5
E-book ISBN 978 1 444 71189 9

Typeset in Plantin Light by Palimpsest Book Production Limited,
Falkirk, Stirlingshire

Printed and bound by Clays Ltd, St Ives plc

Hodder & Stoughton policy is to use papers that are natural, renewable
and recyclable products and made from wood grown in sustainable forests.
The logging and manufacturing processes are expected to conform to the
environmental regulations of the country of origin.

Hodder & Stoughton Ltd
338 Euston Road
London NW1 3BH

www.hodder.co.uk

For Carolyn

ACKNOWLEDGEMENTS

When I started musing on the idea of setting this book in Dacia, to take advantage of the appearance early in Commodus's reign of two of the three men who would contest for the throne after his murder, my eye was caught by one magic word. Gold. In seeking to understand mining's place in the imperial Roman economy, I purchased the excellent *Imperial Mines and Quarries in the Roman World* by Alfred Michael Hirt, which swiftly and efficiently outlined to me both the nature of imperial control over this vital prop of the empire's finances and the place that the mining colony of Alburnus Maior played in that grand scheme. I heartily recommend it to the reader with a thirst for historical detail, although I must warn you that it is a finely detailed academic publication and not a particularly light read. As before, my perception of the early 180s as a time period was strengthened by Anthony R. Birley's seminal *Septimius Severus: The African Emperor*. On the nature, weapons, tactics and organisation of the Sarmatians I was superbly well informed by Brzezinski and Mielczarek's *The Sarmatians: 600 BC – AD 450* in the ever invaluable Osprey Men at Arms series, another strongly recommended read which provides a powerful insight to this warrior people who gave Rome such a run for its money and ended up as an integral part of the empire. As for Dacia itself, I recommend *Dacia: Land of Transylvania, Cornerstone of Ancient Eastern Europe* by Ion Grumeza and *Roman Dacia* by Miller, Vandome and McBrewster, although the latter seems to be a handy collection of all the relevant articles to be found in Wikipedia – no bad thing, but worthy, like that source, of cautious treatment. As ever, all errors are down to me and me alone.

Domestically my support has been as steadfast (and uncompromising) as ever. Indeed the credit for this book's title must go to my wife Helen, whom I was boring half to death with last summer's beach musings, post completion of the *The Leopard Sword* (a completion effected whilst on holiday, not my finest domestic hour). 'It's a story about gold,' I told her, 'set in Dacia which actually means "the land of the wolf" . . .' My lovely wife simply looked at me over her sunglasses with that expression all men come to know only too well, said, 'Well, then, obviously it's *The Wolf's Gold*, isn't it?', then turned back to her crossword. Little did she know just how much that simple statement was to help me. My writing efforts have been greatly assisted by the acquisition of an internet-free bolthole on a local farm (and thus free from the constant distractions of share prices, firearms and sports cars), and my gratitude to Gini and Jonathan Trower for having the foresight to go looking for a tenant just as I was looking for a hiding place from distraction is boundless. And one day soon the temperature in The Old Hen House will get back over zero, I keep assuring myself. It would indeed be the splendidly stark writer's garret of legend if not for the twin luxuries of my invaluable coffee machine and the iPod dock on which Handel tinkles elegantly and Motörhead hammers thunderously (and all shades of the musical spectrum in between) depending on my mood and muse requirements.

Graham Lockhart continues to be the business partner who tolerates my overactive imagination and its demands, while Robin Wade and Carolyn Caughey, agent and editor respectively, continue to be the outwardly calm publishing professionals who wonder just what the hell their author is playing at in having a day job when he's contracted to deliver two books a year. Thanks to all of you for tolerating my megalomania.

Lastly, thank you to you, the reader, for picking up this book. The writer's vision is nothing without a mind for it to occupy for a short time and, for the loan of your grey matter for long enough to make Marcus and his supporting cast live somewhere other than my own feverish imagination, I am grateful.

Thank you.

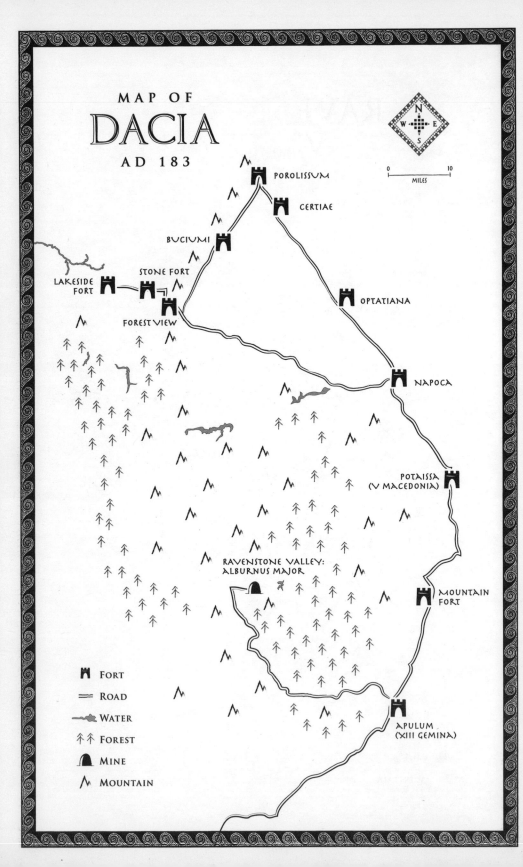

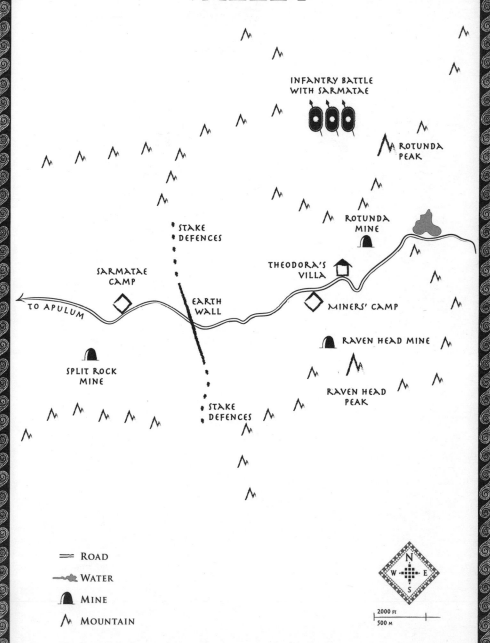

RAVENSTONE VALLEY

INFANTRY BATTLE
WITH SARMATAE

ROTUNDA
PEAK

ROTUNDA
MINE

STAKE
DEFENCES

SARMATAE
CAMP

THEODORA'S
VILLA

TO APULUM

EARTH
WALL

MINERS' CAMP

SPLIT ROCK
MINE

RAVEN HEAD MINE

RAVEN HEAD
PEAK

STAKE
DEFENCES

═══ ROAD

WATER

MINE

MOUNTAIN

N
W   E
S

2000 FT
500 M

Prologue

Dacia, March, AD *183*

A dog barked from the other end of the village, and in a heartbeat another half-dozen canine voices were raised in protest against whatever it was that had alerted the first animal. Snug in his straw nest beneath the house, warm and dry among livestock that had long since become accustomed to the boy's nocturnal presence, Mus smiled sleepily at the chorus of barking. Whatever it was that had set off the dogs would also have resulted in a storm of invective from the men of the surrounding houses, if his father's usual reaction was any indication. He wormed his way a little deeper into the straw, closing his eyes in anticipation of the dogs' protests at whatever nocturnal creature it was that had awoken them dying away into renewed silence.

With a sudden, piercing shriek that had the boy wide awake and sitting up startled in the straw, one of the dogs was silenced. It was a sound that Mus had heard once before, when their neighbour's animal had mauled his master's son and been rewarded with four feet of legion-issue gladius through its back. The dying animal had given out howls of agony in its death throes, struggling against the cold blade's implacable intrusion, until its owner had been forced to rip the sword loose and behead the writhing dog to silence its heart-rending cries. In the brief moment of shocked silence that followed, Mus knew that he had just heard something horribly similar. But who would take a blade to a guard dog for doing its job?

A renewed chorus of barking broke the silence, joined by a swelling sound of gruff voices as the men of the village spilled out from their homes armed with the swords that they had all retained on their retirement from the legion, despite the relative peace of the times. Mus heard his father's voice through the wooden boards above his head, reassuring the family that there was nothing to worry about even as the big man's footsteps thudded towards the door. And then the screaming started. Some of the raised voices were those of men fighting for their lives and losing that fight, the clash of iron overlaid with agonised groans and cries of pain and terror as they were killed and wounded, while others were the higher pitched screams of outrage from their women, howls of imprecation and hatred at whatever was happening down at the other end of the village.

'*Mus!*'

His oldest brother put his head through the hatch to the house's upper floor, and Mus called back to him.

'I'm here! What's—'

'Father says you're to stay there, and *not* to move!'

The head withdrew, and the boy heard the sound of heavy footsteps as his father and three older brothers hurried down the steps and ran towards the swelling sound of battle, the retired watch officer's voice raised to bellow encouragement to his former brothers in arms. Above him he heard the sound of lighter feet as his mother and sisters gathered in his parents' bed, the girls seeking comfort from the night's sudden terror. While he was tempted to run up the ladder and join them, he knew that his father would punish him when he returned to find his order had been disobeyed, and so stayed where he was, raising his head to stare through the narrow opening in the house's wall which served to admit daylight during the day. The view through the slit gave him little more understanding of the events that were unfolding in the village's lower portion than the evidence of his ears, but as he stared out into the dark village he realised what was behind the bobbing flames of torches advancing up the hill towards him.

Driving the remaining men of the village before them, a line of heavily armoured warriors was forcing the retired soldiers' last desperate defence back towards the settlement's higher end. The outnumbered defenders were bellowing their defiance even as they fought and died on the attackers' swords, their distantly remembered sword drills no match for younger men protected by armour and shields. Behind the line of shields, fires were taking hold of the houses already captured, and the howls of female hatred and anguish had become helpless screams of outrage.

As Mus watched in horror, he saw a powerfully built warrior stride out of the attack's line and single-handedly take a long sword to his brothers as the men behind him watched, expertly parrying a cut at his head before swinging the weapon to open the youngest boy's throat with the weapon's point. Sidestepping another furious hack from the oldest of the three, he smashed his shield into the boy's face, then lunged on one muscular thigh to stab his sword through his reeling defences and deep into his chest. As the last of Mus's brothers screamed and charged at him from one side, his spear stabbing out in a desperate attack, the big man simply sprang back from the lunge and allowed the weapon's point to flash uselessly past him, grabbing the shaft and jerking the child off balance. Laughing in the boy's face, he leaned in to deliver a crunching headbutt with his iron helmet, then turned away, leaving the men behind him to finish the semi-conscious child. The boys' father stormed out of the fray with his sword painted black, screaming bloody murder for revenge on his sons' killer.

Tossing aside his shield, the warrior faced the charging farmer with a swaggering confidence that chilled Mus. As his father leapt furiously into his attack, the warrior met the farmer blade to blade and parried the attacking blow wide before twitching his head to the left to avoid a punch that would have put him on his back. Again the helmeted head snapped forward, sending the older man staggering backwards with his nose broken and streaming blood, but the child's heart soared as his father shook his head and strode determinedly forward again. What happened next was almost too fast for him to understand, but the outcome was obvious enough. Parrying the second attack with equal ease to the first, the warrior snapped out a hand to catch the older man's punch and twisted the fist with what seemed effortless power, forcing him to the ground and stamping the sword's hilt from his hand. Putting his sword's blade to the fallen man's throat he stared about him until he found what he was looking for, his prisoner's terrified woman and daughters staring from the house's single window. As Mus watched in disbelief, the victorious warrior pulled the helpless veteran to his feet and dragged him towards the house, pushing him back down into the grass a dozen paces from his son's hiding place and pulling his head back with a hand knotted in his hair, shouting in his ear with a voice made harsh by anger.

'This is your house, old man?! You have women inside, cowering in their beds while you defend them?! My men will pull them out, and fuck them all here in front of you as the price for your resistance! And you will watch . . .'

He gestured to the men around him, waving them forwards, and they poured into the house in a thunder of boots on the boards above the boy's head, dragging his mother and sisters screaming in terror down the steps. Their leader gloated over the fallen farmer, holding his head up with the sword still at his throat and forcing him to watch, as the night clothes were torn from his women's bodies and they were dragged to the ground. Each of their victims was held down by a pair of men while their comrades swiftly mounted them, thrusting vigorously into their helpless bodies with triumphant grins and shouts of pleasure. Staring through the narrow window at his father's anguished face, as the destruction and defilement of his family played out before him, Mus realised that he was looking straight back into his son's eyes. Snapping a hand up from the ground the veteran soldier took hold of his captor's sword hand, forcing the blade away from his throat for long enough to shout one last order to the only member of his family not in the hands of their enemy.

'*Run, boy! Run, and keep running!*'

His captor released the grip on his hair and punched his head again, then ripped the sword's blade across his throat, pushing the dying man away from him and staring at the petrified child's face for a long moment. He screamed an order to his men while the farmer writhed in his death throes at his feet, pointing at the house. A pair of them ran for the steps, and with a shiver of fear Mus realised he had little time before his hiding place was revealed and he faced the same fate as his brothers. Around the house other dwellings were going up in flames, and the few remaining farmers were being slaughtered out of hand while their women were brutally violated by the rapacious groups who had dragged them from their homes. Coming to his senses as footsteps thundered on the steps above his head, he dived out of the straw's cocoon, rushing across the hard earth floor and squirming into a hole in the wooden rear wall which he had long used to escape the attentions of his older brothers. It was a tight fit, now that he was less the child than in those happier days, and he had to push one shoulder into the hole before contorting to ease the other through the gap, scratching his flesh badly in the process. He dragged himself out of the house, getting one foot through the hole and gathering himself to spring to his feet, but a voice shouted behind him and a hand gripped at his shoe, and Mus knew that his unseen pursuer only needed to grab his leg to pull him back through the hole. Struggling desperately, he pulled his foot from the rough boot he'd inherited from the youngest of his brothers a week before, still too big to fit his foot snugly. He scrabbled away on his hands and knees and then staggered onto his feet, running hard for the trees fifty paces distant across his mother's vegetable garden, and kicking off the other boot as he fled for the forest's sanctuary. The old tree that held up one side of the house was in flames, and in the lurid light of its incineration Mus looked back and saw the tall warrior pointing at him, bellowing an order at the men around him.

'Stop him!'

A spear arced over him, a flicker of polished iron in the darkness that thudded into the earth a dozen paces beyond, and an instant later another hissed past him so close that he stumbled with the shock of it and went down on one knee. Looking back he saw a dozen men and more boiling past the house with drawn swords, their shouts unintelligible but all too clear in their delight in the chase. A blaze of terror in the boy's mind gave him one last spurt of energy, and he sprinted the last twenty paces to the trees with his pursuers catching him fast, diving into the foliage with a grateful sob. The forest was as familiar to him in the night as it was by day, for it was here that he had usually come to hide and sulk when his brothers decided to work their frustrations out on him. Several discoveries and subsequent beatings at their hands had taught him very well how to evade capture once he was inside the forest's edge. Jinking to the left and right, his steps silenced by the carpet of needles on the forest's floor and his body made invisible in the long shadows, he slipped into the cover of a long-familiar cluster of trees. Burrowing into the midst of a bush in whose depths he had painstakingly picked out a hole large enough to accommodate his body, he became still, calming his breathing as he listened to the men blundering haplessly about in the darkness around him.

In the space between the house's blazing shell and the trees, the big man waited restlessly until his followers straggled back out of the forest, tapping his sword's blade impatiently against one booted foot. They lined up and waited nervously for him to speak, their eyes shining in the fire's ruddy light, waiting for the big man's verdict with the strained faces of men who already knew only too well what to expect.

'He escaped? A dozen of you, and one small child managed to get away?' He looked along their line with a sneer of disgust. 'You're all cursing your fate that you weren't lucky enough to find a woman to climb onto, and that you've ended up facing me as failures. And with good reason . . .' He turned back to their leader, nodding curtly. 'The usual. They can draw lots to see who pays for their failure. And make sure whoever it is dies cleanly, there's no need to turn an example into a spectacle.'

Striding away around the burning house he found his deputy waiting for him, and the older man fell in alongside him as they walked back down the slope through a scene of devastation, littered with the bloodied corpses of dead farmers lit by the blazing remnants of their homes. The women's initial screams were now reduced to moans and sobs of anguish as their degradation continued without any pause other than for one man to replace another. The big man looked about him with an expression of disgust.

'Let them have one hourglass Hadro, then beat them back into order. I want the animals butchered and salted by morning and every man ready to march. The women are to die, all of them without exception, and you are to ensure that there will be no witnesses. We seem to have allowed at least one small boy to escape, and I'll take no more risks. If any disobedience to this command is brought to light I'll have every man in the offender's tent party beaten to death. Understood?'

The first spear nodded, and when he spoke his Latin was hard-edged and guttural.

'As you wish, Prefect.'

I

Dacia, September, AD *183*

'You must avenge us, my son. The simple fact of your survival is not a sufficient response to the evil that festers at the heart of the empire, or to the gross indignities to which your mother and sisters were submitted before their deaths.'

Senator Appius Valerius Aquila shifted his seat with an expression of discomfort, clearly troubled by the painful joints that had beset him in the months before his son had left Rome for Britannia. In the shadows behind him his wife and daughters stood in silence, their partially visible faces free of any expression, and in the room's darkest recess Marcus wondered if he could see his younger brother standing in equal immobility, the child's features almost entirely lost in the gloom.

'Father, I cannot see—'

The old man raised an eyebrow, his face taking on that lofty patrician demeanour that his son had always found so forbidding.

'You cannot see a way to take revenge for our deaths, Marcus? You have a wife and son now, and responsibilities to the men under your command. You have discarded the name Valerius Aquila, and now live under the assumed name of Tribulus Corvus to avoid association with a family of traitors. A new life has opened itself to you, a life for which you are well skilled. And yet . . .'

Marcus swallowed nervously, unable to move a muscle under his father's scrutiny.

'And yet?'

'And yet, my son, all that you are now has only come about

as the result of what I made you. I took you as a baby, when my friend Gaius Calidius Sollemnis was unable to care for you.'

Marcus found Legatus Sollemnis's sword in his hand, its gold-eagle-head pommel gleaming faintly in the light of the single lamp that was struggling for life while the darkness pressed in all around. He spoke quickly, almost absurdly eager for some approval from the man who had raised him to adulthood.

'Father, I took revenge for the legatus after his betrayal by the praetorian prefect's son Titus. I pursued his murderer Calgus to the edge of the empire and beyond. I crippled him and left him for the wolves.'

'It was simple circumstance which gave you the gift of revenge for your birth father, my son. Retribution for the destruction of your true family cannot depend on Fortuna's whims. You must travel to the heart of the empire, and hunt down every man that took any part in our murder. Until you do this you will never be able to openly raise my grandson under our proud name of Valerius Aquila. Do you wish for him to grow to adulthood under an assumed name? But worse than *that* stain on our honour, you will be forever at the mercy of the conscience that I worked so hard to instil in you while you were still young. Think back, Marcus, past the skill at arms I had the gladiator and the soldier pummel into you until you were a match for either of them with sword or fist. Do you not remember our discussions on the subjects of ethics and philosophy?'

Marcus nodded, reaching for the deeply buried memory of the challenging conversations in which he had for a long time felt more an audience than a participant, as the old man had outlined his own beliefs and values.

'Yes.'

'Then you know only too well that to turn your face from this crime will *not* stand. Only in Rome will you find the men who must be punished for our deaths.'

The darkness was deepening around his family with stealthy inevitability now, and his brother was utterly lost to view. Even as he stared at his mother with a longing to hear her voice one last time, she too sank back into the gloom, leaving only his father's near invisible presence on the couch before him.

'Only in Rome, Marcus . . .'

He woke with a start, and Felicia stirred from her sleep alongside him, her voice edged with concern.

'What is it?'

Marcus put an arm around her, cupping a breast in the way they usually lay before sleep came for them both.

'It was the dream again. Nothing more . . .'

Her body tensed against his.

'My love . . .'

He kissed her ear with a gentle smile.

'I know. I remember your diagnosis. My sleeping mind has found some way to subvert the control I have established over my emotions, and is using images from my former life to conduct some manner of grieving that I cannot indulge in any other way. Although I expect that a priest would tell me that the dreams are sent by Morpheus at the behest of Mithras, who would have me follow a soldier's path to take my revenge.'

She snorted softly into the room's darkness and reached over her shoulder to tap his forehead.

'The problem lurks in here, my love. You must allow yourself to mark the passing of your family in an appropriate manner. Until you do you will continue to be haunted by these ghosts from your previous life, the life you have not yet fully allowed to die.'

He kissed her neck, squeezing his body against her back.

'I know. I will, when the time is right . . .'He cupped the other breast, rubbing his fingers gently across her nipples. 'And now, given that the baby is still asleep . . .'

Later, as they lay together listening to the sounds of the camp coming to life, he held her tightly and mused inwardly upon the dream, just as he had done before several other dawns along the length of the empire's northern frontier.

'Mark the passing of my family in an appropriate manner? Never

*was a truer word spoken, my love. But the time and place is not here
and now, it will be at some time in the future which is not yet clear
to me. But the time will come, of that I am quite sure. And the place?'*
His father's words from the dream echoed in his mind. *'Only in
Rome . . .'*

'So we've marched all this way to protect a fucking mountain?'
The Fifth Century's standard bearer glanced around at the peaks
to either side of the road and spat in front of his boots. 'Gods
below, but we attract every shitty job going, don't we? Got a cold,
wet quarry that needs watching in case some stray barbarians
fancy carrying off the stone? Just send the bloody Tungrians,
they're stupid enough to do anything they're told!'

He shook his head, changing hands on his standard's shaft.

'We can only hope they've got a decent whorehouse up there,
or we'll have come all this way to no purpose whatsoever. Mind
you . . .' Shaking his head ruefully, he glanced back at his audience, the column of men marching four abreast behind him. 'The
sort of woman who's made it this far into the mountains isn't
likely to be big on the softer side of the profession. And I really
hate it when the mattress thrasher sucking my cock can tickle my
balls with her beard.'

Marcus shook his head at his standard bearer's diatribe as he
marched up the road alongside the stocky veteran, resolving as
ever not to rise to the older man's habitual bitter complaint at
any hint of hardship. Eighteen months as Morban's centurion had
taught him that while the twenty-five-year veteran could be
silenced for a moment or two, he rarely relinquished the subject
of his ire for very long. One of the soldiers slogging along in the
ranks behind them raised his voice from the safe anonymity of
the men around him to further provoke the standard bearer.

'There'll be no proper beer neither, eh Morban?'

Catching Marcus's glare the standard bearer wisely held back
his reply, tipping his head to listen for the sound he expected and
softly counting down as he waited.

'Five, four, three, two—'

An incensed bellow from behind them made both men start, despite the fact they had both been expecting it. Marcus exchanged a glance with Morban as Quintus, his chosen man, unleashed a tirade of irritated abuse in the general direction of the anonymous soldier.

'I've a bloody good idea which one of you apes opened his mouth just then, and when I find out exactly who it was you'll be wishin' you never joined up! I'll have you on extra duties for so long your dick will have withered away before you get to do anything better with it than play jerk the gherkin! I'll break my fuckin' pole on your back, and then I'll—'

'Call for another one, will you Quintus?'

The standard bearer's voice was quiet enough that only Marcus heard him, and the chosen man bellowed his challenge into the cold mountain air.

'I'll fuckin' call for another one! That's what I'll do!'

The standard bearer smirked at his officer.

'That's five times today. Morban wins again.'

Ignoring his centurion's raised eyebrow, he cleared his throat and put an end to his colleague's tirade by roaring out the first line of a marching song that had been sung a lot over the previous few weeks, as the Tungrian cohorts had marched the length of the empire's northern frontier along the Rhenus and Danubius rivers.

'*I got five by selling my cloak . . .*'

He paused momentarily to allow the century's soldiers to join in, drowning out their chosen man's indignant voice as they belted out the song in fine style.

> '*. . . five more by selling my spear,*
> *the final five by selling my shield,*
> *that's fifteen fucks, my dear!*'

He winked at his centurion as the men behind them drew breath for the song's chorus, and Marcus was unable to resist a wry smile in return. His standard bearer and chosen man were at daggers drawn for most of the time, and Morban took any and every opportunity to get the advantage in their uneasy relationship.

> *'Fifteen, fourteen, thirteen, twelve,*
> *eleven fucks, my dear,*
> *and when we get to ten fucks,*
> *then I'm stopping for a beer!'*

Marcus stopped marching and stepped off the road, watching the passing soldiers with his hands on the hilts of the swords that had long since earned him the nickname 'Two Knives'. The cohort's centuries ground wearily past him up the long road, whose course twisted and undulated with the valley's floor as it climbed towards the mist-covered peaks that were their objective for the day.

'Having fun yet, young 'un?'

Nodding in reply to his colleague Otho's greeting, and laughing at the wink that creased the older man's seamed and battered face as the cohort's Seventh Century marched past, Marcus stretched his back as he looked down the column's length. Taking a moment to enjoy the sun's warmth on his face, he pushed his shoulders back and rotated his head to work out some of the stiffness in his neck. His body, already wiry with corded muscle from the effort of routinely carrying fifty pounds of weapons and armour on his back day after day, had been exercised to the point of perfection by three months on the long road from Fortress Bonna in Germania Inferior. He looked around him at the towering hills on every side of the road's long straight ribbon, shading his brown eyes against the afternoon sun with a long-fingered hand and musing on the mountainous land around them for a long moment before his reverie was interrupted.

'Still having problems with dear old Quintus are you then? I could hear him shouting from here, and we've reached that point in the day when even the hardest of chosen men are usually hanging from their chinstraps with the rest of us.'

He started walking again as the Eighth Century's centurion passed him, shaking his head ruefully at his friend's question.

'What do *you* think, Dubnus? Mithras knows you were hard enough when you were my chosen man back in Britannia, but you were always fair enough with the men. Yes, you were as harsh with them as you had to be when they needed it, but even *you* knew when to let them have a little slack in their collars.'

The big man acknowledged the point with a nod, scratching at the skin beneath his heavy beard and flicking sweat from his fingers.

'Whereas Quintus . . .'

'Never seems to give them a moment's grace. Every tiny misdemeanour, all the usual silly little things that soldiers do, it all has him screaming at them as if they're recruits rather than battle-hardened soldiers. Quite how Julius used to put up with it baffles me.'

His friend gave him a sideways glance.

'Julius never had any problem with it, Marcus. He didn't get the nickname "Latrine" without good reason, he really can be full of shit when he thinks it's necessary . . .' He paused significantly. 'And he thinks it's necessary most of the time. Not that I don't love him like a brother, but when I was *his* chosen man, before I was set to turning you from a snot-nosed youngster into a half-decent centurion, he regularly used to tell me I wasn't hard enough on his men. So when I was transferred to command your old century last year he took his chance and appointed Quintus for the job.'

Marcus nodded unhappily.

'And now I have to deal with the consequences. I can't demote the man, not without good reason . . .'

'Which you can be sure he'll never give you. He may be a bit of an arsehole, but to be fair he is all soldier.'

'And I probably can't persuade him to be any more lenient.'

Dubnus nodded again.

'You're more likely to persuade Morban to stop gambling. Or drinking. Or whor—'

'*Yes*. So I'll just have to put up with it, I suppose.' Marcus sighed, looking up the column's line at the peaks rising before them. 'At least this incessant marching is coming to an end, if only for a few days.'

Dubnus snorted.

'Yes, but at the price of being perched on top of a mountain with only a bunch of miners and goats for company. That, and any women who've made their way up here in search of either gold or marriage. Although they're likely to be about as good looking as the goats.'

His friend smiled.

'Morban was telling me as much only a moment ago. I'm going to drop down the column and see how Qadir's treating my old century.'

Dubnus laughed.

'In that case you can expect to be getting the cow's eyes from Scarface. I hear he's still telling anyone stupid enough to listen to him quacking on about it just how wrong it was that you didn't take a few picked men with you when Julius put you in charge of the Fifth Century. A few picked men including him and his mate Sanga, of course.'

Marcus shrugged.

'When Julius appointed me to lead his old century he made it clear that I wasn't to try stripping the good men out of the Ninth. I was lucky to take my standard bearer with me, although that might be a strange new definition of the word 'lucky'. Julius told me that there wasn't any need to bring anyone else with me, since I was inheriting "the best bloody century in the cohort". He also mentioned that "the First Spear wouldn't have liked it" if I were to even consider moving men between centuries.'

Dubnus pursed his lips.

'Yes, well I wish he'd stop invoking his predecessor's name whenever he wants to justify something. "Don't allow your men to slack off the march pace, the First Spear wouldn't have liked it."'

Marcus grinned back at him, surprised to find himself appreciating his friend's humour given the trauma of their former senior centurion's recent death in Germania.

'Indeed. "Don't drink too much of that red, the First Spear wouldn't have liked it."'

Dubnus smirked, miming a cup at his lips.

'When we all know very well that Sextus Frontinius would have been guzzling it just as fast as the rest of us.'

Marcus sighed.

'I know he's just doing his best to keep our chins up, but all the same it's time to let Uncle Sextus go, I'd say. Anyway, I'm going to see how the Ninth are doing.'

Marcus stepped back off the road again and waited until his former century drew level with him, falling in alongside their centurion with a nod of greeting. The men were good friends, and for a while they shared a companionable silence amid the jingle of equipment and the rattle of hobnailed boots that routinely accompanied them on the march, until the century's standard caught his eye.

'That thing's clearly been polished to within an inch of its life. It must be a shock for the poor thing after so long under Morban's version of cleaning.'

Qadir nodded solemnly, his reply couched in the cultured terms that had deceived more than one soldier into mistaking him for a soft touch.

'My standard bearer spent a long time in Morban's shadow, as you may recall. He seems to enjoying his moment in the sun, so to speak.'

The man in question, a lanky individual who had been Marcus's trumpeter when he'd commanded the Ninth Century, nodded respectfully to his former centurion, and Marcus found himself smiling back at the man.

'I'd imagine you're still missing Morban, eh, Standard Bearer? Who else is going to keep you sharp with a never-ending flow of complaints, insults and dirty stories, or lighten your purse for you whenever it gets too heavy for comfort?'

Qadir nodded with a wry smile.

'The Ninth Century is certainly a different place without him. Sometimes I find myself missing his continual flow of nonsense and incitement to gambling . . .'

'But the other nine-tenths of the time?'

'Exactly. Blessed peace, and straightforward soldiering for the most part, only broken by the occasional grumbling every time *one* of my soldiers catches sight of you in front of the Fifth.'

He raised his voice for the last comment, making sure the men behind could hear him, and Marcus raised an eyebrow in mock surprise.

'Really? I'd have thought even Scarface would have got over his disappointment at not having to soldier under the tender mercies of my chosen man by now.'

Marching in his usual place a few ranks behind his former and present centurions, the soldier Scarface kept a dignified silence, although he muttered a quiet aside to his mate Sanga once the two men had returned to their conversation about whatever it was that centurions discussed.

'Cruel, that was. Very cruel.'

Sanga shrugged minutely under the weight of his spears, shield, helmet, mail shirt and pack pole, his head thrown back to suck in the cold mountain air.

'So perhaps now you'll be happy to let "Two Knives" take care of his own life, eh, without your having to run round after him all the time?'

Scarface's gaze remained locked on the back of Marcus's head.

'Not right that we shouldn't be allowed to go with him to the Fifth, not right at all . . .'

Sanga shook his head in disgust and fell silent, concentrating on carrying half his own body weight up the road's unremitting incline while his tent mate grumbled away to himself.

Qadir looked out at the mountains to either side for a moment before speaking again, his face creased in a gentle smile.

'At least this far from Britannia there's little danger of anyone having even heard the name Marcus Valerius Aquila. We may not be happy at having been sent east, but at least you'll be able to stop worrying about any further attempt to apprehend you, eh Centurion *Corvus*?'

Marcus nodded, his face softening at the thought.

'It had crossed my mind. Although I'm also forced to conclude that I'm exchanging the chance to be free from pursuit for the likelihood that I'm taking my wife and child into a war. I don't think we've been sent all this way east just to make the numbers up.' Hearing the heavy thud of hoofs on the road's grass verge he turned to see a handful of horsemen cantering up the long column of soldiers. 'And as if to prove me right, it seems that our mounted squadron is about to be allowed off their rope.'

The leading rider reined his horse in alongside the pair, grinning down at them with undisguised glee from beneath his crested decurion's helmet, whose polished face mask was raised to allow him a full field of view.

'Greetings brothers! The time has come for the "First Tungrian Horse" to prove its value once more. After weeks of nothing better than plodding along coughing up the dust raised by your flat feet, we are ordered to scout forward up the road as far as the turn for the mine. The tribune suspects that this country may harbour any number of barbarian scouts, and so bids me ride out to give them the opportunity for some practice with their bows. Since I have permission to seek your participation in this perilous mission, purely in order to improve the odds of my survival by providing the enemy with a wider variety of suitable targets, I've taken the liberty of saddling your usual mounts for the trip. Will you give both your feet and noses a rest by accompanying us on our ride?'

Marcus looked at Qadir, the Hamian's response a shrug of feigned disinterest. Looking up at the grinning decurion, the Roman raised an eyebrow.

'It's tempting, Silus, although it appears that you've saddled that monster Bonehead for me once again, despite your repeated accusations that the poor animal lacks the appropriate discipline for a cavalry horse. And is that the tribune's man Arminius I can see towards the back of your scouting party, clinging to his horse's mane as if it were a handle made of iron?'

The big German, mounted on a heavily built animal judged to be the only beast in the cohort's cavalry detachment capable of carrying his weight without breaking down, scowled at Marcus from the party's rear.

'I can hear you, Centurion, and whilst nothing would make me happier than getting down from this animal now and never remounting a horse in all my remaining years, you know the blood debt I owe you. When my master gives these men leave to take you into harm's way, I have no choice but to accompany them alongside you.'

Silus grimaced, leaning down from his saddle to speak in Marcus's ear.

'Between you and I, even that big bugger Colossus is starting to look a bit resentful at having to carry all that weight around. It's a good thing your man Lugos doesn't have a hankering to follow you into the shit quite so eagerly, or we'd no horses left standing inside a week. So, will you join us, or are you minded to give your German an excuse to dismount?'

Marcus shrugged up at Silus, holding out a hand.

'Very well, Decurion, since I have no option but to respect Arminius's example, I presume you stopped at the medical wagon to pester my wife for my helmet?'

The horseman grinned even wider, raising his left hand from behind his mount's side to display the masked cavalry helmet Marcus had purchased in Tungrorum for the purposes of deceiving the followers of the bandit leader Obduro, much to Felicia's disgust when she had discovered the price he'd paid for its fine workmanship. The Roman took off his centurion's helmet and passed it to Qadir with a wink.

'Can you think of a soldier who might be sufficiently careful to be entrusted with this? I'll take his shield and one of his spears in return.'

The Hamian nodded, dropping back a few ranks and handing the crested helmet to the soldier Scarface, taking one of his spears and helping him to pull the shield from its place strapped to his back.

'There you go, soldier, you're trusted with the centurion's helmet until he comes back from scouting with the cavalry.'

Scarface took the additional burden with a solemn nod, ignoring the guffaws of the men around him, and watched as Marcus and Qadir mounted the horses Silus had saddled for them and rode away up the road's gentle slope.

'Perhaps carrying that lump of iron for the next few hours will teach you to wind your bloody neck in . . .' Sanga fell silent when he realised that his comrade wasn't listening to a word he was saying, but staring down at the helmet with an expression of pride. 'And then again perhaps not . . .'

The horsemen rode forward for a mile or so on the road's hard surface, their horses' hoofs clattering loudly in the silence that hung over the wooded hills to either side. Silus looked back down the road to be sure they were sufficiently well ahead of the marching column of infantrymen, and then waved a hand at the wooded slopes.

'Time to get off the road and make a bit less noise, gentlemen, we're sticking out like tits on a bull as it is. Keep your eyes and ears open for anything out of the ordinary.'

The horsemen separated into two parties, each half a dozen strong, and rode their horses onto the strips of cleared ground on either side of the road before reining them in to a walk so that their hoofs would be almost silent in the long grass. Qadir steered his beast alongside Marcus's big grey, the graceful chestnut mare's finely drawn lines a stark contrast to the warhorse, while Arminius's mount fell in behind them at the German's urging. The three men talked quietly as the patrol ghosted forward up the road's margins, until Arminius suddenly frowned and wrinkled his nose.

'Do you smell that?'

Marcus inhaled deeply, discerning the very slightest edge of a familiar aroma on the air.

'Woodsmoke. And burning fat.'

Qadir nodded, waving a hand to Silus and putting a finger to his nose as Marcus bent to pull his shield from the grey's flank. As the decurion nodded his understanding an arrow flicked out of the trees fifty paces to their front, snapping past the Roman's head with a whistle of flight feathers. Flicking down the helmet's polished face mask he spurred the grey into action, dropping his spear from the vertical carrying position to point forward, knowing that the sight of its long blade would be enough to spark the big horse's customary berserk charge. A second arrow flew from the trees, its flight a blur of motion that ended with a clang as the missile's iron head glanced from his facemask's many-layered protection. The impact's force knocked his head to one side, momentarily blurring his vision. Raising the shield across his body the Roman rose in the saddle by tensing his thigh muscles against the grey's flanks, hefting the spear in readiness to throw. The hidden bowman loosed another shot, aiming for horse rather than rider this time, and Marcus felt the beast shudder with the blow, but the animal's pace was unaffected as it thundered towards the archer's hiding place. Rising to run rather than stand his ground for a final shot, the enemy scout presented Marcus with a fleeting target as the grey hammered past the spot from which the tribesman had watched the horsemen approach, but his hurled spear flew past the fleeing archer with a venomous power born of his anger at his horse's wound and missed by an arm's length.

Pulling the grey up he raised a leg over the saddle's horns to slide from the horse's back, landing on his feet and drawing his long sword as he strode furiously into the trees behind his raised shield, acutely aware that the layered board's protection was largely illusory against a bow at such short range. In front of him the scout was still dodging through the trees, but seeming to stagger slightly as he ran, one side of his body sagging as if he were a puppet with a string missing. He abruptly stopped running, staggering to a halt and standing still for a moment, swaying on his feet, one hand clenching and unclenching around the shaft of an arrow that dangled unnoticed at his side. Marcus stepped in close, his eyes narrowed in anticipation of a further ambush, raising the long bladed spatha to make the easy kill even as he wondered at such suicidal behaviour. The enemy scout turned, his feet dragging through the fallen pine needles like a sleepwalker's, and the look on his face stayed the Roman's hand as he stared with horrified fascination. Momentarily considering the masked centurion before him with empty, glassy eyes, his mouth hanging open to release a thin stream of bloody spittle, the barbarian slowly raised the arrow he was holding until it was in front of his face and emitted a high pitched moan of distress. Marcus watched in wonder as he realised that his intended victim's legs were shaking hard enough to make his whole body shudder uncontrollably. With a long groaning exhalation of his fear and despair, the archer toppled backward onto the forest's needle-strewn floor and lay twitching, soiling his breeches as he shook spasmodically.

Bending to examine the seemingly helpless man more closely, the young centurion held his sword ready to strike as he pushed the barbarian onto his back with a booted foot. The scout's eyes were pinned wide, their pupils shrunk to the size of tiny dots as he stared sightlessly up at the Roman, and the arrow spilled from his nerveless hand, the shaft's last fingernail length painted a deep and ruddy red. Bending closer to look at something that caught his eye on the man's arm, Marcus heard the faintest of noises, the creak of a bow being drawn back, and used the split second's warning to thrust his shield forward toward the tiny fragment of sound. An arrow slammed into the board with enough power to punch clean through the layers of wood and linen, only stopping when the heavy iron head impacted on his mail shirt's iron rings with a hard rap. A powerful stench of something rotting filled Marcus's nostrils, and he rolled away from the spot into the shelter of a tree, calling out to Silus: 'There's another one here! Flank him!'

The Tungrian troopers advanced into the trees to either side, shouting to each other as they sought to trap the second archer in an enveloping movement, but in a scatter of twigs the man was up and running to Marcus's right faster than the dismounted Tungrians could follow. As the Roman watched through the trees, his ambusher vaulted onto a waiting horse and bolted for the road, looking to make his escape before the Tungrians could remount. Pushing up the cavalry helmet's facemask and fighting his way back out of the undergrowth, Marcus almost blundered into Qadir as the Hamian coolly nocked an arrow to his heavy framed hunting bow and pulled the missile back until its flight feathers were level with his ear. Qadir waited patiently as the scout's horse crashed through the undergrowth towards the road, allowing a slow exhalation of breath to trickle from his lips as he readied himself for the shot. Bursting from the trees, the rider whipped his mount to a gallop, crouching low over the animal's neck to present a smaller target, and for a moment Marcus wondered if his friend might hold back the shot for fear of hitting the horse. Qadir leaned forward a fraction, his eyes narrowing in concentration, then loosed the arrow and lowered the weapon, making no attempt to reach for another. Struck cleanly in the square of his back the barbarian scout arched convulsively, toppling over his horse's hindquarters and smashing down hard onto the road's cobbled surface.

Walking forward with his shield raised against any further attempt at ambush, his nose wrinkling at the fetid smell from the bone arrowhead still poking through a long split in the wooden board, Marcus watched the trees to either side warily. Reaching the fallen rider he prodded the man's arm with a toe, sliding it away from the long knife sheathed on the man's belt.

'No need. He's as good as dead.' Glancing up, he found Silus approaching with a look of disgust. 'It's a shame. I'd like to have shared a few quiet moments with him to discuss this . . .'

The decurion reached out and broke the shaft of the arrow stuck through Marcus's shield, pulling out the barbed head and sniffing at it. Pulling a face, he held the offending missile at arm's length and called for an empty feed sack.

'Poisoned?'

The cavalryman nodded grimly at Marcus's question, wrapping the arrowhead in several layers of sacking before snapping it from the shaft and knotting the little package closed.

'Here, it'll be a souvenir for you. Just don't cut yourself with it.' He kicked the dying man hard in the head, his face white with anger. 'No, let the fucker lie here and die as slowly as he likes. And if you've got any problem with that, you'd better go back and see the state your horse is in.'

Marcus started guiltily and hurried back to where the big grey lay rigid on the verge with its legs sticking stiffly out from its body, trembling violently and rolling its eyes in terror while Arminius and Qadir stood over it, turning to greet Marcus with shaking heads. A single arrow protruded from the horse's right shoulder, its shaft painted the same deep red as the one in the dying archer's open hand. A froth of foam was trailing from the animal's open mouth, every shallow exhalation of breath accompanied by a soft groan as the arrow's poison tore at the horse's innards. Shaking his head in sorrow Marcus squatted beside the horse's head, stroking the long face gently as he pulled a hunting knife from its place on his belt. The blade was almost supernaturally sharp, one of a dozen he had paid a swordsmith to forge and edge with metal from the Damascus steel sword he'd taken from the bandit Obduro in Tungrorum. To his brother officers' great delight he had given them all one of the resulting blades, although whether he had managed to neutralise the evil he had sensed in the sword from his first touch of its hilt by doing so, or simply distributed it more widely, he was unable to tell. Tracing a hand down the horse's throat he put the knife to the beast's sweat-slickened neck and made a single fast cut, opening the veins hidden beneath the twitching flesh and staring down with a sad smile as a stream of hot blood poured out onto the ground.

'Farewell, Bonehead. You were a good mount.'

Waiting until the horse's eyes closed he stood, wiping and sheathing the knife with a regretful sigh.

'Properly done, brother. We'll make a cavalryman of you yet.' Silus turned away from the dead animal, shaking his head at the waiting troopers standing around him. 'We won't be eating horse tonight, not unless you lot want to risk meat with enough poison in it to knock this big sod over in less than a hundred heartbeats.'

Marcus walked into the trees and found the spot where the first archer was stretched out in his death agonies, cutting his throat with a single expert pass of the knife's fearsome blade and picking up the quiver of arrows that lay beside him. Bending close to the corpse, he saw that the mark on the man's arm which had drawn his attention briefly during the fight was a scratch, the skin discoloured around the small wound. He went back to the spot on the road where the scout was slowly expiring under Qadir's impassive stare.

'Kill him. He's not going to give us anything that's not already obvious from their presence here, and if I'll do it for a horse then I owe him the same dignity.' He handed the Hamian the quiver, waving a hand at the dying man before them. 'You'd better collect his arrows as well. They may come in handy, and I'd rather not leave them lying about here. And watch out for the ones with the red paint, the slightest puncture will kill a man, from the looks of it.'

He walked on up the road's gentle slope until he reached the place where the dying man's mount had come to a halt after its rider had toppled from the saddle. The horse was cropping contentedly at the verge's grass without any apparent concern, and the Roman walked slowly towards it, speaking soft words of reassurance as he advanced with unhurried care until he was within touching distance of the beast. Reaching out slowly and carefully he took hold of the horse's reins, stroking its flank and blowing in its ear.

'Here. Give her this.'

Silus tossed the Roman an apple, wrinkled from a long time in the store but still tasty enough, and the horse took it off his palm with an eagerness that had the other horsemen snorting with laughter. Silus whistled at his pay and a half, and the soldier threw him another apple with a resigned look.

'They think I'm soft on the horses, and in truth they're right, but how can any man resist that?' The animal was nudging at Marcus with its snout, nostrils flaring at the prospect of another treat, and the decurion held out the apple before standing back for a proper look at his comrade's new mount. 'She's nothing fancy, not a looker, but I'll bet you good money that beast will run all day and get by on a few mouthfuls of grass when she has to. What will you call her, since the previous owner didn't have time to discuss the finer details?'

Marcus laughed, staggering backwards slightly as the horse nudged him again, and held out the apple in surrender.

'Here, take it before you tread on my foot.' He grinned ruefully at Silus, nodding at the decurion's knowing look. 'Her name? I'm tempted to call her "Gobbler", but that would hardly be fitting for an animal bred for war. Let's see how she works out before saddling her with anything premature . . .'

Both men turned to look back down the road as a horn blared distantly, watching as the Tungrian cohort's leading century came into view around the shoulder of the mountain looming over them to the west. Silus turned to his men, barking orders.

'Get into the trees and gather firewood. Once the grunts have staggered past us we'll put poor old Bonehead to the torch, as much to spare his dignity as for the protection of any animal that decides to dine on his body.' He raised an eyebrow at Marcus. 'And you, Centurion Two Knives, had better go and meet with your superiors and warn them that we're marching into a fight.'

First Spear Julius looked with professional dismay at the scene before him as his leading century crested the road's last ridge, and came into view of the mining settlement they had been sent to protect. After a moment he shook his head at the sight opening up before him, an apparently disorganised sprawl of buildings that littered the valley floor as if some distracted god had flung a straggling handful of settlements to earth with no care as to where they fell. The valley ran east for another mile or so before the mountain that reared up at its far end closed it off like the bowl of a gigantic amphitheatre. His superior officer, a tall man with a wiry build that had initially deceived the Tungrians into believing he was unsuited to combat, laughed at the look of disgust on his senior centurion's face.

'So this is the Ravenstone valley, eh? Not up to much, is it Julius? I know what you're thinking – is this why we were sent up here from Apulum without so much as time for a cup of wine in the officers' mess?'

Julius had not yet got over the indifference with which the Thirteenth Legion's broad stripe tribune had treated them at the Apulum fortress's gate. He'd passed on his legatus's orders for the three-cohort-strong detachment to march on into the mountains with the disdain of a patrician ordering a slave to clean out his toilet, and had allowed them no more of a pause in their march than had been required for a cohort of disgruntled Thracian archers to be chivvied out of their barracks and tagged on to the column.

'You know what they say, Julius? If you can't take a joke then you shouldn't have joined up.' Tribune Scaurus smiled at the dismay on the other man's face as Julius found himself on the butt end of one of his own favourite jibes. 'So, disappointed with what you see, are you, First Spear? Afraid you won't find enough drinking dens and whorehouses for your liking, or had you forgotten that you've a woman to keep you away from all those distractions now?'

The senior centurion shook his head without losing the look of disgust as he took in the scattered buildings spread across the valley before them.

'It's not that, Tribune. Annia would have my balls off with a blunt and rusty spoon if I even considered such a thing. Although now that you mention it, given that we've been on the road for the best part of three months, the men are going up the wall for the want of some entertainment. No, what's bothering me is the lack of defensive preparation.'

The tribune nodded, his eyes roaming the scene unfolding before them as they marched up the valley with professional interest.

'Agreed. So what would you make our priorities, if you were my colleague Domitius Belletor?'

Julius's reply required little time for consideration.

'A wall. Something tall enough to keep unfriendly tribesmen from mobbing us. That, and I'd want to be sure that I had control of the heights.'

Scaurus nodded his agreement and then raised a hand to point at a figure advancing down the road towards them, the man's legion uniform complemented by a staff held in his right hand where a soldier would normally have carried a spear.

'Ignoring the fact that an enemy warband might well keep us a good deal more occupied than we'd like, if it's entertainment you want I suspect this gentleman may hold the answer. I suggest you stop the column so that we can find out what it is he has to say to us.'

The lone soldier marched purposefully up to the two officers and snapped off a smart salute, coming to attention with a vigour and precision that raised eyebrows among the veteran troops at Julius's back. On closer inspection the first spear realised that the legionary's staff was in fact a standard, albeit one of a type he'd never seen before, the shaft of a spear with a strangely ornate head that seemed to have no obvious military function.

'Greetings Tribune, Centurion. Welcome to the Ravenstone valley, and to the mining facility of Alburnus Major.' His blue eyes darted to both of them in turn, giving each man a swift perusal with a glance that seemed both open and calculating. 'I am Cattanius, a soldier of the Thirteenth Gemina Legion and beneficiarius to the legion's legatus, sent to assist with the arrival of your detachment. You are the tribune commanding this force, I presume, sir?'

Scaurus stepped forward, returning Cattanius's salute.

'Gaius Rutilius Scaurus, tribune commanding the First and Second Tungrian Cohorts, but not, I should point out, the commander of this detachment.' He jerked a thumb over his shoulder at the long column of soldiers waiting under the mid-afternoon sun. 'My colleague Domitius Belletor has overall command of our combined force. If you look down the column you will doubtless see a man on a horse coming to see what it is that has prompted this unscheduled stop. But since he will take a moment or two to reach us, perhaps we could pass that time by discussing a few topics of interest to me and my first spear here? And stand at ease man, there's no need for ceremony.'

Cattanius relaxed a little.

'What would you like to know, sir?'

Scaurus smiled wryly.

'You could start by enlightening us as to why we find this precious imperial asset apparently stripped of any military presence. Surely one of the Dacian legions' main tasks is to keep this place safe, given its critical importance to the province?'

The legionary nodded earnestly.

'Indeed it is, Tribune. If it weren't for the threat from the Sarmatae there would be a full cohort in the barracks, but Legatus Albinus decided to concentrate his forces—'

Scaurus raised an eyebrow.

'Albinus?'

Cattanius nodded quickly.

'Yes, sir. Legatus Clodius Albinus, officer commanding the Thirteenth Legion, and my beneficium.'

The tribune nodded, his demeanour outwardly unchanged, although Julius wondered if he had imagined the slight narrowing of his superior officer's eyes when Cattanius had first mentioned the legatus's name.

'I see. My apologies. Do continue.'

'Yes, sir. The legatus decided that in light of the Sarmatae threat—'

Julius raised a hand to stop him again.

'You've mentioned that name twice now. Exactly who or what are the Sarmatae?'

Cattanius stooped, using his finger to draw a half-circle whose circumference pointed upwards in the dust at their feet, running a wavy line along its bottom where there would normally have been a flat side.

'This is a very rough approximation of a map of Dacia. The wavy line is the river Danubius, and we are here . . .' He made a mark in the dust just inside the half-circle's radius, halfway between the wavy line and the curve's topmost point. 'And here . . .' He pointed to the ground outside the half-circle, waving his hand around its perimeter. 'Here are the Sarmatae. They're a loose collection of tribes, nomadic and with an equine-based way of life. The grasslands beyond these mountains are swarming with them, a tribe called the Iazyges, and they breed like rabbits.'

Julius nodded his thanks, gesturing for the soldier to continue.

'So, my legatus decided that he should concentrate his force at the legion's fortress, ready to strike decisively in accordance with the governor's wishes. Our scouts tell us that the main enemy threat is mustering on the north-western border. The knowledge that there were reinforcements from Germania within a few days' march persuaded the legatus that the risk to the mine complex would be minimal, given what we know of the enemy's dispositions.'

Scaurus leant forward with a look of concentration on his face.

'Which would seem to have been somewhat courageous of him, given that my horsemen encountered barbarian scouts not ten miles back down the road. Exactly what do we know about *them*, Soldier Cattanius?'

The beneficiarius opened his mouth to respond, but his answer was stillborn in the face of an interruption over Scaurus's shoulder.

'What have we here, Scaurus?'

The Tungrian tribune turned away from the beneficiarius, looking up at his colleague Belletor as he loomed over them both from his position on the back of his horse. His fellow legion tribune had reined his horse in behind Belletor's, and was looking down at Scaurus and his first spear with the poorly concealed curiosity that had been his perpetual expression ever since they had left Fortress Bonna. Scaurus nodded his respect to the horseman, indicating Cattanius with an extended hand.

'A legionary legatus's beneficiarius, colleague, sent to guide us into the valley and ensure that we settle into the defence of the mine as quickly as possible.'

'Excellent!' Belletor nodded down to Cattanius, who had snapped back to attention. 'How very thoughtful of your legatus! You can guide us to the bath house, soldier, I'm positively filthy after so long on the road. I assume you can manage to get the men into whatever barracks the legion left for us, colleague.'

Scaurus nodded in reply, his face a study in neutrality.

'Of course. I'll talk to you later, Soldier Cattanius, if you can spare me the time. I suspect there's a good deal more you can share with us as to the legatus's plans.'

Cattanius saluted, shooting a swift glance of incredulity at Scaurus and Julius before looking up into the tribune's smug face with his own features carefully composed into perfect neutrality.

'This way, Tribune. There are both a heated room and a plunge pool in the commander's quarters, and I took the liberty of having a fire lit an hour ago when we sighted you coming up the valley. We'll have you sweating that road dirt out in no time.'

Scaurus and Julius watched the two officers ride away up the road, the first spear shaking his head in wonderment.

'Every time I think there's no way for that prick to go any lower in my opinion he finds a new way to look even less of a soldier.'

Scaurus nodded, turning back to the waiting column of men.

'I know. But standing here mouthing insults at his back isn't going to get these men into barracks and fed, is it? Get the First Cohort moving, First Spear, and we'll rely on your colleague Sergius to have the sense to do the same for his legion troops.'

Julius saluted, his forehead creased questioningly.

'It occurs to me to ask you, Tribune, what a beneficiarius is?'

Scaurus grinned back at him, hooking a thumb over his shoulder.

'Given that the man in question was clever enough to have Belletor's bathwater hot, I'd say that in this case a beneficiarius is at the very least a bright boy, wouldn't you?

Once Julius had dismissed the Tungrians from the mine's parade ground to their camp-building duties, Marcus found his wife and her new assistant sitting in their wagon. Bowing to Annia, he stretched his neck to plant a kiss on the sleeping baby cradled in Felicia's arms.

'Well *he* seems happy enough.'

His wife raised an eyebrow.

'Remind me to check your ears for wax, Centurion. He was howling so hard while you were all parading that I was forced to hide in the back of the wagon and feed the little monster again, despite having filled him up no more than an hour before.'

Marcus wrinkled his nose.

'Is that . . .?'

Felicia nodded wryly, offering the sleeping infant to her husband.

'Yes, as night follows day, so your son has followed a good feed by filling his undergarment with his usual impression of a well-ploughed field, grunting away in his sleep like a pig digging for truffles. The gods only know how Annia manages to tolerate it, because I can assure you that I'll not be having any more of these little beasts for a good long while. Perhaps you'd like to change him?'

Her assistant laughed, her voice rich with a happy humour that had seemed impossible only months before, after her ordeal at the hands of the gang members she had believed to be her protectors, during the events of one fateful night in the city of Tungrorum.

'It seems your lady is off-limits, Centurion, at least until the memory of constant feeding and bowel movements fades. Here, give him to me . . .' She reached out for the sleeping baby, taking him from Felicia with a smile of reassurance. 'You two have a moment together and I'll see if we have any more clean linen for his delicate little backside. Come on Appius, let's see what we have back here . . .'

Felicia watched her climb into the wagon's rear with a smile before turning back to her husband.

'So, what news, Centurion?'

Marcus shrugged.

'The usual, it seems. There are sufficient stone barracks for one cohort, plus two dozen wooden huts which are in various stages of disrepair since they've not been used in years. Tribune Belletor's legion cohort will take the barracks, of course, and we'll camp in tents tonight, ready to start work putting the huts into habitable condition tomorrow.'

'Which means that Julius will have every man working on the usual marching fort.'

Marcus smiled in reply.

'Of course, with your tent right in the middle, and fifteen hundred Tungrians between you and anyone that wants to take us on. I must go and help my men put up the turf rampart, so I'll see you later, once it's all done. Where will you sleep tonight?'

She smiled, putting a hand to his cheek.

'In my tent, with Annia and that little monster you insisted on dedicating to your father with a name no-one else has used for three hundred years. Come and see me later, and perhaps Annia will sit with the baby and give us a chance for a quiet moment together, once you've had a chance to wash away the mud you're doubtless about to plaster all over yourself. I may not be *entirely* off-limits to a determined approach . . .'

'More wine for you, Tribune?'

Scaurus shook his head, raising a hand to indicate the tent's door flap.

'No thank you Arminius, I can cope well enough. You have a child to be training, I believe.'

The big German bowed slightly, and exited the tent with the same purposeful manner he did everything, closing the flap behind him to afford his master some degree of peace. The tribune poured himself a cup of wine, and another for his first spear, then set the spare cup down on the campaign chest that doubled as his desk. He sat down on his camp chair with the air of a man who had seen better times. Unlacing his boots he eased them off, sighing with the pleasure of putting his bare feet onto the tent's grass floor, then stood and walked to the door, pushing the flap aside to stare out at the camp's bustling scene. His Tungrians were hard at work digging out turf blocks for the customary earth fortifications that a commander ignored at his peril with an unknown enemy in the field. The four-foot-high wall rising around their tents was as ever arranged in a precise rectangle with only one opening, and high enough to slow an enemy's charge and render them vulnerable to the defenders' spears.

'It doesn't ever get any easier to watch our lads labouring while the legion cohort sits on its collective fat backside.'

He started, finding Julius standing at his shoulder with a look of distaste on his face.

'No, First Spear, it certainly does not. Wine?'

The big man nodded his grateful acquiescence, and stepped into the tent behind his tribune, putting his helmet down and running a spadelike hand through his thick black hair. Both men had long since mastered their amazement at their situation, but neither had yet managed to swallow his deep dissatisfaction.

'Do we have any orders beyond setting up camp, sir?'

Scaurus shook his head.

'Tribune Belletor was as unforthcoming as ever, apart from telling me that he'll be sending for the mine's procurator once he's settled in properly. I find myself gratefully surprised to have been invited to join the meeting at all.' He shared a knowing look with the other man. 'I'll be taking you as my deputy and Centurion Corvus to carry my cloak. He can act as another pair of eyes and ears for us both, and look for anything that we might miss.'

Julius sipped at his wine, watching his senior officer over the rim of the cup and seeing the same pain in his eyes as the day their revised circumstances had become painfully clear to them both. Having marched his cohorts east to the First Minervia's headquarters at Fortress Bonna on the river Rhenus, now over a thousand miles behind them, Scaurus had emerged from a meeting with the legion's legatus with a thunderous expression. Knowing his tribune's implacable temper once roused, Julius had guessed that his superior had restrained himself from ripping into the legion's commanding officer by the narrowest of margins. Scaurus had stalked out of the headquarters building with Julius trailing in his wake before sharing the news in the street outside, his jaw clenched tight with anger.

'We're to march for Dacia, First Spear, under the command of a cohort of the First Minervia. In point of fact, I am subordinated to Tribune Belletor, who is to act as my superior officer in all matters.'

Julius could still remember his amazement at the news, and the blazing anger in his tribune's responses to his disbelieving questions.

'My orders from Governor Marcellus not to become subordinated to any other officer? Tossed aside without even being read. One of the legion's equestrian tribunes, a man from my own social class if you like, took me aside before the meeting and quietly warned me that the legatus doesn't care much for the governor of Britannia, having served under him during Ulpius Marcellus's first spell in command of that miserable island. It was just as well he gave me that small clue as to what was coming, and therefore time to compose myself, or I might have taken my fists to the damned fool. And then where would we all be?'

After a moment's pause to further calm himself, Scaurus had related the meeting's events to his first spear through gritted teeth, shaking his head at the situation that had played out before him.

'The bastard took a long leisurely piss all over our achievements in Tungrorum, Julius, and I had no choice but to keep my mouth shut and listen to his bullshit. He noted our victory over the bandit leader Obduro, in passing mind you, and then spent far longer decrying the destruction of Tungrorum's grain store. "Levelled to the ground" was the phrase he used, while my halfwit colleague Belletor stood in silence with that shit-eating grin on his face. Never a word of commendation for the fortune in gold we recovered, or any recognition of the fact that the granaries we torched were largely repaired by the time we left, in fact quite the contrary. It was "disgraceful that imperial property and enough grain to feed this legion for a year" had been destroyed. Clearly I wasn't fit for independent command, and would have to operate under the control of a "more measured officer and a man with better breeding".'

He'd spat out the last words, drawing interested stares from the guards on duty outside the legion's headquarters and the soldiers passing them in the fortress's street. Julius had found the presence of mind, despite his respect for both the man's rank and his fearsome temper once roused, to take him gently by the arm and lead him out of their earshot.

'We are to be commanded, Julius, by a member of the senatorial class, a man from an impeccable family. In short, we are to
be commanded by that buffoon Belletor. The man who couldn't
even make it to the battle outside Tungrorum for sore feet and
lack of wind is now my superior.' He'd laughed at the anger in
Julius's face, shaking his head in dark amusement. 'Oh yes, *now*
you know why I nearly went across the man's desk and took him
by the throat. But there's more. Our orders from Governor
Marcellus, to return home to Britannia once we've dealt with the
bandit threat to Tungrorum, are out of the window I'm afraid.
We're to march for Dacia in company with Belletor's cohort as
reinforcement for the two legions holding the line there. Apparently
some tribe or other is getting uppity and needs slapping down,
so we get to march twenty miles a day for the next two months
in the wrong direction to provide them with more spears. I asked
about the chances of being transported by river, but *apparently*
the fleet is tied up watching the northern bank of the Rhenus in
case the German tribes choose to take the opportunity to renew
their attack on the province.'

Julius had grimaced, shaking his head in dismay.

'The men won't be happy marching east.'

Scaurus had laughed sardonically.

'What, they won't like not going home? Wait until they've
endured a few weeks of Belletor's leadership! He is, as the legatus
took great pleasure in telling him in my presence, to keep me on
a "very tight rope indeed". If I show any signs of failing to accept
my situation with the appropriate deference to his rank, he is
authorised and indeed *encouraged* to replace me with a young
man of equally good family who is to come along for the ride.
Lucius Carius Sigilis, another young tribune from the senatorial
class, still wet behind the ears and already driving the senior
centurions to distraction, I expect. It's an opportunity for the
legatus to rid himself of a pair of daddy's boys who are no practical use to him, and to gain favour with their fathers for giving
them their chance for glory and advancement. If I don't like it
then Belletor can remove me from command and send me home

with a snap of his fingers, put this boy soldier in my place and, of course, impose a pair of new first spears from his own cohort on our soldiers, just to make sure they do what they're told. I'd imagine the only thing that will stop him from doing so the moment we're out of camp will be the sweet anticipation of my humiliation, and after that my happy acceptance of whatever indignity he chooses to throw at me. And if I go, First Spear, then you'll find yourself back in command of a century with a legion man in control of the cohort. If you or any other of our officers make their feelings on the subject clear then the outcome's likely to be your dismissal from the service on whatever charge of misconduct Belletor feels like inventing for the purpose, without either citizenship or pension. So we're all going to have to learn to bite our tongues and wait for the big wheel to turn, aren't we? Just make sure that your officers are perfectly clear on my expectation that we can all display sufficient maturity to see this temporary inconvenience through . . .'

In the event, Scaurus's good reputation with his officers and men had resulted in a conspiracy of silence across both of the cohorts under his command, and the soldiers had contented themselves with bringing a particular gusto to those of their marching songs with any relevance to the legionaries marching alongside them. Julius walked to the door, cup in hand, and looked out at the toiling soldiers for a moment before turning back to his tribune with a shrug.

'If it's of any consolation, Tribune, my colleague Sergius is as embarrassed as ever at being told to sit on his hands while we do all the work.'

Scaurus nodded his understanding.

'I can imagine. But any soldier sharp enough to reach the rank of first spear in a legion cohort knows very well when to keep his mouth shut. He's of far more value to us as a friend in Belletor's camp than for any brief excitement he might whip up by protesting our case. And in any case, I think the worst part of our ordeal is over. Now that we don't have to dig out a marching camp every night we can get back to some real soldiering. There's a decent fight waiting for us somewhere out there, and I don't intend for my men to be found wanting.'

Marcus walked wearily into the Fifth Century's lines as the sun was falling toward the western horizon, finding Arminius and Morban's grandson Lupus waiting for him outside his tent, the child still wet with the sweat of his evening lesson with sword and shield. The big German got to his feet and pointed to the tent's door.

'Inside if you will, Centurion, and get that gear off so that the boy can get to work with his brushes. It's all very well you working on the turf rampart alongside your men, but we can't have you covered in mud on parade tomorrow morning. The boots too. We've laid out a clean tunic and your soft shoes, and there's a bowl of warm water in there for you to wash your face. The doctor came to see us a while ago and asked me to pass on the message that she would indeed be delighted to take a cup of wine with you before bed, if you can tear yourself away from your usual feats of military engineering.'

Marcus washed, taking pleasure from the sensation of the clean water drying on his skin after a full day's labour, then pulled on the clean tunic and belted it so that the hem was above his knees in the approved military fashion. Re-emerging into the evening sun he found Lupus hard at work on his boots, buffing them back to their customary morning shine. He squatted next to the boy, noting that the sword he and Arminius had purchased for him in Tungrorum was laid alongside him in the grass in its battered metal scabbard.

'We haven't spoken much recently, Lupus . . .' He paused, struggling for words as the boy continued his polishing without looking up. 'I've been really busy, and little Appius, well . . .'

Lupus rescued him, still intent on his work as he spoke into the silence, his voice still high and clear.

'Arminius told me that my job is to keep your equipment clean and to learn to fight as well as he can. And that nothing else matters. When I can fight well enough he says I can be a soldier, and serve in your century like my daddy did.'

Abashed at the boy's matter-of-fact acceptance of the harsh facts, Marcus thought for a moment before replying.

'Your father was a brave man, and when you can hold your own in a fight with Arminius I'll be proud to serve alongside you. But you do know that your grandfather loves you too, don't you?'

Lupus grimaced at the boot.

'My grandfather loves me well enough, but he also loves drink, and ladies, and most of all he loves to gamble. But all I love is this . . .'

He lifted the metal scabbard, and Marcus thought his heart was going to break.

'Give me the boot, Lupus.' The child frowned and handed it to him, and Marcus looked down at the shining leather with a quick nod. 'Perfect.' He tossed it into the tent behind him, then reached over for the other, still streaked with mud, and repeated the act.

'But it's not clean . . .'

Lupus fell silent as he realised that the centurion's hand was held out palm upwards.

'Now give me the sword.'

The boy's face crumpled, on the verge of tears.

'But . . .'

Marcus took the weapon from his hands, forcing a smile onto his face.

'You can have it back later, I promise.' He reached over and plucked the weapon from Lupus's unresisting hands. 'It can sit alongside mine while we're away. Nobody's going to risk taking liberties with a pair of dangerous swordsmen like you and me.'

He leaned back into the tent, and laid the scabbard down next to his blades, shaking his head at the stark simplicity of the weapons' purpose.

'Now then, come with me. We'll worry about the boots and the armour in the morning, eh? Tonight you can join Felicia and me for our meal, and little Appius too, if he's awake.' He squatted onto his haunches, looking up at the boy's mystified face. 'Lupus, you're going to make a perfect soldier, when the time comes. By the time you're fifteen you'll probably be able to do more with a sword than I can now, but we're making you into a soldier before your time, and it's not fair.' He put a finger under the boy's chin, lifting it until the boy met his eyes, his voice soft with the memories of his own younger brother. 'There's another life you need to live before you take the oath, Lupus, you need to be a boy for just a while longer, and have as much of a family as we can make for you. Come on, let's go and see which one of us can get little Appius to give him a smile first . . .'

Tribune Scaurus was busy with a long-overdue review of the cohort's records when the beneficiarius appeared at the door of his tent with an apologetic salute.

'I'm sorry to disturb you, Tribune, but you did ask me to find you again when I had the chance.'

The tribune sat back from the table and nodded to his clerk, running a hand through his hair.

'That will be all for the time being, there's nothing much wrong with it all from what I can see. Do come in, Beneficiarius.'

Cattanius stepped inside the tent, and the two men waited in silence while the clerk gathered his scrolls and left. Scaurus gestured to the chair that the administrator had vacated, and allowed the soldier to take a seat before speaking.

'Where are you from, Soldier Cattanius?'

'The province of Noricum, Tribune, from a little village in the mountains above Virunum.'

'And you're how old?'

'Twenty-four, Tribune, I joined the legion when I was sixteen.'

Scaurus raised an eyebrow in recognition of the younger man's achievement. Whilst his failure to progress beyond the rank of soldier might be considered disappointing for a bright young man in some quarters, Cattanius was clearly far better suited to the careful calculation frequently required of a legatus's representative than the casual brutality needed to rule a century as a watch officer or chosen man. As if reading his mind, the beneficiarius smiled knowingly.

'I'd have been a soldier for the rest of my life if not for Legatus Albinus, and not a particularly good one either.'

He fell silent, waiting while Scaurus appraised him more closely. After a long pause the tribune sat back in his chair with an inquisitorial air.

'So who is it?'

'Tribune?'

'Don't play it coy with me, *Soldier* Cattanius. Beneficiarius or not, I outrank you quite severely, and I'm not a pleasant man when I believe I'm being played for a fool. You're bright enough to understand the question, and quite possibly devious enough to know the answer too. So, in your opinion, who is it?'

Cattanius shifted uneasily.

'I don't know, Tribune.'

'You do think there's an insider though, don't you? In fact I'd bet all the gold waiting for shipment down the road to Apulum that you believe there's a traitor somewhere in the mine's hierarchy. Come on man, either give me the truth or your recent run of good luck will very likely take a turn for the worse.'

The beneficiarius shrugged.

'There was a time when we thought there might be someone inside the mine organisation with a line of communication to the Sarmatae, which is why the legatus had me spend so much time here over the last few months, but if such an individual exists I am yet to discover any trace of them. Besides that, *we* have a spy deep in Sarmatae territory; a former soldier turned merchant who has spent the last five years working his way into a position of trust. He curses the empire that enslaved him in the service with every opportunity he gets, and poses as a man that has turned his back on his past. He sends intelligence out to us with the traders that work both sides of the frontier, and his most recent message stated that the tribesmen are getting ready to attack into Dacia. He tells us that there are two war leaders, Boraz and Purta, tribal kings who are both unwilling to subordinate to the other, but who have reached an agreement as to their joint plan of campaign. One of them will attack Porolissum, the most important of the forts that defends the north-west of the province, aiming to smash through our defensive line before raiding deeper into the province, while the other will take advantage of the confusion caused to capture Alburnus Major at a time calculated to ensure that there is a full shipment of gold ready for transport to Rome.'

Scaurus digested the information for a moment.

'Which I presume is currently the case?'

'It will be in a week or so, Tribune. We tend to ship the gold down to Apulum once a month, three thousand pounds or so in each shipment.'

Scaurus thought for a moment.

'I see. And how can you tell that this man's messages are really from him, if he never leaves Sarmatae territory?'

'We have a means of knowing whether the men who bring his despatches are genuine. He sends messages out to us every few months, using a different trader every time to avoid developing any pattern that might betray him. The men he uses are given sealed containers to carry across the border in return for a significant amount of gold, most of which is not paid until they have made delivery with the message tube's seal intact. The message warning of the coming attack arrived in Apulum last week, carried by a horse trader who described our man's identifying feature in perfect detail.'

'He described the man's face?'

Cattanius shook his head, smiling at the senior officer's innocence.

'Oh no, Tribune, he's very careful never to let his face be seen, so that the men he chooses can never link the message back to him if they are caught in the act. What he shows the traders to whom he entrusts his messages is a finely made gold ring in which is mounted a large and beautifully finished garnet. They describe it to us, and so we know that the message is genuine.'

Scaurus raised an eyebrow.

'And so when this intelligence of a Sarmatae attack was received, Legatus Albinus decided to beat them to the punch in the north, didn't he?'

The beneficiarius nodded.

'Yes. The withdrawal of the mine's guard cohort wasn't just a response to the threat to Porolissum, although the Thirteenth Gemina is marching there to join up with the Fifth Macedonica, ready to repel the northern attack. Knowing that your cohorts were only a few days away, and having a good idea as to how long it would take the Sarmatae to make their attack on the mine, the legatus gambled that—'

'Sacred Father, he gambled with the richest goldmine in the empire!' Scaurus shook his head in disbelief. 'It just goes to prove what his centurions always used to say about him during the German wars. There's bold, there's downright reckless, and then there's Decimus Clodius Albinus.'

Marcus walked back down the line of his century's tents later that night to find a small brazier set up outside the entrance to his own tent, and several men sitting in its cherry-red glow, talking quietly. The nearest of them got to his feet and nodded a greeting, a leather boot held in one hand and a polishing rag in the other. The Roman shook his head in mock amusement.

'You appear to be cleaning my boots, Arminius?'

The German flicked his long hair away from his face, having released it from his customary heavy topknot.

'And a good thing too, I'd say. You'd either have lost precious time cleaning it yourself in the morning, or else appeared on parade with one boot gleaming and the other still covered in mud. I came to get the boy for dinner, knowing that his grandfather had managed to find a jar of wine and was happily pouring it down his neck without a care in the world, only to be told that you'd walked him down to your wife's tent. It was clear enough that your gear would need some attention, and so . . .'

The one-eyed warrior who had been sitting next to him stood up and joined them, stretching extravagantly in the fire's warmth and gesturing for his bodyguard to stay in their places by the fire. A prince of the Votadini tribe,which dwelled in Britannia's northern mountains beyond the Roman wall, Martos had gone into voluntary exile with the Tungrians after his people's ill-fated participation in the tribal revolt that still wracked the province.

'And so we decided to make a party of it. The German here and I found the standard bearer and took possession of his wine before he managed to get through all of it. We told him to view it as the fee to be paid for leaving his grandson to the care of others.'

Arminius grimaced.

'In truth, it was the prince's tame Selgovae monster who did most of the dispossessing . . .'

Marcus raised an eyebrow at Martos, who nodded in agreement.

'It was a sight you would have enjoyed, Centurion. Lugos just took the jar from Morban and then put a hand on his head to hold him off at arm's length until he got bored of trying to get it back.'

The Roman smiled quietly at the way in which the Selgovae giant had quietly and patiently become a regular companion to the Votadini prince during their long march to the east, despite the burning hatred his friend still felt for Lugos's tribe after their betrayal by the Selgovae's king Calgus. He nodded, looking hopefully at the jar.

'If you have any wine left . . .'

A cup was passed, and Marcus drank a mouthful of the rich wine.

'You left the boy with your wife?'

He nodded at Martos's question.

'He fell asleep next to Appius's cot, and I didn't have the heart to wake him. It must be hard on him to have travelled all this way from home without the company of anyone his own age.'

The men around the fire nodded, and for a moment there was silence as each of them considered the boy's isolation within the cohort's hard world. After a moment Lugos stood up on the far side of the brazier, passing Marcus his swords with a bow and a rumble of explanation.

'Have made sharp.'

Arminius snorted out a bark of laughter, pointing at the weapon in disbelief.

'You sharpened *those*?'

The enormous Briton shrugged easily, as resolute as ever in failing to take offence at the rough humour of his fellows.

'No blade ever too sharp.' He looked at the weapon resting on the Roman's knee with a reverential expression. 'Is sword fit for mighty god Cocidius himself.'

Marcus returned the bow with a gentle smile.

'My thanks for your efforts, Lugos. As you say, a sword can never be too sharp.'

Arminius snorted again.

'Even a blade that was forged so keen that it will cut through a shield as if the board were made from parchment?'

The massive Briton answered on Marcus's behalf, his expression foreboding in the fire's half-light.

'Centurion need sharp iron soon. This place be watch from hills around. Lugos feels eyes.'

The Roman looked at Martos and Arminius, and found both men nodding in agreement. The Votadini prince spoke first.

'We all feel them, Centurion. Our enemy, whoever they may be, is close at hand. This place will know a bloody day soon enough.'

2

The detachment's officers gathered in Tribune Belletor's new headquarters soon after sunrise to meet with the mining complex's procurator, the man charged with extracting the maximum possible output of gold from the mines whose entrances pocked the valley's hillsides. The centurions had climbed up the road from their camp to the straggling town of Alburnus Major, casting disapproving glances at the seedy drinking establishments and whorehouses that seemed to be the town's major form of commerce. Now they were crowded into the headquarters' briefing room, listening intently as the mine's administrator briefed them on the valley's value to the empire.

Procurator Maximus was a tall, painfully thin man with a half-starved look about him that Marcus found slightly disquieting in the company of so many heavily muscled soldiers as he watched the man from the back of the room. The detachment's senior officers stood closest to him as he went through an obviously well-practised explanation of the mine's operation. Scaurus carefully positioned himself a half-pace behind his colleague and superior Belletor, who was wearing the smug expression of a man who felt in complete control of his situation and was unable to keep that knowledge from his face. The youngest of the three senior officers stood at Belletor's other shoulder, his tunic decorated with a thick purple senatorial stripe identical to that of his colleague's, and in obvious contrast to Scaurus's thinner equestrian line. Marcus was watching him with careful glances, being sure not to stare at the man for very long so as not to draw attention to himself. Scaurus had told his centurions to form an opinion of the youngest tribune before they had set off for the meeting.

'Keep a good eye on young Sigilis, gentlemen, and take his measure now while you have the leisure to do so. You may find yourself under his command if I fail in this continual struggle not to break my esteemed colleague's nose, so you might as well try to understand what sort of man he is now, rather than the first time you find yourselves taking orders from him.'

Marcus observed the young tribune carefully, taking good care to keep a man between them and watch from the shadows so as not to attract his attention in return. His main impression of Lucius Carius Sigilis was that of his younger self, albeit seen from the far side of the chasm that had opened between himself and Roman society with his family's mass execution on a false charge of treason raised by the shadowy men behind the emperor, in order to clear the way for the confiscation of their huge wealth. Watching the tribune through the throng of men between them, he realised that the confident set of the young man's face was achingly familiar. Sigilis was clearly possessed of the same utter self-belief that had been his in the months before his uncompre-hending flight to Britain. They were so alike, and yet . . . Marcus smiled darkly to himself, musing on the barbarian uprising that had swept northern Britannia soon after his arrival. The Tungrians' first desperate battles to survive in the face of the revolt's ferocity had been the fire in which he had been transformed from son of privilege to capable centurion, his former prejudices and expecta-tions of life burned away in the white heat of a succession of pitched battles. He wrenched his attention back to the procurator's words, shaking his head slightly to dispel the memories.

'And so I welcome you all to the Ravenstone valley, gentlemen, and to our mining colony of Alburnus Major. I have roughly five thousand miners currently engaged in extraction and refining processes, working for three investors who fund the necessary resource and expertise, and who in turn take a share of the profits of our enterprise. Most of our mining operations are below ground these days, since the potential for surface mining is all but done, and that makes the process much more laborious and labour-intensive. What with digging into the mountains to find the gold-bearing rock, processing the ore to extract its gold, ventilation to keep the miners alive and hundreds of men working day and night to drain off the water from the mines . . . well, I can assure you that it's all *very* costly.'

He beamed at the gathered officers knowingly.

'I can however, also assure you gentlemen that it's very much worth the expense. My last posting as a Procurator of Mines was in Mount Marianus in Spain, and we were lucky if we dug out ten pounds of gold a day. Here in Alburnus Major we're averaging ninety pounds of gold per day, which makes the mines hugely profitable by comparison. That's over thirty thousand pounds a year without any sign of the seams thinning out. There is said to be enough gold in these mountains to pave a road from here to the Forum in Rome itself, and I can well believe it.' He looked around the room with a portentous expression. 'Which means that the loss of this facility would have the direst implications for the imperial treasury.'

'Not to mention his career.'

Ignoring Julius's whispered comment, Marcus focussed his attention on the procurator, who was still speaking.

'So you see, gentlemen, my original request to the governor for some soldiers to back up my own security force wasn't made lightly. I have men from just about every province in the north-eastern portion of the empire working in this valley, and from pretty much every one of the tribes beyond our northern frontier for that matter, and there is no real way to be certain of their loyalty to the empire. I don't doubt that among them will be a few spies sent in by the Sarmatae to wait until the time is right and then guide their warriors through the mountains to fall upon us without warning or mercy. It was something of a surprise when Legatus Albinus chose to withdraw his men from the valley, even if we did have the report that you were only a few days away.' He looked about him with an expression of relief that to Marcus's eye appeared in no way feigned, and spread his hands to encompass the gathering. 'But here you are. Alburnus Major is safe again, and just in time if your encounter with enemy scouts on the road yesterday is any guide. Might I ask how you plan to establish the appropriate degree of security for my mines?'

The question was directed at Belletor, who started slightly, then scratched at his bearded chin in the manner of a man deep in thought.

'Well, ah . . .'

The silence stretched out just long enough to be vaguely embarrassing and then, just as every man present was weighing up how best to speak up without making the young tribune look foolish, Scaurus's voice broke the silence.

'I would imagine that my colleague's careful thought is attributable to his desire not to provide embarrassment to the previous defenders, even in their absence. The Thirteenth Gemina Legion was responsible for the defence of the valley until recently, I believe?'

The procurator nodded knowingly, and Belletor's face assumed the appropriately neutral cast of a man who had indeed been searching for a way to critique the mine's defences without criticising his predecessors.

'They were, Tribune Scaurus, and your superior is right to avoid offering offence to their deeds here, even in their absence. Although when they were recalled to Apulum to concentrate with the other cohorts of the legion I was forced to note that they left us without either manpower or physical defences to protect the emperor's gold against the Sarmatae, other than the few men I employ to guard my strongroom.'

Scaurus nodded his understanding.

'Knowing that we were only days distant, I would imagine that the legatus commanding the Thirteenth considered this an acceptable gamble. You've seen no sign of any threat from the hills to the north and west, I presume?' Maximus shook his head. 'I thought not. Which means that the main body of the enemy must be sufficiently distant for them to have to be content with scouting around the valley. In that case, I believe that we should proceed with Tribune Belletor's plan for the valley's defence. The tribune and I discussed this matter at some length yesterday, and I find myself in full accordance with his plan. Perhaps I might outline your thoughts, Domitius Belletor?'

Marcus sneaked a glance at Cattanius to find the soldier's face a study in self-control. Arminius had confided in him that Scaurus had talked with the legion man until long after the lamps had been lit the previous evening, gleaning as much information as he could as to the dispositions and contingency plans of the previous garrison. The beneficiarius had clearly realised that the answers he had given would be at the root of the tribune's thinking. Belletor nodded graciously, a hint of relief on his face.

'By all means, colleague.'

Scaurus's face hardened in concentration, and the men standing around him gathered a little closer in subconscious recognition of the real military authority in the room.

'In simple terms, this facility is basically a four-mile-long valley with one end open and the other closed by two successive mountains which rise to heights over a thousand feet above the plain. The valley walls rise to much the same height, and there appears to be only one route in that isn't either straight up the road that runs along the valley floor from the west, or over steep and easily defended peaks on the valley walls with excellent fields of view. It's worth noting that the mining activity is mainly concentrated in the area of the mountains at the closed eastern end.'

Procurator Maximus nodded.

'Indeed Tribune, that's much as the Thirteenth Legion's tribune described it.'

'In which case, there are two main defensive measures necessary. Firstly, we must be ready to repel a strong attack up the valley floor. The Sarmatae might well muster a force of many thousands of men to attack a prize as rich as this, many of them mounted, and we'll have to be ready to fight them off with only the four cohorts you saw come up the road this afternoon. Nobody else is coming to this particular party. And that means we'll need to build a wall at the valley's most advantageous point, Procurator.

A wall high enough that it can't be scaled without a ladder, and topped by a stepped fighting platform to allow a relatively small number of men to fight off several times their own strength. Given that the valley's teeming with strong men I'm assuming that such a construction wouldn't tax you too badly?'

The procurator frowned at the suggestion.

'I'm not sure that the various businessmen who work the mines on the empire's behalf would take well to having their workforces turned away from the mines . . . not to mention the lost revenue to both them and the empire.'

Scaurus smiled at him, showing his teeth in a fierce grin.

'I have no doubt that you're right. But as Tribune Belletor was saying to me only yesterday afternoon as we marched into your facility, it might well be better to lose a few days' income than risk losing the entire mine, not to mention our own lives, wouldn't you agree? He made the point to me that the man that loses this facility must either fall in its defence or face a rather more protracted death at the hands of a disappointed imperium, and I have to say I can't fault his logic.'

Belletor shot him a surprised glance, but kept his mouth shut. The deception Scaurus was weaving around his superior's supposed views on defending the mine had advanced too far to be gainsaid without more embarrassment than Belletor's dignity could bear. For his part Scaurus was making the most of his chance to put the procurator straight as to who was in command of the mine's resources.

'Besides, I'm sure you're not entirely without leverage over the men you've entrusted to extract the empire's gold? Perhaps you might intimate to these businessmen that their accounts are overdue a particularly thorough audit, unless, of course, the urgency of defending their investments makes such an investigation superfluous?' He raised an eyebrow at the procurator. 'I presume there are a variety of stringent penalties open to your discretion, if any of these businessmen is found to have more than his fair share of the profits sticking to his fingers. I can assure you that you'll find my colleague Domitius Belletor more than sympathetic with any request to assist you in delivering imperial justice under such circumstances.'

Left with little alternative his fellow tribune nodded his firm agreement, and Scaurus held the procurator's gaze for a long moment, waiting until the other man acknowledged his point with a slight bow of his head.

'Excellent. So while your partners help the bulk of our men to build this wall to our specifications, the remainder will be conducting repairs on the temporary barracks accommodation to get my men out of their campaign tents and under some sturdier cover. We'll be needing several dozen wood-burning stoves, which I assume your smiths can turn out easily enough, given they'll have a temporary respite from making and mending mining tools. And the soldiers who aren't busy repairing their own accommodation will be standing guard duty in the watchposts up on the peaks, looking out for any sign of a Sarmatae attack over the valley walls, unlikely though that may be. We'll have your facility laced up as tight as a maiden's bodice before you know it.'

He turned to Belletor, whose expression of imperious neutrality had slowly slid into one of slight bemusement as his supposed junior had taken control of the situation.

'That *was* what you had in mind, colleague?'

Left without any choice, the younger man nodded graciously, although his face bore an edge of the suspicion that he had in some way been manoeuvred without having any clear understanding as to how or why. Scaurus bowed respectfully, turning to Cattanius with a slight smile.

'I'm gratified to have reflected your thoughts so clearly. And perhaps, with your agreement, we might trouble the beneficiarius here for a better understanding of the enemy we're facing?'

Belletor nodded again, his frown deepening as he realised that the conference had now utterly escaped his control. His colleague Sigilis was clearly working hard to keep his face immobile, but to Marcus's eye a hint of contempt had entered his expression, although the young man was careful to keep his gaze away from either Belletor or Scaurus. Cattanius stepped forward, clearing his throat with no sign of any discomfort at the size or status of his audience.

'Be under no illusion, gentlemen, our enemy is a proud and noble people. I warn you, if we allow them to use their mobility and fight in their preferred manner we will face almost certain defeat. Their horsemen ride with the skill of men raised in the saddle, and carry a long lance which they call the kontos. Our legionaries have a fighting chance against them in good order, but on the wrong ground, or if the formation has been weakened by their archers, this enemy can be truly murderous. Indeed their prowess was impressive enough to persuade the last emperor to take a legion's strength of their lancers to serve in Britannia, as part of the peace agreement after we defeated them at the battle of the Frozen River. And now it seems that some part of their nation has decided to turn their backs on that treaty and make war on us again.'

He related to the gathered officers the story he'd imparted to Scaurus the previous evening about the two Dacian kings, Purta and Boraz, although the tribune noted that he omitted to tell them about the method by which the intelligence had been gathered.

'Our spies tell us that Purta is gathering a warband of thirty thousand men beyond the mountains to the north-west of the fortress at Porolissum. Our auxiliary forts along the border make an obvious initial target for them, after which we expect he'll be aiming to march down the road to the south-east and knock over the legions one at a time. The governor has given orders that our two Dacian legions are under no circumstances to be separated for fear of losing them individually, and it seems he's happy enough to give up ground in order to keep his force intact.'

'And the mine? Will he surrender that too?'

Cattanius shook his head with an apologetic glance at Scaurus.

'If he has an opinion on the subject then Legatus Albinus hasn't seen fit to share it with me, Tribune. What he did tell me was that the force moving on this valley and led by Boraz is believed to be relatively weak by comparison with that being fielded by Purta. It is expected that you'll be able to hold off the barbarians without too much trouble, given the favourable nature of the terrain.' He shot a look at Scaurus. 'However, he also told me that if this proves not to be the case, he believes that Albinus Major can be recaptured easily enough once the main force under Purta is defeated. His exact words were "it's not as if the Sarmatae can take the mountains with them, is it?".'

Scaurus shot a wry smile at Belletor.

'So there's no pressure then, eh Tribune? We should be able to win easily enough, and if not the legions can clean up later with nothing much more lost than our reputations. That and our lives, of course.'

'Gods below, but I can see why the boys from the Thirteenth would have been keen to have it away from here on their toes given half a chance.'

Marcus looked back down the slope at his toiling standard bearer, grinning at the man's red face and puffed-out cheeks. The rest of the century were strung out down the slope below him, climbing easily enough in Morban's wake as he led them in their journey towards the morning's objective. To their right the mountain that the miners called 'The Rotunda' loomed over them, while to the left the valley's side was formed by a long, steep-sided and easily defendable ridge, but to their front was a flat expanse between the mountain and the ridgeline some three hundred paces wide which had been dubbed 'The Saddle', through which an attacking force would be able to enter the valley with much greater ease. The Fifth Century had been tasked with investigating the observation post that had been built to watch the gap, and to provide early warning of any such approach from the north.

'A good breakfast followed by a gentle walk in the hills? Could a man want for anything more, Standard Bearer?'

Morban looked up at him with an expression of disbelief.

'Where would you like me to start, Centurion? Staying in my bed past the first sparrow's fart would have been good. Eating something better for breakfast than a piece of stale bread and a slice of last night's pork with water to wash it down would have been even nicer. After that . . .' He paused to suck in a breath before resuming his climb, legs stamping at the grassy slope for grip. 'After that my ideal morning would include an energetic spell in the company of some expensive professional ladies, followed by a relaxing hour or two in a private bath house in the company of those same ladies. Put all those things together and it would be more or less perfect. Instead of which, I find myself climbing a mountain in the company of quite the ugliest collection of soldiers it's been my misfortune to fall in with for many a year, and with not one but three centurions, all of whom are apparently intent on draining what little enjoyment there is to be had from the situation.'

Qadir shrugged, a faint smile touching his otherwise inscrutable face.

'I only pointed out to your colleagues, Standard Bearer, that I saw you deep in conversation with Beneficiarius Cattanius shortly before you started offering odds on how long it would take us to reach the lookout post.'

Morban snorted and stuck out his bottom lip, ignoring the Hamian centurion's comment and concentrating on the climb. Dubnus raised an eyebrow at his friend, his voice lowered conspiratorially.

'Morban? Lost for words? I really must pray to Cocidius a little more often if he's going to answer me in such a spectacular fashion.'

The standard bearer kept climbing, sending an embittered rejoinder over his shoulder.

'I heard that. You're a cruel man Dubnus, given that we once served alongside each other.'

The big Briton barked out a sardonic laugh.

'Hah! Not really, given the regularity with which you used to fleece my purse with all manner of wagers. You even ran a book on how long it would take me to get off my back after I stopped a barbarian spear last year.'

Morban raised a disgusted eyebrow.

'Yes, a book on which I lost money due to your rude state of health and your urge to get your hands on a century again . . .'

Marcus put his whistle to his lips and blew a quick blast.

'Fifth Century, form line! We'll make the rest of this climb ready to receive an attack.' The soldiers quickly formed up into a two-deep line and the front rankers stepped forward with hard stares at the hill's summit, pulling on their helmets and unstrapping shields from carrying positions across their backs. In the space of a dozen heartbeats the century was transformed from a line of individual soldiers into an impersonal engine of murder bristling with razor-edged spear blades and faced with iron and layered wood. They were the century's older and more experienced men for the most part, their arms and faces bearing the scars of a succession of bloody battles in Britannia the previous year. These, Marcus knew from experience, were the men who would stand and fight without calculating the odds against them, in the knowledge that to run would be a worse option than any danger they might face. Marcus walked out in front of them and pointed up the slope's last two hundred paces at the wooden watchtower waiting for them, its roof intermittently wreathed in wisps of grey, scudding cloud.

'At the walk . . . advance!'

The Fifth Century followed their centurion up the hill's last slope, the first time that any of them bar Morban had faced the potential for a fight under Marcus's leadership, each man with a spear held ready to stab or throw as ordered by the young officer leading them forward to the summit's uncertainty. As they approached the hill's crest they found the watch post unoccupied, its timbers creaking softly under the wind's intermittent caress. The building was built snugly into a half-hollow just below the summit, the bulk of it shielded from both the worst of the wind and observation from the other slope, while a wooden tower jutted up fifteen feet to provide the occupants with a view over the country beyond the ridge's peak.

'Halt! Kneeling defence!'

The soldiers dropped onto one knee at Marcus's command, bracing their shields on their forward legs and lowering their heads so that their only remaining point of vulnerability was a thin vision-slit between shield and brow guard. Quintus frowned from his place behind the century, and the soldiers exchanged puzzled glances at being dropped into a defensive stance a good fifty paces short of the building.

'Chosen Man!' Quintus stepped forward through the century's ranks with a salute to his centurion. 'You are to keep the Fifth in defensive line and await my orders. In the event that you hear or see anything to indicate that I have been engaged by enemy forces, you are to use your own judgement as to whether an attack or a fighting retreat is the better option, but you must ensure that the news of whatever happens here reaches the tribune. Do you understand?'

The chosen man nodded.

'Are you going in there alone, Centurion?'

Marcus shook his head with a smile.

'Not quite. Gentlemen, shall we?' Dubnus and Qadir stepped forward, both men drawing their swords. 'I very much doubt there's anyone within a hundred miles of here, but the post has been abandoned for long enough that I'll not simply blunder in to see what might be waiting for us. Arabus!'

The scout stepped forward from behind the century's line where he had been waiting in silence. A skilled scout and tracker raised in the forested hills of the Arduenna forest in Germania, he had been captured by Marcus in the act of attempting the Roman's assassination, and turned to the cohort's service by the revelation of his son's sacrificial murder by the same bandit leader who had subverted him. He was acknowledged by even the most skilful of the cohort's barbarian scouts to be the best of them, a master of both tracking and the art of seeing without being seen, and lethal with a short blade. When the Tungrians had marched away from the Arduenna he had chosen to follow them rather than return to the forest, telling the young centurion that with his family dead at the hands of the bandit leader Obduro there was nothing to keep him there. The Roman pointed up the hill and the scout nodded, loping silently away up the slope, drawing puzzled glances from the soldiers as he ran to the century's right and headed purposefully for a fold in the ground that crossed the hilltop. Dropping onto his hands and knees, and then flattening himself fully against the damp grass, he wormed forward into the cover of the fold and vanished from sight.

Marcus led his fellow centurions onwards with only one of his swords drawn, the evilly sharp patterned spatha that he had purchased from a sword smith in the Tungrians' home city of Tungrorum. The weapon had cost him a price that had set his colleagues' heads shaking in disbelief, until they had seen the sword's murderous edge and the speed with which the light and flexible weapon could be wielded. He put a reflexive hand to the eagle's head-pommelled gladius bequeathed to him by his birth father, but left the short sword sheathed for the time being. The three centurions moved swiftly, giving little time for any enemy lurking in the watch post to react as Dubnus and Qadir spread out to either side of their comrade, while Marcus ran to the building's main door and flattened himself against the rough timber wall, listening intently. There was nothing to be heard other than the wind's soft susurration, and the occasional creak from the wooden structure. Putting a booted heel to the wedge holding the post's main door closed, he drew in a long, slow breath, sliding the legatus's gladius from its scabbard and savouring the feeling of the twin blades' heft in his skilled hands.

'Go!'

Kicking the wedge away he ripped the door open and threw himself through the opening, minimising the moment of danger when he would be silhouetted against the doorway's bright rectangle. Pointing the swords into the building's unlit gloom, he turned to track movement against the rear wall.

'Nothing. And you can stop pointing that sword at me with quite so much relish, thank you.'

Dubnus stepped out of the shadows with a look of disdain, while Qadir surveyed the post's wooden floorboards with a critical eye.

'No, nothing at all. No mud, no bootprints. Even the dust is undisturbed. Either nobody has been in here or they were very skilled at hiding any trace of their presence.'

Marcus nodded, turning to the watchtower's stairs. He climbed slowly, with one sword held in front of him, emerging into the cold morning air crouched low to avoid presenting any silhouette to a potential watcher. Looking through the viewing platform's vision-slits he saw his Fifth Century waiting in their defensive line as he had left them, ready to fight or retreat as ordered. Moving to the tower's other side he found an uninterrupted view down the hill's gentle northern slope for three hundred paces, open ground that stretched as far as the forest's edge. Climbing carefully back down the steps he exited the building to find Arabus waiting for him. The scout bowed, gesturing to the north.

'As you suspected, Centurion, there are footprints on the far slope. Also the marks left by hooves. There have been mounted men here, and less than a day ago. I saw no sign of them in the trees, no movement at all. But they were certainly here when we marched up the valley yesterday.'

On the valley floor, five hundred feet below, Julius watched as his centuries toiled up the slopes of the mountains that surrounded them on three sides, nodding his satisfaction as they neared their immediate objectives.

'That's better. With the hills manned we can breathe a little easier.'

Alongside him Scaurus grunted his agreement.

'Indeed. Defending this valley is going to be interesting enough without the risk of being showered with arrows from those heights, or finding that our enemy has found a way to outflank our wall.'

The parade ground before them was empty of men, other than a few dozen veteran soldiers from Scaurus's Second Tungrian Cohort waiting at ease to one side. With the First Cohort tied up retaking the mountains around the valley, Scaurus had sent half of the Second Cohort's remainder down the road under their new First Spear, charged with laying out the line of the defensive wall he was planning to erect across the valley's narrowest point.

'You may not be an engineer, Tertius old son, but you've enough sense to pick the best place to stop a cavalry charge.' Julius had taken his colleague aside after their dismissal from the command meeting, pointing out across the valley. 'Just find the narrowest point, preferably with a nice little slope in front of the line where we'll be dropping the wall in, and make sure we can get water to run to it.' He pointed back up the valley to the point where the huge rock slab of the eastern peak sealed off the far end. 'We don't want all Sergius's hard work up there to leave us with a bloody great puddle on *our* side, do we?'

The men of the First Minervia's Cohort were toiling away at the foot of the eastern peak's steep slopes, energetically clearing away vegetation in a line down the slope from a good-sized lake that sat high above the valley floor to their rear, and Julius looked about him with a smile of satisfaction.

'Give me a month and I could make this place impossible to take with anything less than three legions, and even then they'd pay a heavy price to break in.'

Scaurus raised an eyebrow.

'A month? I'd say you've got two days, three if we're lucky, before enough men to fill the ranks of two legions come thundering up that slope. What do you think you can do in that time?'

Julius opened his mouth to respond, but closed it again as the first of the mine workers came into sight, heading for the parade ground in a long, straggling column. They crowded onto the flat open space until it was full, and the slope which overlooked it filled up in turn, the buzz of their conversation loud enough that the two men had to raise their voices to speak. When Scaurus judged that there were no more to come he nodded to Julius, who signalled his trumpeters to blow a long hard note. Their horns' peals echoed from the rocky hillsides, and the miners fell silent and stared at the tribune as he stepped out before them. Clearing his throat, he shouted a question at the mass of men.

'Where are the mine owners? I believe there are three of you!'

A balding man stepped forward from the crowd, his clothes both cleaner and smarter than his fellows'.

'I am Felix, owner of the Split Rock mine.'

He pointed down the valley to the west, and Scaurus exchanged a meaningful glance with Julius who shrugged slightly.

'Thank you, Felix. Who's next?' A second man stepped out of the throng, but where his colleague had clearly bathed recently, and was dressed in fine cloth, he wore the same heavy, dirty clothing as the men around him. 'Your name?'

'Lartius, my Lord.'

Scaurus nodded, though not without a slight smile.

'Tribune will do, thank you, Lartius. And you own which mine?'

'The Rotunda, my . . . Tribune, on the southern slope of that mountain.'

He pointed to the round-topped mountain to the north.

'I see. One more of you to come then. Will I have to resort to . . .'

He paused in mid-sentence, raising an eyebrow as a woman in her thirties stepped out from the protection of the men around her and acknowledged him in a cursory manner. Her functional clothing was drab, cut for comfort rather than display, but the soldiers standing behind Scaurus were sufficiently audible in their appreciation that Julius turned around to silence them with a glare and a meaningful tap of his vine stick against his mailed chest. She stood and waited until the sudden rumble of male voices had died away, pushing an errant lock of her light-brown hair back into place in a gesture the tribune recognised as an artifice even as his body responded to her overt sexuality.

'Good morning, madam. And you are?'

'Theodora, Tribune.'

'Theodora? From the Greek?'

The woman nodded, a pair of large golden discs hanging from her ears bobbing at the movement.

· 'It means god's gift, or so my father told me when I was small enough to believe every word that came out of his mouth. I am the owner of the Raven Head mine, on the southern side of the valley, beneath the rock for which this place is named.' She pointed at the distinctive rock poised over the mountain that formed the valley's southern side and smiled at the Roman, and Scaurus realised that for all her aggressive swagger she was fairer of face than any of the harried-looking women he'd seen about the settlement. Warning himself not to stare, even if he hadn't laid eyes on so welcome a sight for months, the tribune turned away from the trio and walked for a dozen paces before turning to speak again, his voice raised to carry over the throng.

'Very well then, let's be about our business for the day. How many men do you estimate we have here, First Spear?'

Julius grimaced, more used to counting men arranged into convenient lines.

'Three thousand or so, Tribune.'

'And yet the procurator with responsibility for this facility informed me that you had nearly five thousand men working your mines. Where are the rest of your people?'

Not one of the trio standing before Scaurus showed the slightest sign of discomfort at the acerbic tone in which his question was pitched. Theodora spoke again, waving a hand at the valley sides.

'Contrary to appearances, Tribune, the mountains around us are not the dry towers of rock that they appear from the outside. They are riven by faults, cracks in the rock through which water runs down from the ground above them. If we abandon a mine for as much as a day the lower levels will be knee-deep in water, and a week would make them unworkable. Those men that you don't see here are performing essential work to keep the workings dry, and to prevent our absence from causing problems when you finally allow our men back to work.'

Scaurus exchanged a long glance with her, gauging the truth of her statement.

'Indeed. I recall Procurator Maximus mentioning the requirement for constant water removal. He also told me that you need hundreds of men to keep your mines dry, but not, I should point out, thousands. Once we've finished this discussion and your labour is put to work making this valley defendable against the Sarmatae, I shall pick a mine at random and take a tour, *unguided*, I should add, and see what I can see. And be assured, madam, if I should find as much as a ten-year-old child digging for gold with a spoon, then all three of you will taste the harsher end of Roman military justice. So I suggest that you all send men to your mines, just to be sure that my prohibition is being obeyed to the letter. I *will* have every fit man not required to keep your investments from drowning out here in the sunlight building our defences, whether you like it or not. It's either that, or all three of you can take a turn on *that*.' He waved a hand at the parade ground's whipping post, a constant reminder of Roman military discipline. 'It's not the best way to start off what we all must hope will be a short and productive relationship, but the three of you will all take five strokes of the scourge if any one of you disobeys me in this.'

Lartius smiled a lopsided grin, revealing white teeth in his grimy face.

'If you catch us, that is.'

Scaurus shrugged, his return smile hard and mirthless.

'Try me. If *any* of you forces my hand I'll have all three of you naked and bleeding in front of your workers. *When* I catch you.'

Felix stepped forward, his face set in the uneasy, placating smile of a penniless debtor confronted by thugs sent to collect his dues, and raised a manicured hand to the soldiers.

'This is easily remedied, Tribune. I'm sure the message simply has yet to reach the furthest parts of our businesses. With your permission?'

Scaurus nodded magnanimously, and Felix drew his colleagues away for a moment of whispered discussion.

'Would you really put a woman on the whipping post, Tribune?'

Julius's quiet question creased Scaurus's face into a smile, and he turned away from the miners to ensure that his words were not overheard.

'No, or at least not from choice. But if they believe that I will then that, First Spear, is really all that matters. If we show these men – and especially, I suspect, that woman – the slightest hint of weakness, then they will treat us like the fools we probably are here in their world. This is a confidence trick, Julius, so let us hope that we've gulled these three, at least for the time being. I just wish that bloody fool Maximus had warned us that one of them was a woman.'

Nodding their mutual agreement, the mine owners turned to their closest aides with hasty instructions, then stepped back in front of Scaurus.

'All is resolved, Tribune. Messengers will be sent to our mines to ensure that all men not drawing off the water will attend whatever work it is you have planned for us.'

Scaurus nodded graciously.

'A wise decision, and one that will hopefully spare us all from any unhelpful indignity. And so to business. You're doubtless wondering what you people can do in defence of your mines that three cohorts of well trained and fully equipped soldiers can't, and my answer is simple. Nothing. But what you can do is make our preparations to defend this valley, and your investments, complete in much less time. And time is the key to this situation, my friends, because to be blunt we don't have very much of it.'

All three of the mine owners stared at the tribune blankly, and Julius realised that they hadn't the first clue as to what he was talking about. Scaurus shook his head, muttering an imprecation at the absent procurator.

'I see all of this means nothing to you. In which case I should inform you that this part of the empire is at war.'

'With *who*?' Lartius's question was both loud and incredulous, his big dirty hands spread wide and his head shaking in disbelief. 'The whole reason I took on this mine was because Procurator Maximus assured me that the Sarmatae were no longer any danger. He told me that the legions beat them all ends up, and sent most of their warrior strength to some shithole island on the other side of the empire to keep the savages there in their place . . .'

He fell silent in the face of Scaurus's knowing smile.

'And that's exactly what the histories will say. Victory coins were minted, the Blessed Marcus Aurelius took the name "Sarmaticus", a triumph was held in Rome, and the Sarmatae were declared to be a broken threat. And yet here we are, getting ready to fight those same tribesmen once again. Will our efforts here ever be recorded for posterity?' He shook his head with a smile. 'Given that any formal war with the Sarmatae is not possible without undermining the glory of the current emperor's recently deceased father, then whatever happens here will most likely be recorded as "a border dispute". But trust me when I tell you that a man can die in a skirmish just as easily as in the course of a full-blooded war. These tribesmen mean business, which requires us to all be ready for them, if you value your own lives.'

He looked across the silent crowd, judging his moment.

'But ready for what, you ask? Let me show you.'

He gestured to Julius, who in turn nodded to his chosen man. A quartet of soldiers led forward an aging mule, and the chosen man carefully pulled a red-painted arrow from the quiver taken from one of the dead Sarmatae, jabbing the jagged bone head deep into the animal's flank. For a moment the beast's reaction was no more than an indignant bray and a kicking struggle against the ropes securing it, but within a few heartbeats its demeanour changed abruptly. Emitting a high-pitched squeal of distress the animal staggered sideways, away from the chosen man, then sank to its knees, its eyes rolling as the poisonous mixture coated onto the arrow's head took fuller effect. Collapsing to the ground it lay still, panting hard with a dribble of bloody foam running from its open mouth, and Julius had to force himself to keep watching as the beast twitched spasmodically. Scaurus reached out for the arrow, taking it from the chosen man with delicate care before raising it over his head for all present to see.

'That, my friends, is the death that awaits us all if the Sarmatae reach this valley before we complete the fortifications needed to defend it. They combine snake venom with fresh cow dung to make a paste, age it for a while to allow the two to combine, then smear it onto bone arrowheads which soak up the mixture. My men have shields and armour, but you're all completely unprotected, and so when they send showers of these over our defences it'll mostly be *you* dying like that. You, and your families. Speaking of which, if you have women with you then you can be sure that they will be raped out of hand, and many of you men will probably suffer the same indignity. After which you will be put to work in the mines to quarry gold for your new masters.'

A man spoke out from the safety of the crowd's anonymity.

'Working the mines? What's so terrible about that?'

Scaurus smiled at the shouted question.

'Well for a start you'll be unpaid, because they'll have robbed the procurator's strongroom of every coin. However little it is that you receive now, I'm sure it will be better than working for nothing. Then they'll rob you of anything and everything of value. And you'll be sharing your rations with twice your number of armed men who care nothing for your survival. Times will get lean very quickly and so, I expect, will all of *you*. But worst of all, don't forget that any Sarmatae occupation can only be a temporary one, until two angry legions come marching up that road and drive them off, and they'll know that all too well. They'll work you day and night, driving you like animals to dig every last tiny piece of gold they can get out of these hills before that day. Many of you will die from exhaustion and for lack of enough food to support your exertions, and others will be executed simply to give the rest of you an example of what will happen if you slacken your work rate.'

He looked across the men gathered before him with a harsh expression.

'By the time the legions manage to chase them off, the Sarmatae will have turned this valley into a charnel house, and all that will be left for the survivors when the legions free you, if the Sarmatae don't slaughter you all as one last kick at the empire, will be to burn the rotting corpses of your fellow workers. I'd suggest that you think on it, but as you can see, I really don't have time for this to be an exercise in persuasion. So, you *will* do exactly what you're told, under the guidance of my soldiers, and any of you that feel like discovering what it feels like to be scourged *will* get their opportunity simply by stepping out of line. We have only a day or two to make this valley impregnable, which means there's no time to be wasted. First Spear?'

Julius stepped forward, his gruff bark stiffening more than one back in the throng of miners.

'My soldiers are going to build a turf wall right across this valley, with your assistance. It will be fifteen feet tall and fifteen feet deep at the base, with a fighting platform to the rear of the wall ten feet off the ground to allow my men to fight off attackers with their spears. Some of you will be cutting turf blocks, some of you will then carry them to the wall for laying by skilled builders, and we will work as long as we have enough light. The turfs weigh five pounds apiece, which doesn't sound like much, but we'll be laying about a million of them, so I think it's safe to say that you've all got a full day ahead of you.'

At his command the waiting centurions stepped up to the mass of soldiers, detailing each of their men a party of ten miners to command. Scaurus, his lips pursed in speculation, watched Theodora walk away in the company of a pair of heavily built bruisers, whose role in life was clearly to ensure that she remained untroubled in a sea of sex-hungry labourers.

'What do you think?'

Julius stared at the miners for a moment, seeing a combination of resentment and disgusted resignation in their eyes before answering Scaurus's question with an amused expression.

'What do I think, Tribune? Are you asking me about this rabble of work-shy tunnel rats, or the woman?' He waited until Scaurus turned back to face him with a rueful grin. 'I think they hate us marginally less than they fear the Sarmatae, which is only marginally less than they fear us. I think they'll show us their arses when we march away, and piss in our water supply given half a chance. But I also think we'll have a wall across the valley by nightfall tomorrow, and a few nasty little tricks up our sleeve besides. And that, Tribune, is all I really care about.'

He saluted and went off to join the officers marshalling their work gangs into some sort of order, leaving Scaurus staring out across the valley with a calculating gaze.

Left behind in the Tungrian camp when the centuries marched out about their various tasks, Lupus found himself alone for the first time in months. Knowing that the few remaining soldiers left to guard the camp would be of little entertainment, he took up his practice sword and shield and set about going through the set fighting routine that Arminius had taught him, and which he was expected to practise every morning and evening without fail. The boy was beginning to understand the German's purpose in teaching him by means of the routine's apparently endless repetition, as his wrists and ankles strengthened and his stamina improved to the point where he was no longer walking through the moves after an hour's practice, but still fresh enough to perform in almost as sprightly a fashion as when he had begun. Stabbing and cutting at imaginary enemies, ducking and weaving in response to their attacks, he flowed from attack to defence and back again, building towards the routine's final move, a stab to the front while thrusting his shield to the rear to deflect an attack from behind, followed by a lightning-fast spin and hack with the sword's blade. Grunting with the effort as he made the penultimate attack, he spun into the routine's last move only to find himself face-to-face with a slightly smaller boy whose eyes were wide at the sight of his gyrations. Surprised, he stepped back with the shield instinctively raised.

'Who are you?'

The answer was instant, the younger child untroubled by their apparent age difference.

'I'm Mus. What are you doing?'

Lupus frowned, thinking the answer altogether too obvious.

'Practising. Arminius says practice makes perfect.'

'Who's Arminius?'

A proprietorial note entered Lupus's voice.

'My sword teacher. He's German.'

'Do you live with the soldiers?'

Lupus nodded, and Mus's eyes misted over as he fought back tears.

'My father used to be a soldier. Some bad men killed him and burned down our village. They hurt my mother and my sisters. And they killed my brothers . . .'

Lupus responded solemnly, his own father's death suddenly

raw, as if the younger boy's revelation had ripped away a long-hardened layer of scar tissue.

'My father was killed by barbarians too. I live with my granddad now, but Arminius looks after me most of all.'

The two boys were silent for a moment, before Mus spoke again, wiping away a tear that was trickling down his cheek with the briskness of a child who had quickly learned there was little to be gained from crying.

'I don't have any family left, so I work in the mine, but there's no digging allowed today or the miners get whipped. I went to help build the wall, but the soldier said I was too small to help, so I just thought I'd have a look around here.'

Lupus shook his head.

'You shouldn't be here. If the soldiers catch you they'll probably whip you.'

Mus's eyes widened.

'You won't tell them, will you?'

Lupus thought for a moment.

'No.' He eyed the boy with a calculating glance. 'Not if we're going to be friends.'

'Friends? I don't have any friends. The miners are alright, but they curse at me when I get in the way in the mine, and sometimes even when I don't I put oil in the lamps to keep the passages lit, and I know every passage there is. I even know some that the miners have forgotten about.' He looked at Lupus with a sideways glance, as if he were weighing the other boy up. 'Do you want to see?'

'My word . . .'

Tribune Scaurus stood in the strongroom's lamplight and looked at the wooden boxes stacked neatly against the far wall.

'Every box contains fifty pounds of gold, and we currently have . . .' Maximus paused for a moment to consult his tablet, 'forty-three boxes, or two thousand, one hundred and fifty pounds. We fill two boxes a day, on average, and we can accommodate six months of production without any problem, so as you can see there's no immediate need to send a shipment to

Rome given the risk of it being intercepted by the barbarians.'

Julius walked across the small room and put a hand on one of the boxes, grinning at the look of discomfort that slid across the procurator's face.

'So if there's a quarter of an ounce of gold in an aurei, each of these boxes contains enough to mint over three thousand coins. Which makes the contents of this strongroom worth . . .'

The first spear frowned as he did the calculation, but Maximus was ready for him.

'Worth almost one hundred and forty thousand aurei, First Spear.'

Scaurus nodded with pursed lips, turning back to face the procurator.

'Enough gold to qualify a man for the senate a dozen times over must be enough of a temptation in peace time, never mind now. No wonder the Sarmatae are marching on this valley . . .' He stood and looked at the boxes for a moment. 'Of course, it can't stay here.'

Maximus's reaction was faster and more shocked than he'd expected.

'What do you mean "*it can't stay here*"? Do you doubt my trustworthiness, Tribune?'

Scaurus raised an eyebrow to Julius and turned to face the indignant official.

'What I doubt, Procurator, is your ability to hold on to this rather large fortune in the event that the Sarmatae manage to breach our rather hastily laid defences. Surely you'd sleep better knowing that the gold is hidden away somewhere it'll never be found? We could move it at night, and—'

'*Out* of the question.' Maximus's face was stony, and the Tungrian officers shared a glance at the finality in his voice. 'The gold stays here, and you'll just have to do your job and make sure the barbarians don't come anywhere near it. And now that you've seen the arrangements by which I keep the emperor's gold secure, I trust you have no other cause for concern?'

'No *other* cause for concern at all, Procurator. You have adequate guarding in place, the keys to this room are evidently well controlled, and this place can clearly only be entered by means of the door.' He gestured to the massive iron-studded slab of oak that filled the room's only doorway. 'But it's not theft that concerns me half as much as what happens if we all end up face down in the mud, and the Sarmatae have the time to break in here at their leisure.'

Maximus shook his head again, and both men could see from his expression that he would remain obdurately opposed to any talk of relocating the strongroom's contents to a secret location.

'So do your job, Tribune. And let me warn you, I've spoken with your colleague and superior Domitius Belletor, and warned him that I won't tolerate any more interference in the workings of this facility like this morning. Once that wall of yours is built, my men will go back to work and they will stay there.' He smiled thinly at the Tungrians. 'I pointed out to him that it didn't seem to me as if the idea to stop mining had actually been his in the first place, and that the lost production would certainly look bad for someone when this is all done with.'

Scaurus stepped close to him, resting a hand on the hilt of his sword in a gesture whose casual nature was belied by the hard look on his face.

'Divide and rule, Procurator? How very astute of you. I should be careful though, or you might end up rueing the day that you made your opposition to putting this fortune out of temptation's way quite so clear to us. If the Sarmatae do manage to defeat us, then when they break in here they're more than likely to find one last defender waiting for them.' He put a finger in the other man's face. '*You.* And I won't be asking for Domitius Belletor's permission before I lock you in here to wait for them. Come along First Spear.'

Maximus flushed red as they brushed past him, his voice echoing up the steps that led back up into the daylight.

'Are you *threatening* me, Tribune?'

Scaurus barked a single word over his shoulder and kept walking.

'*Yes!*'

★   ★   ★

'This is *my* mine. Raven Head.'

Still breathing hard from the climb that had brought them a third of the way up the mountainside, Mus gestured proudly to the massive rock that loomed over the mine's entrance, the peak's beak-like overhang giving it the dark silhouette of a carrion bird against the clear blue of the sky above. A hole opened in the mountainside before the two boys, heavy wooden props to either side of the black space supporting a massive cross-beam above the entrance. Lupus stared dubiously at the black square, shaking his head slightly.

'It's dark.'

The smaller boy smiled, stepping forward to the mine's threshold.

'It's better once you're inside. Your eyes adjust, and there are lamps too. Come on, let's go and have a look around.' He reached for a jar of lamp oil from a stack by the open doorway and then walked into the darkness, disappearing from view as if he had been wiped away, although when Lupus strained his eyes he caught the barest shadow of his new friend waiting for him in the gloom. Summoning up his courage he forced himself to walk into the blackness, advancing in small steps until, with a start, he found himself beside Mus, the younger child's eyes gleaming with the light from the doorway's pale rectangle. When he spoke the boy's voice was no more than a whisper.

'See, it's no different from being out there.'

Lupus shivered.

'It's cold.'

'That's why I said to fetch your cloak. It's colder when you get deeper into the mountain.'

Mus reached out with fingers made expert by long practice and found a lamp in a small alcove.

'Here we are.'

He fiddled in the darkness for a moment, then Lupus heard the familiar sound of iron and flint. Blowing gently on the sparks that flew onto the lamp's wick Mus coaxed a flame to life, bringing a meagre but to Lupus's eyes very welcome light to the darkness.

Standing with the lamp in his hand the younger boy grinned happily at his new friend.

'Come on, I'll show you round.'

He turned and padded away into the darkness, his small body framed in the lamp's pale light, leaving Lupus staring at his receding figure. Turning back to the mine's entrance, he was momentarily gripped with an instinctive need to run for the rectangle of daylight, but knew in his heart that doing so would not only expose him to the younger boy's derision but that some part of him would be dissatisfied with the choice to retreat in the face of his fear. Still troubled by the darkness around them, he paced forward in Mus's wake, concentrating on not losing sight of the boy's back. The passage walls, dimly illumin-ated for a few feet on either side, were rough, snagging at his fingers as he reached out for their reassuring touch, and the floor was damp and uneven beneath his boots as it sloped gently *up* into the mountain. Even the faintest of sounds were magni-fied by the tunnel's echoes, each scrape of the boys' boots sounding like a dozen footfalls. The pair walked in silence down the passage for long enough to reduce the entrance to a distant speck of light, and to Lupus's surprise he found his initial panic increasingly forgotten as the means of its relief receded grad-ually from view.

'Here we are, here's the first ladder.'

Lupus frowned, looking at the wooden ladders that ran both upwards and downwards from the spot, unable to see where they led to.

'We have to climb?'

Mus turned back to him, perhaps sensing the uncertainty in his voice.

'We have to go down to reach the place where they mine the gold. Don't worry, it's safe as long as you only move one hand or foot at a time, at least until you get used to it.'

'But you're carrying the lamp?'

'Don't worry, I can climb the ladders one-handed. Here, you go first.'

Suitably reassured, Lupus climbed gingerly onto the ladder and started down with slow, cautious movements, quickly gaining enough confidence to speed up his pace to what seemed like a breakneck descent.

'Good, just take it nice and steady, and don't look . . .'

The other boy's sentence was still incomplete when Lupus found himself compelled to stare down into the darkness. He stopped and hung from the ladder's rungs, an abrupt and irresistible terror gripping him as he realised that he had no idea what depth of empty air waited beneath his feet. Mus spoke to him from above his head, bringing the lamp close to his face to reveal a reassuring smile as Lupus looked up at him.

'It's not far now, just climb down slowly and be ready for your foot to reach the ground. *Trust* me.' Screwing up his nerve, Lupus lowered one foot to the next rung down, waiting for a moment with sweat running down his face before moving the other. 'Good! Keep going, we can get a drink of water when we get down.'

Lupus climbed down another dozen rungs before his foot touched rock, and he staggered away from the ladder as Mus alighted gracefully behind him. The boy took him by the arm and led him to a channel cut into the floor.

'See, water. Have a drink, we've a little way to go yet.'

They drank from cupped hands, and Lupus found the ice-cold water refreshing and clean to the taste.

'Where does it come from?'

Mus grinned back at him in the half-light.

'Come down another ladder with me and I'll show you. And where the gold comes from.'

Marcus walked up to his tribune and saluted smartly, repeating the gesture for Tribune Sigilis's benefit but giving his attention to Scaurus and thereby turning his face away from the younger man as much as possible. The two men were standing by the wall's only opening, a ten-pace-wide gap in the centre of the rampart's eight-hundred-pace length into which a heavy wooden gate was to be set before being backed with enough turf to make it a temporarily immovable part of the defences. They were looking along the line of the planned fortification, and Sigilis was gesturing along the shallow wall with an enthusiasm that the young centurion found surprising given his previous reserve, and his apparent contentment to stay in Tribune Belletor's shadow.

'And perhaps we might make their task even harder by embedding stakes in the upper part of the wall, pointing down to keep them from placing ladders against the parapet?'

Scaurus smiled with what looked suspiciously like a trace of indulgence to Marcus's trained eye.

'Indeed we might, in fact my first spear was muttering something to the same effect when we were designing this edifice. Centurion?'

Marcus snapped to attention, playing the part of an obeisant officer with all his wit.

'Tribune, sir, you asked me to scout the valley's northern side. I can report that the watch post between Rotunda Mountain and the ridge to the west is intact and undisturbed, but that the ground around it shows signs of having been trodden by Sarmatae mounted scouts within the last twenty-four hours. Additionally, the ground beyond the Saddle is open and has been deforested for several hundred paces, making it highly suitable for an enemy attack.'

Scaurus grimaced.

'I suppose it was inevitable they'd have a watch on the valley. How easily can the Saddle be defended against an attacking force?'

Marcus shrugged, unconsciously calling on the military knowledge he'd gleaned in the previous eighteen months of brutal lessons at the hands of the barbarian tribes of Britannia.

'I wouldn't want to lead any strength of cavalry up the north slope, Tribune, it's shallow enough for a mounted approach, but littered with rabbit holes and boulders. Any infantrymen that might be sent up it will be tired from the climb up through the forest, and would have to attack uphill into prepared defences, but if they're going to get around that . . .' He gestured to the turf wall's length. 'Their leader may decide to spend his foot soldiers lavishly if it's the price of putting men in our rear.'

Scaurus nodded, turning to Sigilis.

'So colleague, while this wall and the fortifications we'll use to deny the enemy the slopes to either side of it are of the utmost importance, we'll need to be on our guard against just such an attempt to outflank them. Our colleague Belletor might well decide to mount a guard on this weak spot, with the right encouragement from a man he considers to be of equal standing? I fear I've used up all the presumption our fragile relationship can bear for the time being, but if you were to make such a suggestion . . .'

The younger man nodded his head with a look of understanding, and Scaurus smiled easily.

'Good. I do so dislike having to manoeuvre him when a man he considers his social equal can be so much more persuasive with a good deal less effort. In the meanwhile the only question that really matters now is just how far away the warband is, because if they arrive in front of this wall before it reaches an effective height, we might as well not have bothered going to all this effort. Perhaps a mounted reconnaissance . . .' He turned to look down the line of the defence work, the space around it teeming with labouring men cutting turfs and carrying them to the slowly ascending structure, while Marcus stood in silence, acutely aware of Tribune Sigilis's unblinking scrutiny. 'Yes, I think a scouting party would be our best means of finding that out. Carry a message to Decurion Silus, if you will Centurion Corvus, and invite him to join me here at his earliest convenience, along with yourself and your Hamian colleague. I believe the time has come for us to gain a somewhat better understanding of what's on the other side of this particular hill than we have at the present.'

He paused, having noted the approach of Felix, the owner of the Split Rock mine further down the valley. The businessman was clearly in a state of agitation, practically running up the slope towards the officers, and Scaurus turned to his colleagues with a wry expression.

'Ah, I've been expecting this all day. I have to say I'm surprised it's taken him this long to realise he's got a problem.' He called out to the troubled mine owner. 'Greetings, Felix, can we be of any assistance to you? You do seem a little distressed.'

Felix covered the last few paces between them in the attitude of a supplicant, his hands pressed together as if to solicit a favour, and the look on his face openly pleading.

'Tribune Scaurus, a dreadful mistake has been made, a terrible error that must be put right! I beg of you . . .'

Scaurus tipped his head to one side, his face taking on a sympathetic cast.

'I will do whatever is within my power to assist you. Tell me, what is this "dreadful mistake"?'

Felix turned and pointed at the wall with a look of horror.

'This wall, Tribune! It is too far up the valley, and my mine is left outside the defences! When the enemy come they will have my business at their mercy, undefended and open to their pillage!'

'I see . . .' Scaurus stroked his chin as if in deep thought. 'Yes, that is a problem.'

Felix's face brightened.

'So you'll move the wall, Tribune?'

Scaurus shook his head sadly.

'I'm afraid not. Not only would that be an insane waste of the progress we've already made, but this rampart's current line requires it be no more than eight hundred paces long. Whereas, were I to command it to be moved in order to defend the *emperor's* property to the south, including a mine which you are fortunate enough to be allowed to work on his behalf . . .' he paused to allow the statement to sink in, 'then I would need to double its length. We would need twice as much turf, which would take twice as long, and I would then need at least twice as many soldiers to defend it. So, as you can see, I have neither the time nor the manpower to incorporate the Split Rock mine into the valley's defendable ground, Felix. You and your men, however, will be safe enough behind this.'

He patted the eight-foot-high foundation beside him. Felix gestured helplessly in response.

'But my mine . . .'

'Will indeed be undefended, although I'll be happy to lend you a sword if you're that keen on fighting to keep what's yours?'

The mine owner's eyes narrowed.

'You're making fun of me. I don't believe you ever truly intended to defend the Split Rock, did you?'

Scaurus shrugged, his response couched in a breezy tone which did little to mask the steel that underlaid it.

'In all truth, Felix, it was never my main concern. I simply told my officers to find the best line with which to defend the valley and its occupants, and this is what they settled on. If I were you I'd count my blessings, given that we're here to stand between you and enough barbarians to put a very severe crimp in your day. I'd get as much of your equipment as you can out of the mine and prepare whoever's left down there to evacuate when the Sarmatae get here. Unless you want to find yourselves fighting to defend the emperor's gold?'

'It's *so* cold!'

Mus shrugged at the comment, even though the unconscious gesture was invisible in the mine's gloom.

'That's why I told you to wear your cloak.'

They paced through the darkness, Lupus making sure he stayed close to the dim glow of Mus's oil lamp. The younger boy stopped several times to add oil to the lamps perched on shelves cut into the passage's stone walls, their flames providing tiny islands of light in the pitch-black that seemed to bear down on them from all sides. Eventually a slightly brighter light appeared around a bend in the passage, and Mus turned to him with a finger to his lips, whispering in his new friend's ear.

'Be very quiet. I don't want them to see us.'

They crept down the corridor, and when he judged that they were close enough to the light from whatever it was that was waiting, Mus put the lamp down before leading Lupus forward again. Keeping low, they peeked around a corner into a chamber lit by torches, the open space dominated by a massive wooden wheel, three times as tall as a full-grown man and mounted on a heavy axle. A pair of muscular labourers were toiling at the device, using their strength to turn the wheel by means of bars protruding from each of the spokes, their powerful arms bulging with the effort. Another two equally powerful men sat off to one side with an hourglass and a water jug. Mystified, Lupus whispered a question.

'What are they doing?'

Mus pointed to the wheel.

'Look at the bottom of the wheel. Can you see the water?'

The wheel's bottom was submerged in a pool of water, and as Lupus stared harder he realised that as it turned, the device was dragging wooden buckets attached to the rim through the pool. Whilst a little of the water captured by the buckets splashed out as they rocked to and fro, they were clearly still quite full as they swung on their mountings. From his own experience of carrying the medical wagon's water bucket to and from whatever river or spring the cohort camped by, he knew that they were bound to be heavy. At the height of their travel the buckets were tipping over into a wooden trough carefully aligned with the top of the wheel.

'Now you can see why the passage we climbed down from slopes uphill. The wheel takes the water up to the level of the passage we climbed down from, and the water runs down the slope and then away down the hillside.'

As they watched, the last sand ran out of the glass and the resting workers climbed to their feet and took over the task of dragging the wheel around, while the men they had replaced stretched their aching bodies before sinking down onto the rock floor to rest.

'Is that all they do all day?'

'If they don't do it then the chamber would fill up with water and soon the mine would be flooded. And it's safe now. My friend Karsas is having a rest.'

Lupus followed Mus into the chamber, and one of the workers got to his feet with a smile of greeting.

'Welcome, little one. Who's this you've brought to see us?'

'He lives with the soldiers. He's got a sword, and he let me hold it.'

'So you repaid the favour by bringing him down here? You chose the right time to come forward though. If Gosakos there were not at the wheel, I expect he'd be chasing you round the chamber with his prick in his hand.' Lupus frowned and turned to look at the men on the wheel, meeting the hungry stare of the closer of the two with a shiver of fear. 'Not to worry, he knows what happens to men like him if they make the mistake of touching my friends. And he'll be turning that wheel for a while now, so we've got time to talk if you like? It still helps to talk . . .'

Mus shook his head.

'Not today. Can we have a look at the face?'

Karsas put his head back and chuckled, winking at Lupus.

'You want to see some gold, eh young 'un? Come on then, follow me. There's no one to get in our way today since they're all upstairs getting chased round the valley by your mates, and good bloody riddance to the lot of them. Always swaggering about and gobbing off about how they're the real miners when all they ever do is quarry out the rock, while us men practically live down here to keep the place going.'

He took a torch from the wall and walked away up another passage, gesturing to the boys with his free hand.

'Come on then, my lads, come and see where all the gold comes from.'

Scaurus was enjoying his first cup of wine of the evening when Arminius put his head round the tent's open flap and held out a message tablet. Scaurus frowned at his unexpected appearance.

'Shouldn't you be away training the boy Lupus in which end of a sword makes the nasty holes?'

Arminius shrugged.

'He seems to have found something more interesting to do, so I contented myself with a swift kick of Morban's backside for letting him wander off without seeking permission. I'll go looking for him again once you've got some food in front of you. Anyway, take this . . .' He held up the message tablet. 'One of the woman Theodora's bruisers brought it to the camp entrance, and a soldier ran it up here. Apparently the messenger's waiting for you.'

The tribune sipped at his wine.

'Well, what is it? I know damned well you'll already have read it.'

The German smiled.

'Not only read it, I've smelt it too.'

Scaurus raised an eyebrow, taking the tablet and sniffing at it.

'My word. I see what you mean. And?'

The German shrugged.

'It's from the lady mine owner herself. She's inviting you to dinner with her and her fellow businessmen.'

Scaurus grinned up at his bodyguard.

'I see. So my choice is either to sit here, drink this decidedly average red and eat whatever unidentifiable meat it is that you're busy burning, or go and break bread with the people whose livelihood I'm either protecting or ruining, depending on one's point of view. That's a tough one . . .'

The German shook his head in disgust.

'Let's hope they're not planning to do a re-enactment of Caesar and the senators with you, given the havoc you've been causing with your wall. You'd better wear the breastplate, just in case.'

Scaurus nodded in agreement, looking at the heavy sculpted-bronze armour in its place in the tent's corner.

'Quite so. Not only will I feel safer, but I've always found the old bronze to be a sure-fire winner with the ladies. Family heirloom, worn by my noble ancestor in the Year of the Four Emperors, that sort of thing. It helps not to mention that he ended up on the losing side, mind you. Give me a hand with it, if you will?'

'Begging your pardon, Centurion, but have you seen that damnable boy?'

Morban made a quick salute to his centurion, looking about Marcus's tent with a harried-looking stare as the Roman turned from the sword blade he'd been polishing.

'If you mean your grandson, I've not seen him. I'd assumed that he was training with Arminius.'

'That's just the problem, sir, he's nowhere to be found. Arminius is chewing on my leg for wasting his time waiting for the lad, and so I wondered . . .'

He looked about the tent again, as if hopeful that Marcus might have Lupus hidden in one of the corners, then shook his head in exasperation and withdrew. The young centurion followed him out into the still early evening air, both men reflexively looking up and down the line of tents. Seeing the big German approaching, Marcus waited for him to reach them before speaking.

'No sign?'

Arminius shook his head darkly.

'Nothing. The gate guards say they saw him a few hours ago, practising with his sword, but after that there's been no sign at all. If he's wandered off into the town there's no saying what trouble he might have . . .'

He fell silent, raising a hand to point at something behind the other two men. Marcus turned to see Lupus sidling down the line of tents with another boy a few paces behind him. The child's companion wore an expression that told the Roman he was poised and ready to run.

'Not a word, either of you, or whoever that is will be on his toes and we'll never know the truth of it. Arminius, take the standard bearer here away to the town's beer shop for a discussion about a donation for the boy's equipment needs. His mail looks to be getting a little short to me . . .'

The German nodded knowingly, taking a firm hold of Morban's arm.

'Come then, Morban, we'll combine your favourite activity with your biggest fear.'

As they walked away Marcus squatted down on his haunches,

watching the two boys approach. Lupus walked up to his officer and saluted as the soldiers had taught him, his eyes alive with excitement.

'Centurion, I've been in a gold mine!'

Marcus nodded calmly, smiling at the other boy who was lurking out of arm's reach.

'I guessed by the state of your cloak that you'd been somewhere dark and dirty. A gold mine, eh? Did you find any gold?'

Lupus's eyes widened with the memory, the enthusiasm spilling out of him in the absence of any punishment for going missing.

'No. Mus's friend Karsas took us to look at something called a seam, but it was only rock. But I saw the men turning the waterwheel, and we put oil in the lamps, and Mus . . .' he turned to the other boy, 'Mus showed me how to climb up the *thirty*-foot ladder like he does, with a lamp in one hand, and we went to the other side of the mountain to see the Raven, and—'

Marcus smiled at the smaller child, making no effort to move in the face of the boy's obvious readiness to run. He gently over-rode Lupus with a question.

'Hello Mus, I'm Marcus. Are you boys hungry?' Lupus nodded eagerly, and his new friend's face brightened slightly. 'I'll tell you what, why don't we go and see Felicia and Annia and see what they're cooking for dinner. You can tell me all about where you've been and what you've done while we eat, and after that the pair of you can clean my boots and armour together, eh?'

He turned away from the children as he stood, hoping not to send the younger boy running simply with the movement, and walked slowly away down the line of tents without looking to see if they were following. Lupus turned to his friend, who was staring at the Roman's back in a misery of indecision, and held out his open palm.

'In the mine today, I was scared of the darkness and the ladder, and you told me to trust you?' Mus nodded, still watching Marcus, and Lupus waited in silence until the boy's gaze turned back to his outstretched hand. 'So now *you* have to trust *me*.'

★　　★　　★

Scaurus followed the waiting messenger up the valley in the early evening's dim starlight with one hand on the hilt of his sword, but the taciturn man led him past the miners' camp and straight up the road into the heart of Alburnus Major, a cluster of houses that huddled in the shadow of the Rotunda Mountain. A figure walked down the road out of the gloom, and a familiar voice spoke in a tone which to the tribune's ear was clearly edged with more than a hint of bitterness.

'Well now, Tribune Scaurus, you seem to be getting around smartly enough.'

The tribune nodded tersely, putting both hands on his hips and forcing a note of civility into his voice, while the messenger lurked almost unseen in the darkness.

'Good evening, Procurator. Are you joining us for dinner?'

Maximus laughed, and again Scaurus was left with the feeling that there was something he was missing.

'No, Tribune, I won't be joining you.' He stepped around Scaurus, calling out over his shoulder as he continued on down the road, his last words floating away across the darkened landscape. 'I wish you a pleasant evening, although I have little doubt you'll find the entertainment to your taste. Unless, of course, all those stories we hear about soldiers preferring masculine company are true . . .'

Watching the procurator vanish into the darkness, Scaurus shrugged and turned back to his guide, gesturing with a hand for the man to continue on his path. The messenger led him into a walled courtyard, across a wide, paved garden lit by a dozen blazing torches and decorated with tastefully planted trees and shrubs, and up to the front door of the large villa sheltered behind the high walls. He hammered at the door, which was promptly opened by an imposingly rotund slave who beckoned the tribune inside. Closing the door behind them, the man turned back to him with a slight smile.

'Good evening, sir. Might I take your sword, before I escort you through into the dining room?'

Scaurus shrugged and eased the weapon's baldric over his head.

'I'll keep the dagger if it's all the same to you. A man needs something to eat with. And take care with that blade, it's been in my family since the blessed Claudius was on the throne.'

The portly servant nodded, taking the weapon with the appropriate reverence and then ushering the tribune through a door and into an empty room with two couches set out on either side of a low table, on which stood a wine bottle and two beakers.

'The lady will join you shortly, sir, I believe.'

'The lady?'

Whether deliberately or not, the slave had withdrawn too quickly to have heard the question, leaving a bemused Scaurus to pace around the room with one hand on the dagger's hilt, and a distinct feeling that he was being misled in some way. Glancing at the murals that decorated the walls he frowned momentarily, then raised an intrigued eyebrow as he realised exactly what it was that they depicted.

'Good, aren't they? I had to pay an absolute *fortune* to find an artist with the skill and experience to get them right, but it was worth every denarius if the reaction of the men who see them is any indication of their value. I particularly like that one, where he's mounting her from behind. Do you see the way her back's arched? You can almost hear the cries of pleasure as he grinds her into the couch.'

Scaurus nodded, turning to face the speaker with the distinct feeling that his face was a little pinker than might be desirable. Theodora was carefully posed in the doorway on the opposite side of the room, leaning against the door frame with her elegant chin resting on her raised hand and the other hand at her side, gently stroking at whatever gauzy, semi-transparent material had been used to make her gown. He bowed deeply, using the moment to gather his thoughts.

'Ah, madam. I must admit you have me at a disadvantage. Your messenger led me to expect a dinner party, but your rather exotic clothing indicates that the gathering might be a more select group than I'd imagined?'

She laughed, the sound light and breathy in the room's silence, and stepped away from the door with a calculating look on her face.

'The confusion is purely intentional, Tribune. I wanted you all to myself, but I wasn't sure how you would have responded to an invitation that would appear to be aimed at seeking favouritism with you.'

He raised both eyebrows, putting his hands on his hips.

'Which is exactly what this is, I presume.'

Theodora smiled with genuine pleasure.

'Oh yes, of course it is, and how clever of you to see through me. Mind you, I was also hoping to provoke you to come here dressed up in all that lovely armour. I do so *love* a man in uniform. I wish my artist were here now, I'd have him paint you just like that, looking all stern and manly . . .' She walked across the room and ran a finger down his breastplate. 'And shiny too. All my birthdays come at once. If only you'd worn your helmet.'

Scaurus smiled.

'If only I'd known.'

'Ah, but half the fun of these things is the surprise, wouldn't you say? Now, what happens if I undo this?'

She pulled at the fastenings that secured his breastplate, her delicate fingers unpicking the hooks.

'Let's have all that bronze off, shall we? It's all very well for intimidating civilians, but it's not really evening wear, now is it?'

His smiled broadened.

'I must warn you, madam, that I've had a fairly hectic day, and the timing of your invitation allowed me no opportunity to bathe. I may be a little . . . ripe?'

She finished teasing open the tight knots securing his breastplate's two halves, lowering the heavy bronze armour to the floor before bending close and inhaling.

'Marvellous! That, my dear tribune, is the smell of a man. And presumably down here we'll find . . .' She darted a hand beneath his tunic and rubbed at his rapidly swelling penis. 'Exactly what I'm looking for!' She stood, laughing into his expression of delighted astonishment as she tugged him towards the door by the now thoroughly engorged member. 'This way, Gaius. I may call you Gaius, I presume, given that I'm just about to mount this rather impressive specimen? Let's get that first desperate coupling out of the way, shall we? I don't want you leaking all over my furniture in anticipation when a few minutes of vigorous enjoyment can calm it all down until later.'

'Later?'

She smirked knowingly at him, knowing she literally had him in the palm of her hand.

'Oh yes. After a nice long dinner, with enough wine to dull your sensitivity whilst not destroying your ability, during which we can have a chat about how you're going to defend the Raven Head mine against these beastly barbarians, I'll be expecting you to impale me on *this* a few more times. Until, to be perfectly frank, there's no more impaling left in you.'

3

Julius was busy describing the many and varied faults of the day's gate sentries to them in the most graphic and violent terms possible when the message from Annia reached him. He had already left the two tent parties in question in no doubt whatsoever that another such failure in their duties would result in significant loss of pay, not to mention a certain flogging.

'And no, the fact that the boy came back safe doesn't make it any fucking better, because he shouldn't ever have been able to fucking well leave unnoticed, and nor should the other lad have got into the fucking camp in the first fucking place!' He took the message tablet that was being held out to him by a visibly wilting soldier from his own First Century, and scanned the contents before turning back to the waiting man with a wave of dismissal. 'Tell the lady I'll be there shortly. And fetch enough of the evening meal for six people. If it's not at the doctor's tent when I get there you can join this lot on punishment duty and get your spade dirty cleaning out the latrines.'

The soldier swivelled on his heel and ran, having been on the butt end of his first spear's evil temper more than once, while Julius turned his attention to the nearest of the current gate sentries, his sharp eyes quickly finding a pair of men clearly struggling to restrain their mirth at their comrades' predicament. Raising his voice to a parade-ground roar, he bellowed at them loudly enough for half the camp to hear.

'And I don't know what you two are laughing at, because according to that message the other lad got back into the camp with our boy just now, and once again not one of you stupid bastards noticed! I want the entire guard paraded in front of my tent when you come off duty, no exceptions!'

He was delighted to discover that by happy coincidence the night guard's duty centurion was Otho, the most foul tempered of his officers, who had long since been christened 'Knuckles' by soldiers and centurions alike for his pugilistic tendencies. In a short and vigorous discussion he suggested that the veteran officer might do well to sharpen up the camp's guards, using both tone and language he judged were sufficiently terse to result in a rich crop of black eyes and fat lips. Still shaking his head in angry disbelief at his men's failure to detect two children sneaking around the camp in broad daylight, he stamped off to the doctor's tent where, the tablet written by Annia had informed him, he was invited to dine as long as he provided the evening meal. Poised to walk through the tent's doorway, he was met by the lady in question who put her hand on his chest and pushed him firmly away from the opening. Her look was enough to make him hold his tongue long enough for his woman to put her face close to his, her features set in the expression that he'd come to understand signified that she meant business. Her whispered warning was delivered in what he'd taken to describing as her 'command voice', when he was sure that she wasn't listening.

'I knew you were coming this way because I could hear you beasting anyone that crossed your path! We've a guest, Julius, and if you barge in shouting the odds about the "fucking sentries" in your usual manner he'll be out and away before you've stopped to draw breath. I'm not sure exactly what happened to the boy, but what little I do know is that some soldiers tore his life apart, as a result of which he's terrified of a uniform – *any* uniform – especially one filled by a self-important centurion with the temper of a prize bull who's been shut away from the cows for too long.'

Julius watched in disgust over her shoulder as the soldier tasked with fetching the party's dinner took grateful advantage of his first spear's unplanned delay by hurrying into the tent with a large pot, presumably filled with whatever the man had been able to beg, borrow and in all likelihood steal from his fellow soldiers. He opened his mouth to protest, only to find a hard finger pressed against it. 'So *if* you want to be warming your feet in anything better than your cloak tonight, then you'll put a smile on that big ugly face and follow me into the tent as if the lad's presence is the best thing that's happened to you all day. *Won't you?*'

Opening his mouth to agree with alacrity, given that he'd learned from grim experience not to take the lady's favours for granted, he found himself not only silenced but utterly amazed by her parting comment as she turned back to the tent.

'And besides, it's about time we found out just how good a father you're going to make, isn't it?'

'Whatever it was she told him, he went as white as a legionary's arse, according to the soldier he sent to run for his dinner. And when the evening guard reported for a kicking as ordered, rather than ripping them all a new one he just sent them away with no more than a warning not to let it happen again. My mate in the Seventh Century said that the poor bastard looked as if he'd been smacked with an axe handle. And now look at him . . .'

Morban and Arminius turned as one man to look at Julius as the first spear strode down the line of the Fifth Century's tents, his expression that of a man with a deep preoccupation. The standard bearer raised a knowing eyebrow at his companion.

'I've closed the book on whether she's with child or not, and I'm offering two to three on a boy, evens on a girl. Let's see if we can get some confirmation, eh?'

He snapped off an improbably precise salute, which Julius ignored other than casting a brief sardonic glance at the standard bearer.

'Good morning, First Spear, sir!' Julius's lack of reaction to his artificially breezy greeting only provoked Morban to continue his salutation. 'It's a beautiful clear day, sir, perhaps we'll get that wall . . .'

He fell silent as the first spear stopped in his tracks, turned his head to stare expressionlessly at him, then rotated his body and stepped forward to put his nose only inches from Morban's face. When he spoke his voice was a low growl.

'Good morning, Standard Bearer. Yes, it is indeed a good day for building a wall, and yes, we will indeed be completing the initial construction today. As to any questions you may have for me, I'd suggest that this is one of those times when discretion would most definitely be the better part of bravery. Whisper your gossip and lay your odds all you like, but don't be expecting me to provide you with any encouragement. Now get on fucking parade.'

Julius turned away from the standard bearer, who pursed his lips in silent comment but otherwise sensibly kept his mouth firmly closed. The first spear turned back to Arminius.

'Centurion Corvus?'

The German pointed down the line of tents to where the medical wagon stood beside Felicia's hospital tent.

'Is with his wife, saying his farewells.'

Julius found his colleague sitting on a wooden chest with his baby son cradled in his lap while Felicia fussed around him.

'Are you ready?'

Marcus nodded, standing and handing Appius to his wife, kissing her gently before turning to follow the first spear from the tent. They walked down to the section of the camp where the cohort's cavalry detachment had taken up residence, finding five horsemen standing by their mounts, ready to ride, with Marcus's captured mare in their midst. Julius nodded in return to their leader's salute and to the tracker Arabus who seemed to have been drafted into the party.

'Morning, Silus. Have you worked out how you're going to carry out the tribune's orders?'

The grizzled decurion pointed to a rough map sketched in the earth before them.

'According to the miners there's only one road down which an invader would be likely to make his approach to the mine. The same track we marched up runs on past the end of this valley and away to the north, eventually joining up with another valley, which contains a stream that the locals call the Gold River, aptly enough, which in turn feeds the Marisus, deep in hostile territory. If you were aiming to lead a warband out of the plains and bring them here, then I doubt you could do very much better than to lead them up the banks of the Marisus, turn up the Gold and follow it all the way up its valley. That many men will need a lot of water, and the stream will also provide reliable navigation. I plan to ride down the Gold's banks, with the centurion's scout here to look for any tracks they might have left, and if we find nothing of note then I'll set up a watch post on the valley side and wait to see what turns up. When it's evident that they've arrived we'll ride back and warn you. Just make sure you leave us a way back inside the wall, eh?'

Julius nodded grimly.

'You'd best be careful not to outstay your welcome once the barbarians make their appearance. I'd rather find out they've arrived some other way than watching your heads bobbing about on spears.'

Silus turned away, jumping into his mount's saddle.

'Don't worry about us, we'll give the unwashed hordes the appropriate measure of respect. You'll have plenty to keep you busy, I expect, what with finishing off the defences and choosing a name for the impending arrival?'

Julius nodded without any change in his expression.

'Indeed. I was discussing that very subject with the baby's mother-to-be last night, and the two of us were pretty much agreed to call the baby after you . . .' He waited for a moment, allowing the idea to sink in and then, before Silus could muster any reply, shook his head sadly. 'Until Annia pointed out that any child called "Nosey Arsehole" was going to be at a disadvantage in life.'

Silus threw back his head and laughed uproariously.

'Harsh but fair, First Spear, harsh but fair. Come along then, Centurion Two Knives, let's get you mounted and be on our way. I want to be tucked up in our hiding place before the sun gets too high. And since the subject of our first spear's impending arrival is clearly forbidden, we'll work out what to call that greedy little mare of yours instead.'

★   ★   ★

The assembled centurions of the two Tungrian cohorts snapped to attention as Julius stalked into the morning officers' meeting. Some of them stared fixedly at the hills behind him, not daring to meet his eyes, while others, men that had known him longer and in one or two cases had previously outranked him, met his stare with hard, impassive eyes.

'Gentlemen, the rumour's all over the camp so let's lay it to rest. Yes, I am going to be a father. At some point in the future when we're all staggering drunk in celebration of beating off the barbarians and toasting those of us that don't survive the experience, you're all welcome to take the piss as much as you like, as long as you don't mind having your many and varied shortcomings exposed in return. For now though' – he looked around at his officers, taking stock of their grim, bearded faces – 'I couldn't give a shit about any of that. We have one objective today, to get that wall built high enough and strong enough to resist a determined attack by thousands of gold-crazed barbarians. The tribune is away making sure that the legion centuries on the slopes to either side of the wall will have their defences in place, but we all know that if they're going to come at us it has to be straight up the valley. Yes, they'll send patrols round the flanks but they'll get no joy there. It will all come down to a straight fight to get over the wall, and as far as I'm concerned, we have to have it ready to defend by the time darkness falls tonight.'

He looked around at his officers with a hard stare.

'So it's time to stop the soft treatment. We need those miners working like animals today, not taking this as an opportunity to get some sunshine on their backs, so here's a direct instruction for all of you. The first man you see slacking off, soldier or miner, you take your vine stick to him and you make it clear to all of them that the next one will be getting a tickle from this . . .' He held up the whip, allowing its braided leather straps to hang free. 'And if you have to, then you send the next man you have to pull up to me. I'll be setting up a whipping post by the main gate so that anyone who gets to ride it does so in full view of the rest. Now get to it, and don't let me down.'

★   ★   ★

The scouting detachment rode down the road beyond the rapidly growing wall at a swift trot, each man keeping watch in a different direction as a defence against the potential for roaming Sarmatae scouts to surprise them from the dense forest around them. At the Ravenstone valley's end they turned north, rejoining the path up the road that the cohorts had left to reach the mine complex. Two hours' riding saw them over the ridge at this valley's far end and taking their lunch in the shelter of a sparse copse of straggling trees, whose trunks and branches had been twisted and bent to the east over long years of exposure to the wind. Silus sat chewing his bread with his coarse wool cloak wrapped tightly about his body, looking down the valley's length with professional interest.

'Not so different from the mountains to the north of the Wall in Britannia, is it? We could almost be hunting down Calgus and his bluenoses, rather than riding out for a game of cat and mouse with these Sarmatae. Now, as to this horse of yours . . .'

Marcus leant back and rubbed the mare's neck affectionately, provoking an immediate nudge in his back from the animal's snout.

'It seems to me that the giving of names can bring bad luck, if poor old Bonehead is any indication. It might be better to leave her as she is, safely anonymous.'

The decurion snorted derisively.

'That's all very well for you, when you'll only be getting onto her every now and then, but we'll have to feed and exercise her every day. What am I supposed to do, tell my men "go and feed the mare"? I can just imagine the confusion. No, if you won't name her then we will. What do you think lads?'

One of the riders spoke up from behind them.

'She tried to bite me this morning, the crafty bitch. What about Nipper?'

Silus nodded.

'Nipper. I like the sound of that. There you go, Centurion, problem solved. We'll just . . .' He turned back to the view down the valley, his eyes narrowing. 'Nobody move.'

Holding himself stock-still, Marcus swivelled his head slowly
to look at whatever it was that had caught the decurion's attention. A mile or so down the valley's length, at the point where the
river far below them swung in a tight horseshoe to the north, a
party of horsemen had come into view. Silus grimaced at the
sight, shaking his head.

'At least fifty of them. There's no way we can fight them, and
if we try to run there's a good chance they'll chase us down before
we can get clear. I reckon the best we can do is keep our heads
down and let them pass us by. Get down behind the trees, slowly
and smoothly, and keep your mouths shut. With a bit of luck
they'll stick to the river and give us a nice wide berth.'

The soldiers watched as the enemy scouts made their way down
the valley floor at a careful pace, the riders looking about them
suspiciously.

'They're ready for trouble, almost as if they know we're
hereabouts.'

Silus nodded at Marcus's whispered comment.

'They know we've taken occupation of the valley alright. You
can be sure that the scouts whose tracks the centurion here found
yesterday will have made a careful count of our numbers as we
marched in, and they'll have noted that we had hardly any cavalry.
That's why this lot have been sent forward in enough strength to
deal with any riders that we might have out looking for them. It
was as well that we were snuggled down here behind these trees.'

'And once they're past us?'

'The decurion smiled tightly at Marcus's question.

'Once they're past us, Centurion, that's when the fun starts.'

The Tungrian scouts sat in silence as the enemy party rode
slowly down the valley, watching from the scanty shelter of the
copse as the Sarmatae picked over the valley floor, clearly looking
for any signs of Roman cavalry activity. Silus shook his head in
professional exasperation, staring down at the riders in their
apparently listless examination of the ground to either side of the
river.

'Whoever's in command down there must have a head that's

all skull. I'd have spaced them across the valley and swept every last inch, not just ridden up the riverbank.' He sighed. 'I suppose we should be grateful, but I hate to see a job done badly.'

They waited until the enemy scouts had ridden out of sight around the shoulder of the hill on which the Tungrians were perched, and Silus got slowly to his feet.

'We can expect the main body to come down the river behind them soon enough, so it's time to be on our way just in case they double back and put us between the hammer and the anvil. You three, you're to ride south over the hill and through the forest until you find a clear path back to the Ravenstone. Warn Julius he's got the rest of today to get that wall raised at the very best. If you spot the Sarmatae again then you go to ground and wait for them to piss off unless they've seen you, in which case you ride like madmen for the mine and the best of luck to you. The rest of us are going to find somewhere a bit less exposed to watch from.'

The three men mounted up and rode down into the valley at a fast trot, Silus anxiously craning his neck to look to the east for the riders who had already passed them, but his men forded the shallow river and ascended the far side without any sign of the advance party.

'This ought to do nicely.'

They led the horses deeper into the forest that crowned the hill, leaving Arabus to guard them while Marcus and Silus watched the valley from the cover of the trees. After an hour or so the first riders of the Sarmatae vanguard trotted past their hiding place, some of them close enough for Marcus to see their faces. Silus watched them with a professional scrutiny, muttering quietly in the Roman's ear.

'At least this lot are doing their jobs properly, although I'd have been tempted to comb these woods as well as the valley's slopes. And by the gods, there's some stunning horseflesh out there. Watch what they do when they reach the end of the valley.'

As the two men watched from their shelter the riders turned

south toward the Ravenstone, some two thousand strong beneath blood-red banners decorated with white swords which danced prettily on the breeze. Silus nodded to himself.

'If we ever doubted that they would be heading for the mine, there's the proof. At that pace they'll reach the wall well before darkness. Let's hope that Julius has managed to build it too tall for a horseman to jump, because that many pigstickers would make a nasty mess of the defenders if they were to get behind it.'

'A blood-red flag decorated with a white sword? That will be Boraz, he goes to war under just such a flag.' Cattanius looked around the officers gathered on the wall with a faint smile. 'And I think that we can be grateful that our intelligence was correct. As you can see, Boraz is very much the junior partner in terms of the size of his warband.'

While the tribunes and their first spears stood and watched the barbarian outriders move cautiously up the valley, their men were still labouring around them, the soldiers catching turfs and laying them along the top of the rampart to form the five-foot-high parapet, behind which the defending troops would be protected from enemy spears and arrows. Julius looked out at the oncoming mass of horsemen with a long stare of appraisal.

'If that's the size of their advance guard then I'd say it's of little matter to me which of your two kings has come to play. Either way we're all dead men, if this wall fails to stop them getting among us.' He looked about him with a grim smile. 'Mind you, their arrival seems to have put a little more urgency into the construction.' Where the mine workers had previously been working hard enough to avoid the ever present threat of a flogging for anyone caught slacking, their efforts had redoubled at the sight of the barbarian cavalry making their way up the valley. 'Let's not tell them that the wall's already high enough to deter that lot, eh? I quite like them putting the extra effort in.'

The officers watched as the Sarmatae vanguard rode cautiously up the valley, until they were no more than fifty paces beyond the best distance that an archer atop the wall's fighting platform could hope to coax from his bow. A single rider came on, the tail of a scarlet banner trailing over his shoulder. Reining his horse in a few paces from the wall's foot, he sat in silence for a moment and looked up and down the rampart with an amused smile before calling out to them.

'How very Roman.' His voice carried to the officers easily enough in the afternoon's calm, the confident tones of nobility obvious to the listening Julius. 'You hide behind your walls without any regard for the cowardice you display. Far better to meet an enemy on the field of battle, sword to sword, than to disgrace yourselves like *this* . . .'He waved an expressive hand at the wall, shaking his head in apparent sadness. 'When you go to meet your ancestors they will ask you whether you died like men, and all you will be able to say is that you built a tall, strong wall and then hid behind it with your knees knocking together.'

Scaurus looked down at him dispassionately.

'Possibly, but I won't be talking with my grandfather any time soon, whereas you my friend have already booked a place at the table with yours tonight, unless you get to whatever point it was you came to make and then shift your arrogant barbarian backside out of the range of my bowmen.'

The horseman nodded up at Scaurus.

'As you wish. I am Galatas, son of King Asander Boraz and commander of his horsemen. My father has sent me before him in order to offer you a most generous gift. You will be permitted to depart this place with your lives, and with your weapons and armour, if you will quit your defences tomorrow at dawn. My father is willing to allow you this magnificent gift of mercy if you will swear to withdraw from this part of your province, and promise never to return.'

Scaurus looked down at the horseman for a moment before speaking, shaking his head gently from side to side.

'A generous offer indeed, and I must ask you to thank your noble father for his magnanimity. I am forced, however, to refuse this"gift of mercy". It seems to me that while we would be leaving this place with our lives and our equipment intact, our honour and dignity would be left here shredded beyond any repair. I'm sure that your father, man of honour that he undoubtedly is, will understand my reluctance to accede to his request.'

Galatas smiled darkly back up at the Roman.

'This is both as I expected and hoped. It is a mark of pride for our people that no man can truly consider himself a warrior until he has taken the head of one enemy soldier, and has the dead man's helmet to bear witness to his conquest. Your crested helmet will look fine on the wall of my great hall when I succeed my father. Perhaps I will cut off your ears before I kill you, to nail up alongside it?'

Scaurus pulled the highly polished helmet from his head, deliberately tilting it to send bright reflections flickering at the Sarmatae noble.

'This old thing? This helmet has been in my family since long before your great-grandfather was pissing in his napkin, and not one of the seven generations that have worn it have ever brought shame upon it. By all means come and find me, Galatas son of Asander, and I will spare a moment to demonstrate to you why it is unwise to promise to do a thing so patently beyond your capabilities. Now be off with you. If you are still within bowshot after a count of thirty, I will have these archers turn you into a pin cushion.'

They watched as the Sarmatae prince rode away.

'So, now that they're here and likely to set up camp just over there, I suppose we really ought to get a couple of centuries of the Thracians up here to keep an eye on them. It's all very well threatening a man with bowmen, but it's probably a little empty as a gesture unless there are actually bows in the wall. First Spear, I suggest that it would be sensible to send a runner to their prefect and ask him to send some men down here with plenty of spare arrows. I'd better go and wake up my esteemed colleague to the fact that the war seems to have come and found us.'

★ ★ ★

Marcus and Silus watched in silence as the main body of the Sarmatae host marched down the valley past their hiding place, waiting until the barbarian infantry and the body of horsemen at their rear had all passed before risking even the most cautious of discussion.

'Perhaps four thousand foot soldiers, and another four thousand or so horse to add to the two thousand that passed us earlier. Cattle too, perhaps two hundred oxen, and did you see the slaves they were driving along in the middle of all that infantry?'

Marcus nodded, his face dark with anger.

'Yes. And I also noticed that a good number of them looked Roman. And they were not all men.'

Silus shrugged.

'There will always be some fools who put the pursuit of profit over common sense. Doubtless when the last emperor declared the Sarmatae pacified there were a fair few idiots who made tracks across the border in search of trading profits. Mind you, why a man would be stupid enough take his woman and children into that sort of risk is beyond me.'

Marcus looked down the valley at the barbarian host's rear.

'We'll have our work cut out if that many men come at us together.'

Silus smiled knowingly.

'But they won't, will they? You found the tracks of scouts around the Saddle on the Ravenstone's northern side, so it's a fair bet that he'll send a party of men up there to make a flank attack behind the wall. Not too many, mind you, or we'll know there's something going on just from the lack of numbers in front of the defences, but if a couple of thousand foot soldiers were to come down that north slope behind us it'd be about over. They'll come at us from two directions at once, I reckon, and depend on us having to split our strength to cope with both attacks. Come on . . .'

He led the Roman back into the trees, and they remounted their horses and rode cautiously after the Sarmatae, allowing Arabus to lead and interpret the tracks left by the enemy host.

'These men are travelling heavily laden.' The scout pointed to the bootprints left in the soft ground by the passing foot soldiers, comparing them with one of his own deliberately laid alongside. 'The print is deeper than mine. And see . . .' – he bent and picked an ear of corn from the mud – 'they are carrying sacks of grain. It seems that they have come prepared to besiege the valley, if an outright victory is not gained at once.'

They followed the tracks as they turned south towards the Ravenstone valley, and after a mile or so Arabus stopped, pointing to the ground before them.

'The warband has split. Most of the men, and all of the horses, carried on down this way towards the entrance to the Ravenstone valley. But here' – he pointed to their left, up a narrow defile almost hidden by trees – 'a large party of warriors on foot has turned off the main route. They are marching for the Saddle, I expect. It will take them hours to reach it since the path into the hills will be difficult, but they will have scouted it well enough to be sure of reaching it before darkness falls. Either tonight or tomorrow at dawn they will attempt an attack on the valley by that route.'

Marcus nodded, staring up into the hills.

'And they may well succeed, unless we can bring this news to the tribune.'

'Whether this Boraz is a junior partner in this war or not, it seems that our defences are ready just in time to confront the barbarians with something a little more difficult than what they may have been expecting. Our scouts estimate six thousand horsemen and perhaps three or four thousand foot soldiers from their dependent peoples.' Tribune Belletor looked at the assembled officers for a moment before continuing. 'We expect them to make a serious attempt at getting over or around our wall soon after dawn, so I want every available man either on the wall or behind it, and ready to fight from first light. Yes, Tribune Sigilis?'

The youngest of the senior officers stepped forward, pointing at the map with one finger to indicate the long ridge that ran along the valley's northern side.

'Sir, it seems from Centurion Corvus's scouting report as if the enemy plan to attempt a flanking attack from the north.'

Marcus and his companions had made their way into the valley over the Saddle just before dark, having used game paths scouted out by Arabus to lead their horses around the Sarmatae warriors they had tracked up the side valley. Picking their way carefully through the traps laid out across the flat ground earlier that day by the Tungrian pioneers, they had descended wearily into the valley as darkness fell. Their arrival had resulted in a combination of relief that they were safe and consternation at their news, and Sigilis had swiftly agreed to go through with Scaurus's suggestion that he attempt to influence Belletor into defending their Ravenstone's obvious weak point. He indicated a spot on the map of the valley, putting a finger on the Saddle's location.

'I must admit that I had anticipated such a move, given the centurion's report of the open ground up there, and so I suggested to our colleague Rutilius Scaurus that he might get his pioneers to give the ground up there a bit of attention, in anticipation of a fight for that particular piece of high ground . . .'

Scaurus stepped forward with his face carefully composed.

'Which I was happy to do, given the wisdom I saw reflected in the suggestion. Although as we all know, to a determined enemy an undefended obstacle is no obstacle at all. It might be wise to detach a part of our strength to watch this potential point of attack – perhaps five centuries from my First Cohort and three centuries of the Thracian archers? Indeed further to that, colleague, I think that the command of such a critical part of the valley's defence is a job for a senior officer, and so I suggest that Tribune Sigilis might be given an independent command in this instance? Perhaps Centurion Corvus here might act as his second in command, and assist him in the control of un-familiar soldiers?'

Sigilis looked to Belletor in question, and after a moment the tribune nodded graciously to Scaurus, who saluted gravely before turning to the younger man.

'Thank you, colleague. Tribune Sigilis, I hereby detach half of the First Tungrian Cohort to your command, with Centurion Corvus to assist you. Use them wisely, Tribune, I'd like them back in good condition when you're done with them. You are to organise the movement of the required forces this evening, and put your men in place before nightfall. I'd expect the attack to come at first light, but we've no way to know this Boraz's intended schedule, so let's not run the risk of the show starting before your men are in place. On your way, gentlemen. Now, as to the rest of the defence, if I might make a suggestion . . .'

Marcus and Sigilis slipped out of the briefing through ranks of centurions, intent on Scaurus's instructions as to how the battle would be fought the next day. Outside the command building the young tribune held his hands up in a gesture of surrender, shaking his head at the quizzical look he received in return.

'We both know why Gaius Rutilius Scaurus put you under me for this task, Centurion, so let's not be under any illusions. You know because you're experienced enough to know how these things need to be done, and I know because he took me to one side and told me so, slowly and clearly and without any room for doubt. You're the experienced soldier and I'm a neophyte, and if anyone's going to get hundreds of soldiers up on that hillside and ready to fight it's going to be you, not me. So just to be really clear, I'm intending to watch and learn, and most of all not to get in your way over the next few hours.'

Marcus nodded.

'In that case, Tribune, I suggest we both go and fetch our thickest cloaks and an extra pair of socks, because it's going to be bitterly cold up there once the sun's gone down. And be sure to bring your most important piece of equipment.'

Sigilis nodded earnestly.

'I will. And that would be?'

'Your spoon, Tribune.'

Scaurus returned to his quarters to find Theodora waiting for him outside the tent, her face reflecting the anxiety she was clearly feeling. He bowed formally, raising an eyebrow in question.

'I trust you're well, madam? You'll have to excuse my rather fleeting attention, but I have rather a lot on my mind at this point in time.'

She smiled warmly at him, stepping close in a wave of perfume and taking his hands in hers, staring up into his eyes.

'Do forgive me, Tribune, I have no desire to waste your time. I just wanted to tell you that we're all very grateful that you're here to defend us from the barbarians. I believe their attack is expected in a matter of hours?'

The tribune put a ressuring hand on her arm.

'It seems that nothing escapes your vigilance, Theodora. But you can rest assured that we've completed the valley's defences to my satisfaction. Nobody's going to get inside this facility without a good deal more strength than I believe this man Boraz can muster.'

'But I saw men climbing the northern side of the valley?'

'A precaution, nothing more.' He bowed again. 'And now I must beg for your forgiveness. If you'll excuse me?'

She released his hands, trailing her fingertips across his palms.

'On the contrary, Tribune, you must forgive me for keeping you from your duty. I wish you the best of luck.'

He smiled wistfully at her back as she swept away down the line of tents, then ducked inside his own with a call to his bodyguard.

'Arminius? Where is that blasted—' Realising that the big German's blanket was missing from its usual resting place at the bottom of his bed where the bodyguard routinely slept, he nodded his head in belated realisation of where he was likely to be. 'I hope you dressed warmly, old friend . . .'

'Don't be put off by Arminius's forbidding exterior; he's the most amenable of men once you get to know him properly.' Marcus popped a chunk of pork into his mouth, blowing steam out into the night air as he gingerly chewed at the hot mouthful. 'I was lucky enough to be in the right place to save him from harm a year or so ago, and he still won't allow me anywhere near unfriendly men without looming over my shoulder like a particularly unaccommodating doorman.'

Sigilis laughed through his own mouthful, and earned a raised eyebrow from the German.

'Don't worry, I'm very much used to intimidating barbarians. My father has half a dozen house slaves who were taken during the German Wars. He used them to accompany the female members of the family out in the city, depending on their fearsome looks to keep the ladies safe from robbers and charlatans. Mind you,' – he looked over at Arminius with a calculating glance – 'there's none of them quite the match of your friend here. What do you feed him on?'

'Tribunes.'

Marcus shook his head at the German's retort.

'Rutilius Scaurus has been trying to cure him of the habit of answering back to his superiors for as long as he's owned the man, but to no avail. And since he won't let me go anywhere the slightest bit risky without the pleasure of his company, I've found it best to tolerate his occasional flashes of wit, rather than rising to them. Though why he still feels the need to stay so close when Lugos here is getting on for twice his size is a bit of a puzzle.'

The massively built Briton grinned at Arminius across the fire, earning a snort of derision in return.

'When that monstrosity can best me with a sword – with a *sword* mind you, Lugos, not that bloody great hammer – then you're all his. Until then I'll do what I'm sworn to, and hope that young Lupus will make a good enough swordsman to replace me at your side before my master is ordered to a different command.' He gave Sigilis a dirty look. 'Or to put it another way, until your friend Belletor decides he's had enough of being made to look like a fool.'

Marcus and Sigilis exchanged glances. The well-known fact of the young tribune being the obvious choice to succeed Scaurus in the event of his provoking Belletor one time too many had been hanging over their conversation all evening. Sigilis sighed and put down his bowl, looking about him at the cooking fires that studded the hill's northern slope, then leaned forward and looked first Arminius and then Marcus in the eyes.

'I wouldn't do it, you know.' The German's return stare was hard with disbelief, the Roman's carefully neutral, and the younger man shook his head in irritation, showing a spark of maturity beyond his years. 'Don't patronise me, Centurion! *Don't* pretend you don't know what I'm talking about.' He pointed at Arminius, his lip curling. 'See, the truth of it is there in his eyes. I told Domitius Belletor that if he were to try getting rid of our colleague Scaurus I wouldn't be prepared to take on his cohorts. For one thing I lack the experience, and for another . . . well it just wouldn't sit well with me.'

Marcus raised his eyebrows.

'And your career? Surely refusing such an opportunity would be an ignominious start to the sequence of offices?'

Sigilis laughed loudly enough to turn heads at the nearest cooking fires.

'The sequence of offices can be buggered, Centurion. Unlike my father I have no appetite for politics, that's the whole reason I insisted on being posted to the frontier rather than allowing him to manipulate his contacts and slide me into some carefully purchased position in the empire's heart. If he'd been doing the choosing I would have ended up in a role that was all kudos and no real responsibility. Besides, it seems that even Roman politics isn't all that safe a calling at the moment.'

He held Marcus's stare for a long moment before looking away, with the disquieting air of a man who knew more than he was saying, then took another mouthful of stew. While he was chewing the gristly meat a figure appeared out of the gloom and took a seat next to Marcus, gratefully taking the bowl of food waiting for him and speaking in a softer tone than the young tribune had expected.

'I have checked all of the scouts. None of them has seen or heard anything to indicate that the enemy is attempting a night approach.'

Marcus put down his empty bowl, swallowing the last of his stew before addressing Sigilis.

'Tribune, this is my friend Centurion Qadir. He is from Hama in the east, and his men are expert hunters. If they say that we are under no threat then I think we can be assured that the Sarmatae will not attack tonight.'

Arminius stretched, lying down on the grass and making himself comfortable.

'They will come with the dawn, most likely. Wake me when the sky in the east turns from black to grey.'

The Roman stood up, putting a hand on Qadir's shoulder to prevent him following suit.

'You've done enough tonight, my friend. Get some sleep, and I'll wake you in plenty of time to be ready for the fun and games. It's time for me to do the rounds of the men and make sure that my brother officers understand tomorrow's plan.'

Sigilis jumped to his feet.

'I'll come with you, Centurion.'

They walked away from the fire, Marcus putting out a hand and pulling the tribune's sleeve.

'Walk further to the right, Tribune, unless you want to end up with your foot full of holes and faeces. Titus's men have the endearing habit of emptying their bowels into the stake pits they dig.'

Sigilis was silent for a moment, looking up to contemplate the blaze of stars above them before he spoke again.

'Centurion, my father told me something a long time ago that I've never forgotten, back before the last emperor's death. He said that all that was necessary for evil to flourish was for the decent men in the empire to be cowed into taking no action when injustices are perpetrated. And then two years ago he repeated that statement in connection with the death of a well-respected senator, a man known for putting his family's long tradition of service to Rome ahead of his own interests. He told me that this man, whilst held in high regard by his peers and at the height of his powers, had nevertheless been murdered on false charges of treason whose main objective seemed to be the seizure of his considerable fortune. Understandably, given his closeness to this senator, a man with whom he shared much of his political attitudes, he took particular pleasure in the fact that the man's son had apparently been spirited away to an unknown part of the empire and seemed to have escaped this perversion of justice. It was the talk of the Forum for a while, until it became clear that the son was not going to be found any time soon.' He looked long and hard at Marcus in the firelight. 'And now here I stand before an obvious Roman whose background is shrouded in mystery but who seems to me very much alike to that murdered man's son.'

Marcus shrugged, long prepared for the moment when he might be recognised.

'It wouldn't be the first time a man's been mistaken for another, Tribune, and it's not as if you've much of a physical description to go on. We should turn uphill a little, I suspect we'll find Otho just about to beat the snot out of one of his—'

Sigilis shook his head, putting a hand on Marcus's arm as he made to turn away.

'Hear me out, Centurion. Before I joined the legion my father made a point of making sure that I understood the nature of service to the empire by arranging for me to make a series of visits to military units stationed close to the city. I sailed on a warship out of Misenum, I watched as the Third Augusta paraded in the dust at Lambaesis in Africa, and most interestingly of all, I spent a day at the Praetorian Fortress on the Viminal Hill. I remember the view of the city from the vantage point of the fortress's walls, I remember the spotless turnout of the soldiers, but most of all, Centurion, I remember the young officer who was given the duty of showing me around the fortress. You were younger then, unscarred by either iron or your fate, but you were very much the man standing before me now. You recognised me the instant you set eyes on me back in Fortress Bonna, of course, I could see it in your eyes even if I didn't realise what it was that was bothering me about you for a while.' Marcus stopped walking and turned to the other man with a rebuttal ready, only to see Sigilis shaking his head, his eyes hard in the fire's red light. 'Don't waste your breath denying it, Valerius Aquila, I won't betray you. There's been too much murder in Rome of late without adding another name to the list.'

Marcus nodded, his face set in stonelike immobility.

'So why tell me all this now?'

'That's simple. Tomorrow, if your expectation is well founded, we will face thousands of barbarian warriors across this narrow strip of ground, and for me this coming battle is a thing of mystery. It may well find me lacking. It may even kill me. If I fail to speak my mind to you now I may never have the chance to do so again. In which case you will continue to live in ignorance of information that might well be of inestimable value to you if indeed you are, as I believe you to be, Marcus Valerius Aquila.'

Marcus looked up at the stars for a moment before speaking.

'In truth, I have almost ceased to consider myself by that name. I am Marcus Tribulus Corvus, centurion, husband and father, and nothing more than that. My former life is a grey memory of something I once had, but which is burned and gone for ever. I'll admit that there are times when I dream of revenge, and I am haunted in my sleep by the ghosts of my family . . .' He shook his head wearily. 'And yet I also wonder why I should give any more thought to something I cannot change, inflicted upon my family by men whose names I will never know and whose damage can never be reversed? How can one man hope to take on the throne and hope to find anything other than death both for himself and his loved ones?'

Sigilis nodded, his voice taking on a note of urgency.

'And in your place I expect that I would feel the same uncertainties. But before I left Rome I was party to several discussions between my father and like-minded men of influence, men with the money required to buy the best investigator to be found in the city. He came to our house just once, sliding in through the servants' entrance with one hand on the handle of his knife, a grey man who seemed happiest merging into the shadows. He told us what he had discovered of your father's murder, details which, if I were you, would fill me with both despair and hope, and fuel my desire for revenge. And if I die tomorrow with these facts unshared, then your chance to hear what he had to say will be gone for ever.'

Marcus shook his head, looking away into the darkness.

'I cannot listen to this now.' He waved an arm at the fires burning along the hill's slope. 'You call me Centurion, and in all truth this is my family now. Every one of these men is my responsibility, and if I allow thoughts of murder and revenge to cloud my thinking I will lose my concentration at the time when I need it the most. I appreciate your wanting to help me, but it must wait until a time when I can afford the distraction. And now, Tribune, I suggest we find my brother officer Otho, and find out how many black eyes he's handed out to his men today.'

The Tungrians and their Thracian archers took up their positions across the slope in the dawn's grey light, centurions pacing out their sections of the defensive line and adjusting their men's places until the infantrymen's frontage was a single unbroken line of soldiery. Fifty paces behind the line the defence was anchored at either end, as the ground rose to meet the mountains on each side, by impenetrable barriers formed of trees expertly felled by the pioneers of the cohort's Tenth Century to present their branches to any attacker. Martos and his two hundred or so warriors lurked behind the barriers on either side of the Tungrian line, the Votadini prince having insisted on leading his men up the slope behind the soldiers the previous evening, ignoring the nervous looks cast at them by the Thracian archers. Martos had shared a swift breakfast with the officers before rejoining his men, exchanging crude banter with Arminius while Sigilis had listened with a face white with tension. He'd clasped arms with Marcus, raising a scarred clenched fist, and grinning savagely at the thought of impending battle.

'When your men are getting tired, you just shout for the Votadini. We'll show you the meaning of war.' He leaned closer to the Roman, muttering in his ear. 'And watch out for the boy there, a pale face before battle is the sign of a fighter, as well you know. He'll be in the line and trying to carve up the enemy before you know it, if you let him.'

Marcus gathered his brother officers on the slope behind the line, sipping at a beaker of water and watching as their soldiers stood in line waiting for the Sarmatae to make their appearance. The Tungrians were for the most part talking with each other as matter-of-factly as men discussing their favourite gladiator or chariot racer, although he could see a few small huddles of men as veteran front rankers prepared their comrades for the terror of what was to come with hard words and rallying cries.

'It occurs to me that we've been here before, brothers, or somewhere very much like it.' The other four centurions nodded sagely, their minds going back to a similar hillside on which the cohort had fought for its life the previous year. 'Only this time we've had long enough with this ground to make any army that comes at us up that slope deeply regret the idea. I saw the Sarmatae force that's pitted against us up here this morning while I was scouting yesterday, and I'd say there were barely fifteen hundred of them. And that, brothers, is clearly not enough men to assault experienced heavy infantry in a position like this, especially given the fact that I expect our archers to neutralise theirs.'

He looked around at his comrades, the pugnacious Otho, Caelius with his usual deceptive look of innocence, Qadir's customary imperturbability and Titus's glowering scowl, and felt his spirits rise at the sight.

'No tribal warband of that size can threaten us, brothers, not while we retain our discipline. So we'll stay safe behind our defences and let them come to us, as we discussed last night. And at the right moment . . .'

'We go for the knock out, eh young 'un?'

The Roman grinned at his colleague.

'Very apt, Otho. Yes, at the right moment we'll go forward and land the killer punch. Wait for my signal, and when I give it back me up with everything you have left to throw at them.'

A horn blared from down the slope, swiftly followed by another, and the officers turned to see their Hamian scouts breaking from the treeline three hundred paces distant and running up the hill toward the safety of the waiting soldiers. As the Tungrians watched, the first enemy warriors came out of the trees behind them, some putting arrows to their bows. Qadir, seeing the danger to his men, raised his voice to bellow a command.

'Dodge!'

The fleeing scouts angled their runs from side to side, changing direction every few strides to put the barbarian archers off their aim, running hard to get beyond the Sarmatae bowmen's maximum range, but one unfortunate was hit squarely between the shoulders and dropped to his knees, writhing in agony from the arrowhead's deep intrusion. Half a dozen barbarians ran forward with their swords and knives drawn, clearly eager to take their first trophy. Qadir looked grimly at Marcus and then strode across to his century, taking a bow and a handful of arrows from one of his men and nocking the first missile to the weapon's bowstring as he pushed his way through the Tungrian line.

'Surely the distance is too great for any accuracy?'

Otho snorted through his battered nose, shaking his head at Sigilis with no regard for the younger man's rank.

'Just you watch and learn, young sir.'

Sigilis raised his eyebrows and turned back to the scene just in time to see Qadir's first arrow hit his stricken comrade squarely in the chest, dropping him to the ground to lie unmoving.

'That's astound—'

Otho snorted again.

'He ain't done yet.'

While the Sarmatae warriors who had been advancing on the wounded scout were still digesting the stricken Hamian's merciful death, a second arrow punched into the closest man's body and toppled him into the long grass. Another warrior staggered to his knees with a fletched shaft protruding from his side as he turned to run, and Qadir shot the last of his arrows at the rearmost man as the rest of them sprinted back down the hill, missing by a hand's breadth as his target dodged to one side. He turned with a look of disgust at the miss and walked back up the hill, handing the bow back to its owner as he passed.

'That will keep their archers from getting too pushy until they've got some numbers gathered.'

Marcus nodded at the blunt statement, turning back to the other centurions.

'Return to your centuries, brothers.'

He strode out in front of his men, ignoring the Sarmatae warriors mustering at the edge of the forest three hundred paces down the slope, stalking along the Tungrian line with his eyes fixed on the soldiers of the five centuries under his command. Some of them returned the stare with faces set hard against the coming violence, others looked straight through him as they retreated into private places to protect themselves from the coming horror. Stopping before them he drew his spatha, holding the long patterned blade above his head until he had their attention and shouting his challenge across the hillside.

'Tungrians, we have marched a thousand miles to stand here and face these barbarians. And you, the men that our tribune has entrusted with the defence of this edge of the valley, you have been selected for the hardest task of all. Our brothers make their stand from the top of a wall too high to climb, or behind a wall of wooden stakes too dense for any horse to penetrate, but we will defeat this enemy in the way in which we have become accustomed. We will stare them in the face close enough to reach out and take their lives with our iron . . .' Realising that most of the front rank were watching the enemy behind him, he turned to look down the slope, seeing with a sinking feeling in the pit of his stomach that the enemy host forming before them was already far stronger than he had expected, with men still pouring out of the trees to their rear. He faced his men in silence until the soldiers turned their attention back to him. 'Yes, there are many more of them than there are of us, but we have laboured to prepare this ground before us, and we have the support of three hundred archers. Be sure of this, my brothers, we will win this fight, as we have won so many times before, by standing together and fighting for one another. Ready yourselves to meet this enemy, and know that you are more than a match for whatever they have to throw at you!'

He ducked through the line, pulling a man from the second rank and taking him out of earshot of his fellow soldiers.

'Give me your spear and shield. Now, run to Tribune Scaurus. Tell him we face three thousand enemy warriors up here and need urgent reinforcement. *Go!*'

The soldier took to his heels, vanishing over the ridge with more than a few of his comrades casting envious glances at the spot where he had disappeared from view.

'How do you do that? How do you manage to sound so confident when the odds are so clearly against us?' Marcus turned to find Tribune Sigilis at his shoulder, and paused long enough before answering that the younger man felt compelled to fill the silence. 'Forgive me for asking, it's just . . .'

'I understand, Tribune. You find yourself on the verge of entering a world of which you have no experience. You wonder just how you will react when the killing begins.' Sigilis nodded, and Marcus shrugged with a mirthless smile. 'I stood in your boots less than two years ago.' He shook his head at the memory. 'An old centurion who came out of retirement to help save me from the empire's assassins once told me that some leaders of men are born, screaming out their need to command their fellows even as their mothers push them from the womb, but that others among us are less driven, and are made into leaders by either choice or circumstance, forged in battle to reveal whatever strength lies within them. And in that forging, he told me, we learn things that we might rather never have known. We gain scars and lose friends, and by the time we're hardened enough to cope with what's waiting for us down that hill we're not the men we were at the beginning. In facing our fears and forcing them to surrender to the need to survive, we become so hardened as to lose some part of what made us the men we were. He was right, of course, although I couldn't ever see myself changing at the time.'

'You've lost friends?'

Marcus nodded at the question, staring down the slope at the approaching Sarmatae with unseeing eyes.

'Yes, but there was one man in particular, the retired centurion I mentioned. His name was Rufius, may Mithras honour him. I very nearly followed him across the river, such was my rage at his death. Battle touches us all in different ways, Tribune, and it finds our weaknesses as surely as it unveils our abilities. My weakness is a tendency to unmanageable fury once I am sufficiently provoked, a clear, cold anger that will sharpen my abilities but destroy all sense of what is either wise or even decent. I have it in me to become a mad man, Tribune, with no purpose other than to spill the blood of my enemies until I am too exhausted to lift my sword. If for any reason I am sufficiently roused to step into the enemy line in what is to come, you should under no circumstances follow me. I did it once, driven mad by the death of my closest friend, and was fortunate enough to escape that act of gross stupidity with my life. I doubt that sort of luck is granted to a man twice in one lifetime.'

The tribune nodded, his face still white at the prospect of the battle.

'I understand.'

Marcus turned back to face the tribesmen. The Sarmatae force had now fully emerged from the forest, and were forming up in readiness for their attack.

'We seem to have underestimated their leader's intentions. He fooled us by sending a smaller party of men up the valley that leads to this hillside than we see before us now, but he must have reinforced it last night once our scouts were all pulled back.' He exchanged glances with Sigilis. 'And if he's chosen to make this his main point of attack, then I doubt that four hundred infantrymen and three centuries of archers are going to hold him off for long, even if we do have Martos and his Votadini straining at their collars to get into the fight. But given that we have little choice in the matter, I suppose we might as well make a decent job of it . . .' He blew his whistle to get his officers' attention, raising his vine stick and pointing it at the oncoming mass of tribesmen. 'Tungrians, prepare to form the shield wall!'

The Tungrian front rank went down on one knee, angling their shields so that they could just barely see over the iron rims as the second rank stepped up close behind their comrades. He nodded to Sigilis, tipping his head to the archers waiting in a line behind the Tungrians, and the younger man shouted a command in a voice tense with the pressure on him.

'*Archers, make ready!*'

The Thracians hurried forward into the line's shadow, each of them pulling an arrow from his quiver and nocking it to his weapon's string. Marcus watched the oncoming enemy with his breath unconsciously held, calculating the distance between the two lines. At one hundred and fifty paces the Sarmatae stopped, and their archers stepped out in front of the line of shields some five hundred or so strong. They went about stringing arrows to their bows with the deliberate care of men at archery practice rather than preparing to go about the grim task of battlefield murder, seemingly confident that the Romans had no means of replying.

'*Rear rank, shields!*'

The rear rankers lifted their shields into place, overlapping them with those of their kneeling comrades to form a wall of wood fully eight feet tall. Peering between two of his men, Marcus watched as the Sarmatae archers drew their arrows back, clearly awaiting the word of command.

'Here it comes . . .'

He ducked into the cover of the line, pulling Sigilis by the arm to make sure the tribune was sheltered from the coming attack. At a shouted command the enemy bowmen loosed their arrows, and the Tungrians listened in silence as the missiles whistled across the gap between the two lines. With a sound like hail on a wooden roof the storm of arrows broke along the Tungrian line, hundreds of iron and bone arrowheads hammering into the raised shields, some protruding through cracks in the wood while the occasional missile found a gap in the defence, flicking between raised shields and past the men behind them. One of the Thracians staggered out of his place behind the infantrymen with an arrow protruding from his thigh, falling to the ground as the poison painted onto its barbed bone head took the life out of his twitching legs. Marcus raised his voice to bellow along the line at the Thracians.

'Wait! Let them spend their arrows on our shields!'

Parting two shields to risk a swift glimpse of the enemy, Marcus saw that the Sarmatae warriors were making no attempt to advance, waiting instead while their bowmen peppered the Roman line with arrows. Judging that the enemy archers were starting to slow the rate at which they were loosing their missiles, he raised his voice to bellow a command along the length of the line.

'Archers . . .' Along the length of the line the Tungrians eased their shields fractionally sideways, each man allowing the archer standing next to him a thin gap through which to sight his bow on the enemy. *'Loose!'*

The unshielded enemy bowmen were easy meat for the Thracians, and dozens of them fell with the first volley of arrows, some falling to lie motionless while others staggered away from the clumps of arrows they had shoved point first into the ground by their feet. Another volley whipped out from between the Tungrians' shields, reaping a further harvest from the wavering bowmen, and at a sharp word of command that rang out across the slope they turned and ran, more of them falling even as they fled for the cover of their fellow warriors' shields.

'Archers, cease! Rear rank, rest!'

The Thracians stopped shooting, nodding to each other at the ease of their quick initial victory over the tribesmen, while the Tungrian rear-rank soldiers lowered their shields and rubbed at their aching arms, waiting for the Sarmatae leader's next move. After a moment's pause the mass of enemy warriors began hammering their spears rhythmically against their shields, working themselves up to attack up the hill's rippling, boulder-strewn slope.

'The man in charge down there must still fancy his chances even without his archers . . .'

Marcus turned to look at the tribune, but to his relief found no sign in the younger man's face that he was in terror of what was to come.

'And so would I, if I were him, given their numbers. But then what we lack in strength we've made up for in the fact that Titus and his pioneers had a day with this ground yesterday. Let's just hope that our men have it in them to stop running when their centurions tell them to stand and fight.'

He raised his voice to be heard over the Sarmatae warriors' din, bellowing the command that his men were waiting for.

'*Tungrians, prepare to retreat! Archers, retreat!*'

The centurions standing behind their soldiers watched in dark amusement as the Thracians obeyed their orders, turning away from the line and heading away up the slope at a fast jog. Spotting the movement the Sarmatae roared in delight, individual warriors stepping out in front of their line to wave their spears at the Romans, screaming threats and curses in crude Latin as they capered in front of their comrades, swinging their swords in extravagant arcs and bellowing their imminent victory at the sky above. The hammering of weapons on shields quickened in pace, and with a piercing shout of command the warband's leader sent them forward at the Roman line. Before the shout had died away Marcus was roaring out his own orders.

'*Tungrians, retreat!*'

The soldiers turned away from the oncoming enemy, running away up the slope at a pace which matched that of the archers moments before, their centurions swiftly outpacing them as they ran full pelt in front of their men. Howling in delight, the tribesmen lost any cohesion they still possessed, the faster men sprinting out of the oncoming mass in their determination to get at the retiring Romans. Fifty paces up the slope from where the retreat had begun the centurions stopped and turned to face their men, pointing their vine sticks at the ground in command, and as the retreating Tungrians reached them the soldiers stopped running and performed a swift about-face, quickly resetting their line and hefting their spears ready for combat. Both ends of the defence were now anchored against the fallen trees felled by the pioneers the previous day, presenting an unbroken defensive face to the oncoming tribesmen.

Undeterred by the apparent rallying of their enemies, the tribesmen came on at the gallop, still screaming their hatred and triumph as the first of them blundered into the mantraps that waited for them beneath thin carpets of turf laid with meticulous care just the day before. The ground collapsed beneath their feet to drop them into knee-deep pits sown with fire-hardened wooden stakes smeared with excrement. Marcus and Sigilis watched grimly as the Sarmatae advance foundered, each fallen warrior tripping two or three of his comrades in their uncontrolled rush. Marcus waited for a moment more as the tribesmen pushed forward, ignoring the pockets of chaos caused by the traps laid out for them, until he judged that enough of them had passed the marker laid out for the purpose.

'Pull!'

The Votadini waiting at either end of the line dragged hard on their ends of a rope laid across the line's entire frontage and looped around trees to provide an anchorage, snapping the fist thick line out of the narrow trench in which it had been concealed. Dozens of Sarmatae warriors were sent sprawling by the unexpected obstacle, and the mass of men behind them swiftly descended into chaos as they fought to get around or over their fallen comrades, giving them little chance to rise.

'Archers! Loose!'

The Thracians had reformed at the head of the slope, ready to use their height advantage to send arrows skimming over the Tungrian's helmets and plunging into the disordered mass of barbarian warriors. At Marcus's command they loosed a volley at the warband's sprawling target, and while the archers poured their missiles onto the milling mass of unordered warriors, the Roman turned his attention back to the men who had managed to struggle through the field of mantraps so carefully laid out for them.

'Tungrians! Ready spears!'

Several hundred men had made their way through the obstacles, some simply climbing over the bodies of their less fortunate comrades, and were gathering themselves to storm up the slope at the Romans, but their earlier reckless charge had left them tired and Marcus knew that the time had come to take the offensive.

'Front rank . . . throw!'

The Tungrian line took two quick steps forward to build momentum, then slung their spears with all the power they had, sending their iron-tipped javelins arcing into the mass of enemy warriors. A chorus of screams rent the air as the heavy missiles ripped into the barbarians, killing and wounding enemy warriors and painting their comrades with sprays of their blood.

'Rear rank . . . throw!'

The remaining soldiers slung their spears over the heads of the kneeling front rankers, shivering the advancing line of Sarmatae again with a second barrage of sharp-edged iron, then closed up to their comrades, ready to fight.

'Swords!'

With a rustle of blades on scabbard throats the soldiers drew their swords, setting themselves to receive the enemy assault with feet planted and shields raised. Hundreds of the barbarians lay dead and wounded on the ground before them, but the mass of the enemy was still far stronger in numbers than the perilously thin line of defenders. Roaring their rage at the Romans the Sarmatae stormed past and over their dying comrades, hurling themselves onto the defenders' shields with howls intended to chill their blood as they battered and tore at the Tungrian line.

'What do we do now?'

Marcus looked down at his spatha's patterned blade for a moment before answering Sigilis's question, pulling the eagle-pommelled gladius from its place on his other hip as he spoke.

'Now, Tribune, we stand and wait to see if our plan succeeds. The archers will keep shooting into the enemy rear until they've run through their arrows, and my men know very well that they must either stand fast or die here.'

'Should we perhaps pray to Mars for victory?'

Marcus nodded, raising the spatha to show Sigilis the finely carved intaglio of Mithras stabbing the sacred bull, which he had paid a priest to attach to the sword's pommel with fine gold wire during the cohorts' long journey down the river Danubius. The engraved oval of amethyst was a dull purple in the early morning light.

'If it will help you, Tribune, then yes, indeed you should pray to your god. As you can see, I give my faith to Mithras to strengthen my sword arm, but divine help from any of the gods you care to mention would be very welcome about now.'

He turned away, waving his sword at the reserve century under Centurion Caelius, who were waiting at the slope's crest behind the Thracians. Caelius waved back, shouting the order for his men to march around the archers and make their way down the slope. The Sarmatae numbers were already starting to tell, pushing the Tungrians back up the slope towards the archers. The Tungrians were still butchering the barbarian warriors whenever the soldiers could bring their swords to bear, but were nevertheless slowly but surely losing the fight as the Sarmatae inexorably drove them off their ground by sheer crush of numbers. The air was filled with the hum of arrows as the Thracians launched volleys of arrows over the top of the soldiers' helmets and into the enemy's tightly packed throng, but the missiles seemed to be no more than an irritant to the enraged tribesmen. Caelius's century dived into the battle, adding their weight to the centre of the Tungrian line, but their additional muscle seemed to have almost no impact on the struggle. Marcus shook his head at the sight of the reinforcements' booted feet churning the soft ground as they too were pushed back by the crush of the enemy, realising that his command was all but doomed.

'They don't even have to kill us. All they have to do is push us back another hundred paces and it's all over. Once we don't have the slope to help hold them back they'll force us over the crest without any trouble at all, and then they'll break the line and hunt us down individually.'

Marcus looked back, hoping for any sign that his message to Tribune Scaurus had born fruit, but he knew the runner would barely have reached the valley floor. Sigilis stepped forward with a clenched fist.

'Surely we can't just let this scum push us off the field? What can we do? There must be something . . .'

Marcus looked levelly at the young tribune and shook his head slowly, but it was Arminius who spoke first, his face hard.

'What can we do? Nothing, except fight and die like men when the time comes. Are you ready to fight and die, Lugos?'

The huge Briton standing beside him grunted, hefting his hammer and staring at the warriors raving against the Tungrian shields.

'Lugos ready. I send many warriors before me.'

A shout from the archers on the ridgeline one hundred paces behind them caught Marcus's attention, and he craned his neck to peer over his men's shields at whatever it was their centurion was indicating with his pointing hand. Realising what it was that the Thracian officer was trying to tell him, his shoulders slumped momentarily as the enormity of their predicament became clear.

'Holy Mithras above, there are *more* of them!'

More men were emerging from the trees behind the first wave, at least a thousand well-armed men in full armour and wearing metal skullcaps in the Sarmatae fashion, some wielding bows, other armed with axes and long spears. Marcus shook his head grimly at Sigilis again, raising his swords ready to fight.

'Well if ever there was a time for that prayer, Tribune, this is it.'

4

The detachment's senior officers watched from the top of the turf wall as the Sarmatae cavalry cantered across the defensive line's frontage in a straggling mass of horsemen. They were showing no sign of any eagerness to mount an attack beyond the occasional speculative bowshots whose arrows fell dozens of paces short of the wall. Tribune Belletor raised an imperious eyebrow as he stared out across the space that the soldiers had cleared of all vegetation for a distance of several hundred paces.

'Well they certainly don't seem to be in any hurry to come in and get us. I thought these barbarians were fearless animals, but all I see here is fear and uncertainty. Perhaps this is going to be easier than you expected, eh colleague?'

Scaurus nodded his agreement, staring out at the motionless infantry waiting well out of bowshot as their masters rode up and down the wall's length in a compact mass of riders.

'It certainly doesn't fit with the behaviour I'm used to. In the German Wars these men would have been fighting to get over the wall since an hour before dawn.'

His colleague shrugged, huddling deeper into his cloak.

'Perhaps these barbarians are a little more concerned for their own skins than the men you fought in Germania? It looks to me as if they're looking for a weakness in our defences.'

Scaurus snorted his laughter.

'Well if that's the case, they're unlikely to find any. We've had too long to get this place ready. But that still doesn't ring true for me . . .'

The ground in front of the wall was sodden, saturated with water drained from the lake high on the Ravenstone's eastern wall and carefully channelled down a stream bed carved into the valley's long slope by Sergius's legionaries, then carried under the wall by pipes set in position before the first turfs had been laid. Archers waited with nocked arrows along the defence's entire length, each of them flanked by a pair of Tungrians ready to repel any attempt to climb the earth defence. The valley's sides to either side of the wall were defended by forests of wooden stakes backed by Belletor's legionaries, and the watching Romans could well understand why the Sarmatae commander was loath to commit his men forward into the teeth of such a formidable defence. Julius watched for a moment longer as the horsemen wheeled and rode down the wall's length again, still careful to stay beyond the reach of the defenders' bows. He frowned, tilting his head to one side in puzzlement.

'Something isn't quite adding up here.'

His tribune raised an eyebrow, while Belletor stared morosely out at the wheeling horsemen.

'What's troubling you, First Spear?'

The big man stepped forward, pointing out at the warriors waiting patiently behind the line along which the Sarmatae cavalry were cantering up and down.

'A discrepancy, Tribune. Centurion Corvus estimated that four thousand infantrymen passed his position yesterday. How many infantry can you see?'

Scaurus fell silent for a moment, scanning the men waiting in silence on the valley's sloping floor.

'Not many. A thousand?'

'Exactly. There ought to be more of them. And if they're not here . . .'

'Then where are they?'

The two men looked at each other for a moment before Scaurus nodded decisively, turning for the steps cut into the wall's rear and ignoring Belletor's incredulous gaze.

'Well spotted, Julius! You stay here with Tribune Belletor in case they decide to become a little more aggressive. I'll take the reserve centuries, and with a bit of luck it won't be too late!'

He hurried across to the remaining four centuries of the Tungrians' First Cohort who were waiting fifty paces behind the wall under the command of Dubnus, ready to be used as reinforcements in the event of a serious threat to any section of the defence. Before he had time to explain his fears as to the suspiciously small Sarmatae force facing them, a single soldier ran breathlessly up to him and panted out his message. Scaurus listened for a moment before pointing up at the Saddle, his voice taut with urgency as he addressed the centurions.

'It's as I feared. The enemy have turned what we took for a diversionary attack into their main thrust. They've left enough men down here in the valley to avert our suspicions while their infantry deliver the decisive blow. We have to get up there and reinforce our comrades, before they're thrown down into the valley with a mob of blood crazed barbarians at their heels.'

The Tungrians followed him up the hill as fast as they were able to climb the steep slope in their heavy armour, hearing the sounds of battle swelling above them as they approached the crest. Scaurus stopped just short of the top, panting for breath and pointing to the ground before him.

'Form up and prepare to fight!'

He led the soldiers up the slope's last fifty paces in a double line of battle with his heart pounding, knowing that they might well be marching into a fight that was already lost, but found himself gaping in amazement as the scene unfolded before his eyes. The Tungrians were holding their ground by the slightest of margins given the strength arrayed against them, and for a moment the tribune's eyes narrowed in disbelief until he realised what it was that his first glance across the scene had missed. While the Sarmatae closest to them continued their assault on the Roman line, the men to their rear were themselves under attack by a mass of warriors whose rearmost men were still emerging from the forest, throwing themselves into the attack in a manner quite different from the ordered advance in line that would have typified a Roman assault. Snapping out of his momentary amazement, he pointed down at the beleaguered Tungrian line and shouted a command that his centurions swiftly echoed with their own shouts.

'*Reinforce the line!*'

His men hurried forward, calling encouragement to their comrades as they joined the embattled line and pushed past the exhausted front rankers, pulling men out of the fight and stepping swiftly in to confront the bloodied tribesmen with fresh determination. Along the Sarmatae line the barbarians recoiled in shock as the unblooded Tungrians tore into them with furious purpose, spears stabbing out over their shields to reap a fresh harvest from the exhausted men facing them. Marcus walked stiff-legged with fatigue away from the line with both of his swords bloodied and his armour sprayed black with the gore of the men he had killed, Arminius and Lugos at his shoulders. He pushed the patterned spatha into the soft turf and saluted his tribune wearily.

'That was well timed, sir; we were all about ready to drop.'

Scaurus looked past him.

'Where's Sigilis?'

The young centurion hooked a thumb over his shoulder.

'In there. He insisted on taking his turn in the front rank.'

Scaurus nodded meaningfully at Arminius, and the big German stepped into the crush, pulling the junior tribune out of the fray by the neck of his bronze chest plate. Breathing heavily, Sigilis dropped the shield he had taken from a wounded man and leaned on his sword, looking up at Scaurus from beneath the brow of his helmet as the older man nodded his head and smiled.

'Well met, Tribune Sigilis, and indeed well done for showing these men how a Roman gentleman takes his share of the fighting, but I think you can be indulged with a moment's rest, eh?'

Sigilis nodded blankly, looking down at his sword arm as if only just noticing the blood that painted it dark red all the way to his elbow. His knees started to buckle as his legs shook with delayed reaction to the shock of the fight, but Arminius shot out a muscular arm and held him upright with a hand wrapped around his bicep. Scaurus turned back to Marcus.

'That was a closer run than you'd have liked, I expect, Centurion?'

Marcus nodded, his eyes still fixed on the newcomers who were forming the other half of the trap that was closing with slow but irresistible power about the embattled Sarmatae.

'Without them we would have been broken before you reached us. Who are they?'

Scaurus shook his head soberly.

'I have absolutely no idea, Centurion, but whoever they may be, they've probably saved this entire valley. And now, if you'll permit me, I think it's time we finished this fight and took some heads to mount over our battlements.'

Marcus nodded, and the two men stepped back up to the rear of the Tungrian line, now three men deep and holding its own with relative ease. Scaurus raised his voice to the parade-ground roar that always came as a surprise when heard for the first time, given the urbanity with which he usually spoke.

'Tungrians, we have them by the balls! Now we finish them!'

An arrow flew past the tribune's head close enough for both men to hear the breathy whistle of its passing, but neither of them flinched as the rear rank's eyes turned to them.

'Front ranks, with your spears, ready!'

A cheer resounded along the line's length, as the fresh replacement soldiers readied themselves for what they knew was coming.

'Rear ranks, with all your strength, *push!*'

The Roman line ground forward, the remorseless pressure of their shields pinning the warriors facing them against the mass of men trapped helplessly behind them, lifting some of the Sarmatae off their feet and rendering them all but powerless as the sheer crush prevented them from wielding their swords. The fresh Tungrian front rankers went to work with their spears again, stabbing repeatedly at the men three and four ranks back in the warband, plunging their iron blades deep into throats and chests before ripping them free to strike again. Marcus looked to Sigilis, who was watching the slaughter with a sick expression, and waved a hand at the battle's bloody mayhem.

'*This* is war, Tribune! Not the fighting you come to expect from the histories, but the simple bloody slaughter that leads to one side drunk with bloodletting and the other either dead or enslaved!'

The young centurion fell silent as he spotted something in the crush of men, a flash of gold that was gone in a second, then seen again as the barbarian ranks opened for a moment. Looking closer he realised that a blood-red banner decorated with a white sword waved above the spot. He strode back towards the fight, ripping his spatha free from the turf and calling a command over his shoulder.

'Arminius, Lugos, with me!'

Muscling his way into the line with the barbarians close behind, he bellowed an order to the men about him over the battle's furious din.

'Tungrians! On me! Form! *Spearhead*!'

Grabbing the soldier in front of him by the shoulder, he bent close to shout in the man's ear, loud enough for the men around him to hear.

'Their king is a dozen paces in front of you, and he's wearing enough gold to earn your tent party a fine reward. When I give the command we're going to cut our way through to him and either kill or capture him. Are you ready?'

The soldier nodded, setting his feet ready to attack, while his mates shuffled in closer around him. Marcus glanced around to see the men to either side looking to him for the command, while Arminius and Lugos pressed close in behind the spearhead's point.

'Tungrians, *advance*!'

The formation lurched forward, spears flicking out to fell the men to either side. Exhausted Sarmatae warriors flinched away from the advance and turned away in a fruitless attempt to escape into the crush of men behind them, falling to wounds in their backs and necks as the Tungrians mercilessly ground forward. Within a dozen paces they had the Sarmatae noble who Marcus had sighted through the battle's shifting tide in plain view, the warriors who had stood between them left dead and dying by the spearhead's remorseless advance. A pair of giants wielding long swords pushed through the retreating tide of their fellows with contemptuous ease, stepping into the space between the Romans and their leader to assault the Tungrians with desperate ferocity.

The soldier at the point of the spear died quickly, beheaded by the sweep of a long blade, and his decapitated corpse fell forward at his killer's feet while the warrior bellowed his defiance at the Tungrians. His partner raised his own sword high before swinging it down onto the man beside Marcus, cleaving open his helmet and sending him reeling away with an uncomprehending grunt and his eyes rolling upwards until only the whites could be seen. Before the young centurion could react Lugos shouldered past him, swinging his war hammer up and over his head with a guttural bellow of challenge. The rough iron beak's crushing impact smashed the first man's iron cap deep into his shattered skull, felling him like a slaughtered ox while Arminius's sword blocked the other bodyguard's swift attempt to take revenge. Parrying the blade's thrust to one side the German stamped forward and punched the bodyguard in his throat with a half-knuckled fist, the crackle of cartilage loud enough for Marcus to hear over the battle's din. With a look of fury the king himself stepped out of the press of his warriors and raised his sword to fight. In his strong bearded face Marcus saw nothing more than the desire to kill, and he crouched slightly into the two-handed fighting pose as time seemed to slow around him. As the king strode forward to fight blade to blade, beneath the banner that still flew close behind him, he screamed his defiance at the men facing him.

'*Boraz!*'

The Roman met his opponent's attack head-on, countering the shout with his own battle cry.

'*Mithras!*'

Their blades met in a shriek of metal on metal, but before the king had time to raise his sword again Marcus took another step forward, swinging the gladius in his left hand in a viciously swift arc to stab its point through the Sarmatae leader's armour and into his side. Boraz crumpled, his eyes staring up at Marcus as he sagged to his knees with a face contorted by the crippling pain. Kicking the wounded man aside the Roman slashed at the bannerman behind him, dropping the blood-red flag into the battlefield's churned and gore-soaked mud along with the hand that still gripped at its wooden shaft.

Faced with their king's defeat, his bodyguard smashed and the Tungrian attack driving deep into their line, while the unknown force assailing them from the forest savaged from the rear, the Sarmatae were trembling on the edge of defeat. Raising his swords to renew the fight with Lugos and Arminius to either side, Marcus grinned cruelly as the warband broke like a flock of sheep attacked by a pack of wolves, men twisting this way and that in their efforts to run from the remorseless enemies to front and rear, the fight going out of them in the space of half a dozen heart beats. Straining like hunting dogs on their leashes, the Tungrians looked to their officers for the last command that would be required to bring the fight to a conclusion. At the line's rear Scaurus nodded, putting his head back to bellow the words every man was waiting to hear.

'*Sound the pursuit!*'

The soldiers were sprinting forward even before the first notes of the trumpet call sounded, every man intent on capturing any of the tribesmen not too badly wounded to work as a slave. Sigilis watched in amazement as the tidy Roman line disintegrated into a frenzy of running men, tent parties working together to wrestle individual tribesmen to the ground and disarm them, before leaving a man with his sword at each captive's throat and setting out to repeat the feat. Scaurus watched the scene with dark amusement, raising an eyebrow to his junior colleague as Marcus walked out of the chaos holding the king's banner at his side, while Arminius and Lugos were carrying the stricken Sarmatae leader between them, the big Briton raising a justly feared fist to any soldier entertaining designs on the king's gold accoutrements. Arminius held a finely made helmet and a golden crown in one hand, having discovered the latter on the body of one of the bodyguards who had been carrying it while his king's head was encumbered with his helmet.

'Well done, Centurion! It seems that our last-minute reinforcement and your customary loss of reason on the battlefield have turned the day.' He turned to Sigilis, pointing at the battle's aftermath. 'As you can see, colleague, the financial incentives for taking prisoners alive and in fit condition for labour make defeat in a battle like this all too final, wouldn't you agree? If we'd lost then they would have been butchering our wounded and leading the living away down that hill and into slavery, never to be seen again. But as it happens, praise to our Lord Mithras, our unknown rescuer arrived at the very last moment and pulled our grapes out of the press in good style. Which means that we are the victors, despite the skill with which this poor man fooled us as to his intentions.'

He smiled down at the stricken Sarmatae king, bending to pat the man's shoulder.

'My compliments on your strategy, sir, you very nearly had us at your mercy.'

The wounded man was perhaps forty years of age and clearly in the prime of his life, arrayed in armour and clothing that stood out from the rough horseshoe-scale armour worn by his comrades. The helmet that Arminius had pulled from his head was fashioned from silver inlaid with gold, and his armour was made with finely wrought iron scales, each of them polished to a shine. An ornately decorated scabbard hung from his belt, its engraving matching the designs that adorned the beautifully crafted sword carried by Lugos, and similar craftsmanship had been lavished on the greaves still protecting his calves. The tribune tapped at the heavy gold bracelets adorning his prisoner's wrists with a sardonic smile.

'Well done, gentlemen, I'm pleased you've managed to keep all of his finery intact and resisted my soldiers' predictable desire to strip him bare. I expect we'll need it all to convince his people that their war with Rome really is over.'

The king spat a wad of bloody phlegm onto the ground at his feet, his words grating out from between teeth gritted against the agony of his wound.

'This victory is only temporary, Roman. My son still commands enough horsemen to wipe your presence from this valley as if you had never existed.'

Scaurus smiled back at him beatifically.

'Quite so, I've already seen them riding up and down the length of our rather fine wall with no clue as to how they are to get over or around it. And since this seems to have been the only place you deemed worthy of attacking, I shall improve the defences here and make it utterly impassable, once we've finished burning your dead.' He turned to his bodyguard, drawing the German away out of earshot. 'Arminius, please be good enough to find a bandage carrier and get the king's wound bound, then take him down to the hospital as quickly as you can. Ask the doctor to work her magic upon him, and tell her that his survival may well be the key to our achieving a negotiated peace with these people.'

He turned back to the waiting officers.

'And now, colleagues, let us go and offer our thanks to the officer commanding these men who seem to have stepped in with such commendable timing, whoever he is. Will you come with us, Centurion Corvus, and provide us with the additional security of your swords?'

Marcus raised his spatha once more and walked across the corpse-strewn battlefield several paces ahead of the tribunes, his eyes roaming the human carnage for any sign of movement. A wounded warrior groaned loudly to his left as he passed, holding out an imploring hand for succour while the other barely held his guts in place. The young centurion reached out and pulled the hand aside, scanning the severed ropes of the wounded warrior's intestines for a moment before whipping out his sword and cutting the Sarmatae's throat. Wiping the weapon's blade he stood, shaking his head and ignoring Sigilis's horrified gaze, to resume his slow, cautious pace across the field of battle.

'A kindness . . .'

Scaurus's words must have had the desired effect on his younger colleague, for a long moment of silence followed before Sigilis spoke.

'The smell is just . . . I mean it's indescribable . . .'

Marcus could hear the bitter humour in Scaurus's response.

'Revolting? Without doubt. Beyond description? Hardly. That's the same simple fragrance that has wafted over every battlefield I've ever trodden. All you have to do is liberally slop the fresh blood of a thousand men across the grass, then open their bellies to let the contents release their aroma into the air. Evocative, isn't it? But believe me, this smell of freshly spilled blood and faeces is nothing compared to the rare delicacy that results from leaving that same mixture open to the air for a day or two, and adding some decomposition to the mixture. And a week-old battlefield where the winner had no time to clean up after himself, or perhaps just no inclination, now *there's* the thing. You can smell the rotting bodies from five miles distant, if you have the misfortune to be downwind of them, and by the time you've passed the spot it's a hard man indeed who hasn't thrown up the contents of his stomach, either due to the smell or simply because so many of his comrades are vomiting around him. And that's why we'll set a pyre and burn every corpse here, both ours and theirs, once we've stripped away their armour. Here we are . . .'

The party stopped walking ten paces from the line of men who had intervened in the fight from the forest behind them, looking intently at their well-ordered line and obvious discipline as they collected up their dead and led the wounded out for treatment. To Marcus's eye they seemed to bear the hallmarks of regular soldiers, their armour, helmets and shields all conforming to a single pattern, clearly the output of a single armoury, and yet as he examined their ranks he frowned at other aspects of their appearance. Each man seemed to have been allowed free choice of weaponry, and a profusion of swords, spears, axes, hammers and even clubs had resulted, while many of them wore their hair long and were heavily bearded. As he watched, a massively built man wearing the bronze chest plate and crested helmet of a Roman senior officer stepped out of the mass of his men and raised a hand in greeting. And then, to Marcus's utter amazement Arminius took one look at him and went down on one knee, his head bowed in obeisance. Scaurus raised an eyebrow at the sight and muttered under his breath as he stood and waited for the man to approach.

'Mithras above . . .'

The big man saluted, greeting the tribunes in Latin only barely edged with a German accent.

'Greetings Tribune, I have the honour to be Prefect Gerwulf, commanding officer of the Allied Cohort of the Quadi tribe.'

Scaurus stared at the other man in open curiosity for a moment before returning the salute.

'Apologies Prefect, I was trying to work out just where it was I knew you from, although my man Arminius's somewhat uncharacteristic behaviour was more than enough of a clue. You're the Quadi prince who was captured early in the German Wars, unless I'm mistaken?'

Marcus slid a stealthy hand to the hilt of his spatha, fearing that the big man might take offence, but to his relief the prefect's only response was a nod of recognition, his lips pursed and his head nodding in acknowledgement of the accuracy of Scaurus's memory.

'I'm impressed, Tribune. Not many men recall that sort of small detail. I was taken hostage in the aftermath of a battle at the very start of the war between Rome and my father's people . . .' He gestured to the kneeling man at Scaurus's side. 'If I might?'

The Tribune nodded, and Gerwulf reached out to take Arminius's hand.

'Stand brother. The days when any Quadi warrior was expected to bend the knee to me are long gone. These days I'm more accustomed to the salutes of my men.'

Arminius stood, his face bright red.

'Forgive me Lord . . . Prefect . . . I had not thought to see your face again. We were much the same age when the war started, and . . .'

'And war seemed a wondrous thing, eh? We soon learned otherwise, of course, but we both ended up on the right side I see.' He nodded to the big German, clapping him on the shoulder. 'And we can swap tales of how that came to pass sometime soon, but not now. Now I must make my report to the tribune here.'

Scaurus snorted, a smile cracking his face as he stepped forward to clasp Gerwulf by the arm.

'Your bloody report can wait for a better time, man! For now it's more than enough that you appeared in our enemy's rear when you did, for if you'd been very much later you would have been able to do no more than watch these barbarous gentlemen as they rampaged through the valley below us. As it is, your timing couldn't have been any better, for which reason you have the gratitude of an entire cohort of men who would otherwise either be dead or contemplating slavery. And now, once my Tungrians are done with taking slaves, we have a valley to defend, so I suggest that we get to work on improving these defences and gathering the dead for burning, before the carrion birds start their grisly work.'

'You're sure you still want to do this? You could back out now and not a man among us could have any complaint. Not even that idiot Belletor could complain if you had second thoughts.'

His friend's voice was perilously loud, and Marcus shook his head, shooting a warning glance at the group of senior officers gathered barely out of earshot.

'Keep your voice down, Julius, or "that idiot Belletor" will be taking far too close an interest in you. And now that I've put my hand up for the job I think I'll see it through. It'll be a novel experience to see inside a Sarmatae tribe's encampment. Here, take these for me.' He put down the Sarmatae king's helmet and unbuckled his sword belt, handing the weapons to his friend. 'And if for any reason . . .'

The first spear grinned at him in the early morning gloom.

'I know. You want Dubnus and me to have your swords.'

Marcus smiled darkly at his friend, feeling the tension ease from his taut neck muscles as he picked up the ornately decorated helm.

'Not unless the pair of you want to suffer the wrath of a woman rather too skilled with the surgical blade for comfort.'

Julius nodded slowly back at him, his grin softening to something gentler.

'You'll be fine. Just remember—'

'To show no weakness? How could I forget? You've been knocking that particular nail home ever since Gerwulf opened his mouth on the subject of our captive this morning.'

Tribune Belletor had initially been adamant on the subject of their prisoner's fate, when he'd been informed of the Sarmatae leader's capture at the previous evening's command conference. He was still brimming with excitement at the close-fought victory at the Saddle, and doubtless already mentally composing his triumphant report to the governor.

'We must execute him! I'll have him beheaded up on the wall while his tribesmen watch and shiver with terror! That'll send them away quickly enough!'

The reactions around the command conference table had varied from the incredulous to the politely amused, although Belletor had been too far lost in his righteous anger to notice the stares of the gathered officers and civilians. Scaurus had wisely chosen to hold his own counsel and see who would be the first to risk their commander's ire by daring to disagree. To Marcus's surprise, watching from where he stood behind his tribune in the role of his aide, it was Procurator Maximus who had been the first to speak, his voice shaded with doubt.

'It seems to me that we have a delicate situation here, Tribune. Outside the walls are enough men to slaughter us all, were they to break in, but for the time being they content themselves with waiting for some news of their attack on the northern side of the valley, and the fate of their king. Surely if we keep him alive we can . . .'

'*Unacceptable!*' Belletor had become used to shouting when he felt he was being disregarded, and the volume to which his voice had risen was a clue to the depth of his anger. 'This man led an attack on the empire with the simple aim of plunder, and he can pay the price for seeking to profit from Rome's industry. I'll have him executed before he has the chance to die of his wounds. I'll have his head put on a spear and see that his body is thrown to the dogs as soon as there's enough light for those animals beyond the wall to see it carried out.'

An uneasy silence had ruled the gathering for a moment, as each of the attendees had imagined the likely response of the thousands of warriors camped in the lower valley to their leader's execution, until Prefect Gerwulf had coughed softly. All eyes had turned to him, most of them registering surprise at the mannered way in which he waited for permission to speak. Belletor had raised an eyebrow, but nevertheless nodded to the German.

'You have something to say, Prefect?'

Gerwulf's blue eyes had been free of any trace of guile, but to Marcus's ear his voice had been edged with a faint trace of irony.

'Tribune Belletor, I have fought these people camped in front of our wall for most of my adult life. When I was taken hostage in my people's war with Rome I determined to learn your language and adopt your customs. As both a warrior and a willing convert to the civilised way of life, I was appointed as a junior officer in the army that went to war against the Marcomanni and my own tribe. Through good fortune I was appointed to command the forces that my tribe had volunteered for the service of Rome, under the treaty that ended that war . . .'

Belletor had stirred uncomfortably, clearly already bored.

'There is a *point* to your life story, I presume, Prefect?'

Gerwulf had nodded equably, ignoring the impatient note in Belletor's voice.

'Indeed there is, Tribune. Since the treaty to end the German Wars was agreed, most of the army's efforts have been directed at the control of the Sarmatae tribes that live on the great plain that lies north of the Danubius. And if taking part in those operations has taught me one thing, it is that killing this man will only prolong a fight that might otherwise be brought to a successful close within a day or two.'

'Within days? How so?'

Gerwulf had bowed slightly.

'Tribune, it is my experience that when a Sarmatae tribal king wishes to make war, he first sacrifices a bull, cooks the animal's meat and lays the skin out on the ground. He then sits on the skin with his hands held behind his back as if bound at the wrist and elbow, and each of the men who consider themselves his followers approach to offer him their fealty. They eat their share of the meat and then place a foot on the bull's hide, which is the symbol of their thunder god Targitai, pledging whatever strength they feel able to bring to his cause. My point, Tribune, is that this man will undoubtedly have blood brothers out there beyond our wall, and more than likely sons too. If we kill him now we will simply perpetuate their shared cause against Rome, and make it highly likely that they will attack again.'

Marcus had seen the German's face harden slightly, as he had flicked a calculating glance at Belletor.

'Tribune, whilst you have worked marvels given the time you had, our defences cannot be considered to be perfect by any stretch of the imagination. In the event of continued hostilities with this people, the best that we can hope for is that they will ride away to join up with the forces further to the north, and remain a problem for the empire. Whereas if we return him to them with both his skin and his honour intact, demanding that they swear to depart in peace in return for his release and perhaps even demanding hostages in return, then perhaps we can send him away with his army bound to his word not to make war against Rome. With one stroke *you* would have saved this valley from capture and taken a sizeable piece of the enemy's strength out of the field.'

Belletor had fixed the German with a hard stare.

'And you're sure that these people will respond to such an approach?'

Gerwulf had shrugged, rubbing at his closely cropped blond hair with a big hand.

'No Tribune, I am not. The Sarmatae have always tended to be scrupulous about their honour, but there is an exception which is the proving of every rule. And whoever goes over the wall to negotiate with the tribesmen must clearly be at some risk.'

Belletor had started with surprise.

'Over the wall? You suggest that we send a man to speak with them?'

Gerwulf's expression had remained neutral, although to Marcus's ear the tone of his response was perhaps a little more strained than before.

'Of course, Tribune. We must open discussions with whoever rules the tribe in his absence in order to show them that we hold their king, and are doing everything we can to restore him to good health. Such a matter is one for men to discuss face-to-face, not for shouting from our defences, and besides, whoever leads that warband in the king's absence will never consider venturing within bowshot. A man will have to go down into their camp if we are to achieve a treaty. I'd do it myself if I wasn't sure that my cohort would dissolve into chaos without me.'

He looked around the assembled officers with a sombre expression.

'Be under no illusions, whoever goes to open discussions with them is putting himself at considerable risk.'

Belletor had looked around at his officers.

'Your thoughts, gentlemen? Should we attempt to make peace with these savages, and if so, who should we send to discuss terms with them?'

After some further debate, with both Scaurus and the Thracian cohort's tribune agreeing with Gerwulf that the possibility of concluding hostilities with the Sarmatae was too strong to be ignored, Belletor had reluctantly agreed with the idea. While his change of heart had come as something of a relief to the men who knew him well, the stipulation that accompanied it had narrowed Scaurus's eyes with fresh anger.

'Very well, if you're all certain this is the right approach to these animals, then I am happy to go with the weight of opinion. But I won't risk any of my senior officers being taken and butchered in front of our wall. Tribune Scaurus, you can send one of your centurions to talk to the tribesmen instead. That way if they decide to indulge their desire for revenge on the man we send to negotiate with them, we'll have limited our losses. There, that's a decision made. Wine, gentlemen?'

With the conference completed Marcus had promptly volunteered for the task of going over the wall, and had resisted Scaurus's efforts to persuade him that another man might be better suited.

'With all respect, Tribune, who else can you send with a clear conscience? Both Otho and Clodius could start a fight in a temple of the Vestals, neither Milo nor Caelius has the words needed, and if you send Titus he'll just spend the whole time looking down his nose at the Sarmatae and making it very clear to them what scum they are without ever saying a word. It has to be me.'

Scaurus had played a calculating look on him for a moment before responding.

'And Dubnus? I note you didn't mention him? Dubnus doesn't have a wife and small child to be left alone in the world, whereas *you*, Centurion, have responsibilities to worry about.'

Marcus had shaken his head, putting a hand to his face.

'But Dubnus isn't *Roman*, Tribune. His skin and his eyes are the wrong colour. For this to work, these people need to believe they're negotiating with a man with the power to make decisions. And that means it has to be me.'

Scaurus was standing alongside Belletor in a small group of officers a dozen paces distant from where Julius was preparing Marcus for his descent from the wall's top, his face set in stony lines as he listened to Belletor holding forth on some subject or other, shooting the occasional glance at his centurions. Tribune Sigilis made an excuse and walked the short distance to join the Tungrian officers, holding his hand out to Marcus.

'You're a brave man, Centurion, and you have my respect. I'll pray to Mars that you come back to us without suffering any harm.'

Marcus smiled back at him, a wry grimace twisting his lips.

'It seemed to work yesterday, Tribune.'

Sigilis laughed, shaking his head gently.

'Up there on the hillside? I never actually got round to praying, if the truth be told. I was rather too busy discovering what it was like to take sharp iron to my fellow man.' He gave Julius a sideways look. 'If I might have a moment with the centurion, First Spear?'

Julius raised an eyebrow, nodding slowly.

'Of course, sir.'

He walked away down the wall, and the two men smiled at the sight of the soldiers in his path stiffening under his scrutiny.

'Any second now he'll see something that doesn't match his expectations, and then there'll be fur in the air . . .'

Almost on cue Julius snapped down on a soldier who had unwittingly attracted his ire, withering the offender with a swift and vicious tirade of abuse, and the two men shared a look of sympathy. Sigilis leaned forward and spoke quietly.

'We still need to talk, Centurion. I had thought to wait until you decided that the time was right, but since you seem determined to put yourself in harm's way it's important for you to know that you may still have some blood relatives left alive. I don't know who or where, but my father's investigator told us that he suspected some other members of your family might also have avoided the destruction of their line, although he was unable to prove anything.'

Marcus nodded, his face set in stonelike immobility.

'That's not a hope I can afford to encourage, given the likelihood of disappointment should I ever find myself in Rome again, but I thank you for the concern.'

Sigilis shook his head urgently.

'One more thing. When they lower you down from the wall, just remember that there is still revenge to be taken for all those who died unjustly alongside your father. Make sure you climb back onto this parapet, Centurion, since you are likely to be the only man left alive in the entire world with the ability to exact that revenge.'

He nodded to Marcus and turned to his colleagues. Julius walked back to join his friend, signalling to his chosen man, who promptly issued orders for a rope ladder to be lowered from the parapet. Turning to his friend, he took Marcus's hand and put an arm around his shoulders.

'Good luck. Come back alive.'

The Roman eased his weight up and over the raised turf parapet, climbing carefully down the ladder until he felt solid ground beneath his boots, then looked up, gesturing to Julius for the ladder to be pulled up. Turning to face the Sarmatae, he saw that his presence on the ground before the wall had already been noticed. Half a dozen men had run forward to the edge of the safe distance from the defences, just outside the Thracian archers' maximum range, and now stood with arrows nocked to their own bows, while another ran shouting to the sprawling mass of tents that had sprung up late the previous evening when the barbarians had realised that a swift victory would not be forthcoming. Taking a deep breath he stepped forward out of the wall's shadow, pacing slowly forward with both arms raised well away from his sides. As he walked towards the barbarian camp, a group of horsemen cantered out of the tents, trotting steadily up the valley's slope until they were abreast of the waiting archers. Continuing at the same slow pace, he walked to within a few paces of the bowmen, close enough to see that the bone heads that tipped their arrows were blackened and discoloured with the same poison that had killed his horse. One of the riders waiting behind them called out to him, his face grim below a helmet that was the matching twin of the one taken from their captive the night before, and which Marcus was carrying in his right hand. A long lance was couched loosely in his right hand, the point only feet from Marcus's mailed chest.

'No further, Roman. If you've come to gloat then you've picked the wrong man to make sport of. We saw the glow of your pyres on the northern peak reflected in the clouds last night, and I see you carry my father's helm.'

Marcus bent slowly, placing the helmet on the ground before him with what he deemed to be appropriate respect for its wearer's status. The rider placed both hands on the horn of his saddle, bending forward to look at the Roman more closely.

'I am Galatas Boraz, son of King Asander Boraz and in my father and my uncle's absence, the leader of this host. State your purpose in putting your life in my hands, and do so quickly. My patience is not at its best today.'

Marcus stepped forward a pace, and the arrowheads tracked his movement, the archers' knuckles whitening on their bows. The men arrayed around the prince were hard faced, their expressions giving him nothing beyond simple enmity, while the warrior mounted on Galatas's right stared down at him with evident disgust from beneath the brim of a dented legionary's helmet clearly looted from the scene of a recent Roman defeat.

'I am Marcus Tribulus Corvus, Centurion of the First Tungrian Cohort and deputed by my tribune to enter discussions with you as to your intentions. I—'

Galatas leaned back in his saddle, his laughter both harsh and terse.

'My *intentions*? I *intend* getting my horsemen around that wall and riding down every man that hides behind it before I carry off the gold that waits for me.' He sat forward in the saddle and regarded Marcus levelly for a moment before speaking again. 'I will trade information with you, Roman, since you face my kontos without any sign of fear. Only a few of my father's men have returned to our camp with the tale of defeat, and none of them know what happened to the king. Tell me truly, what was the fate of my father and my uncle?'

Marcus grimaced.

'For a time it seemed as if your attack would force us off the hill, but we were reinforced at a vital time in the fight, and took the field with much slaughter. We burned a thousand bodies and took twice as many prisoners, including your father. He is being treated with the appropriate respect due to a king, but he is badly wounded. Our doctor is providing him with the best medical care possible, but it is not yet clear whether he will live or die. As to your uncle, I have no news.'

The rider nodded grimly, shooting a meaningful glance at an older man on his left.

'Very well. Your turn. What would you know from me?'

Marcus looked up at him for a moment before speaking again.

'You speak excellent Latin. I would very much like to know how this is.'

Galatas pulled a face at the unexpected mundanity of the question, but answered quickly enough.

'My father had all of his sons taught the Roman speech and letters. He said that we could never really understand our enemy unless we could read their writings, and so it has proven. Which makes it my turn again. What is so important that you have been sent out here to discuss? The news of my father's capture could just as easily have been shouted down from your wall without putting a man such as yourself at risk of being killed by an over-eager archer, or dragged apart by my household guard. I must warn you, the men around me are eager to have you for a plaything to avenge the harm done to our king.'

The Roman looked up at the hard-faced man on Galatas's right, meeting the murderous intent in his eyes with a flat stare.

'You will have noted that I came to you unarmed, as a mark of our seriousness in seeking to negotiate some form of agreement to end this dispute.' His voice hardened from its carefully controlled tone of reason, an edge of iron creeping in as his anger swelled at the looks being cast down at him. 'But I will back down before no man. Grant me the loan of your sword and then release your dogs, and we'll see who's left standing by the time twenty heartbeats have passed.'

The Sarmatae leader laughed again, a little less tersely this time, and the smile that spread across his face appeared genuine.

'If only you sat where I did, Roman! You must have fruits the size of an ox's danglers to threaten this man.' He gestured to the warrior wearing the captured helmet. 'Amnoz here is the champion of my father's bodyguard and a murderous bastard besides. There is not a man in this camp who could best him in combat.'

Marcus shrugged.

'No-one lives forever. Arm me, Prince Galatas, and I will demonstrate the truth of that statement to him. Either that, or tell your champion to treat an envoy who has come only to talk, and is not equipped to fight, with a little more respect.'

Galatas's smile was replaced by a frown.

'For "an envoy that has come only to talk" you're a little more aggressive than I would have expected. I have enough strength out here to wipe your army away without trace, given the favour of the gods, and yet here you are offering to take on my greatest warrior just for breathing heavily at you?'

Marcus smiled and bowed slightly.

'My apologies, Prince Galatas, it's a bad habit of mine. By all means please tell your man Amnoz that his appearance is as terrifying as it is martial, and that I am quaking with fear just to be in his presence.' The tone of his voice, and the smouldering look he cast at Amnoz left the bodyguard in no doubt as to his real feelings, but Marcus switched his gaze back to the prince and softened his tone. 'So, to business, your highness?'

The Sarmatae prince nodded wearily.

'Say what you have to say.'

'Simply this, Prince Galatas. We will do everything in our power to aid your father's recovery from his wound, and your defeated kinsmen will not be harmed in any way as long as they remain peaceable. We have more than enough food for a long siege, and your warriors will be fed just as well as our own soldiers. You are more than welcome to camp here in the valley and stare at our wall for as long as you like, or at least for as long as you have the food to sustain you, but any further attempt to break into our defences will be met with the same rough treatment as your attempt to take the northern hill. We have an inexhaustible supply of wood for pyres, and we will burn as many men as you see fit to send at us. Or . . .'

He paused, and the prince leaned forward in his saddle again.

'Or what? Is this the point where you offer me some honeyed words to make the bad taste in my mouth go away?'

Marcus shook his head.

'Far from it, Prince Galatas. I am simply instructed to point out that Rome and the Sarmatae people have a rich history of collaboration over the last century. We fought together against the Dacians back in the time of the Emperor Trajan, and more recently your king Zanticus sent eight thousand horsemen to serve with our army in Britannia. Might this not be another opportunity for us to unite our forces, or at least to coexist in peace?'

The man sitting to Galatas's left laughed long and hard, then lifted a leg to jump down from his horse. Hawk-faced, and with a beard that was grizzled with grey, he stood before Marcus with his hands on his hips and a hard, challenging smile. His Latin was equally as polished as the prince's.

'Zanticus? That fat, bald, pop-eyed old fart? Zanticus found himself over a barrel with three legions up his arse, *that's* why he gave up the horsemen, and returned one hundred thousand of your people he was holding captive. When my brother Asander heard the tidings of that defeat, he and I went out to the sacred sword that is proudly sheathed in the soil of our homeland. We poured a libation of the best wine to its spirit, and gave the blade a taste of our blood. The king swore never to give fealty to Rome, and that he would find a way to make your emperor regret his presumption that the defeat of one hapless fool is the defeat of us all.'

Marcus inclined his head in recognition of the point, glancing up at Galatas with an eyebrow raised in question. The prince sighed quietly.

'This is Inarmaz, my uncle on my mother's side, and my father's strongest ally. Over one third of the men in our host owe their fealty to him.'

Marcus nodded his understanding.

'And he was the first to make common cause with the king when he went to the ox hide?'

This time Galatas's smile was without mirth.

'You know our ways then, do you Roman? Yes, my father skinned a bull with his own hands and sat on the hide still bloody from the task, challenging his kinsmen to join him in this sacred deed.'

'And if the king dies? I swear to you that I will bring his body to you should he lose this last fight, just as I have brought you his helmet as a sign of good faith. What if I stand before you again with your father's body in my arms?'

Inarmaz replied before Galatas had the chance to respond, his answer both instant and stern.

'We drove a plentiful supply of cattle along behind our spears, and the blade of *my* kontos is still sharp. Asander Boraz's death would sadden us all, but it would change nothing, Roman. And that, I think, is enough of your efforts to turn us from the path of war. The next time we meet you would be well advised to come armed and ready to back your words with your blade, but whether armed or not you can be assured that I will put your head on my long spear. This I will swear on the bloody hide that brought me here to make war on your accursed empire.'

He spat on the ground at Marcus's feet and turned away, and the king's son shrugged expressionlessly down at the Roman.

'I suggest you return to your own side of the wall, before the temptation to sheathe iron in your flesh becomes too much for my men to resist any longer.'

'They could be bluffing, of course, to make us believe that it's in our interests to keep the king alive rather than quietly put him to the knife in the hopes of ending the war he started?'

Marcus shook his head in answer to his tribune's question.

'I'd say not, Tribune. The prince struck me as being sincere enough in following his father's lead, and the king's brother by marriage has the look of a rabid dog. If the king dies I believe we'll face exactly the same threat as if he lives.'

'Whereas if he lives, perhaps he'll feel sufficiently grateful to end the war?'

The officers turned to face Belletor, but it was left to Gerwulf to voice what they were all thinking.

'Not likely, Tribune. Once a king has taken oaths on the bloody hide he is bound to pursue his destiny to either victory or defeat. And the men waiting beyond our walls can hardly be said to have suffered defeat yet, even if we did stop their attack on the north ridge.'

Belletor sighed with frustration.

'Then we should strike back at them and clear them away. Surely a surprise attack, perhaps at night . . .'

'Would in all likelihood only end in disaster.' Every eye turned back to Scaurus in his place at the far end of the table. 'Five cohorts, all but two of which have never worked together before and most of whom are inexperienced at night fighting? It would be the toss of a coin, but my money would be on these Sarmatae being better at fighting in the dark than most of our men.' He gestured to Gerwulf. 'Our Quadi allies excepted, of course. It would be a brave commander who would abandon the security of a well-defended position to risk such a gamble, given the empire's rather robust approach to punishment in the event of such a spectacular potential failure.'

Belletor sat in silence for a moment, clearly musing on the rumours they had all heard from Rome on the subject of the young emperor's rule, tales of military officers ordered to commit suicide for the smallest of perceived failings, then spoke again.

'So all that we can do is wait behind these walls for the enemy to get bored, or more likely to run out of supplies? In that case, I'm going to my bed. Wake me if anything happens.'

He stood, stretched and left the room. After a long silence Scaurus looked around at his remaining colleagues with a raised eyebrow.

'For my part I've had far too interesting a night to get to sleep that easily, and with that many of the enemy at our walls; I think it would be wise if someone were to stay awake. An early lunch, perhaps?'

The group repaired to his tent and ate a hearty meal while Scaurus and Gerwulf exchanged stories of their respective military careers and Marcus, Sigilis and the Thracian prefect listened with interest. As Scaurus related the story of their war with the British tribes the previous year, Gerwulf listened intently, nodding as the Roman described their various actions in detail.

When the story was done he looked at Scaurus with a new respect.

'That's quite a year you had. It seems Britannia is every bit as troubled as the German and Dacian frontiers. I'd wondered why there wasn't more reinforcement for Dacia from the fortresses along the Rhenus.'

Scaurus reached for his cup.

'With the Sixth Legion losing half its strength in one ugly afternoon, there wasn't really any choice for the empire but to reinforce Britannia from Germania. It was either that or pull back to the south of the country to regroup. We would have lost the northern half of the island for years, perhaps for good, and even if it is a desolate land, good for nothing but breeding slaves and hunting dogs, it would still have been a defeat.' He smiled at the men around him. 'And everyone knows what happens to governors who deliver defeats to the throne.' He took another sip as the officers nodded knowingly. 'Mind you, even with all that extra manpower it was still hard to tell just who was more likely to end up holding the loser's severed head for a while . . .'

He gestured for Arminius to refill their cups.

'But what of you, Prefect? How does the son of a tribal king end up in the service of Rome?'

Gerwulf leant back, smiling gently, while Arminius refilled his cup with an expression of poorly concealed interest.

'As you may know, Tribune, the story of my people is a strange one. The Quadi tribe is a friend of Rome, and yet we have taken part in some of the bloodiest wars against the empire that the northern frontier has ever seen. And on more than one occasion, men who have been sent to serve as soldiers of Rome have found themselves facing their own people across the battlefield, although not, thank Thunaraz, myself. Not yet, at least.'

He paused for a sip of heavily watered wine.

'I was taken hostage by Rome more than fifteen years ago, as a boy of thirteen years. My tribe took part in the invasion of Germania Superior that the scholars now tell us was the start of what they've taken to calling the German Wars. You have to remember that this was in the days before the plague from the east ravaged the German legions along with the rest of the empire, which meant that the forces to hand were still strong enough to defeat us with ease. I was given over as one of the royal hostages who were taken in return for the legions not simply liquidating the tribe as revenge for our incursion onto imperial territory. Of course, in reality we were only facing part of the First Auxiliary Legion and a heavy cavalry wing, but we weren't to know that, and so my father made peace rather than risk his people's complete destruction. I was shipped off to Rome where a rather more enlightened gentleman than most of his peers decided to take me in hand and turn me into the son he never had. By the time the war had turned hot again five years later, I was too civilised to be considered an enemy of the empire, and in any case I was on the brink of joining the army as a junior tribune due to my new "father's" influence.'

He drank again, holding the cup up for Arminius to refill.

'Thank you. So off I went to war, and by the Gods I loved it! I started off as a glorified message runner, but once I'd proved myself with the sword I was soon commanding my own cohort. My first proper fight was the disaster at Aquileia, when we marched under the command of the praetorian prefect Titus Furius Victorinus to rescue the city from a barbarian siege, and gentlemen what a fuck up *that* was! We fought our way out of the battle with half the strength we'd had the day before, and left a carpet of dead and wounded soldiers for the tribesmen to make sport of as we pulled back, still under sporadic attack even as night fell. The official histories say that Furius Victorinus died from the plague, but I saw him go down fighting. They hoisted his head on a spear to terrify the shit out of the rest of us, which worked well enough, I can tell you.'

He sipped at his wine again.

'We spent the rest of that year on the back foot, just fighting to stop them from penetrating any further south and trying to avoid another pitched battle, because believe me, we were in no fit state. Of course, the two emperors managed to reinforce us in the end, and eventually we went back on the offensive and pushed the tribes back across the Danubius, but it's true when the old sweats tell you that a man can learn more about soldiering from a single defeat than from a summer of victories. We were hardened by that year, my men and I, and after that we neither gave any quarter nor expected it when we faced barbarians. We fought almost a dozen times in five years, marching up and down the frontier to get to each tribal incursion in turn, and by the time the war had ground to a halt it was clear to everyone around me that I was ready to command more than a single cohort.'

'The problem was,' – he drank again, smacking his lips in appreciation – 'the problem was that in the eyes of the army I was still a barbarian. A useful barbarian, mind you, handy for turning raw soldiers into veterans and enemy warriors into carrion, but not one of "us".' He raised an eyebrow at Scaurus, who nodded back with a knowing expression. 'No, I was never going to get my own legion, or even command of a legion detachment if there was someone with darker skin and the right shaped nose to hand, and for a while it looked as if I'd be a junior tribune for the rest of my time with the army, until a detachment of men from my own tribe arrived at the fortress where my legion was in winter quarters. I was the obvious choice to command them, despite the fact that they already had a prefect of sorts. One of my cousins had volunteered to lead them when the Romans had demanded the service of two thousand men as the price for their latest defeat. He made the mistake of taking me for a Roman – I suppose I'd been changed out of any recognition by my experiences – and he compounded the error by insulting me in front of the cohort when it became clear to him that I was taking his place. To have backed down would have been to justify his insolence, so I took him on in single combat, there and then, revealing my true identity as I lifted my sword ready for the death stroke. I half expected the legatus in charge to stop it at that point, but he seemed to find the whole thing hilarious, and allowed it to play out to the end. The men of the cohort were a little suspicious, of course, but we soon got over that, and here we are, still fighting whichever of Rome's enemies we're pointed at. We were ordered out here when we marched into Apulum two days ago, and it's obviously just as well that we were sent here rather than just being kicked up the road to the north to join the Thirteenth Legion.'

He took another draught of wine, and then looked around the tent with a questioning expression.

'So that's my story, how about you men? Tribune?'

Scaurus tipped his head in salute.

'For my part, I consider myself fortunate to have reached my current rank. Like you, I am a man who was always most unlikely ever to command anything bigger than a single cohort. Whereas you suffer from your barbarian origin, I was born into the right family, only a hundred years too late. My ancestor made the mistake of siding with Vitellius during the year of the Four Emperors, and while we were fortunate that Vespasian decided to be magnanimous in victory to the extent that he avoided execution, our family was reduced to relative obscurity in one dismal afternoon.' He raised his hand and gestured to Marcus. 'And the centurion here goes by the name of Corvus, a young man from Rome whose letter of introduction got him a place in the cohort just as the rebellion in Britannia started.'

Gerwulf snorted his amusement, raising his cup in salute.

'That must have been a nasty surprise for a lad fresh from the capital. You've seen some action since then?'

Marcus nodded, his expression solemn.

'Yes Prefect, I've taken heads and lost friends.'

'I'll bet you have. And this young gentleman?'

Sigilis answered quickly, before Scaurus could introduce him.

'I'm Lucius Carius Sigilis.'

Gerwulf looked him up and down.

'Just starting your path along the sequence of offices? You've had a rude introduction to the ugly face of battle, but you did well enough. I'm pleased to make your acquaintance. And you, my brother?' He looked at Arminius with a raised eyebrow. 'How do you come to be in the service of Rome? The last time I saw you, you were still little more than a child.'

The big German nodded, dipping his head in an unconscious gesture of respect.

'I grew to become a warrior, Prince Gerwulf, and when war came to the Quadi once more I took my stand alongside my brothers. But we were betrayed by Thunaraz, and he sent thunder and lightning to bring us defeat just as we stood poised on the verge of a great victory.'

Gerwulf smiled again.

'Ah yes, the famous Rain Miracle. You should have heard how that played in Rome at the time. Where you blame the thunder god for the defeat, the received opinion in the legions was that Mercury responded to the prayers of a Roman priest and struck the crucial blows that consigned you to your fate. But like me, you have adapted to that fate and made a new life in the service of Rome. And now, gentlemen, with thanks for both lunch and wine, I must take my leave. My men have a tendency to become troublesome without a good firm hand on their collars.'

He stood, saluting the tribunes and turned for the tent's door. Marcus got to his feet and flashed Scaurus a quick salute, following the prefect out into the afternoon's warmth.

'Let me escort you to—'

Gerwulf was standing stock-still, staring down the line of tents at something hidden from Marcus's view. The Roman stepped sideways and realised that the German was looking at Lupus and Mus with narrowed eyes as the two boys walked towards them, too busy chatting to realise that he was in their path.

'Well now, the things a man sees when he least expects it!'

The sound of Gerwulf's voice stopped both boys in their tracks, and while Lupus looked up in simple puzzlement, the effect on Mus was quite the opposite. Barely pausing to digest who it was standing in front of them, he turned and pelted away through the camp without looking back, clearly terrified of the big man.

'Come back here, you little bastard!'

The German leapt after the fleeing child, knocking Lupus aside in his haste and swiftly catching Mus, grabbing him by the back of his tunic. He laughed with triumph as he lifted the boy off his feet.

'Got you, you little fucker. You might have escaped us back then, but . . .'

'*Prefect?*'

Something in Marcus's voice must have sounded a warning to Gerwulf, who turned quickly, changing hands on the struggling child and reaching for his dagger. The centurion was striding down the line of tents with a fierce scowl, and one hand reflexively dropped onto the hilt of his spatha in response to the German's move. The German put his free hand out towards him palm first, shaking his head with a forbidding scowl.

'This has nothing to do with *you*, Centurion, and I'd say you're somewhat outranked. Back off, and I'll be away with this thieving little bastard.'

Far from standing down, Marcus stepped in closer, his nostrils flaring with anger as he ground out his words through bared teeth.

'*Release the child.*'

Gerwulf hesitated, his grip on the dagger tightening as he calculated the odds in favour of his managing to get away from the Tungrian camp, but the Roman shook his head forbiddingly, his voice cold.

'If that knife leaves its sheath you won't have a hand to put it back with. Release the child.'

With the two men balanced on the point of fighting, Scaurus stepped out of his tent with a look of amazement, walking quickly to stand between them with a horrified Arminius at his shoulder. He barked out an order in a voice that brooked nothing less than immediate obedience.

'What in Hades is going on here? Give me that child . . .' He reached out and took Mus by the arm, pulling him away from Gerwulf and passing him to Marcus. 'Hold on to him, Centurion, until we've got to the bottom of whatever it is that caused our colleague to react so forcefully.'

Marcus drew Mus to one side, feeling the tension and the urge to flee coursing through the child's trembling body. The tribune turned back to Gerwulf with raised eyebrows.

'So, Prefect?'

Gerwulf glared at Mus, pointing an accusatory finger at him.

'We caught the child stealing from our stores a few months ago, and when we tried to catch him he put a knife through one of my men's hands and left him unable to grip a sword. He escaped by the skin of his bloody teeth, and I swore that if we ever crossed paths again I'd have his life for that devious little trick.'

'That's interesting.'

Scaurus turned to find Julius standing behind him.

'When my woman managed to get the boy to talking the other night, he told us that his village had been razed to the ground by armed men dressed much like us – and very much like your men for that matter – and that he'd escaped being killed by these soldiers by fleeing into the forest. The acts he described sounded like wholesale murder and rape to me. And here's the worst part of it, Prefect. The boy's village was a colonia, a village founded by veterans of the Thirteenth Legion on the edge of the province. Whoever it was that tore their world apart was knowingly murdering Roman citizens, men retired from the service with honour. What sort of man do you think could order such an atrocity, and what sort of men would follow such an order?'

Gerwulf laughed angrily, waving a dismissive hand.

'I can recognise a lie when I hear one, First Spear. I wonder if *you* can?'

Julius stepped forward until he was nose to nose with the German, his face set hard.

'I'd like to think so, Prefect. In my experience, one of the clearest signs of a liar has always been the trick of answering a question with a question, rather than the truth.'

Before the fuming German could respond, Scaurus shook his head and stepped in forcefully.

'And that's quite enough public argument, gentlemen. We'll settle this discussion in private at a later date, when all the facts are completely clear and when, more importantly, we don't have ten thousand angry tribesmen camped outside our walls. Is that clear?'

He looked to Marcus and Julius, both of whom nodded quickly, then turned his attention back to Gerwulf whose face was a study in disbelief.

'You're going to take his word over—'

'Is that *clear*, Prefect?'

The German mastered himself with a visible effort.

'Yes, Tribune.'

Gerwulf saluted and turned away, white-faced with rage, and Scaurus stood and watched him go until he was safely past the guards at the camp's low earth wall.

'Well, there goes a new enemy. And it was going so well . . .' He sighed and looked at Mus, still shivering violently in Marcus's firm grip. 'I think you and I need a serious conversation, young man. Bring him to my tent, Centurion, but do it gently. I think he's been through enough coercion for one day. You too, First Spear, since you seem to know more about this than any of us.'

Back in the tent he gave Mus a long, searching stare, then turned to Julius with a raised eyebrow.

'So what's the story he told you?'

Julius pursed his lips wryly.

'He didn't exactly tell it to me, Tribune. As far as he's concerned we're all soldiers, and soldiers aren't to be trusted. He told it to Annia, while Centurion Corvus and I sat in the background and did as she told us.'

'Which was what?'

Marcus spoke up.

'Which was to keep our mouths shut and allow the boy to tell us his story in his own time.'

Scaurus sighed.

'I've always known in my heart there was a reason why soldiers aren't allowed to marry. It seems we break some rules at our peril.'

Julius raised an eyebrow.

'With all due respect, Tribune, the lady and I aren't married.'

Scaurus laughed hollowly.

'From what I'm hearing it sounds as if you might as well be. No matter, tell me what it was that the boy had to tell you.'

Julius and Marcus looked at each other, and after a moment's pause Marcus spoke.

'The boy seems to have witnessed the massacre of his entire village. They were prosperous enough from the little he could tell us about the place, and their status as retired soldiers made the tribes wary of raiding them, knowing that the Thirteenth Gemina would come down on them like a collapsing bathhouse if they took any liberties with the legion's veterans. The army even supported them by buying food from them on a regular basis, it seems, because the boy talked about a soldier with a crest like ours that he saw several times. And then one night it was all torn apart by armed men who ripped through the place in minutes, killed all of the men whether they fought to defend their homes or not, raped the women and butchered their animals for food. Mus saw his father and brothers die, and he gave a description of his father's murderer that sounds quite a lot like our new friend Prefect Gerwulf. And—'

'It was him.' The soldiers turned to face the boy, almost forgotten in the corner. 'That is the man who killed my father.'

He fell silent again, his face streaked with fresh tears.

'The worst of it is that the boy told us his mother and sisters were being raped when he ran for his life. And then he told us how old the girls were.'

'And?'

'The youngest of them was seven, the oldest thirteen.'

The tribune turned away with a troubled expression, staring at the boy for a moment.

'We have no proof, and only the word of a nine-year-old child against that of a valuable ally of the empire, a man of proven loyalty and in command of over two thousand battle-hardened troops. If, no, *when* Gerwulf goes to Belletor with this matter, my colleague will simply tell me to hand the boy over and be done with it, and any attempt to argue with him will be all the excuse he's been waiting for, doubly so since I've had to expose him as the incompetent he is to mount an effective defence of the mines.'

He stared up at the tent's roof with a thoughtful expression.

'So perhaps the time has come for me to stop dancing to the tune that was set out by the First Minervia's legatus, and to start treading on Domitius Belletor's toes.'

5

'What baffles me is how a hundred bored soldiers can keep control of that many tribesmen. Surely if they rushed their guards there'd be no way a single century could stop them?'

By the time darkness had fallen across the valley a fine drizzle was drifting across the hills in curtains that found their way inside the soldiers' armour and trickled down necks and backs with dispiriting ease. Dubnus was duty centurion, and since the Fifth Century had the duty of standing guard on the Sarmatae prisoners, Marcus had joined him as he made his rounds of the sentry positions. His friend grunted at the question, shrugging and then shivering in disgust as the gesture allowed another line of cold rainwater to run down his back.

'They're damp, cold and hungry, and every one of them looks at the guards' spears and imagines ending his life here to no purpose. Besides, there are easily twice their number of troops within two hundred paces. They'll offer us nothing worse than dirty looks, because any man that shows a sign of having any spirit left in him will be pulled out for a swift beating. Just look at them.'

They paused at the side of the four-foot-deep ditch which had been dug around the prisoners' enclosure, and whose bottom had already collected enough water to present a mirror for the blazing torches that burned every twenty paces. On the other side of the entrenchment the captured Sarmatae warriors were huddled into a space carefully laid out to be barely large enough to accommodate their numbers. Clustered around a few braziers whose contents glowed red through the sea of bodies, they were clearly far more concerned with keeping warm than with any attempt to escape. Dubnus shook his head in disgust.

'They'll be freezing cold after a day doing nothing in the open at this time of year, and there are only enough fires to keep them all warm if they're constantly changing places to give everyone a turn in the heat, which of course never happens. And since they're fed just enough to keep them quiet, some of them inevitably go hungry, which divides them against each other. Even if they did have the stones to have a crack at the guards, they'd still have to climb down into *that* . . .' He pointed down into the trench that had been dug to contain the prisoners. 'And then they'd have to hoist themselves up on this side straight into the shields and spears of the guards. Not to mention the fact that half of them would have broken ankles from the leg-breaker Julius had cut into the floor of the ditch. No, we're safe enough from . . .'

Dubnus paused, having realised that an armoured figure was approaching them down the entrenchment's edge. Having apparently realised that his centurion was present, Marcus's chosen man strode up to the officers with a determined look on his face, stamping to attention in front of the two men and saluting Marcus with his usual punctilious precision.

'Centurion Corvus, *sir!*'

Marcus returned the salute with as much gusto as he could muster.

'Stand easy, Chosen Man Quintus, I trust we find all well with you?'

Quintus nodded quickly.

'Yes, sir, all's well here. The prisoners are all behaving themselves quietly enough, although we did have one small problem earlier. Soon enough dealt with though.'

He grinned at the two centurions, raising his fist and kissing the knuckles with a hard grin. For the sake of politeness, and in the hope of building some better relationship with the man by dint of finding something for which he might offer his deputy some praise, Marcus decided to show some interest.

'A problem, Chosen? What sort of problem?'

Quintus launched into his explanation, still stood rigidly to attention.

'One of the prisoners approached a guard and asked to see the officer he heard had been over the turf wall and into the barbarian camp. Said he was the king's brother or some such nonsense. I gave him a clout and sent him packing, the cheeky bastard.'

Dubnus raised a sceptical eyebrow.

'And how would he have heard about the centurion's little adventure, eh Quintus, unless your lads have been fraternising with the prisoners? Has Morban been up to his old tricks with them perhaps, sniffing for gold?'

The chosen man shook his head indignantly, his expression apparently genuinely scandalised.

'Certainly not, Centurion! You know how it is though, the men do talk, and if a prisoner can speak Latin then he's likely to over-hear what—'

Marcus snapped awake, bending to look into Quintus's face with an expression that widened the chosen man's eyes in alarm.

'Latin? He spoke to you in *Latin*?'

Quintus nodded slowly, his smug expression melting fast under the heat of his centurion's intense scrutiny.

'Yes, sir, as well as you or I. All the same, I wasn't going to have him—'

Marcus's suspicion became incredulous anger in a heartbeat.

'Get your arse back into that enclosure and find him, Chosen Man Quintus! And if you don't find him alive then don't bother coming out again! *Move!*'

Quintus turned and fled, while a thoroughly incensed Marcus looked about him at the men guarding the prisoners, searching for any target on which to vent his spleen. Dubnus laughed softly at him, drawing his attention away from a pair of soldiers who were, he guessed, only barely holding onto their self-control.

'Well if Quintus has been missing Julius and his rough and ready ways, I'd say you've probably just cured him of that particular yearning. That was just as hairy-arsed as our good friend ever managed when I was his chosen man, and you can take that as a compliment if you like.'

Quintus returned after a tense wait with a bedraggled prisoner in tow, and his obvious sense of aggrievement was left unsalved by Marcus's swift dismissal with instructions to find a plate of food and a hot drink for the man.

'Hot food, mind you Quintus, I'm sure there's a pot bubbling somewhere close to hand to feed the guards. We'll be in the duty officer's tent.'

He led the way with Dubnus bringing up the rear in best menacing form, but the prisoner seemed untroubled by the potential for violence, looking about himself with an interest apparently undimmed by either a day in captivity or the lump beneath his right eye. Once inside the tent's welcome warmth Marcus called for more lamps and sat the man down, placing his damp cloak close to the brazier that was heating the enclosed space.

'While we wait for my deputy to bring you something to eat, perhaps it would be best to find out whether you're going to earn it. Who are you?'

The captive looked back at him with a steady gaze.

'If it's true that you met Prince Galatas Boraz today, then you already have a good idea of my identity, Centurion.'

Marcus shook his head, crossing his arms over his chest with his vine stick tapping impatiently at one shoulder.

'We're not playing party games here. Whoever you are, the outcome of this discussion is of far more concern to you than it is to me. If you turn out to be nothing more than a man with a gift for languages, then you'll be back inside that ditch with your fellow captives before you even get a sniff of a bowl of stew. So I'll ask you one more time, who are you?'

The prisoner shrugged, apparently untroubled by the Roman's impatience.

'Galatas will have asked after his father, of course, and in the same breath I'd expect him to have wondered as to the fate of his brother and his uncle. I am Balodi Boraz, his uncle. I could have proved that statement yesterday, by showing you my gold chain, but I hid it on the battlefield before your men took me prisoner.'

Dubnus nodded.

'Very wise. It would either have been stolen or identified you as a noble, and worthy of special treatment. You can find it again?'

Balodi shrugged.

'We can only hope so.' He shot a sideways look at Marcus. 'Is Asander still alive?'

Marcus shook his head.

'We'll keep the questioning to this side of the discussion, Balodi, if that's your real name. You asked to see me. Why?'

The Sarmatae noble leaned back in his chair and smiled.

'Because I was told you had been over that wall of yours, and gone down into our camp to attempt a negotiation with my brother's son. I just wanted to meet the Roman who went face-to-face with my brother's kinsman by marriage, Inarmaz, and lived.'

He watched the expression on Marcus's face closely while he was speaking, and on seeing the Roman's reaction to the Sarmatae noble's name his smile became a grin.

'Oh yes, now we both have the proof we wanted. You know that I am who I claim to be, and the look on your face when I mentioned his name assures me that you did indeed speak with Galatas, because I'm sure Inarmaz would have been close to his shoulder. Most likely he was trying to work out where best in his nephew's back to put the knife, when he inevitably seizes power for himself.'

His wet cloak was starting to dry in the brazier's relentless heat, tendrils of steam drifting up from the damp wool. Marcus stared at the prisoner for a moment before speaking.

'You suspect that Inarmaz covets the throne?'

The noble shook his head impatiently.

'No, I suspect no such thing. I know it for a fact. My brother's brother by marriage has always been the most fiercely opposed member of our tribe's rulers to our having any truck with your empire, whereas our father always raised both of his sons to be realists in these matters. He once took both of us out onto the great plain, to the place where our tribe's sacred sword juts proudly from our soil, and pointed to the east, then the south, and finally the west. Every time he pointed, he said just one word.' He paused for a moment. 'And that word was "Rome". "My sons," he told us both, "in every direction other than to the north, our peoples' lands are bordered by Rome, a people so rich that they have armies of tens of thousands of men who do nothing but fight wars and practise for war, and whose leaders constantly scheme to increase their empire's wealth. If we provide these men with sufficient reason they will slaughter our warriors, enslave our women and children and turn our grasslands into farms, which we will be forced to work for them. All my life I have sought to keep these people at a distance by means of guarded friendship backed by the promise of unremitting war should they venture north of the river Danubius, and when I die that task will fall on you both, may the sword help you."'

He glanced at the cloak, more moisture steaming out from those parts of the garment closest to the brazier.

'But my father made one mistake, late in his reign when the light in his eyes was starting to dim. He married my older brother Asander to the daughter of a neighbouring king, a sweet little thing while she lived, but with her came her brother Inarmaz, and with Inarmaz came all the poison with which *his* father had been feeding to him all his life. My brother's brother in marriage is, as you will have gathered, deeply hostile to your empire, and much of what he says on the subject finds an echo in my people's hearts. Over the years, like the water leaving that cloak as steam, the heat of his hatred has burned out the good sense our father worked so hard to establish in the tribe's thinking. His constant outpouring of hatred has made them ready to take arms against Rome once more.'

'But your brother?'

Balodi shook his head.

'Asander's wife died delivering Galatas into the world, and her brother has proven merciless in using her memory to drag the king toward his enmity with Rome. Asander Boraz was our father's son in this matter, always more disposed towards what you might describe as an accommodation with Rome. But over the years Inarmaz's influence slowly pulled his thinking away from any relationship with your empire, to the point where he was content to be goaded into this war by promises of easy victory while the Roman armies are preoccupied in the province's north. Inarmaz also promised my brother a mountain of gold ripe for the taking. And in the last few months our people's anger has been sharpened by the tales of rape and pillage from the settlements bordering your province, atrocities perpetrated by soldiers in the uniform of your empire.'

Marcus and Dubnus exchanged glances while the Sarmatae noble continued.

'But in all of these decisions, of course, he was always the man *behind* the throne, constantly seeking to advise and cajole the king, but taking great care never to expose himself as the real decision maker. As far as the tribe is concerned this was Asander's war, and Inarmaz always took care to be seen as his faithful follower. When the sweet wine of victory that my people expect turns out to be a sour brew it will be the king's decisions that are questioned, rather than the counsel on which they were founded.'

He shook his head wearily and fell silent just as Quintus returned with a wooden bowl of steaming stew. Marcus took the food with a word of thanks to his deputy and passed it to Balodi, who took a bone spoon from his clothing and started eating. The two centurions watched as he ate the food with relish, and as he scooped the last of the stew into his mouth Marcus reached out for the bowl, raising an eyebrow in question.

'So, what will happen now?'

Balodi looked up at Marcus with an expression of resignation, chewing on the last piece of meat and swallowing before answering.

'I am not gifted with the ability to see the future, Centurion, but a man doesn't need the skills of a seer to know that with my brother and I unlikely ever to see our people again, my nephew is very much alone in a sea of enemies. He finds the easy prize that Inarmaz promised his father fiercely guarded, preventing him from giving the tribe a swift victory, and the huge wealth they have been promised will be theirs. And at his back lurks a man of infinite cunning whose sons, Amnoz and Alardy, give him an edge of terror over the tribe's nobles. They are mad dogs, both of them, and neither of them would have either difficulty or scruple in killing my nephew "for the good of the tribe". He will make his move in the morning, I would imagine, suggesting to Galatas that he must lead a fresh attack on your defences, and pledging his sons to fight on either side of their prince to ensure his safety. And at some point in whatever battle ensues, whether our warriors be winning or losing the day, one of Inarmaz's sons will slip a small blade into my nephew's armour and let his life run out, shielded from view by the press of the king's bodyguards who, I strongly suspect, have already been turned to their service.'

Dubnus nodded his understanding.

'And you? If you were standing on the other side of that wall, what could *you* do to change this prediction?'

Balodi got to his feet, taking a deep breath and eyeing the burly centurion with a gentle smile.

'You take me for a beaten man, do you, resigned to the end of my father's line? The blood that carved a kingdom out of the plains beyond these hills is strong in me, Centurion, and were I to stand against Inarmaz I would command the support of thousands of those spears you see camped before your walls. I would not stand by and watch my father's legacy be stolen by the second son of a rival king, and neither would my nephew go to his grave with a knife in his back if I stood alongside him. He might still die, of course, but the wound would be in his front, and his defeat inflicted in a fair fight, not by deception and assassination.' He shook his head with a bitter smile. 'But since I stand here under your spear points that's all of precious little import, wouldn't you agree?'

The tent's flap parted, and a soldier put his head through the gap with a respectful salute.

'Begging your pardon, Centurions, but I have a message for you from the hospital. The doctor gave me this for you and she said it was urgent.'

Marcus took the tablet and read for a moment, then handed it to Dubnus, calling for Quintus.

'Chosen Man, keep this man under guard. Centurion Dubnus and I must consult with the tribune.'

'You really don't have to do this.'

Marcus continued with the painstaking task of re-strapping the leg windings that secured the bottom of his leggings around his boots, working carefully, ensuring that nothing could flap loose in a fight.

'I really *do*. I promised . . .'

'You *promised* to love and care for me, and for Appius, that was the promise I remember. What will we do if you climb down that wall and never come back? What if the next time I see your face it's stuck on a spear point? What if the—'

Marcus shook his head, retying the other legging and getting to his feet. Taking Felicia in his arms he pulled her close, wrapping both arms about her.

'I promised to deliver the king's body to his son if he died. And I am a man of my word.'

She looked up at him with tear-filled eyes.

'And his uncle promised to kill you if you were ever to cross paths again.'

Shaking his head again, he smiled grimly.

'That's the last time I tell Julius anything I don't want you to know.'

'But it's true, isn't it?'

Marcus nodded.

'Yes. And I take *him* for a man of his word.'

'So you'll go unarmed into a barbarian camp in broad daylight without even wearing your swords?'

He looked reflexively at the twin scabbards propped against his field chair.

'There's little point in provoking them by an ostentatious display of weaponry. I expect they'll provide me with a blade if I'm called upon to defend the empire's honour. Just make sure you get a good price for mine, if . . .'

Felicia snorted derisively.

'You're sure you haven't *promised* them to one of your friends?'

Marcus opened his mouth to reply, but the tent flap was abruptly pulled aside to reveal Julius waiting outside.

'It's time to do this thing, if you're set on putting your head into the trap?'

He nodded curtly at Julius and, kissing Felicia on the cheek, turned to leave.

'I'll be back soon enough.'

'And if you're not?'

The Roman turned, stroking a tear from his wife's cheek.

'Then I'll be with Mithras. In which case, my love, honour my memory?'

He stepped out of the tent and started walking towards the wall's looming bulk, Julius falling in alongside him and speaking quietly in the morning's calm.

'You're a stubborn bastard, I'll give you that much. Will you reconsider?' The only reply his friend offered was a curt shake of his head, the pugnacious set of his jaw making the first spear sigh in only partially affected despair. 'I know, you gave your word, and the trustworthiness of a Roman gentleman is the last thing he can afford to lose. Except you're not a Roman gentleman any more, are you Marcus? You're a centurion in an arse end of the empire auxiliary cohort, and to those people out there your word's not worth the steam off your piss. So give up this lunacy, and we'll lower the stiff off the wall by rope. They can have a truce to come and get their dead king. You'll never see this man Galatas again, so there'll be no-one any the wiser. What do you say; shall we all decide to live to see tomorrow's dawn?'

Marcus stopped walking and turned to face him.

'And if you'd given your word to a man that you would do a thing? What then, Julius? What if your only reward was likely to be cold iron, but you'd looked a fellow warrior in the eye and made a solemn vow? How would you be able to tolerate your own company for the rest of your life if you walked away from that promise?'

The first spear shook his head in bemusement.

'Marcus, nobody's going to think any the less of you for not committing suicide at the hands of this pack of howling barbarian scum. Think of your wife and child.'

The Roman nodded, turning back to the wall and resuming his steady pace.

'I am. I'm sparing them the indignity of watching me deal with the bitterness and self-castigation that will be my fate if I deny my instinct in this matter. Now let us get this done, with no further attempts to dissuade me from following the path my honour dictates.'

Realising that he was beaten, the first spear fell silent for the remainder of the walk to the wall, following his friend up the rampart's steps to where the king's body waited on the fighting platform in its tight wrappings. Tribune Scaurus was standing alongside it looking out over the enemy camp, and when he saw Marcus he pointed a finger at the archers waiting patiently outside of the range of the Thracian's bows in the grey of dawn.

'You'll be inside the reach of their arrows by the time you've taken fifty paces, Centurion. You won't be able to make a run without them peppering you with arrows before you can cover half the distance back this way. I suggest you give up this insane idea before I find myself lacking yet another experienced officer.'

Marcus shrugged.

'I won't be running, Tribune. Whatever it is that's waiting for me in that camp is better than dying within sight of our wall with an arrow in my back. You can give me a direct order not to go out there, but you'll be sacrificing two things if you do.'

Scaurus chuckled softly.

'I can guess one of them – your sense of honour, yes?' Marcus nodded gravely. 'And the other?'

'The chance that we might yet manage a negotiated peace with these people.'

Scaurus raised an eyebrow.

'More likely that we'll manage nothing of the sort, but I can see the way you're thinking, and if you're not to be dissuaded . . .' Marcus shook his head, and the tribune turned to Julius with a helpless shrug. 'Very well. Let's get on with it then, shall we?'

Marcus watched in grave silence as the dead Sarmatae ruler was lowered over the wall's edge and down to the bare earth below. Once the corpse was safely on the ground, he faced Julius with a grim smile.

'It's time to go and see what fate I'm due. Look after my wife and child, if the worst possibility comes to pass.'

Before any of them could answer he gripped the knotted rope and stepped over the wall's parapet, lowering himself down to join the king's corpse. Regaining his feet he cast a glance at the enemy camp and saw a sudden bustle of activity as more warriors issued from the gates to stand ready to repel any attack. Squatting, he untied the rope around the corpse and gathered the dead king's body into his arms. Struggling to his feet he turned, and began the long, slow walk towards the barbarian camp without looking back at the cluster of officers watching his progress from the wall above. As before, his approach was greeted by a group of horsemen headed by the dead king's son, although this time, he noticed, the prince had dispensed with the obvious threat of his long lance. Reining his horse in a few paces from the Roman, he stared down at the centurion's burden with a look of fear and sorrow.

'You bring my father to me, do you, Roman?'

Marcus nodded, standing stock-still with the king's heavy body held across his chest.

'As I swore I would, Galatas Boraz. He surrendered to his wounds in the night.'

The prince bowed his head.

'Tell me truly, did he die alone?'

Marcus shook his head.

'No. When it became clear that his end was near, my tribune, a warrior of proven courage, paid his respects as was only fitting, and sat with him until the end. The king died with his sword in his hands.'

Galatas sighed, staring down at the body in Marcus's arms.

'For that much I am grateful.'

The prince gestured to his men, and a pair of slaves came forward to relieve the Roman of his burden. Marcus stood still, acutely aware of the iron and bone arrowheads pointing at him. After a moment Galatas lifted his head again, unashamed of the tears streaking his cheeks.

'There are men all around you, Roman, who will be strongly tempted to put their bone heads into you and watch you die in agony as their revenge for my father's death. Have you seen what our crimson arrows can do to a man?'

Marcus returned his gaze steadily.

'I have. One of your scouts managed to scrape himself with such an arrow when we disturbed his hiding place during our march here. It did not look to be any sort of death for a warrior. I gave him peace, rather than stand and watch a warrior die in so unfitting a manner.'

'I see.' Galatas shook his head, and Marcus felt a slight easing of the tension in the air around him. 'And for that I give you my respect.'

He shifted uncomfortably in his saddle, glancing sideways at the bodyguard beside him, the man Amnoz who had shown such enmity during the Roman's previous visit. Beneath the looted Roman helmet the bodyguard's face was set in obdurate lines, his eyes fixed on Marcus with an undisguised, smouldering hatred. Alongside him was another man with their father's features, clearly several years older and heavier set, and he recalled Balodi telling him that Inarmaz had another son. Where Amnoz's expression was one of a simple lust to kill the Roman, his brother Alardy's face was altogether more calculating. Galatas spoke again, and Marcus heard a note of resignation in his voice.

'You will recall that my uncle Inarmaz swore an oath to have your head the next time he saw you. Amnoz is his son, and he has repeated his father's oath. I have discussed this matter with them both at length, and expressed my disappointment that they should violate the hospitality of my camp, but my uncle has declared that he will serve only the king. Since I am not yet acclaimed by the nobles, he is refusing to accept my command to desist in this matter. It is a thin distinction, but in the absence of my uncle I am not strong enough to force obedience upon them. Not yet . . .'

Marcus looked up at him and realised from the weariness in his face that the young prince had problems enough of his own to deal with. He nodded, casting a level stare at Amnoz.

'I understand. You cannot protect me from this man without weakening your own position, perhaps to the point of provoking a rebellion.'

Galatas nodded, and the Roman looked at the warriors gathered behind him, seeking out those men whose faces betrayed their uncertainty as to whether they should back the young man at their head. He found enough men who appeared undecided to support Balodi's assertion that his nephew's position was by no means secure.

'I see. You are yet to be acclaimed as the new king of your tribe, since your father's death has only just been confirmed. And every man here will watch and judge you if you prevent Asander Boraz's men from seeking some vengeance on the men who killed their ruler. And yet to murder the man returning your father's body to you in cold blood, that might also earn you the ire of your gods. I see your quandary, Prince Galatas, and I might offer a suggestion that will suit both our needs?'

A curt laugh sounded from behind the prince, and Inarmaz pushed his horse to the front of the group, his powerful stallion biting bad temperedly at the beasts in its way.

'Go on then, Roman, show the prince here the way out of his dilemma. Doubtless it will involve your being allowed to leave unharmed?'

Marcus opened and raised his hands, stepping slowly forward while the arrowheads tracked his movement. The polished iron head of Amnoz's kontos dropped to meet him, its point digging lightly into his mailed chest in a clear warning, and Marcus smiled up at the man with his teeth bared.

'As to your last point, Inarmaz, the answer is more than likely yes; I assure you that I will be walking away from this place. But to understand why that would be the case, you might want to consider the possibility that far from protecting me from you and his father's men, Prince Galatas might be trying to protect you from *me*?' He stared at Amnoz for a moment longer, then spat on the ground before the horses' feet.

Galatas whipped out a hand, taking a handful of the tunic protruding from beneath Amnoz's mail shirt and preventing him from dismounting with a sudden harsh word of command. Turning back to Marcus he narrowed his eyes in question.

'You wish to forfeit the traditional protection I am obliged to offer you, given that you have returned simply to bring my father's body to me?'

Marcus nodded curtly, staring at Amnoz with an intensity that was only partly feigned.

'I do. I challenge *him* to a duel in the manner I am told is traditional for your tribe, one sword and two men, with only one allowed to leave the ring of shields. Does he accept, or is his bravery nothing more than a show to impress the boy he keeps in his tent?'

Inarmaz looked down at him with an ugly grin.

'My son may not speak your tongue the way I do, but I'm sure he'll have recognised the term you just used. Unless you're as good in the circle as you seem to believe, Roman, you'll soon find yourself on your back in the mud with your guts split open and the dogs pulling at your entrails.'

He nodded to his son, and the bodyguard shouted a string of orders to the peasant infantrymen gathered behind the horses. While Marcus watched they hurriedly formed a wide circle around him, planting their shields in an uninterrupted barrier of wood and iron that would hem the combatants into the arena in which their fate would be decided. The prince dismounted and took a shield from one of them, carrying it across to Marcus and handing it to him with a grimace.

'You're possibly the bravest man I have met, Centurion, or the most stupid. Probably both. Unless your supreme self-confidence is justified, Amnoz will play with you for a while before crippling you in order to have his sport, and then when you are too weak even to beg for the mercy stroke, he will most assuredly open your body and leave you here, alive but helpless for the dogs. I've seen him fight a dozen such duels, and trust me, there's no contest involved. For Amnoz such matters are simply sport.' He looked Marcus hard in the eyes, shaking his head slightly. 'The conditions for this contest are simple. Firstly, you must fight bareheaded.'

Marcus loosened the strap of his helmet and took it off, handing the heavy iron bowl to Galatas, who in turn passed it to one of the men forming the circle. Amnoz shouted a comment across to the warrior, and the men around them laughed at his words while Galatas smiled darkly, drawing his sword from its scabbard. Marcus looked down at the blade, wondering how heavy it would be in comparison to his own patterned spatha. The weapon's hilt was decorated with a pommel fashioned in the shape of an eagle's talons gripping a ball of metal.

'If you are needing any motivation then it might help for you to know Amnoz is telling him to take good care of that helmet, since he'll be wearing it from now on. Very shortly now I will place this sword in the ground in the middle of the ring, and at my signal the fight will begin. The first man to the sword has the right to draw it from the earth and attack the other in whatever way he chooses, while his opponent can resist that attack by any means at his disposal. Do you understand?'

Marcus looked across the ring at his opponent, seeing the confidence in Amnoz's eyes as he swung his arms in a perfunctory warm-up.

'I understand. And for my part, I'm told that Amnoz is a good swordsman, not supremely talented but faster and stronger than most of your men. He's also somewhat overconfident, and stronger on his right-hand side than his left. And your uncle Balodi sends you his regards. Do *you* understand?'

Galatas nodded in response to the question with an expression of slight bafflement and then turned away, firmly planting the sword's blade in the turf between the combatants before stepping back out of the ring of shields which closed behind him, isolating the two men within an arena roughly thirty feet across. Amnoz

nodded to his father before turning to face Marcus, and silence
fell across the circle as the men around them watched the Roman
square up to their champion with grins of anticipation. Galatas
gave the necessary signal to a warrior holding a horn, and as the
instrument touched the man's lips Amnoz sprinted forward to
rip the sword from the turf with a triumphant shout while Marcus
stood and watched, allowing his shield's rim to rest on the ground
at his feet. The Sarmatae turned to his comrades and raised the
weapon in triumph, receiving their cheers with the outstretched
arms of a victorious gladiator, but his look of glee faded when he
turned to the Roman only to find him watching the spectacle
with apparent disinterest. Raising the sword to his lips, Amnoz
kissed its blade reverentially to renewed cheers, then swung it
with a smirk to point at Marcus, stepping into a fighting stance
and advancing slowly towards his intended victim.

Still the Roman waited and watched, holding back from making
any move until the weapon's point was only feet away from his
face. Sliding one foot back he raised his right arm to bring the
shield into place, watching Amnoz's eyes over the rim and waiting
impassively for him to make the first move, hoping that his immobility would be taken for fear by the grinning barbarian. With a
casual shrug to his comrades the champion stepped in closer,
swinging his sword in a vicious attack at Marcus's bare head. The
blade clanged off the Roman's raised shield in a flash of sparks
from its iron rim, and the centurion stepped back again, pulling
the shield back close to his body, while the men in the ring of
shields jeered at the tactic. Amnoz swung the heavy blade again
without any pause, attacking with a horizontal cut that hammered
a deep groove in the wooden board and jarred Marcus backwards
to renewed cheers from the men around them. Again the Roman
stepped back, pulling the shield so close to his body that his nose
was almost touching the iron rim, reaching stealthily to his belt
with his left hand behind its cover. Sensing victory, Amnoz swung
the sword up over his head, clearly aiming to chop it down into
the shield with enough force to split the iron rim and cleave the
wood behind it asunder, but as the heavy blade reached the height

of its swing Marcus stepped decisively forward, taking a deep lungful of air as he did so. Pushing the right-hand edge of his shield behind his opponent's board he bellowed defiantly into Amnoz's face, then used the momentary advantage of surprise to wrench the other man's shield away from his body. Discarding his own shield he stepped in close and reached up to take the other man's raised sword arm in a powerful grip that held the weapon uselessly in the air above them.

Amnoz had only an instant in which to realise that the Roman was armed before the knife was between his ribs, shuddering as Marcus pushed a hunting blade of polished metal the length of a man's hand through his mail armour and into his chest. Looking down he frowned in disbelief at the sudden shock of the wound, staring with blank eyes at the odd swirling pattern which decorated that portion of the blade not buried deep in his chest. A shocked hush fell across the circle, and the warriors around them watched in amazement as Marcus, keeping a firm hold of the wounded warrior's sword hand with his left hand, twisted the knife's handle to bring the blade's cutting edge uppermost and dragging a groan of pain from the agonised champion's lips. Setting his teeth in a snarl, the Roman wrenched the steel up through his ribs, angling the blade to carve its point into his opponent's heart. Amnoz died where he stood, his eyes rolling upwards, and his body sagging loosely on pain-stiffened legs. Releasing his grip on the knife's handle Marcus pried the sword from the dying man's slack grip, leaving the smaller blade buried deep in his chest and kicking hard at the tottering corpse to send it sprawling into the centre of the circle.

After a moment's stunned silence, Galatas stepped into the ring of shields, but as he opened his mouth to speak Inarmaz shouldered his way into the circle from behind him, his other son a pace behind. Ripping his sword from its scabbard the noble pushed his nephew aside and stalked forward to pick up his dead son's shield, ignoring the angry words his prince was shouting at him, while Amnoz's brother Alardy took a shield from one of the men lining the circle. Marcus took stock of Inarmaz's older son in that brief moment while Galatas railed at the nobleman, watching as the heavily built warrior hefted his sword and stared back at him over the shield's rim. Pointing his blade at Marcus, Inarmaz barked a terse sentence over his shoulder in his own language, smiling grimly as Galatas fell silent. Stepping forward until the two men's swords were close enough to touch, Inarmaz spat out his fury in a tone edged with hatred.

'My nephew tells me that I risk the dishonour of our tribe by offering you further violence. He tells me that you defeated my son in a fair fight and that we should now respect your victory and allow you to leave. And I, Roman, have told him that I will either have your head or *his*.'

Marcus smiled grimly back at him, raising the sword to point it at Alardy.

'You're sure you want to do this, Inarmaz? You've only one son left now. What if I put Alardy on the pyre alongside Amnoz? Who will you plot to put on the throne in place of Galatas then? Yourself, perhaps?'

Inarmaz's eyes narrowed.

'Accusing me of treason won't save you from my revenge, Roman. Defend yourself!'

The two men advanced to either side of Marcus, and at Inarmaz's signal they attacked fast, hammering at his defences with the fury of men whose world had been ripped to shreds before their eyes. Ducking under a sword-cut aimed at his head, Marcus spun, slashing the prince's sword at Alardy's legs with the aim of hamstringing him, but the sword was heavier and slower to wield than he was used to, and the warrior danced away from his attack with a mocking grin as the sword's blade ended its swing practically resting on the centurion's shoulder. Inarmaz waded into the fight, smashing at the Roman's shield with his sword, and Marcus met the weapon's threat with the polished iron centre of his shield, wincing as the collision of blade and boss instantly numbed his left hand. Barely hanging onto the board's handle he stepped decisively inside Inarmaz's defences with Galatas's sword still held with its long blade pointing back over his shoulder and the heavy iron pommel decoration pointing forward. Dropping the shield he grabbed the noble's heavy gold chain to prevent him from pulling back, and while Inarmaz was still trying to bring his sword to bear, the Roman smashed the pommel into his forehead with all the force he could muster.

A bellow of rage gave him an instant's warning that Alardy was upon him, and in a flash of inspiration he used his grip on the chain to drag Inarmaz towards him, ducking away as he pulled the dazed noble into his son's path. The warrior battered his father aside with his shield, ignoring him as he sprawled full length in the mud and squaring up to the Roman with a furious glare, kicking his enemy's discarded shield away to prevent him from recovering it.

'I shouldn't imagine your father will be very happy when he recovers his wits.'

Alardy half laughed and half snarled his response, wristing his sword in an extravagant swishing arc.

'He'll be happy enough when I show him what's left of you being dragged apart by his hunting dogs. You're without a shield now, and no fancy sword tricks are going to save you.'

He attacked with fresh energy, and the Roman found himself hard-pressed under the flurry of his sword blows, falling back under the onslaught, able to do little more than deflect the strikes while waiting in vain for an opening in his opponent's defence. Stepping back again, he felt the hard surface of a shield behind his rearmost heel, and at that moment a hand pushed hard into the square of his back, momentarily unbalancing him. As he staggered forward Alardy sprang to attack him, swinging his heavy blade in a lethal arc that Marcus barely managed to deflect with his own weapon, hooking his booted foot behind the Roman's ankle and pulling him off balance before barging him to the ground. Standing on the blade of the prince's sword, Alardy lowered the point of his own weapon to Marcus's throat and grinned mirthlessly down at him, breathing hard from his exertion.

'See? No shield, and now no sword either.'

Marcus looked up at him, then switched his focus to stare at the other side of the circle.

'True. But I do still have one last weapon. Your uncle Balodi.'

For a moment Alardy frowned down at the Roman, uncomprehending, and then his eyes widened in shock, his back arching and the breath explosively bursting from his mouth as something hit him hard in the back. Rolling away from the sword's point, Marcus got to his feet to see the young warrior drop his weapons and put a hand to the spot where a red-painted arrow protruded from his back. Gathering up the prince's sword the Roman strode across to the dazed Inarmaz who had managed to get back to his feet, putting the weapon's point to the Sarmatae noble's throat while he was still staring aghast at his son's plight. Tottering for a moment as the impact of his wound sank in, Alardy abruptly dropped to one knee as a line of bloody saliva ran down his chin and onto his mailed chest, lifting his eyes to meet Marcus's pitiless gaze for a moment before his eyes rolled up to show only their whites. Pitching full length into the mud he lay twitching beside his brother while the Roman watched several warriors push their way through Inarmaz's men with their swords drawn, shouting loudly in their own language and using the flats of their blades on those who were slow to yield to their advance. Moving quickly, they strode across the circle to stand around their prince while Balodi, now dressed in the furs of a noble, pushed through the shields and into the circle at the head of another larger group of his followers. His assured swagger was clearly intended to give the impression of a man who knew that events were running his way.

Motioning Marcus away from Inarmaz, Balodi pulled the heavy gold chain from around the nobleman's neck and then brutally kicked his feet out from beneath him before pulling the king's narrow gold crown from inside his clothing and raising it above his head in a clenched fist. Turning to Galatas he bowed ceremoniously before placing the crown on the young man's head, then turned back to Inarmaz's warriors and bellowed a brief command to them, gesturing to the prince with an opened hand before going down on one knee with his head bowed. From behind the shield holders a sudden rattle of iron announced the presence of dozens more of his men, with yet more still pouring from the camp behind them. At their leader's shouted order they started rapping their swords and shield bosses together in unison and chanting Galatas's name. After a moment of stunned silence one of the men in the ring of shields sank slowly to his knees, swiftly followed by another, and in a heartbeat every one of them had followed their fellows' example in recognition of the fact that they were outnumbered and leaderless. Galatas stepped forward with his arm raised to take their salute, sharing a look of amazement with Marcus as men flooded from the camp behind him, adding their voices to the adulation.

'So the king's brother intervened just in time?'

Marcus nodded wearily at Tribune Belletor's question.

'Yes, Tribune. He put a poisoned arrow into Inarmaz's son Alardy just as he was about to fillet me and serve me up to his dogs, and surrounded his warriors with men loyal to the old king. His possession of the dead king's crown was the masterstroke, he just marched up to Galatas and put it on his head, which meant that Inarmaz's men either had to fight then and there or proclaim their loyalty to the new king.' He took another drink of water from the beaker in front of him before continuing. 'The prince got me out of there as quickly as he could, but he gave me a message to bring back to *you*, Tribune.'

He turned to Belletor and opened a writing tablet, working hard to put the right tone of respect into his voice.

'Tribune, it is apparent to me that my father, the king Asander Boraz, sought battle with you at the ill-advised urging of my uncle Inarmaz. Given my father's honourable death in battle, and the attempted insurrection by my uncle, I would prefer to establish peaceful terms with your empire and withdraw my army to our tribal lands without any further conflict between us. I will be happy to meet with you on ground of your choosing in order to formally agree this end to our hostilities.'

Belletor raised an eyebrow at his colleague.

'I find it intriguing that this man Balodi seems to have gained possession of the Sarmatae king's gold crown, a valuable item which I was assured was in safe keeping ready for shipment to Rome as a prize of battle. How might that have happened, Tribune Scaurus?'

Scaurus maintained an admirably straight face.

'There's no secret there, colleague. I gave the crown to Balodi when I freed him, soon after the centurion here discovered him among the prisoners.' Belletor gaped at him in amazement, but Scaurus continued as if he were discussing nothing of any greater importance than the weather. 'I had another of my centurions escort him over the northern edge of the valley and then via a circuitous route to within a mile or so of the enemy camp while we prepared the king for return to the Sarmatae, so that at about the time Centurion Corvus here walked up to the side facing our wall, Balodi was slipping into a section guarded by his own men on the opposite side.' He smiled blandly at Belletor. 'This has all turned out very well, I'd say, a rebellion put down before any really serious damage was done and a new king with good reason to be grateful to the empire.'

Belletor snorted his disapproval, waving a hand in dismissal of his colleague's argument as he proclaimed his verdict on the matter.

'On the contrary, Tribune Scaurus, you have once again acted without the approval of your superior officer—'

Scaurus laughed out loud, the jaundiced tone of his outburst as much as the simple fact of its expression widening the eyes of the gathered senior officers.

'Enough of this nonsense! Your *approval* would have taken half the morning *not* to be forthcoming. Why would I even bother? You're not interested in anything that doesn't suit your own needs, and you're the closest thing to a military illiterate I've yet to meet in uniform. This was a decision that needed making immediately, not after the time required for you to wake, bathe, deign to see me and then spend an hour teasing the question through your clearly limited intellect, and so I made it on the spot. And now, I'm afraid, you'll have to do as you see fit.'

Belletor's response was an instantaneous, spluttering retort.

'I'll remove you from your command, that's what I'll do!'

Scaurus shook his head slowly.

'You won't, I'm afraid. That was a threat that only held good while we were on the southern side of the Danubius, never far from a legion fortress and the informed opinion of a legatus whose senatorial view of the world would match your own. Now that we're on the empire's very edge there are two problems with that course of action. For one thing, without a senior officer standing behind you, you've no means of backing up the threat. I have two cohorts of battle-hardened men to your one cohort of recruits and wasters, so you've no credible threat of force to offer. And secondly, I'll not surrender those two cohorts to your incompetence, and neither will I allow you to put our inexperienced colleague Sigilis in charge of them, decent enough man though I believe him to be. So unless you've got a suicidal urge to take your iron to me, there's no recourse to military discipline available to you until we both stand before a legion's legatus, and while I'll happily accept whatever it is that such an august personage decides should be my fate for ignoring your orders, until that day we'll just have to rub along. Won't we?'

Belletor looked about the room in search of some means of enforcing his impotent will. The Thracian cohort's prefect looked down at the floor, clearly hoping to remain uninvolved, but Gerwulf met his gaze steadily.

'Prefect Gerwulf?'

The German saluted respectfully.

'Tribune?'

'Will you obey my orders, Prefect?'

Gerwulf nodded.

'I will, Prefect.'

'Then disarm this mutineer and take command of his cohorts!' Belletor's expression went from enraged to crafty. 'I believe there's something he has which you want?'

Scaurus waved a dismissive hand at his colleague.

'That won't work either. You won't be buying the prefect's

loyalty with the blood of a child because the boy has been hidden away where you'll never find him.'

Gerwulf shook his head, ignoring Scaurus's outburst.

'With respect, Tribune, whilst your colleague is clearly in flagrant breach of your orders, I cannot come between you in this matter since it's far from obvious to me that you're really the senior officer here. Your best option now that the Ravenstone is safe from attack would surely be to march for Apulum and then head north, to seek the judgement of the Thirteenth Legion's legatus. You could order me to do your will, of course, but my inevitable refusal can only provide you with more embarrassment, wouldn't you say? The matter of the child will sort itself out soon enough, I expect.'

Belletor shook his head in frustration, and then came to an abrupt decision.

'Very well, we'll take this Galatas at his word and negotiate a peaceful end to this rebellion, after which I'll march our three cohorts north to join with the main force. I'm sure the Thirteenth Legion's legatus will be happy to receive reinforcements, and equally happy to sit in judgement of your insubordination. You, Prefect Gerwulf, can guard the mines in our absence and *you*, Tribune, will soon be receiving a harsh lesson as to what the price is for failing to obey the orders given to you by your betters!'

'And that's their king? That young lad riding in the middle of all those ugly looking bastards?'

Marcus replied without taking his eyes off the Sarmatae party, watching the men around Galatas carefully for any sign of a problem, with the fingers of his right hand touching the patterned spatha's hilt.

'Yes, Standard Bearer, that is indeed the king of the Sarmatae.'

Galatas was surrounded by the party of fifty horsemen that had been agreed in the initial negotiations, enough to represent a show of the tribe's mounted strength without posing any threat to the defenders' infantry cohorts, which had been drawn up on an open-sided square before the wall's gate. His uncle Balodi was riding at their head, and the would-be usurper Inarmaz was mounted behind Balodi with his hands bound in front of him. The party stopped and dismounted, Balodi signalling to his men to help Inarmaz down from his horse before the three men stepped forward to meet the Roman senior officers waiting for them. After a moment's discussion between the two sides Scaurus stepped away from the group and signalled to Marcus to leave his century and join them. Pacing out to meet the young centurion halfway, he spoke quietly as they walked towards the waiting men.

'The king specifically requested you join us for the negotiations. I think he has a soft spot for you, and Belletor's in no better position to refuse the request than he was when dear old Balodi insisted that I should be party to the treaty.'

Galatas smiled when he saw Marcus in the tribune's company, stepping forward to take the Roman's arm in a formal clasp.

'Greetings, Centurion! It gives me great pleasure to see you again.'

Marcus bowed deeply.

'As it does for me to see you in your rightful place, *King* Galatas Boraz.'

He bowed to Balodi, who nodded in return and gestured to Inarmaz at his side.

'Greetings, Centurion, and well met once more. I'm sure my brother-in-law would greet you in effusive terms had I not taken precautions against him spreading more poison against the king as he's done so many times before.' The Sarmatae noble's mouth was tightly bound with a strip of cloth, and Balodi laughed at the evil glare he received for drawing the Romans' attention to his discomfiture. 'Ah, if looks could kill, but then I'm afraid that looks are all my brother's brother by marriage has left in his quiver. I've told him that any attempt to speak while he is thus restrained will only result in my having his mouth stitched closed, which would be a shame since I have a mind to deliver his final punishment before the sacred sword rather than watching him starve to death before we reach our homelands. But now to business, Tribune.'

Scaurus gestured for his colleague Belletor to step forward, and the other tribune did so with a venomous look of hatred at him which Balodi noted with a raised eyebrow. Gathering himself up, the Roman raised his head to point his chin at the Sarmatae nobles.

'Very well then, King Galatas Boraz, I am Tribune Lucius Domitius Belletor, the officer commanding this mining facility and thereby responsible for your defeat. You have requested a negotiation of peace terms between your people and the Emperor Lucius Aurelius Commodus Antoninus Augustus. What terms do you seek?'

Galatas stepped forward to meet him, his expression neither humble nor proud.

'We will withdraw from your lands and return to our own, seeking no further confrontation with your people, and we will provide you with enough foot soldiers to make up your battle losses. In return we desire only the return of the prisoners you have taken . . . and perhaps some small token of the renewed friendship between our peoples?'

Belletor nodded graciously.

'Your gift of men to serve in our ranks is most generous, and we will, of course, liberate those warriors we captured in the course of defending our emperor's property.' He turned and smirked at Scaurus, knowing that the Tungrian cohorts would thereby be deprived of the spoils of their victory. 'You will arrange for the repatriation of the prisoners, colleague.'

The Tungrians' tribune nodded tersely, having already told his officers that he would seek no further opportunity to clash with his colleague, given the size of the rupture between them.

'Further, I propose an accommodation between our two peoples. Procurator?'

Scaurus stared at the back of Belletor's head with his eyes narrowed, and Procurator Maximus walked forward into the open space bounded by the ranks of soldiers, clicking his fingers to summon four men carrying a heavy strongbox. They walked forward, clearly struggling under the weight, and placed it before Galatas. Belletor smiled at the young king, holding up an iron key.

'The box contains ten thousand gold aureii, Galatas Boraz,

which you may consider to be an *initial* payment from the empire, if you respond favourably to two suggestions. Firstly, I propose a treaty of friendship between our two peoples, with both sides sworn to come to the defence of the other in time of war. Secondly, in recognition of the current state of war between the empire and your fellow tribes, I request the service of one thousand horsemen from your tribe. If you agree to both of these suggestions I will petition the governor to continue with regular payments for as long as there is friendship between our two peoples. Good and faithful service by your horsemen, and continuing peace on our shared border will, I am sure, be enough to encourage his agreement in due course. Do take a moment to consider this matter with your advisers . . .'

Belletor turned back to face Scaurus with a triumphant grin, clearly savouring the look of disbelief on his colleague's face.

'What in the name of Our Lord are you playing at, Domitius Belletor?'

'Simply taking a lesson from the histories and applying it, Rutilius Scaurus. Barbarian kings are easily swayed by Roman gold, and this way we can ensure they stay out of the fight whilst also increasing our own army's mounted strength. I have no doubt that the Thirteenth Legion's legatus will snap up a thousand horsemen happily enough.'

'I see.' Whilst Scaurus's reply was pitched too low for the Sarmatae nobles to hear, his tone was acerbic. 'You seek to gain favour with the authorities by bringing them a gift of cavalry, whilst returning the prisoners we took in battle to put my nose out of joint, and so you spend the emperor's gold like water in order to buy peace with a defeated enemy. And what of the slaves? I thought we agreed that the freedom of any Roman citizens among them was an absolute requirement? We know that they hold Roman citizens captive.'

Belletor laughed softly, shaking his head at his colleague's anger.

'So reality bites, does it colleague? Yes, I'll do whatever it takes to show the men in power I know how these things work. Unlike *you*, I have no intention of being a tribune for the rest of my service, and this will make it clear to the men that matter just what I'm capable of. Besides, the mine generates nearly two million aureii a year for the empire, against which a payment of ten thousand is relatively small change, wouldn't you agree? And as I said to Maximus here when he was busy wringing his hands at the loss of so much gold, we have to consider the bigger picture. Surely that's a price worth paying, if it means the empire doesn't have to post half a legion here to keep the place safe? And as to the slaves, if those people were foolish enough to put themselves in such danger, it's hardly an imperial priority to rescue them from their own idiocy, is it?'

Scaurus spoke slowly, as if he were explaining a complex problem to a child.

'The problem with paying protection money, colleague, as any stallholder will tell you, is that the men providing the protection are seldom satisfied with the sum initially agreed when they get the scent of more money. And the whole point of native levies is that they are sent to serve at the other end of the empire, not to put them into battle against their brothers. And to leave Roman citizens in bondage and certain depravity? Words fail me.' He shook his head sadly. 'At least you're right in one respect, colleague. This will indeed say more about your abilities to the men who control this province than I ever could.'

A soft cough from the Sarmatae indicated that their thinking had come to an end. The Romans turned back to face them to find Galatas and his uncle waiting.

'I have discussed this matter with my nobles, and we are in agreement with your suggestion. In return for your gold we will provide you with one thousand horsemen who will give you faithful service in the defence of your province. Perhaps we might examine the quality of your gold?'

Balodi stepped forward and bowed to Belletor, taking the proffered key and opening the heavy chest. Digging his hand into the coinage stored within, he pulled an aurei out from near the box's bottom and examined it closely, testing the metal with his teeth. He nodded to Galatas, who turned back to Belletor with open arms.

'Tribune, your generous gift proves the sincerity of your desire for friendship between our peoples. I accept this gold, and vow to return to my lands in peace.'

The Roman bowed.

'And I accept your gracious terms, and your most esteemed gift of men and horses. I would have one more thing of you though, something without which I may struggle to persuade my master the governor of this province as to the likely longevity of this agreement.' Galatas raised his eyebrows in question, but Marcus saw a look of complicity steal across his uncle's face. 'Give me your would-be usurper Inarmaz, and I will subject him to Roman justice every bit as unforgiving as your own. After all, he assaulted the centurion here despite his peaceful intent in returning your father's body to you, and he clearly harboured ambitions to your throne.'

Galatas looked to his uncle, who returned the unspoken question with a slow, thoughtful nod. He turned back to Scaurus with a look of uncertainty.

'Our punishment for Inarmaz's crime would be for his head to be severed from his body before the sacred sword, making his execution both quick and honourable. Can you assure me of a similarly swift end to his life, if I hand him over to your justice?'

Belletor nodded soberly.

'At your request, King, and despite his crimes, I will ensure a clean death for this man.'

Galatas gestured to the men surrounding Inarmaz to bring him forward.

'Very well. Once I have left this place you will send him to meet his ancestors with the appropriate dignity for a member of my family.'

Belletor smiled.

'I will. And with our agreement concluded, I would deem it a great personal honour were you and your uncle to join myself and my colleagues in a celebration of this alliance between our tribes.'

Later, when the gathered nobles and centurions had drunk enough for the evening to have turned rowdy, the feast tent was filled with the shouts and cheers of good natured if lively games of axe throwing and arm wrestling. Balodi, who had narrowly bested Dubnus in an axe-throwing contest, much to the big Briton's noisy disgust, strode across the tent to salute Scaurus.

'I give you my respect, Tribune. It was your quick thinking in releasing me that saved us all from a long stalemate, and my nephew there from murder!' Galatas was sitting in earnest conversation with Belletor, who was holding forth on a subject of great significance, to judge from his intent expression. 'Although I suspect he now faces a new and terrible danger – death by boredom!'

Scaurus smiled at the joke, but his eyes were hard as he stared at the Sarmatae noble.

'It seems that I have made a big mistake, Balodi Boraz. I have underestimated you, and as a result the terms of your defeat have swung somewhat further in your favour than I might have believed possible.'

Balodi raised his drinking horn in salute, his smile unflinching in the face of the Roman's evident disapproval.

'You did the right thing, Tribune, you freed me and in doing so you ended this war. Can you blame me for using every tool at my disposal to settle the terms as favourably as possible?'

Scaurus shook his head.

'No, I cannot, although you seem to have found our Achilles heel rather more easily than I'd have hoped. You *did* negotiate this whole agreement with my colleague Belletor before we ever came to discuss peace, didn't you?'

Balodi grinned, nodding happily.

'Well spotted, my friend! As my father told me often enough for me to grow heartily bored with his urging, a man never stops learning! A man watches, and he listens, even in the depths of adversity, even in *captivity*, and eventually he will learn something that he can use to his benefit. And soldiers will talk, so once I knew of the enmity between you, and that he was likely to be the more suggestible half of your partnership, I knew what I needed to do.'

The Roman nodded his understanding.

'In which case I can only salute you, Balodi Boraz, you played the game too well for me. You have a fortune in gold, you have a young king to mould as you wish, and your only potential rival's death can be conveniently laid at our door, keeping your own hands clean and Inarmaz's men from revolting. Belletor didn't even manage to persuade you to free the Roman slaves that we know you brought with you.'

The nobleman shrugged.

'I told him the truth, that many of my brothers would rather kill their slaves than hand them over to you under duress, and since you have no idea of how many of them we possess, many would most assuredly die if the king were to enforce their freedom. It will be much easier to have them freed quietly, and without fanfare once we have departed from this place. You have my word upon it.' He eyed Scaurus speculatively. 'And speaking of Inarmaz, what of this quick death your colleague has assured my nephew you'll grant him?'

The Roman shrugged, hooking a thumb back over his shoulder at Marcus.

'My centurion here has a sword sharp enough to slice fine cotton dropped onto the blade, and little enough love for Inarmaz. He'll take the man's head off with a single blow, when I tell him to do so.'

Balodi stared at him for a moment.

'What other methods of punishment are usually employed to punish traitors to your empire?'

Scaurus raised an eyebrow.

'We would usually give the convicted traitor thirty or forty lashes with a whip whose braids contained nails and fragments of glass. A skilled executioner can scourge a man to within an inch of his life without allowing him any easy exit. After that he's nailed to a cross through his wrists and ankles with only three nails, by a man who knows how to drive in the iron without severing a blood vessel. After that it's only a question of time before he dies of suffocation as his weight sagging from his arms stops his breathing. With his legs left unbroken a strong man can hoist his weight up on that single nail driven through his ankles for long enough to avert suffocation, although clearly at the cost of the most intense pain. Such a man might last for two or even three days, but the crows have usually taken his eyes before the end comes. It's not a death you would wish upon anyone for whom you retained any family feeling.'

He looked steadily at Balodi, waiting for the noble to speak.

'Tribune, my brother's brother by marriage is responsible for the death of my brother, and for the slaughter of some of the bravest and best warriors in our tribe. I do not find the prospect of his swift and merciful death an attractive one, and if it were my choice he would endure the fate you have just described. I feel that the promise of such an end for Inarmaz would be the best possible way of ensuring a lasting peace between us. And besides, the men I will be gifting to you are Inarmaz's followers, as I am sure you will have guessed. My people respond best to demonstrations of strength, and so I will counsel your colleague Belletor to begin their time in your army by showing them your iron fist, *if* you take my meaning?'

Scaurus nodded slowly, his voice flat.

'I do indeed. I don't expect you'll find him any less malleable on this subject than you did before.'

Balodi clapped him on the shoulder and then stood up, a little unsteadily, bellowing a challenge into the tent's noisy interior.

'Excellent! Now, where's that big ugly ox of a first spear of yours? He promised me a contest of arm strength and the time for that mighty battle' – he drained his cup of wine and held it over his head with the last drips raining onto his hair – 'has come!'

'Not looking quite so full of himself now, is he Centurion?' Marcus stared across the parade ground at the cross onto which Inarmaz had been nailed the previous day, noting dispassionately that the slumped body was now motionless, in stark contrast to the frenzied struggle for life the Sarmatae had put up the previous day. Morban leaned closer to his officer, muttering quietly from the side of his mouth. 'I heard that someone came out here in the night and put a spear in his heart. When the guards came to give him a prod in the morning he was already stiff as a plank. Some soft-hearted idiot who ought to have known better . . .'

Marcus looked down at him with pursed lips, ignoring the disapproving gaze that his standard bearer was directing at him.

'Your point is taken, Standard Bearer. I will remember to apply it rigidly when your continual flow of insubordination and invention of schemes to defraud your fellow soldiers leads to your taking your turn to dance on the shaft of a nail. Or would that be different?'

The two men stood in silence and watched as the Second Cohort marched onto the parade ground and took their place behind the First. The Tungrians were loaded for the march, their carrying poles topped with the bundles that contained their lives, and it wasn't hard to detect a certain lack of enthusiasm for the day's march in the soldiers' bearing. Once the Tungrians were settled in place the legion cohort made their entrance, and the soldiers standing behind Marcus started their accustomed stream of insults and jibes, albeit muttered at a volume low enough to prevent them carrying beyond their own ranks. Swinging to face his men, Marcus lifted his vine stick to Quintus who was standing in his usual place behind the century's ranks.

'Chosen Man Quintus, you have my permission to put your pole through the head of the next man to speak! And on this occasion I won't be finding fault with your selection of targets! Should you give a nasty headache to the most unpleasant man in the century in error I'm sure he'll know who to blame once the initial shock has worn off.'

He turned back to watch the legion cohort's arrival, smiling at the sudden complete silence behind him as the likely consequences of the next smart comment sank into his soldiers' minds.

'I see the German's come to see us off.'

The Roman turned his head at Morban's muttered comment, quickly finding Gerwulf standing alone at the side of the parade ground in full uniform.

'Indeed so. I wonder . . .'

A hurrying figure caught his eye, a woman dressed in a heavy cloak against the morning cold and escorted by a pair of solidly built men, one of whom was carrying a long bundle in his arms. She hurried across the parade ground looking from side to side, obviously seeking out somebody in particular.

'It's the floozy that owns the Ravenstone mine. Gods below, but she could make a man forget that he ever had any troubles. Good legs, fair-sized tits, a pretty face . . . and all that *gold*.'

Marcus ignored the standard bearer's musings and watched as Theodora made a beeline for Scaurus. With a sudden presentiment of what could have upset the woman quite so badly, he stepped out of his place in front of the century and strode down the cohort's line to join the tribune and the first spear as they listened to her near hysterical recounting of the night's events.

'They broke into the villa at dawn and held my staff at swordpoint. They killed the boy, Gaius!'

Scaurus leaned closer, staring into the woman's eyes with a slitted gaze, his voice hard in the sudden silence as she fell quiet at the sight of his murderous expression.

'Who were *they*?'

His answer was a wail of despair and fury, as she turned and pointed at the stationary figure of the German prefect still staring at them from the parade ground's edge, a smile creasing his lips.

'They didn't say, but it must have been *him*! Look at him standing there with that smug expression on his face and tell me that they weren't *his* men!'

Looking at the bodyguard's burden, Marcus realised that it was Mus's body, wrapped in a sheet. A small bloodstain had leaked through the material, and the realisation that the child must have been killed with a blade sent a wave of icy fury through him, but before he could move Scaurus barked out a command.

'*No!*'

The tribune stared at his furious officers with a face set hard.

'If we have no proof then we *cannot* act. Gentlemen, return to your duties.' Neither Julius nor Marcus moved, both men staring across the parade ground at Gerwulf with murderous intent, but before either of them could translate intention into action the tribune spoke again, his tone suddenly matter of fact.

'This one we lose, it's as simple as that. I thought asking Theodora to hide the boy was enough to safeguard him, but I was wrong. He's dead, which destroys the last chance of anyone bearing witness to Gerwulf turning his men loose on that village. And if any of us attempt to make him pay for Mus's murder Belletor will be provided with exactly the evidence he needs of my insubordination. The bastard's got away with it this time, and he knows it.'

The German stared at them for a moment longer and then raised his arm in an ironic salute. He turned and strode away down the hill without a backward glance, leaving the three men staring at his back until he vanished from view among the tents of his cohort's camp.

6

'The legatus will see you now, Tribunes.'

Scaurus motioned to the door, gesturing for his colleague to enter the legatus's office in front of him. Belletor accepted the invitation with alacrity, clearly keen to put himself in front of the man who would be the arbiter of their fate ahead of his rival. The legatus rose from the desk behind which he was sitting and walked round it to greet him, his face professionally bland as he accepted first Belletor's salute and then Scaurus's. Whilst his facial bone structure and hair colour were clearly North African in origin, from the coastal lands previously occupied by Rome's ancient enemy Carthage, his skin was surprisingly pale by contrast with the darker hue that usually accompanied such an appearance.

'Domitius Belletor, welcome to Porolissum. I am Decimus Clodius Albinus, legatus of the Thirteenth Legion and joint field commander of imperial forces in the province.'

Belletor saluted formally, a frown creasing his brow.

'My thanks, Legatus, although I am at a loss as to how you were able to discern which of the two of us was which?'

Albinus smiled slightly, indicating Scaurus with a wave of his hand.

'It was easy enough, Tribune, given that I've known Gaius here since he was a fifteen-year-old. I'm surprised that he's never mentioned our long association to you.'

Belletor's eyes narrowed as the implications of the legatus's statement sank in. He dithered for a moment before speaking again.

'In that case, Legatus, you will doubtless be aware that I am the commander of the auxiliary detachment that arrived here this morning. My command comprises a legion cohort, two auxiliary cohorts, a squadron of auxiliary cavalry and one thousand native horsemen.'

Albinus nodded easily, seating himself behind the desk again and waving to a pair of chairs set out ready for the two men. The slab of wood in front of him was devoid of any clutter, and only two objects marred its otherwise clear surface: an infantry gladius sheathed in a magnificently ornate scabbard and a small silver bell which had been polished to a brilliant shine. Once the tribunes were seated he answered Belletor's statement, his face wreathed in a beneficent smile.

'Indeed, Tribune, my beneficiarius arrived here two days ago with news of your impending arrival, and a *detailed* briefing as to the events around the successful defence of Alburnus Major. Well done gentlemen, I'm sure the governor will mention you *both* favourably in his next despatch to Rome.'

He paused, looking closely at Belletor to see how the tribune would react.

'*Both* of us, Legatus? Since I am the commander of the detachment that defended the mine complex I would have expected . . .'

Albinus smiled again, putting up a hand to silence him.

'All in good time, Tribune. I think that our first topic for discussion ought to be this disciplinary matter my clerk tells me you wish to register. I believe it is a matter of concern regarding Rutilius Scaurus's conduct during your recent encounter with the Sarmatae? That is, I hardly need to point out to you, a serious accusation that might well cast a severe and possibly terminal blight upon a man's career. Are you sure you wish to persist with this request?'

Belletor responded stiffly, his suspicion as to where Albinus's sympathies might lie clearly aroused.

'I feel it my duty to report Rutilius Scaurus's insubordinate behaviour, Legatus, and to ensure that he receives the appropriate penalty for his wilful ignorance of my orders.'

Albinus shrugged, holding out a hand.

'I see. In that case perhaps I'd better have a look at that scroll in your hand, which my clerk informs me contains your orders from your legatus in Fortress Bonna. I believe it has direct relevance on the matter of who was granted command of the detachment in question.'

Belletor handed over the scroll, shooting a triumphant glance at Scaurus.

'As you can see, Legatus, my own commanding officer's instructions on the matter of *my* absolute power over the detachment are quite unequivocal.'

He waited patiently while Albinus digested the contents of the scroll.

'I see. Well this is most edifying, Domitius Belletor. Perhaps more so than you realise.' He looked up at the tribune with a look that redoubled Belletor's suspicions that all was not going as he hoped. 'Tell me, who was it that composed this order?'

The tribune frowned again, failing to see the point of the question.

'It was Legatus Decula, the commander of the First Minervia at Fortress Bonna, as you can see from the name at the bottom of . . .'

Albinus shook his head with a look of sympathy.

'You miss the point of my enquiry, Tribune.' He sighed, his voice taking on a tone of weary patience. 'In every organisation, Domitius Belletor, there is usually a small group of experienced professionals who understand all too well the empire's requirements of whatever it is that they do, and how these might best be delivered, and who endeavour to ensure that their superiors' instructions are issued in a manner likely to bring about success. And for better or worse, that's doubly true in the army. I've got one, the man who showed you in here. Yes, he's only a soldier, but he has fifteen years of experience in the framing and the writing of orders by senior officers. I make sure to ask his opinion as to every administrative matter that crosses my desk, as I did with this order I'm holding, once you'd shown it to him when requesting this interview. It was very clear to him that this order had been written by a fellow professional as an *interpretation* of the original verbal order given by Legatus Decula at Bonna. Which, of course, the idiot signed without a second thought.'

He smiled into Belletor's incensed glare with complete equanimity for a moment, then shook his head in good-natured amusement.

'Tribune, I've known Sextus Tullius Decula since the bad old days of the German Wars. He's quite the most pompous and hidebound man I've ever served with, utterly convinced that only men of the senatorial class are capable of leading our legions to victory and at the same time somewhat *more lax* with the more mundane aspects of his command than might be wise. Doubtless he barked out a diatribe based on his ingrained prejudices, and then left his clerk to convert the sentiment of whatever it was he'd ranted on about into a written order for you to carry away, as your proof of superiority over your colleague here.'

Belletor shifted in his seat, while Scaurus's face remained rigidly set, and Albinus looked down at the order again, pointing to the paper in his hand.

'The first part of the order is clear enough, so I will paraphrase. You, Domitius Belletor, are to assume command of the detachment comprised of the units you detailed to me earlier, less the one thousand Sarmatae horsemen you've been brave enough to add to your command since then. Further, you are to exercise "absolute decision-making responsibility", with the right to remove your colleague here from his subordinate command of the Tungrian cohorts should he provide you with adequate reason to do so. That was almost word for word with the legatus's verbal instruction, I expect?'

Belletor nodded vigorously, sensing that his argument was easing itself away from the thin ice of the legatus's relationship with his colleague, and onto the more certain ground of his clearly delegated authority over Scaurus.

'Indeed so. And yet when I attempted to exercise that right to remove Rutilius Scaurus from his command he refused to accept my decision.'

Albinus nodded.

'On the face of it then, Tribune Scaurus's refusal to accept your command to relinquish control of his cohorts is a simple question of insubordination?' Belletor nodded sanguinely. 'I see. It is, of course, a matter which I am compelled to punish severely . . .' He paused and fixed Belletor with a flat stare. 'If, that is, I am unable to find any justification for Tribune Scaurus's actions.'

The tribune recoiled in his seat as if he'd been stung.

'*Justification*, Legatus?'

'*Justification*, Domitius Belletor. By which I mean a good reason for your colleague to have ignored your instruction to relinquish his command.' Albinus waved the order at Belletor, his smile now notably reduced in its friendliness. 'And so we turn to the second part of this order, the part I suspect you read rather less well than the section we've already discussed, since it was perhaps less worthy of your interest. By which I mean it serves *your* interests somewhat less well. It is, after all, an afterthought, the usual standard order that headquarters' clerks tack onto every set of instructions received by every detachment commander, and to which no legatus will ever take exception to since it all makes such good sense from the perspective of covering his backside.'

He flourished the order theatrically.

'Let's see what it says, shall we? He read from the scroll. '"You are commanded to fulfil the requirements of your orders with regard to the march from Germania Inferior to Dacia, and to conduct any necessary independent field operations with the required combination of *necessary* aggression whilst also exercising due regard for your command's preservation." Oh yes, this was definitely written by a professional administrator, since you are ordered to act both aggressively and in a cautious manner at the same time. The man's covered every possible angle for his legatus, so that any disaster you might inflict upon your command is clearly your own fault and in no way capable of arriving on his desk. My man does much the same, and indeed I'm sure it's a long-standing art passed from one clerk to the next.'

He smiled at Belletor again, but this time the expression was so thin as to be practically non-existent.

'And so we come to the meat of the issue, Tribune Belletor. This last section, which I doubt Legatus Decula gave even so much as a second glance as he scribbled his name at the bottom of the paper, given he'll have seen it so many times by now for it to be virtually invisible to him. "Should the requirement become obvious, you are to be replaced by your deputy until such time as you demonstrate your renewed ability to command the detachment in question." An innocent little clause, isn't it, and yet I fear it's going to be the downfall of your argument for Rutilius Scaurus's dismissal.'

Belletor's mouth dropped open in amazement, and when he spoke again his words were an incensed gabble.

'But there was *never* any need for Scaurus to replace me! I was always in complete control of the detachment, and at no time unfit to command!' He glared at the legatus with undisguised fury. 'This is outrageous, Legatus Albinus, I can see what you're trying to do here and it won't . . .'

He fell silent as Albinus picked up the silver bell and rang it, the high-pitched note summoning his clerk from the side office where he had clearly been waiting as instructed.

'And that, Tribune, all depends on how we are to interpret *fitness to command*, doesn't it? Ah, Julius. If you'd be so kind as to ask Beneficiarius Cattanius to join us? And perhaps you could take some notes for me? You know how the army likes this sort of thing to be properly documented.'

'So what's going on here, eh? What fuckin' mischief are you apes up to now? And put those fuckin' buckets *down!*'

Sanga and Scarface snapped to attention and stared fixedly at the fort's wall while Quintus strode up to them with a furious look on his face, Marcus trailing in his wake with his eyes narrowed at the sight before him. Much to Scarface's delight the two soldiers had been transferred from Qadir's century to the Roman's, along with the remnants of their tent party after the cessation of hostilities with Galatas's men, replacements for the losses that Marcus's men had taken at the battle for the Saddle. Shortly thereafter their

number had been reinforced by one of the warriors Balodi had
offered as part of the agreement, and as the cohort's officers
had expected, the soldiers were finding ways to express their
disdain for the hapless conscripts. The young centurion and his
chosen man had rounded a corner to find the two veterans in the
act of filling four buckets from one of the rainwater troughs that
were positioned around the fort's exterior. Their intended victim,
a new soldier who Marcus recalled went by the name of Saratos,
was standing stolidly by and watching the buckets being filled with
an expression of faint dismay. Looking past him the young centurion spied Morban, having seemingly exercised his usual sixth sense
with regard to the impending presence of officers, halfway down
the line of tents and walking briskly with his attention ostentatiously
elsewhere. Deciding to leave the standard bearer's comeuppance
until later in the day, Marcus stepped up behind his chosen man,
pursing his lips as Quintus squared up to the veteran soldiers.

'Think we're clever, do we boys? Think we can have some fun
with the new recruits while my back's turned, eh? What were we
doing then, loading him up with four buckets to see how many
times around the camp he could carry them? A big strong lad
like him? My money would be on ten, at least. What was your
money on, eh lads?'

Sanga kept his mouth shut and his gaze locked on the fort's
wall, but Scarface lacked his mate's ability to know when his
mouth would be better kept closed.

'You know how it is, Quintus, we was just seeing how tough
the barbarian really is . . .'

The chosen man raised a finger to silence him, pointing at the
buckets on the ground in front of the two soldiers. Sanga nodded
minutely, his face taking on an expression that told Marcus he
knew only too well what was coming next. Quintus patted the
recruit on his shoulder, pointing in the direction in which Morban
had vanished and gently telling him to be on his way, then turned
back to the soldiers, his voice rising to parade-ground volume as
he put his face less than an inch from Scarface's.

'He's not a barbarian, he's a fuckin' *soldier*! He's in your tent party for a fuckin' reason, you *pricks*! You're supposed to be the responsible men, the lads that can help the new boys to adapt . . .' He shook his head in disgust and moved to face Sanga. 'If I catch you pair, or anyone else in your fuckin' century picking on the poor bastard, I'll have your fuckin' cocks dangling from my belt. As of now he's your baby, so you'd better make sure you start looking after him, hadn't you!'

The veterans nodded in swift agreement, Scarface shooting a quick glance at his mate that made Sanga shake his head in disgust. Quintus grinned evilly at him, nodding vigorously as his voice returned to a conversational volume.

'Oh yes, I saw that. Your thick-headed mate here thinks you're going to get away with just getting a bollocking, but you're far too smart to agree with that, aren't you?' Sanga nodded, turning a jaundiced eye on Scarface. 'So, Soldier Sanga, what punishment would you give the pair of you if you was me, eh? Get it right and I'll let you off lightly, get it wrong and I'll double what I have in mind.'

Sanga looked down at the buckets, then up to see Quintus nodding.

'Good guess. And?'

Sanga thought furiously.

'Ten times round the camp?'

'Good guess! Get on with it then! If you're not back here with them fuckin' buckets still brimming by the time the centurion and I are ready to move on, then you can double the number of times each sentry gets to rip the fuckin' piss out of you.'

The veterans took a pair of buckets apiece and hurried off, water slopping over the sides of the containers. Quintus watched them go with a smile.

'I was only going to make them do it five times, but there's no arguing with keenness.'

'I wouldn't have had you down as being soft on the new boys, Chosen Man.'

Quintus looked up at his centurion for a moment before answering, one eyebrow raised.

'Well, sir, just because I'm a little harsh with the men on occasion doesn't mean I've forgot what it feels like to be the new boy myself. I was bullied half to death before I learned that the best answer is to meet fire with fire, and started knocking men over and then kicking them until they stopped trying to get up again. That Sarmatae lad is going to be stood in line with the rest of us soon enough, and if we treat him right he'll be trying to stick his spear in the enemy and not Scarface's fuckin' arse, begging your pardon Centurion.'

The Roman smiled at him with new admiration.

'I can respect that point of view, Chosen. Shall we continue?'

Quintus nodded deferentially, then turned to stare at the veterans' retreating backs.

'Faster you apes! And stop spilling that *fuckin'* water!' He turned back to Marcus. 'After you, sir. Let's go and find out which one of the sentries it was that tipped off your pet standard bearer that we was on our way, an' whoever it was can join those two in their fun and games.'

'It's not an outcome in which I can take very much pleasure, First Spear.'

Scaurus regarded Julius levelly over the rim of his cup, sipping at the wine it contained. Julius shook his head in only partly feigned exasperation, tossing back his own cupful and putting it down on the table with a bang.

'You'll have to forgive me, Tribune, but I'm nothing less than bloody delighted by the whole thing! I'm going to find Cattanius and get him properly pissed as his reward for making sure that his legatus knew exactly how big a fool Belletor made of himself. Between the two of you, you've got that prick off our backs and you're in undisputed command of the cohorts once again. It's a shame we didn't keep the Sarmatae horsemen, but that's a small price to pay.'

The tribune mused on the meeting's conclusion for a moment, and Belletor's incensed behaviour, as it had become clear that Albinus intended siding with his old friend.

'Nothing good will come of this I'm afraid. He'll be writing a long letter to Rome even as we stand here discussing the matter, telling his father how he's been robbed of the command he was granted by Legatus Decula only as a result of my political connections with Clodius Albinus. And don't forget he can play on *his* famous victory over the Sarmatae, and how he defeated the bandits in Germania before that. I've already told you that my family is still under something of a shadow given our previous history, and then there's the fact that he's from a senatorial family while I'm only an equestrian. No, my instincts are telling me that Albinus has perhaps missed his judgement in this matter.' The tribune shook his head, reaching for the wine flask. 'Boyhood friend or not, I suspect he would have been wiser to have stuck with the status quo in this case.'

Julius shrugged, accepting the offer of another cup of wine.

'You did know that the legatus would take your side though, didn't you?'

Scaurus nodded his agreement.

'In truth, I did. From the moment that Cattanius mentioned his name I knew that I could do what was needed to defend the mines, because Albinus would ultimately protect me from Belletor's sense of inadequacy if I stepped too hard on his toes in the process. I just didn't realise he'd be that harsh with the man. And I don't expect that Cattanius has made any friends in the matter either.'

He winced at the memory of the beneficiarius's unequivocally expressed opinion on the matter of Belletor's command of the mines' defence.

'He tried to avoid being too blunt, but once Clodius Albinus ordered him to stop dancing around the issue he was positively scathing about the man. "It was self-evident that the tribune was keener on his bath than on the welfare of his men" was one of the kinder things he said.'

He took another mouthful of wine, shaking his head as if to dismiss the matter from discussion.

'Anyway, here we are again, masters of our destiny more or

less. If we forget for a moment the two legati at whose whim we'll be dancing over the next few weeks. Yes Tertius? There's no need to raise your hand with me man, just spit it out like your colleague here does.'

The Second Cohort's senior centurion was slowly but surely gaining confidence in the presence of his tribune, and was now willing to venture an opinion where a month before he had been content to allow his brother officer to do the talking.

'Begging your pardon, sir, but given that there's snow on the ground shouldn't we be setting up for winter quarters? Surely there won't be any more fighting now until the spring?'

Scaurus smiled ruefully.

'And so you might think, First Spear, but that would be to underestimate Dacia. This is the land of the wolf, you see, it's literally the meaning of the name in the natives' language, and the wolf hunts all year round. The tribes won't be pulling back from the frontier, and consequently neither shall we. Legatus Albinus has arranged for the legion stores here to issue us with the appropriate cold weather clothing, after which we'll be declared as fit for duty.' He raised an eyebrow at the two senior centurions, shaking his head slightly. 'But whether the gear we'll be getting will genuinely be fit for the weather we'll be facing is another question entirely.'

'Well now, Centurion, do come in. Can I offer you a cup of wine?'

If Tribune Sigilis was surprised by Marcus's presence at the door of his quarter he managed to hide it well enough, pulling up a chair for his fellow Roman and waiting while the other man shrugged off his cloak and sat down. Waving away the offer of a drink with a smile, noting that the bottle was stoppered and that Sigilis was drinking nothing stronger than water, Marcus took a moment to compose himself before speaking.

'Thank you for your time, Tribune—'

The younger man raised a hand, shaking his head in gentle rebuke.

'No. I won't sit here and allow you to show deference to me

when we both know that you're easily as wellborn as I am. On top of which, you're the one with the scars and experience I so badly need if I am to make a success of this way of life. When we have the privacy necessary for you to drop your mask, I would be honoured if you would use my first name.' He gave the centurion an appraising stare. 'In truth I'd long since decided that you and I would never have this discussion.'

Marcus nodded.

'And in truth, Lucius, so had I. When you told me about your father's investigations into my family's downfall I quickly decided not to pursue the matter. I decided that I would be wiser to be content with the life I have here, and to cherish and protect my family, than to go hunting shadows and risk losing everything.'

Sigilis raised an eyebrow.

'So I had assumed, when we marched all the way from the Ravenstone valley to this frozen extremity of the empire without exchanging a word on the subject. So what changed your mind?'

Marcus smiled wryly at the question.

'Not so much what, as who. My wife is adamant on the subject, despite knowing the risks involved for all of us. You see . . .' He shook his head, as if in disbelief at what he was about to say. 'As I think I told you, my father's ghost haunts my dreams. He pursues me through my sleeping hours, sometimes accompanied by my family, sometimes alone. Last night I dreamt about a battlefield scattered with bloodied corpses and stinking of blood and faeces . . .' He gave Sigilis a knowing look which the tribune answered with a minute nod. 'And there, in the corner of my eye, I found him standing waiting for me. His toga was rent and bloodied, and the nails had been torn from his fingers. He raised them for me to see, and told me that this was the torture to which he had been subjected before he was killed, in the expectation that he would betray my hiding place.'

He sighed and put a hand over his eyes, and Sigilis reached for the wine bottle, filling a cup and passing it over.

'Thank you. In every dream he tells me that I have to seek revenge for their murder, and that I can only exact this vengeance by returning to Rome. But the worst dreams are the ones where my younger brother appears beside him, always silent, always staring at me without expression.' He took a mouthful of the wine. 'Felicia tells me that I must resolve this internal conflict if I am to stay sane, and that she fears I will turn to the bottle or kill myself to find peace. She also believes that my customary loss of any sense of self-preservation in battle is rooted in the same problem.'

Sigilis frowned.

'Your wife does not believe that this is your father's ghost?'

Marcus smiled, shaking his head.

'My wife is the most rational person I have ever known. Not many women could have dealt with the ordeal she was put through last year, kidnapped by an imperial assassin who was using her as bait to lure me in for the kill. He lowered his guard for a single moment and she stuck a knife through his tongue in defence of our unborn child. She never seems to have lost a moment's sleep over the matter either. But it makes no difference whether my father speaks to me from the underworld or simply from here,' – he tapped the back of his head – 'I must do as he bids, and find the men who murdered my family. Only when they are cold in the ground will I find the peace I crave.' He raised his gaze to stare levelly at the tribune. 'So tell me if you will, Lucius, and in as much detail as you can muster, what it was that this investigator told your father and his colleagues about my father's death.'

Sigilis stirred in his seat, reaching for a cup and filling it with wine.

'There was much in what he told us that you will find troubling, but one name was woven through the whole sorry story. It seems that there is a group of men who do the emperor's bidding, or perhaps more accurately that of the man who stands behind his throne, the Praetorian Prefect Perennis. When men without conscience or compunction are needed, these men step forward without regard to the consequences of their actions. They carry out the dirty jobs that require the spilling of innocent blood in pursuit of imperial aims, and if a noble family vanishes from the city, as if they have been expunged from life itself, they are usually at the heart of the matter. He named them, not as individuals but by their collective name, a title that sent a shiver of fear through the men listening in my father's house that night. He called them "The Emperor's Knives".'

'Atten-*shun!*'

The gathered officers stiffened their bodies as the two legati entered the room, obeying the legion first spear's barked command without hesitation.

'He's a fearsome old bastard, that Secundus.'

Scaurus nodded fractionally in recognition of Julius's muttered comment, replying in equally muted terms.

'Yes, he's from the old school, a throwback to the days of the republic.'

The veteran senior centurion was apparently well known for his evil temper when his instructions were not followed instantly and to the letter, and wasn't above publicly berating an errant tribune in the most incendiary of terms without any apparent regard for social status. Cattanius had shared a story with the two men while they had been waiting for the command conference to begin, the payoff to which had been his recounting of the man's furious beasting of an errant junior tribune for some mistake or other only the previous day. He had looked around to make sure they weren't overheard before continuing with his recounting of the centurion's words.

'All Secundus said was this: "The Thirteenth Legion is the best fucking legion in the empire, young sir. We're the descendants of the men the Divine Julius Caesar used to conquer the world, and ever since those famous days the Thirteenth has been led by *real* soldiers, from the legatus down. And if you can't manage to behave like a *real* soldier then you, young sir, can fuck *right* off!" I don't expect his daddy warned the young man in question to expect treatment like that when he signed the boy up!'

Under the veteran centurion's gimlet eye the officers stood to attention while the two legati took their places by the map table. Albinus looked about him with a slightly bemused smile, while his colleague Gaius Pescennius Niger's expression was altogether more dour.

'Very well, gentlemen, relax, and gather round the map if you will.'

The assembled officers obeyed Niger's command, clustering round the meticulously constructed map table while he waited for them to settle into place. Julius looked down at the plaster replica of the landscape across which the campaign against the Sarmatae would be fought.

'Lend me your vine stick will you please, First Spear?'

Secundus surrendered his badge of office to his legatus, the look on his face indicating his displeasure at having to allow his commanding officer to make free with his most treasured possession. Oblivious to the centurion's reproving stare, Niger looked around the circle of men with the stick held up until he was sure he had every man's full attention.

'So, gentlemen, here we are, two full legions, or as close as one can get to such a thing these days, and eight auxiliary cohorts, seventeen if we choose to pull in the garrisons of the forts within marching distance, two of them formed of cavalry recruited from Britannia.' He caught sight of Belletor's raised eyebrows. 'Plus, of course, the First Minervia's Seventh Cohort and a thousand allied barbarian cavalry recently recruited in the south of the province. And as of now we're all based here, at Porolissum.'

He pointed with the vine stick at the map table's lovingly constructed replica of the local geography, and Marcus stared with interest at the contours of the ground across which the campaign to come would be fought.

'Our opponent is a Sarmatae chieftain called Purta, who we are informed is fielding approximately twelve thousand cavalry and another ten thousand light infantry. Against our heavy infantry the foot soldiers represent a negligible threat. First Spear Secundus and his colleagues would tear through them in an hour or two of butchery and slave-taking. The enemy horse, however, represent an entirely different and more serious proposition. Gentlemen, to be very clear, that strength of barbarian cavalry, if used decisively and in mass, would without doubt represent a very serious threat, even to a force as strong as ours.'

He paused, looking about him again.

'Some of you, those who haven't ever faced barbarian cavalry of this type, will be wondering if I might perhaps be a little over-cautious in that assessment. I can see it in your faces. Gentlemen, our military history is littered with cautionary tales of otherwise distinguished commanders who underestimated the capabilities of the Sarmatae, and before them the Parthians, and paid a heavy price for doing so. These Sarmatae are men raised on the great grasslands beyond these mountains, taught to ride at an age when most children in the empire are still considered infants. They do not need to use their hands to control their mounts, learning to do so purely by means of the pressure they exert with their knees. That leaves their hands free to use a bow on the move, and they are expert at hitting a target from a moving horse time after time, whether advancing, retreating or just riding round in a damned circle. As if that isn't enough of a threat, they carry a long lance which they call the kontos, capable of spitting a man without having to get close enough that he can use his own spear in return.'

Niger shook his head.

'So call me a pessimist behind my back if you like, but I will not risk my legion in battle with that strong a force of their horsemen on open ground. My colleague here and I' – he gestured to Albinus, who inclined his head in grave agreement – 'have decided that this is a battle that we will win by tempting a head-strong enemy onto well-defended and carefully prepared positions. Once we have the enemy horse nicely bogged down then we will unleash our legionaries to conduct their slaughter . . .' He raised a warning finger and looked around the assembled officers with a stern glare. 'But until then, gentlemen, be warned that I am determined not to give them the chance to wreak the havoc they are all too capable of inflicting upon us, *if* we are unwise enough to let them do so. Colleague, will you explain our plan?'

Albinus nodded, taking the vine stick with a wink to its grizzled owner.

'As you newcomers to Porolissum can see, we're here, on top of this ridge which runs south-west to north-east. These are the Knife Mountains, gentlemen, and they are well named. They are largely impassable to any sort of military formation other than the most lightly equipped scouts, and crossed by passes at a very few points, most of which are laughably simple to defend due to their narrow nature. Our forts to the mountains' rear are perfectly placed not only to resist any direct attack, but also to allow the cohorts that occupy them to move quickly in defence of these passes.'

He looked around the group of officers with a knowing smile.

'Which means that nature has provided us with a very handy rampart against any barbarian attack from the north-west. However,' – he pointed with the stick to the southern end of the ridge – 'all good things will naturally come to their end, and so it is with this line of defence. As you can see, the mountains are split by a valley, here, which provides a natural point which an aggressive enemy commander would undoubtedly consider as the key that will unlock this particular door. For that reason there are three forts positioned along the length of the valley in a line from south-east to north-west.' He pointed with the stick. 'Lakeside Fort here, Stone Fort here, and lastly Two Rivers Fort, here. Two of them are not very much more than glorified lookout posts, but Stone Fort is a far tougher nut to crack and represents the heart of the valley's defence. We've sent two cohorts of Britons, First Britannica and Second Britannorum to man the forts, since they seem to be bloodthirsty maniacs to a man, and given command of the valley's defence to one of our more energetic young tribunes. By now I would expect him to have the place as tightly defended as the praetorian fortress in Rome.'

He pointed at the valley with the borrowed vine stick.

'So, if the Sarmatae look to turn our line by attacking up this valley, aiming to get behind the mountain ridge and into our rear area, they must first deal with the garrisons of these forts. This man Purta's dilemma is that he must either break into each fort in turn and destroy the garrison, or bypass them and tolerate the risk presented by their presence in his rear. Either choice is problematic, of course, since he either accepts a significant delay to his advance, and allows time for stronger forces to be moved into position to block his way up the valley, or else finds himself with our spears to both front and rear.

'Now we have it on very good authority that Purta believes the defences arrayed against him in the valley are too strong. He fears that by the time his army has smashed a path through them, and cleared a route out onto the open ground his horsemen need, he'll find a legion blocking his way. He therefore plans, we are informed, to turn just such a plan against us. He will make a feint up the valley, with the intention of drawing a legion into exactly such a blocking position, and then sending his full strength at a point somewhere else along the ridge. He's going to roll the dice, colleagues, and gamble that he can weaken the province's main line of defence enough to walk through the front door while the bouncers' attention is distracted by a scuffle in the corner.'

The legatus smiled around at his officers, his eyes bright with the prospect of action.

'Whereas we, armed with this inside information, are going to give every indication that we've fallen for his ploy whilst keeping our main strength concentrated, and ready to land the one blow that will end this war in a single battle. Whichever pass through the mountains Purta sends his main force at, he'll find two legions massed and ready to meet him, and on ground that's been well prepared. Questions?'

Scaurus raised a hand.

'Tribune?'

'Legatus, if you're going to keep the Thirteenth Gemina and the Fifth Macedonica concentrated for the main battle, how are you going to convince this Purta that you've taken his bait?'

The legatus grinned back at him.

'Perceptive, Rutilius Scaurus, very perceptive indeed. We'll have mounted scouts out, of course, and once we know that the Sarmatae are making their move on the valley I propose to send an initial relief force from the south-western end of the line. Any

enemy scouts sent forward past the river forts will see the movement and take it for the advance guard of the blocking force.
The report will go back to Purta that we've taken his bait, and
he'll make his move on the main line in blessed ignorance of
what's waiting for him. On top of that, this apparent relief force
will also serve to sweep the valley clear of scouts, and prevent
them from getting so far up the valley that they realise there's
no legion moving up in support. Quite an elegant solution, I'd
say. And now that you mention it, given that your Tungrians
have rather more battle experience than most of our forces, I'd
say they'll make the ideal units for a task which is, of course,
likely to result in an action of some kind. Do you think you can
handle such a mission?'

Scaurus nodded, already hard in thought as he stared at the
map table.

'Legatus!'

Albinus swivelled his head to regard Tribune Belletor, standing
at the other end of the table from his former colleague and wearing
an expression of concern.

'Tribune?'

'My command, Legatus, is every bit as powerful as that under
Rutilius Scaurus's leadership, and has the advantage of mustering
a powerful force of cavalry. I propose that the Tungrians advance
along one bank of the river, while we will manage the other.'

Albinus shared a glance with Niger, but it was the older man
who responded to Belletor's request.

'Your cavalry, Tribune, if my memory serves, are only recently
recruited from the Sarmatae you defeated at Alburnus Major. I
wonder, perhaps, if they represent too great a risk to be put into
the field against their own tribe.'

Belletor, having clearly anticipated the response, reacted with
uncharacteristic understatement.

'I completely understand your concern, Legatus. Perhaps it
would help if I were to tell you that they have already been active
in scouting before us as we marched north. On more than one
occasion the scouting parties of these horsemen that I sent out

to clear our path brought back the bodies of Sarmatae scouts they had managed to kill, along with their mounts. My discussions with them have convinced me that they care little for these other people, owing loyalty only to their own offshoot of the tribe, and in the absence of their kindred, to me as their paymaster. And besides' – Marcus watched his tribune's eyes narrow as Belletor advanced his argument one last step – 'the use of their own horsemen as part of the master plan that undoes this Purta's invasion of the province will surely play very well in Rome, I would have thought.'

'Hmmm. I see.' Niger stroked his bearded chin, looking at Albinus with a calculating expression. 'Military and political advantages combined, eh? Very well, Tribune Belletor, my colleague and I will give your proposal due consideration and inform you as to our decision in due course. Any more questions? No? Very well gentlemen, go back to your cohorts and ensure that your men are in prime condition and ready to fight. Here's your vine stick, First Spear Secundus.'

The Tungrian cohorts marched from Porolissum at dawn three days later, heading down the military road that followed the line of the Knife Mountains to the south-west in the company of the Thracian archers who were ordered to reinforce the defence at Stone Fort, while Belletor's mismatched force bought up the rear. The Sarmatae horsemen rode in a straggling mass at the column's rear, as immune to any form of marching discipline as had been the case since their enlistment.

'I presume your tribune's riding with his new best friends, perched up on that horse of his like some kind of conquering general?'

Julius had dropped back to the rear of his men and by happy chance had found First Spear Sergius marching at the head of his legionaries with a dark and foreboding look. The two men were now marching together with their cloaks wrapped about them to fend off the bitterly cold wind.

'Indeed he is. Since he managed to persuade Legatus Niger

to put him on the right bank of the river for this march down to Lakeside Fort, he's been puffing and preening like a man preparing to ride through Rome with the rose petals floating down around him.' Sergius shook his head and spat on the road's verge. 'I've tried to point out to him that he has no idea as to their real loyalties, but he's like a man besotted with his new wife. All I get back is "my tribesmen this" and "my tribesmen that", and no concern at all for his regular soldiers.' He pointed to Julius's boots, their new fur linings visible around the ankle. 'Our boots are stuffed with straw, not rabbit like yours. The storeman told Belletor that your men had already taken everything they had to spare, and since he didn't have a legatus supporting him he was forced to walk away empty handed. He's got fur linings in *his* boots mind you, and a nice fur cloak. He was given them by his bloody Sarmatae.'

The two men marched in silence for a moment, enjoying the crisp autumn air and the constant rattle of hobnails on the road's cobbled surface.

'They're decent enough scouts though?'

Sergius grimaced reluctant agreement.

'So it seems. You saw just as well as I did what they brought back with them from their patrol over the mountains.'

The deciding factor in Niger's decision had been a patrol that Belletor had sent over the mountains, with orders to range along their northern slopes in search of enemy scouts. The thirty-man party had returned with two empty saddles, but with the heads of half a dozen dead tribesmen dangling from their saddle horns, and the legatus had been an instant convert to the idea of their being used alongside the First Minervia's regulars. Julius nodded.

'Exactly. I may not have very much respect for your tribune, but it does seem as if he's picked a winner for once.'

The twin detachments ground their way to the south-west at a fast pace, reaching Forest View as the sun was dipping towards the horizon. Ushered into the sizeable marching camp alongside the fort's walls, more usually used by several legion cohorts at a time, the Tungrians found themselves alongside men from a cohort of auxiliary infantry whose title excited a good deal of comment. Marcus overheard Morban explaining it to one of the younger men of the Fifth Century.

'First Britannica? You know what that means, don't you? These are men who've descended from the tribesmen who were enlisted in Britannia when the legions were recruiting for the wars in Dacia a hundred years ago. What's the odds of them having come from somewhere near our old fort at The Hill, eh? I'll give you five to one . . .'

As it turned out the Britons were welcoming enough, but it had seemed that in truth they were no more from Britannia than the majority of the Tungrians were really from the farmland around the city of Tungrorum. A hard-faced veteran stepped forward to greet the standard bearer and his hopeful companion.

'Yeah, my granddad was from Britannia. My dad told me that his old man volunteered for service at a time when the province was right peaceful, so he and another five hundred bluenoses were shipped out here to keep the locals in order.'

Morban thanked him and turned back to the young soldier, sliding the man's stake money into his purse with well-practised speed.

'Grandfathers don't count, I'm afraid.'

Scaurus and Julius went looking for the Britons' prefect in company with Belletor and Sergius, and the four of them walked into the fort to where they knew the headquarters building would be, given that its layout was prescribed by army regulations. Scaurus tapped at the wall of a barrack block with his knuckle as they passed.

'The fort may be built to the standard design, but the materials they've put it up with aren't. These men obviously live under a serious threat; you only have to look at the way their buildings are constructed to see that.'

The barrack was built with walls of stone, and the roof was an expanse of thick slate tiles. Wherever wood was used, in doors and windows, the openings were both recessed and protected as much as possible by overhanging stone lintels, designed to prevent a fire arrow from striking the timber. The four men found the fort's commander, a harassed-looking veteran centurion, snatching a quick meal in the fort's headquarters building. He pulled up chairs for them and then called for more food and wine.

'I've only got two centuries, gentlemen, enough to stand guard and prevent the locals from ransacking the place while our backs are turned. The bulk of the cohort is concentrated further down the valley at Stone Fort, along with the Second Britannorum. That's the spot where two valleys come together, so any attacker from the north has to pass through a narrow point in the valley, almost a gorge in truth. If we can't stop an attacker there then we're not going to be able to hold them anywhere else, and from here it's an easy enough march to Napoca.' He smiled knowingly at the tribunes. 'And if you think this fort's well constructed, you want to see the job Tribune Leontius has made of Stone Fort!'

The three cohorts marched on down the valley the next morning, along the road that paralleled the river's winding path. Another hour's march brought them within sight of the second of the three forts defending the valley, and Julius stared at the defences arrayed around its walls with a whistle of appreciation.

'Now there, Tribune, is a fort that's been set up by a man who knows his trade.'

Commanding the narrowest spot in the valley's length, the fort's walls were taller and longer than was usual, clearly big enough to house considerably more strength than the single five-hundred-man cohort that was the usual garrison's complement. Even from a mile's distance the structure was evidently built from stone rather than timber. Heavy towers were set on every corner, and the road ran into the fort's eastern side through a massive stone double-doored gatehouse flanked by two more towers.

'Are those bolt throwers?'

The first spear followed his tribune's pointing hand and shook his head.

'It's hard to say with all that protection.'

The towers were topped by shallow wooden roofs set low enough that the heavy weapons' crews would barely have sufficient headroom to work, a small enough price to pay for the resulting protection from enemy bowshot. As the Tungrians drew nearer they realised that the towers were indeed occupied by bolt throwers, one on each corner of the fort, and that the weapons' crews were tracking their approach. Julius stared darkly up at them, shaking his head in irritation.

'Very funny. If I find out that those things are loaded then I'm going to tear off someone's head and shit down his neck. An accidental shot at this range would pin three or four men together.'

The ground to either side of the road was studded with lilies, the stake-filled pits that would deny an attacker any safe footing other than the road itself, and channel them into the bolt throwers' killing zone. A deep ditch stretched across the valley's four-hundred-pace width, a hundred paces in front of the fort's rear wall. Julius nodded approvingly again, his ire at the bolt-thrower crews distracted by the defences.

'Nice work. A ditch deep enough and steep enough on the far side to have a man climbing on all fours to get out of it, with a four-foot wall for the defenders on the far side and a nice little surprise at the bottom, no doubt.'

Scaurus squinted down into the ditch as they crossed the wooden bridge that spanned the gap, nodding in agreement.

'So I see. And if this is how well they've chosen to defend the back door, one wonders what the side facing an enemy attack looks like?'

'So you're to march down the valley to Lakeside Fort on either side of the river looking for trouble, are you? That's quite extraordinarily adventurous for Pescennius Niger, unless of course he's been chivvied into taking a risk by his colleague Albinus!' The tribune commanding Stone Fort laughed uproariously, tipping his head towards the other British cohort's prefect. 'And I thought my colleague here and I had drawn the short straw, but at least we've got a nice thick layer of stonework to hide behind!'

Scaurus shared a smile with him.

'At least my men will get to sleep under proper roofs tonight, and with stoves to thaw their feet out.'

Leontius nodded.

'Indeed. I'm sorry not to have any better hospitality to offer you, but as you can see, Stone Fort is rather spartan in its construction. No bath house for us, just enough barracks for half a legion and every other bit of spare space given over to storage. On the brighter side, we have enough rations in our storehouses to provision five thousand men for a fortnight, so nobody's going to go hungry, just as long as they're happy with bread and dried meat of a somewhat dubious quality. And let me tell you, gentlemen, your arrival is most welcome, not to mention the archers, given I expect to have a pack of angry Sarmatae dogs baying for blood on the other side of my western ditch within a day or two. What word do we have from Porolissum? Where do the grown-ups expect the Sarmatae will land the first punch?'

Scaurus smiled at his colleague's irreverence.

'The legati are convinced that any attack up the valley here will only be a feint. They have intelligence from within the Sarmatae camp, it seems. Domitius Belletor and I are ordered to reconnoitre forward from this position and attempt to locate the enemy. The 'grown-ups' have decided to convince Purta they've taken his bait by risking a couple of thousand men in a probe down this valley.'

Leontius's face reflected his cynicism.

'You do realise that in the event of any serious Sarmatae attack here you'll be like a pair of boxers leading with your chins? Where I come from, Tribune, we have the saying that if it looks like a duck, waddles like a duck and quacks like a duck, it's probably a duck. So in this case, colleagues, whether the legati are in receipt of secret intelligence or not, we'll be treating any barbarian force that comes up the valley as the real thing. I don't know about you gentlemen, but this country isn't like any other I've served in, not with tens of thousands of men like those barbarian horsemen you marched in with, all spoiling for a fight not fifty miles to the north. And what starts out as a feint to deceive us might end up becoming the main line of attack overnight. You might just find yourselves marching your men head-on into an army of twenty thousand of the buggers. Go down the valley by all means, but I'd suggest that you be ready to come back up it as fast as you can, and join us here to defend the pass, if by some misfortune you find yourselves toe to toe with the entire Sarmatae nation. And now gentlemen, a toast!' He raised his cup. 'To secret intelligence! Let's just pray it's as *accurate* as it is *secret!*'

If the previous week had been cold, the next dawn found the Tungrian sentries clustered around their braziers in search of whatever heat was to be had whenever the duty centurion's attention was elsewhere. A bitter wind was blowing from the north, sweeping curtains of snow down from the mountains onto the fort, and for a time it seemed that the weather would prevent the cohorts from fulfilling their mission. However, and to great disgust, shortly after the soldiers had taken their breakfast and were happily anticipating a day doing nothing more taxing than shivering in their tents, the storm front cleared away to leave Stone Fort under a clear blue sky and with temperatures low enough to freeze the water in the horse troughs solid. Scaurus gathered his centurions together in his quarter and issued the orders that their men were dreading.

'We march. The legati are depending on us to deliver on our promise to make the Sarmatae believe that there's a legion defending this pass, and deliver it we will. Make sure your men are wearing every piece of clothing they can muster, not that they'll need much encouragement in these temperatures.'

Watched by the Britons, the cohorts marched out over the fort's western gate and across the wooden bridge that, as with the eastern approach, was the only way over the ditch that had been dug across the valley's full width.

'What stops an attacker from just taking to the hills to either side and working their way around the ditch?'

Overhearing the question from one of his brighter soldiers, Marcus answered it despite Quintus's look of disapproval.

'What stops them from doing that, soldier, is the fact that the

Britons have had weeks to prepare the ground. Their pioneers have felled enough trees up the hillsides and planted enough sharpened stakes in their branches to make an impenetrable barrier, which means that the only way to get to the fort's other side is to go that way . . .' He pointed at a side valley to their right. 'But that means taking a long detour around to the north, the best part of a day's march. Titus and his boys in the Tenth Century were looking quite jealous when they saw all those fallen trees yesterday.'

The Tungrians crossed the frozen river to reach the left bank, their hobnailed boots slipping and sliding on the smooth surface, while the First Minervia's cohort drove on down the right bank with their native cavalry in close attendance.

'If only I'd known, I could have offered odds on my being able to walk on water. I would have made a right killing,' said Morban.

'Ah yes, but you have taken a bet on the very same subject, if you recall?'

Marcus smiled at the momentary look of fear that crossed his standard bearer's face as Morban recalled the moment when he had been provoked into offering his centurion a bet of heroic proportions during the march north. Marcus turned his attention back to his men, some of whom were already clearly troubled by their numb toes, despite the fur linings in their boots.

'They'll live, as long as they keep moving. I had a good look at their feet before we marched this morning, and there's not one of them with a serious problem. Those poor bastards have it worse, I'd say.' Quintus pointed across the river's thirty-foot width at the labouring legionaries on its far side. 'Some of them look like they're already struggling . . .'

As they watched, a mounted patrol of Belletor's Sarmatae went forward at the trot, the riders apparently impervious to the cold in their thick furs, quickly vanishing from view around a bend in the river. As the two forces made their way down the river's course, the valley widened, broadening from barely a hundred paces on either side of the frozen stream to three times as much in the space of a mile. Cresting a slight rise, Marcus found himself staring down the valley's length for the best part of two miles, squinting into the light of the winter sun as it reflected off the broad, icy expanse of a lake a mile or so distant. A soldier ran down the cohort's line and saluted him.

'Centurion, sir! First Spear says we'll march as far as that lake and then we'll take a rest stop.'

Marcus nodded and waved the man on down the line before turning to call out an order to his chosen man.

'Quintus! They're all yours, I'm going back for a chat with Qadir and Dubnus!'

Waiting until the Eighth Century reached the place where he had stopped, flexing his toes experimentally and finding them disquietingly numb, he fell in alongside Dubnus with a grimace of shared discomfort. The Briton laughed at him.

'I'd forgotten you've yet to experience the joys of campaigning in a proper winter. How are you finding it, apart from the blueness of your toes?'

The Roman shrugged.

'It seems I'm doomed to always either be too hot or too cold, so I suppose it's best just to ignore the weather and think more about the job at hand. Anyway, there's something I wanted to test out when we get to that lake, to see if the histories are true in what they tell us? I've just reminded Morban of the wager he made with me on the subject while we were marching up from Apulum, and he looked decidedly sick when I raised the matter.'

When they reached the lake the soldiers milled about, unwilling to subject themselves to more discomfort by sitting on the freezing ground, while Marcus and Dubnus, joined by an inquisitive Qadir and a nervous Morban, trailed by a few inquisitive soldiers, made their way onto the ice. Across the lake's expanse they could see the First Minervia's legionaries shuffling about disconsolately, First Spear Sergius clearly having decided to rest his men to keep the two advances aligned. The remaining Sarmatae horsemen had dismounted, but as usual showed no sign of mixing with the soldiers.

'Buggered if I know what we're doing out here on the bloody ice!'

Sanga turned to the soldier Scarface with an irritated expression.

'What we're doing out here, you idiot, is following Two Knives around like a pair of three-year-olds hanging off their mummy's skirts as per usual. As to what he's doing out here, did you not hear about the bet?'

He raised his eyebrows in amazement at his mate's uncomprehending expression.

'You really do go around with your head up your own arse, don't you? The *bet?*' Scarface shook his head and shrugged, and Sanga waved a hand at the lake's frozen surface. 'Seems the tribune was telling some of the lads about a battle that was fought on a frozen river round here a few years ago. He said that some of our lads were attacked by Sarmatae horsemen like those pricks over there, but they stood their ground and ended up winning the fight. I don't know how that would work, but the officer seemed very sure about it. Anyway, seems Morban quacked on about what a load of bullshit it was and how he'd give ten to one that it was all bollocks, so *your* centurion slapped down a gold aurei and took him up on it.'

Scarface looked about him with new interest, peering hard at the nervous-looking standard bearer before raising his voice in an amused chortle.

'Well he's not looking quite so fuckin' brave about it now, is he? Ten in gold, eh Morban? That's the best part of six months' takings for you, I wouldn't wonder.'

'Well that's one part of the story proven.' Marcus stood on the frozen surface with his arms open wide. 'It's perfectly possible to stand on this stuff, as long as you dig the hobnails in hard enough. It would be murder on the feet without these skins wrapped around my feet though. Now, pass me that shield please.' One of the soldiers surrendered his board, and Marcus experimentally rested it on the frozen surface. 'Hmmm. I can't see how that's going to be sufficiently stable to put a boot on.'

'Here, I've an idea how it might work.' Dubnus took it from him, drawing his sword and swiftly chopping a rough circular hole the depth and width of the shield's heavy brass boss into the thick ice before dropping the board face down onto the ice, guiding the hemispherical protrusion into the hole he'd created, much to the disgust of the soldier in question. 'And you can stop pulling faces, it's a piece of fighting equipment, not a piece of the family silver. There . . .'

He gestured to the shield, then put a booted foot onto its wooden surface.

'See, you can stand on this ice a lot easier with one foot on the wood. Give me that spear.'

He clicked his fingers, and the now resigned soldier, whose shield was held firm to the ice by Dubnus's foot, handed over his spear. The big centurion adjusted his footing, then posed for Marcus with one foot on the shield while he essayed a series of swift stabbing blows with the spear.

'Very warlike. You might even pass muster as a soldier, if we didn't know you better.'

Dubnus turned to face the approaching Julius. Scaurus was walking a few paces behind him, and both men were gazing at the spectacle with open curiosity. Dubnus took his foot off the shield, gesturing for his man to pick it up.

'Centurion Corvus entered a considerable wager with the obvious person as to whether the battle on the ice could really have happened. And as you can see, your story was clearly well founded, Tribune.'

Marcus stroked his chin in amusement, looking at Morban.

'Well now, Standard Bearer, it *can* be done. How much is it that you owe me?'

The older man raised a pitying eyebrow.

'You should know better than that, Centurion. The bet I took was that you couldn't prove it was possible to fight off a screaming horde of Sarmatae horsemen like that, not that you could persuade Dubnus to stand on a shield and wave a spear about. I thought you'd have realised by now sir, it's all about how the bet is stated.' Growing in confidence that he would once again be on the winning side of the wager, he winked at the big Briton. 'And very fetching you look too, if I might make so bold, Dubnus.'

Marcus turned back to his friend with a smile but found the big man's attention locked on the other side of the valley, where the river's meandering course bent around to the east and took the road down its banks out of view.

'Here come the scouts that Belletor sent out, back already. I wonder what they've seen?'

They watched as the scouting party rode around the river bend and up the valley toward the waiting legionaries, but Dubnus was pointing to a spot behind the horsemen.

'Look! Smoke!'

A line of smoke was rising into the cold, still air further down the valley, and Julius frowned, looking across the lake at the Sarmatae scouts with a look of disquiet.

'Whatever's burning may be out of sight from here, but it won't have been from where they were and yet they're acting as if nothing's amiss. Something isn't right here . . .'

Scaurus stepped forward.

'I warned the idiot!' He cupped his hands around his mouth, shouting across the lake's frozen surface. 'Belletor! *Tribune Belletor!*'

Clearly visible mounting his horse, Tribune Belletor turned his head to the source of the sound. Scaurus waved, then pointed at the smoke, now strengthened to form a thick, greasy column. Belletor looked about him, then waved back to the small group before spurring his horse forward towards the returning scouts. Scaurus's expression hardened.

'Blessed Mithras, the bloody fool's not listening! He can't see the smoke for the hill beside them. *Belletor! The scouts are . . .*'

He fell silent as his colleague's imperious tones reached them, audible across the open ice even if the exact words were lost on the slight breeze, and the tribune raised his fist in salute. The leading rider approached the Roman, his long lance couched to point at the ground.

'That's their leader, isn't it?'

Qadir squinted into the ice's harsh glare.

'Yes, that helmet he wears is quite unmistak—'

He gasped involuntarily as the Sarmatae leader raised his kontos, stabbing the blade forward and ramming it into Belletor's throat. Ripping the bloodied iron free, as the tribune tottered in his saddle, he raised his arms and bellowed a command at his followers. With a chorus of answering yells the Sarmatae flooded forward and past him, their weapons flashing in the clear winter air as they fell on the unsuspecting and unprepared Roman infantry. The men to the rear of the cohort, who had quietly mounted their horses while the legionaries' attention had been elsewhere, took their cue and launched themselves at the resting soldiers with their lances glinting evilly in the winter sunlight. Qadir turned to Marcus in horror.

'Deasura, it'll be a massacre!'

Julius shook his head in disbelief as the first screams of dying men reached them. The soldiers closest to the attacking Sarmatae were mounting a desperate, unprepared defence, fighting without organisation or control, and the enemy horsemen, pressing in on them from front and rear, were reaping a bloody harvest with the long spears that allowed them to out-reach the legionaries.

'And we'll be next!' He hooked a thumb over his shoulder. 'Rejoin your centuries!'

'*Wait!*'

He frowned disbelievingly as Scaurus put a hand up.

'Tribune?'

'I've seen these people fight from horseback before. Even if we form a disciplined line, and stand ready to meet their attack with our spears, they'll just stand off for a while and pepper us with arrows from all directions, retreating whenever we try to get to grips with them, and then when we start to weaken, from the cold and our losses, they'll make a full-blooded charge and scatter us across the valley. If we stand and fight on dry ground we'll lose, I guarantee you that!'

Julius shook his head brusquely.

'But if we run they'll harry us to destruction just like they're doing to the First Minervia. We *have* to fight!'

Scaurus nodded.

'I know. But not up there . . ' He pointed to the lakeside. 'We need to fight *here*, on the ice.'

Julius stepped forward, his face, only inches from his tribune's, set in deadly earnest.

'It's one thing to pull off a trick like that when you've been practising for days, Tribune, and quite another when it's no more than a story in one of the histories that was more than likely dreamed up by the writer to make some bloody senior officer look good! You do realise this is likely to end in disaster?'

The tribune pointed hollow-eyed at the scene of horror playing out before them. Individual soldiers were running now, while Sarmatae horsemen spurred their horses in pursuit, some spearing their victims with swift brutality while others cantered after the fleeing soldiers at a more leisurely pace, giving them time to realise that a grim death was upon them before striking. As they watched, a group of fifty or so soldiers leapt onto the ice and ran towards the Tungrians, shouting desperately for help. A score of the horsemen followed them out onto the frozen surface, cantering on either side with their lances raised to strike. Marcus pointed at them as the first men fell under the riders' blades to leave a trail of bloodied corpses in the runners' wake.

'That's Tribune Sigilis leading them, isn't it?'

Scaurus looked at the beleaguered runners for a moment before nodding sadly.

'Yes, it is.' The Sarmatae horsemen closed in around the helpless soldiers, their lances stabbing out at the Romans from beyond the reach of their spears, and Marcus turned away as his friend was spitted by first one and then two of the long spears, his spasming body held upright for a moment before falling to the ice as the blades were wrenched loose. When he looked back none of the men who had run were still standing, and the mounted tribesmen ironically saluted the watching Tungrians as they turned away.

'Exactly. We're next. They're toying with those boys, First Spear, and I doubt dying out here on the ice will be any worse. Besides,

I'm not of a mind to meet my ancestors without at least having some pride in the manner of my death.'

He nodded decisively, turning to the two senior centurions.

'I'm making a commander's decision. Get your men onto the lake and into two battle lines, back to back and ready to form a circle. *Do it!*'

While the Tungrians flooded onto the ice without question, the First Cohort were running to a point indicated by Julius and quickly forming a line, while the Second pressed in behind them. The tribune stalked through them to find Silus and his mounted squadron waiting at the lakeside. Silus saluted, looking down at his commander with a solemn expression.

'What are your orders, Tribune?'

Scaurus pointed back up the valley.

'Get out of here while you still can, Decurion. Take word of this treachery to Tribune Leontius, and to him alone. There'd be little point in throwing your lives away alongside ours, if what I have in mind fails to work.'

Silus nodded grimly and saluted again.

'As you command, Tribune. Good luck.'

He wheeled his horse and led his men away up the lakeside as the Tungrians swiftly formed up into two lines, the discipline of a thousand drills taking over from conscious thought. Scaurus nodded to Julius, who bellowed a fresh command at the waiting soldiers.

'Second Cohort, about turn! First and Second Cohorts, *Form! Circle!*'

The centuries at the centre of the two cohorts' lines marched forward a smart thirty paces out of formation, the soldiers cursing as they slipped on the ice's slick surface. Each century to their left and right stopped a successive five paces short of their comrades, until both lines were arrayed in an arrowhead formation with one point facing toward the enemy horsemen and the line behind facing away.

'Dress your lines!'

Centurions and their chosen men moved swiftly to push and

pull their men into position, quickly transforming the serried ranks into two curving lines that met to form a rough circle.

'Close it up!'

Pulling their men back, the officers shrank the circle until each front ranker was shoulder to shoulder with the men to either side. Scaurus nodded to Julius and Tertius with a look of respect.

'Excellent drill, First Spears!'

He pushed into the circle with the two men following, and Julius shouted one last command.

'Face inwards!'

With a rattle of equipment the Tungrians reversed their facing, forming an unbroken ring of faces around the tribune. Scaurus strode into the middle and then turned a full circle with an appraising stare.

'You see the value of all that mindless drilling?' He smiled wolfishly at the men encircling him, working hard to exude a confidence he was a long way from feeling. 'Just a moment ago you were standing watching those horsemen over there tear a legion cohort apart, wondering whether we'll fight or flee and expecting to die whichever we chose. Now you stand in a tight formation that will enable us to face down those murderous bastards and beat them!'

He paused again, finding the looks of incredulity and disbelief he'd been expecting on many of the faces around him. The remaining legionnaires were in full, desperate flight now, running for their lives in all directions, and whooping riders were hunting them down as they frantically sought to escape by climbing the valley's side, those men with bows using them to bring down men who succeeded in reaching parts of the slope impassable to the horsemen.

'They can fight alright, and on the right ground that many of them are pretty much unbeatable for two cohorts of infantry, no matter how good we are. Out here on the ice, however, it's a different story! On the ice, gentlemen, victory goes to the man with the best footing! A horse can walk on this surface, and even trot, but there's more to cavalry fighting than simply charging at an enemy!' He lowered his voice slightly, forcing the soldiers to lean in and listen intently. 'A horse, gentlemen, will not charge into a line of soldiers. A bold enough rider might jump that line, except here on the ice there's no footing for the beast to make the jump from. It might be persuaded to back into the line, although the prospect of you ugly characters poking it with sharp iron will doubtless be enough to put most animals off.'

He waited long enough for a few tight smiles to appear in the Tungrian ranks before continuing.

'Make no mistake, gentlemen, they will come across this ice at us very soon now!' The horsemen were milling about on the lake's bank, some dismounting to strip their victims of their weapons and whatever valuables they happened to be carrying. 'Their spears will be red with the blood of five hundred legionnaires . . .'

'And one fucking idiot.'

The men standing beside Scarface nodded their agreement with the muttered sentiment, quickly turning their attention back to their tribune.

'. . . but you men and I know full well that such displays mean nothing. Besting a few hundred untried boys caught unawares in open order is one thing! Defeating two full cohorts of the best infantrymen in the empire who are formed and ready to meet them is entirely another! They will come charging across the ice at us, but at the last moment, when they know that their horses are likely to shy away rather than collide with our line, they will pull their beasts up, looking to use the length of their lances to pick holes in our line from a safe distance. And on this smooth surface those animals *will* slide, gentlemen, they *will* fail to stop soon enough and they *will* present themselves at the end of your spears. And when that happens we *must* take the opportunity they offer us and do to them what they've done to those legionaries.'

He lowered his voice again, and spoke into the hush in a tone that told his men he knew something they did not.

'You see, gentlemen, the man that leads them has made one dreadful mistake. Had he attacked us first, while we were strung out along the road on the march, then he would most likely have been successful. The legion cohort would almost certainly have run for their lives and presented him with an easy kill to finish the day. But as it is he's chosen to start his dinner with the easy meat. We're going to show him that we're built from bone and gristle! We're going to stick in his bloody throat and choke him to death!'

He nodded to Julius, ushering his first spear forward. The big man scowled around the circle, knowing that for all of the tribune's reassurance what his men needed most now was the harsh voice of command to which they had been brutally conditioned to answer with instant obedience.

'No more speeches, Tungrians. You either fight and win here or you'll break and die here. And *I'm* not planning on dying here. Front rankers!'

Scarface and Sanga exchanged a glance, the latter muttering a comment to his mate that had heads around them nodding again.

'Here it fuckin' comes.'

'On the command "Prepare to fight", you will do this!' Julius drew his sword and took up a shield from the ice next to him. Hacking at the ice with measured blows, he swiftly dug out a hole like the one that Dubnus had carved before dropping the shield onto it.

'You see? Give your spear to the man behind you, use your sword to chop out a hole for the boss to sit in, then put the shield down with the boss in the hole you've made and your foot on the shield to give you some footing. Then you sheathe your sword, take your spear back from the man behind you, and *his* shield, and prepare to fight! Rear rankers! On the command "Prepare to fight", start working yourselves up to taking on a horseman at close quarters. When those barbarians come skating up to the line fighting for control of their horses, you're going to dive out and grab their reins and drag them in close for the front rank men to kill. If you can't manage that, then you pull down the rider and do for him with your sword or your dagger! If you go down with him, remember that the ice is slippery. Get your feet in his body and push him away, so you've got time to get back on your feet and get your iron into him!'

The Sarmatae were forming up on the lakeside, their leader

shouting curses and imprecations as the last of his men remounted their horses. Some of the enemy riders were laden with booty stripped from the slaughtered legionaries, wearing captured Roman helmets and weapons.

'All ranks, about-face! Front ranks, get those shields down!'

Scarface and Sanga grimaced, drawing their swords and chopping at the ice alongside each other. The scarred soldier dropped his shield experimentally onto the frozen surface, sliding it around until the boss dropped neatly into the hole he'd made a moment before.

'Fuck me, it actually works. Who said all senior officers were full of shit?'

Sanga spat on the ice, putting a foot on his own shield.

'As I recall it was you, you stupid bastard. Here, you,' – he put a hand out to the man behind him – 'give me my spear, and I'll have that shield . . .'

His eyes met those of the rear ranker, and narrowed in calculation as he realised it was one of the Sarmatae foot soldiers who had been given to the Romans to plug the gaps in their ranks.

'Oi, Saratos, or whatever your name is. Am I going to let you finger your blade behind me while your mates do their best to put their iron through me? Not likely!'

He grabbed the man's mail shirt at the collar and dragged him forward, pushing the man to his right backwards into his vacated place in the circle's rear rank. Switching places with the hapless Sarmatae so that he was sandwiched between the two veterans, he patted his spear with a meaningful glance.

'You so much as twitch the wrong way and I'll put this little darling up your nose!'

Scarface regarded the trembling man levelly for a moment.

'I think you're being a little harsh on our new friend, my old mate. Let's face it, he's wearing our kit and standing in our fuckin' line, ain't he? He either fights for his life or else he ends up with one of them long spears of theirs poking out of his arse like a backwards prick.' He slapped the Sarmatae on the shoulder, thrusting his head forward to shout in the man's face. 'You *fight*?'

While the previous discussion had been unintelligible to the

recruit, the unequivocal challenge left no room for misunder-
standing. He nodded vigorously.

'I *fight*! Horseman *kill*!'

Sanga nodded to his friend.

'Best keep an eye on him all the same. Hold on, Latrine's
shouting the odds again . . .'

Rapping the flat of his sword's blade against his dagger, Julius
was looking about the circle with a look that brooked no
argument.

'Tungrians, make some noise! Tell those horse-fuckers that
we're not going anywhere!'

Within seconds the flat tapping of blade on blade had swollen
to a thunderous pulsing rattle of spear shafts on the bosses of the
soldiers' shields, a wall of sound that echoed across the lake as
the horsemen manoeuvred into a rough line and began to advance
on the waiting Tungrians, their horses stepping gingerly down
onto the lake's frozen surface.

'And so it comes down to *andreia* . . .' Julius turned to glance
at his tribune with a curious expression, and Scaurus shook his
head in self-deprecation. 'I'm sorry, First Spear, random
outbursts in foreign languages are the price to be paid for having
education thrust upon one at an early age, I suppose. My history
tutor used to fill my head with tales of the Greek wars, and time
and time again he used the word *andreia* to describe the nature
of a man's courage.'

'Greek was he, Tribune?'

Scaurus laughed at the question.

'A fair guess. Yes, he was Greek, and if my uncle had known
the disregard in which he held our empire by comparison with
the glories his country once knew, well then I expect that he would
have had the man beaten and thrown out of the house. He used
to take me out on the balcony and point out across the city, all
those buildings as far as the eye could see, and tell me that "All
this will one day crumble, as mighty Greece's time in the sun
came to an end, when we lost the collective *andreia* that allowed
us to triumph over Troy and repel the Persians."'

He watched as the Sarmatae horsemen gathered pace, the horses snorting out their breath in plumes of vapour as they accelerated to a canter across the ice.

'And now this dirty little battle becomes a matter of whose *andreia* is the greater, ours or theirs. If we break in the face of their charge then we are all surely dead, but if we hold long enough for them to skate onto our spears, then we may yet hold the whip over them.'

Julius craned his neck to stare over his men's helmeted heads, then turned to Tertius and muttered a quiet instruction. The Second Cohort's senior centurion nodded, pacing away to the back of the circle where his own men stood. The enemy were closer now, their screams and shouts piercing the air as they waved their lances over their heads. Directly facing the riders' onrushing wall of horseflesh, Scarface rolled his shoulders and ducked into the cover of his shield with his spear held ready to throw.

'Fuck me, but would you look at that lot?'

Sanga laughed grimly.

'Your leggings full then, are they?'

His mate shook his head dourly.

'Not yet. After that shit you cooked up for dinner last night you'll know when my ring gives up the fight, 'cause it'll smell like I've dropped a week-old corpse.' He raised his voice, as the horsemen lowered their lances in a glittering wave of polished iron, speaking to the men to either side of him with a tone that dripped with bored contempt. 'Hold your ground, you fuckin' women! You heard what the tribune said! We can beat these!'

Marcus stepped up behind his men, raising his voice to be heard over the oncoming horses' thunder and the chorus of brutal reassurance and imprecation being shouted by the veteran soldiers at their less experienced comrades.

'*Ready spears!*'

The front rankers leaned back, eager for the command to unleash their spears on the horsemen, but Marcus guessed that Julius would wait until the last possible moment, knowing that his men would be unable to get the usual power into their throws given that the ice would prevent them from performing the forward step to add momentum to the missiles' flight. He watched the first spear intently, waiting for his raised vine stick to fall.

'Ready . . . wait . . . ready . . . *throw!*'

A hail of wood and iron arched out from the Tungrian line in an untidy cascade, spears raining down onto the oncoming enemy and transforming their relatively ordered formation into chaos in an instant. Riders busy aligning the points of their lances with the Roman line were caught unawares by the onslaught, their spitted bodies falling beneath the hoofs of the horses behind them and unnerving or even tripping the hapless beasts, while those men with both wicker shields and the wit to use them managed in the main only to deflect the flying spears onto the men beside and behind them. The charge faltered momentarily, giving the Tungrian front rankers time to reach behind them for a second spear.

'*Steady!*'

All along the Tungrian line centurions and chosen men crouched close to their soldiers, encouraging, cajoling and simply bullying them to hold their positions as the horsemen regained their momentum and covered the last few paces at a canter. Scarface felt a hand on his arm, and glanced round to find Marcus at his shoulder.

'*Wait . . .*'

Staring up at the looming wall of horseflesh, even Marcus was struck by the apparent impossibility of any attempt to resist the attackers' oncoming tide, seeing his men's spearheads wavering in the face of the onrushing charge. He bellowed at his men, knowing that the moment of greatest danger was upon them all.

'*The eyes! Look at the horses' eyes!*'

The animals were panicking, eyes rolling as their riders goaded them forward at the Romans, eager to strike back at the waiting soldiers, but the beasts' attempts to shy away from the waiting spear points only resulted in their hoofs sliding on the smooth ice. As the rider facing Scarface skated helplessly up to the Tungrian line, he lunged forward with his lance, cursing as the soldier raised his shield and allowed the weapon's sharp iron blade to punch through its layered board and stick firm. Wrenching at the shield's grip, the Tungrian fought the rider for possession of the weapon, edging to one side as the soldier to his rear squeezed between him and the Sarmatae recruit alongside him to grab at the horse's reins. Bracing himself off the shield laid on the ice before Scarface and pulling back with all his strength, the rear ranker physically dragged the protesting animal into spear reach, and even as its rider released his grip on the lance and went for his sword the Sarmatae recruit, Saratos, stabbed forward expertly with his spear, burying it deeply in the horse's throat and twisting the shaft before ripping it free.

With an ear-piercing scream of pain the animal reared back, wrenching the reins free from the struggling soldier's grip and pulling him over onto the ice, but then staggered on its feet as a thick rivulet of steaming blood gushed down its neck and legs from the open artery. Bellowing incoherent rage, the animal's rider leapt down from his stricken mount's back, raising his sword to attack only to receive Sanga's spear in his armpit as the veteran took his brief chance with a lunging strike. The barbarian recoiled from the blow against the horse's flank as the beast sank helplessly to its knees, horse and rider both crippled by their wounds. The rider alongside him leaned forward and punched his lance into Sanga's unshielded shoulder, scattering a handful of severed mail rings as the long blade sank deep into the soldier's chest below his collar bone. He staggered back with his right hand locked on the weapon's long shaft even as the Sarmatae tried to tear it free from the wound, maintaining his tenacious grip as his eyes rolled upwards and he fell to his knees on his own shield. Scarface bellowed his rage at the distracted rider as the man fought to dislodge his lance from the wounded Tungrian's grasp, hurling his own spear with a ferocity that buried it deep in the junction of the rider's trunk and thigh and dropping him writhing to the ground. Drawing his sword the wild-eyed soldier took a step forward, only to find Marcus's hand on his arm again, the centurion's raised voice calm amid the storm of iron.

'No! Get him to safety!'

Pulling his gladius from its scabbard the Roman levelled the two swords' blades, pushed past his soldier and advanced out of the line in a whirl of flickering steel. Ducking under a lance thrust he swung the spatha's long blade at his attacker's mount, neatly severing both of the animal's front legs at the knee. Dancing away to the right, away from the collapsing beast, he turned another kontos thrust with the gladius, then chopped the weapon's gleaming iron blade from its wooden shaft with a swing of the spatha. Lunging in close to the horseman's mount, trapped and unable to move in the crush of its fellows, he ducked under the horse's belly and rammed the gladius into its belly, tearing the blade out to sever the muscles beneath the skin. The stricken beast staggered, unable to stay on its feet, and keeled over away from the Roman, sending its rider sprawling onto the ice. Looking back over his shoulder to be sure that Scarface had managed to pull his comrade to safety, his boot caught on a shield's rim, and he staggered for a moment before falling heavily onto his back to lie momentarily helpless as fresh horsemen pushed their mounts forward around the animals he had disabled, their long lances raised to strike.

With a roar of anger Saratos stepped forward and smashed a pair of iron spearheads away with his shield, thrusting his own spear's point up and through the foremost horse's jaw and deep into its head, dropping the animal to the ground so fast that its hapless rider was catapulted from the saddle on top of Marcus's legs. The young centurion thrust his gladius into the stunned warrior's neck, then flexed his knees and kicked him back under the advancing horse's hoofs in a shower of dark-red arterial blood. Hands grasped him by his mailed shoulders and dragged him back into the Tungrian line, and Marcus looked up to find his chosen man standing over him with a grin as he pushed more men into the gap.

'I knew you were a good 'un, Centurion, but I'll buy you a fuckin' cup of wine for that, if we ever see the inside of a tavern again.'

He nodded his head to the scene of carnage facing the Tungrians, dead and dying horses littering the ground while the animals behind them pranced and whinnied at the stink of blood and offal.

'Sanga?'

Quintus shook his head grimly, pointing to where the wounded soldier lay helpless on the ice.

'Scarface did well getting him out of there, and the bandage carrier's stuck a wad over the wound, but I doubt he'll see sunset even if we outlast these bastards.'

Marcus walked over to the prostrate veteran, his hands shaking slightly with the rage still fizzing though his body.

'Get him onto his feet. He'll freeze to death if he lies here much longer!'

'And if he can't stand?'

Marcus looked down into Sanga's face, shaking his head grimly.

'Then he'll die.' He bent to speak into the wounded man's ear. 'Get on your feet and stay on them, Soldier Sanga. I've no time to spend on you now, but when we're done here I'll see you safely back to the fort if you're still upright. Either get up now or go to meet your ancestors!'

The soldier nodded weakly, his face as pale as the ice beneath him, and staggered back onto his feet to stand with his back bent, staring at his own knees. Marcus patted him gently on the shoulder and turned away, looking up and down the Tungrian line to gauge the fight's progress. Roughly half of the circle's circumference was embattled, with soldiers fighting for their lives along the entire length of the side facing the Sarmatae attack, and his gaze flicked to where Scaurus and his first spears were watching the fight with calm patience. The tribune nodded his head decisively, and Julius ran towards his cohort's rear, shouting the instruction Marcus had been expecting.

'First Cohort, pull back! On me!'

Looking to either side to be sure they were keeping pace with the line's retreat, the men facing the Sarmatae stepped back from the half-circle of shields along which enemy riders and horses were scattered, the battle's bloody detritus, some dead while others were still kicking and screaming in their death agonies. At a shouted command those barbarians with bows pushed through the throng of horsemen and started sending arrows at the retreating Tungrians, their leader bellowing his encouragement as he sensed the beginning of a collapse in the Romans' morale. A soldier in Marcus's Fifth Century fell with an arrow in his foot, writhing in agony at the pain and staring in disbelief at the long shaft transfixing his boot. Unable to stand, he pitched forward onto the ice too far from his retreating comrades to reach out and drag him back with them.

'Hold the line!'

The soldiers around Marcus obeyed his command with sullen faces, watching in horror as one of the horsemen leaned from his saddle to push the blade of his lance through the fallen soldier's thigh. Another spurred his mount forward, raising his kontos with a theatrical flourish and grinning at the Tungrians before stabbing it down into his throat with an ululating scream of triumph. Still the Roman line retreated, and with their spirits buoyed up by imminent victory the Sarmatae pressed in closer, forcing the soldiers to defend themselves from their relentlessly stabbing lances. The Tungrians' formation was bowing under the barbarian pressure now, the two cohorts within a dozen paces of each other in two long concave lines, and the Sarmatae leader pushed his horse through the mass of men competing to stab down at the soldiers with a savage grin of impending victory.

7

Silus and his men rode into the fortress under the watchful eyes of the bolt-thrower crews standing ready to either side of the main gate, the decurion smiling mirthlessly as the weapons' commanders ordered their men to remove the heavy iron missiles and release the torsion on their straining ropes. He dismounted, looking to left and right for the duty centurion.

'Back so soon?' Silus turned to find the object of his search approaching him with a questioning look. 'I assume that this isn't good news you're bearing.'

He shook his head, leaning close to the grizzled officer and speaking in tones quiet enough to be audible only between themselves.

'It's news that I've been told to deliver to your prefect, and to share with no-one else.'

The centurion's expression didn't change.

'Which, I suppose, tells me all that I need to know. You!' He plucked a soldier from the men standing at attention by the gate. 'Take the decurion here to the headquarters building.'

Leontius was equally unsurprised by the news, although the report of the Sarmatae horsemens' betrayal of Belletor and the slaughter of the legion cohort did set his head shaking.

'That's a bloody disaster, Decurion. Three perfectly good infantry cohorts lost in a morning, which only leaves me with the men I have here, given that the units posted down the valley will already have been overrun. Very well, we'd best get ready for a fight. Thank you for bringing me this news, despite what it must mean for you. At least your escape means I have a ready supply of despatch riders with which to alert the legati. Not that their knowledge of this situation is likely to bring reinforcement quickly enough.' He smiled bitterly at Silus. 'I strongly doubt that two five-hundred-man cohorts are going to hold the pass against a decent-sized tribal band for long enough for it to matter whether we have a legion marching in our support or not, but we should never give up hope, eh?'

Silus saluted.

'As you wish, Tribune. Do I have time to share these tidings with our cohort's doctor? She was a good friend of one of the centurions.'

The senior officer waved a dismissive hand.

'Do what you need to do, Decurion, and then come back here to collect my first message. We need reinforcement as quickly as possible if we're to prevent these Sarmatae maniacs from getting past us and into the province. Oh, and send a scout party back down the valley, will you? I want a little more notice as to exactly what's coming up the road at us before the blighters knock on the gates and tell us they've come to repossess the place.'

Silus saluted again and left the room, detailing five of his men to carry out the prefect's instructions and ride back down the valley road. He hurried to the fort's hospital where he found Felicia and Annia in the middle of an inventory of the drug stocks.

'Precious little dried poppy sap, no Mandrake, enough Knitbone for half a dozen patients . . .' Felicia shook her head unhappily at her assistant. 'Any man that stops a blade is going to have to take his treatment without the benefit of medication. At least we have a good supply of bandages and honey.' Her eyes flicked up to see Silus standing in the doorway with an unhappy expression, and her eyes narrowed. 'Decurion, can I help you? This isn't good news, is it?'

He shook his head sadly, recounting the disaster which had overtaken Belletor's cohort.

'The tribune ordered me to ride back here before the barbarians finished tearing the legionaries to pieces. If he hadn't then the thirty of us would be dead now, regardless of whether the poor bloody infantry won, lost or drew. So I'm grateful to him for my life . . .'

Felicia tipped her head to one side, her eyes shining with barely contained tears.

'But you wish you'd stayed to fight with them, don't you?'

The cavalryman took her hand and held it in his own.

'No true soldier ever wants to run away from a fight, Doctor, no matter all the jokes we make about the best defence against enemy iron being twenty miles of road between them and us. And your husband and his comrades were my friends.'

Annia shrugged and turned back to the medical supplies.

'A little more faith is called for, Decurion, in both our gods and our men. Neither this woman's husband nor my own big stupid oaf of a man will have rolled over and died as easily as you seem to imagine.'

Silus smiled and bowed.

'I hope and pray that you're right, madam. And now if you'll excuse me?'

'Second Cohort!' The waiting centurions braced themselves for the command as Tertius's voice rang out over the battle's din. *'Attack!'*

The rearmost cohort's line split in the middle to form two wings, both rotating on the pivot points where it joined with the First's with the two central centuries running as fast as they could on the slippery ice to swing the leading edges of the formation out from behind the embattled line. In the space of a dozen heartbeats, and before the Sarmatae leader had time to realise that he had fallen for the tribe's own tactic of the feigned retreat, the two wings slammed into his warband's unprotected flanks in a furious assault. Stabbing with their spears at the horses' vulnerable sides, half a dozen men swarmed each of the riders exposed on either flank, dragging their riders down and bludgeoning them to death with their hobnailed boots and the brass-bound edges of their shields. As the horses either collapsed from their grievous wounds or were simply pulled from the fight by their reins, the cordon to either side of the Sarmatae closed tighter, and their leader looked about him in growing horror as he realised that his warriors must either escape or die where they stood. Waving his arms frantically, he attempted to turn his mount about to lead his men in a bid to escape, but only succeeded in providing Qadir with the target for which he had been waiting with his customary patience. A feathered arrow shaft sprouted from his side, and the barbarian chieftain stared down at it in terror before subsiding onto the rider alongside him, insensible with the wound's pain. Julius turned back to the centurion of his reserve century, standing behind him at the head of his men with both hands resting on the well-worn handle of his axe.

'Your time has come, Bear! Take your men around the right flank and close off the bag we have them in!'

The big man nodded his understanding, growling a command to his men and lumbering away at their head with a purposeful look, winking at Marcus as he passed the rear of the Fifth Century.

'Hold them a while longer, little brother!'

The first spear looked up and down the length of his cohort, recognising the signs of desperate exhaustion in his men as the battle's focus switched away from their line and the Sarmatae pressure on them relented.

'First Cohort!' The centurions looked at him from either side, wearily waiting for his command with the expressionless faces of men ready to carry out whatever order their leader ordered. *'Straighten the line and hold!'*

Marcus nodded, gesturing Qadir to help him push his surviving men forward alongside the centuries to either side, straightening the cohort's formation until, while still ragged from the centuries' losses and exhaustion, it had taken on at least some semblance of a straight line of defence.

'They have little fight left in them, I fear.'

The Roman nodded, surveying his men with a grim but professional expertise, taking in the way that many of them had slumped onto their shields the instant that the line was straight, while others were leaning against their fellows.

'True. But we're not done yet.' He raised his voice in a bark of command to be heard above the battle, smiling inwardly as backs stiffened and heads lifted at the harsh tone in his voice. 'Soldiers, this fight is not yet over! When the Tenth Century attacks the enemy rear, and with no escape route left to them, these barbarians will attempt to flee in panic. And their horses are facing us! You must make one last effort if we are to avoid this victory turning to disaster . . .' He looked up and down the cohort's line to find his fellow officers bellowing similar instructions at their equally weary soldiers. 'One last effort, gentlemen, but then it's hardly a fair fight, is it? On this side we are unbroken, experienced soldiers with more battle experience than most legions, whereas they are surrounded and in terror, their only motivation to escape from this circle of spears! Very soon now, when their last desperate attack fails, these bloodied warriors before us will be begging for mercy! And I say we should give it to them in the only way their treachery has earned. I say we give them the mercy of a quick death! *No prisoners!*'

'*No prisoners!*'

The soldiers took up the cry, bellowing it at the tops of their voices at the horsemen milling about before them, and the centuries to either side took it up until the entire cohort was bellowing the sentiment in unison.

'You really are a bloodthirsty little beast, beneath all that civilised veneer, aren't you?'

Marcus shrugged at Julius, who had walked across to stand alongside him.

'Aren't we all, when the spears fly and the smell of blood is thick in the air? And besides, you know what's going to happen when—'

The battle's noise sharpened, a fresh note of terror raising the hairs on the soldiers' necks as men and beasts screamed in fresh horror at the violence being done to them.

'That'll be the Bear's men engaged. There's nothing puts the shits up a horseman like a century of big bastards with axes carving their way in through the back door. And here they come!'

As if commanded by some secret voice that only they could hear, the horsemen to their front spurred their horses as one and drove them forward at the Tungrians in a desperate, instinctive lunge to escape the ring of sharp iron closing about them. Riders kicked furiously at their mounts, driving them at the Romans despite their rolling-eyed reluctance, until the terrified animals were practically nose to nose with the defenders. The soldiers held their ground, those men with spears as yet unthrown and intact, stabbing them into the oncoming mass of horseflesh to inflict horrendous wounds on the helpless beasts, the front rankers held upright by the men behind them.

A rider leaned out of his saddle to stab down at the Tungrian line with his long kontos, sending a soldier reeling back from his place with his jaw opened to the bone by the iron blade's cold kiss, and Qadir pushed a man into his place with a growled instruction to keep his shield up. The wounded man staggered away to the century's bandage carrier, who simply pulled the scarf from round the soldier's throat and pressed it to the wound before turning away to deal with a more serious casualty. Along the length of the Tungrian line the Sarmatae were railing at their prison of spears and swords, unable to persuade their horses to drive into the array of shields confronting them, and the soldiers facing them gained in confidence with every moment.

Saratos drew his knife and looked at Marcus with an eyebrow raised in question, pointing with his other hand to the sagging Sarmatae leader who was hanging grimly onto his horse's neck with Qadir's arrow protruding from his side. Nodding his consent, the young centurion watched as the man dropped his shield and crawled into the forest of horses' legs, crouched low to avoid becoming a target for the enemy's lances. As his new comrades watched with incredulity, he nestled under the belly of the wounded man's mount and slid the knife between its flesh and the rider's saddle straps, slicing the thick leather with a quick sawing action before pulling at the Sarmatae leader's leg and dragging him down from the horse's back with the saddle still between his legs. As the hapless barbarian hit the ground, the knife flickered out to rest on his throat, leaving the fallen rider gasping in terror and the remaining horsemen utterly leaderless.

Like the last guttering of an exhausted candle, the fight went out of the Sarmatae warband in less than a dozen heartbeats. The men nearest to the First Cohort's line fell from their horses and threw down their weapons, raising their empty hands to the soldiers still tearing into their ranks and imploring the Tungrians to spare them from the massacre that was already in train behind them, looking around in terror at the axes and spears slashing into the steadily shrinking perimeter of their doomed warband. Now that the rage of battle was seeping out of him, leaving the young centurion more amazed than angry, given his men's survival against such odds, he found himself unable to carry though the threat of slaughter that he had bellowed out only moments before. He looked round to find Julius, waving a hand at him and then putting his wrists together to mime the binding of a prisoner's wrists. The first spear looked to his tribune, who nodded solemnly.

Silus was mounted and ready to ride to the north-east with the tribune's message in the company of four of his men, when the scouts sent west to determine the Tungrians' fate came galloping back up the valley, and he dismounted to wait for them to reach the gate while the duty centurion stood his disgruntled bolt-thrower crews down for a second time.

'The Tungrians, Decurion! They won! They're marching back up the road!'

He grinned in disbelief, shaking his head at the duty centurion.

'You'd better send a runner to fetch your tribune, hadn't you?'

The dour-faced officer nodded, then shouted for his chosen man.

'Send a man to the headquarters and tell the tribune that some of the auxiliaries seem to have escaped from the barbarians. Then get the carts moving, those poor bastards are going to be carrying their wounded on their backs. And warn the hospital to expect casualties.'

Silus turned to the men he had picked to accompany him on his mission to deliver the dispatch to Porolissum.

'I'll take that task. You four, ride south with that message. And if you fail to deliver it don't bother coming back, because we won't fucking well be here!'

He mounted up and took a dozen men down the valley, finding the Tungrians labouring up its slope two miles from the fort. Reining his horse in alongside Scaurus he jumped down from the saddle with a swift salute as his superior officer stepped out of the cohorts' slow, weary column of the march.

'I suggest you stop your men, Tribune, there's mule carts on the way for your wounded . . .'

The expression on the other man's face stopped him in mid-sentence.

'We'll march in unaided, thank you, Decurion.'

'But the wounded, sir?'

'Are either already dead or will last long enough to see the inside of the hospital. And you miss the point, Silus. These men are Tungrians, and they will not leave a man behind for the enemy to despoil, not while they have the strength to carry their bodies.'

The decurion looked down the length of the column slowly making its way past him, the cohort's soldiers clearly on their last legs from the effects of the battle and subsequent march. The bigger men were working in pairs to carry either dead bodies which had been stripped of their armour and weapons or those of their comrades too badly hurt to walk, while the walking wounded were each supported on either side by one of their fellow soldiers. He recognised the scarred soldier who was frequently to be seen around Marcus with his arm locked under another man's shoulders, the wounded man barely managing to stagger up the road's steep slope, his face grey with the pain and exertion. Scaurus broke off from their conversation to exhort his men to one last effort.

'Keep moving Tungrians! One last mile, and you can march back into Stone Fort with your heads held up!'

Julius joined them, his expression every bit as exhausted as those of his men, and Silus took his arm in a warm greeting. The first spear nodded at him with a look of calculation.

'Just the man I wanted to see.'

Silus frowned in puzzlement.

'Really? I'd have thought you'd never want to see another horseman for as long as you lived?'

Julius shook his head with a weary smile.

'No, Silus, you're exactly what we need to motivate these men to cover the last distance to the fortress with their heads held up. Get back on your horse and lead your men to the head of the column and you'll see what I mean.'

Scaurus thought for a moment before nodding sagely.

'Indeed. I can't think of any better encouragement for these men.' He patted Silus on the shoulder. 'Off you go, Decurion, lead us home.'

Shaking his head in puzzlement the cavalryman remounted his horse, leading his men back up the column's length at an easy trot. The soldiers he was passing barely acknowledged his presence, and those that did so shot him looks of disdain before returning their gazes to the backs of the men marching before them. From behind him he heard Julius's voice raised to bellow above the rapping of hobnails on the road's cobbles, and with a sudden dawning of realisation he put a hand to his face in disgust just as the words Julius was shouting became clear.

'*The cavalry don't wash their cocks when something dangling itches . . .*'

The reply was instantaneous, hundreds of voices raised in song which quickly swelled to encompass both cohorts as they yelled out the old favourite at the tops of their voices.

'*. . . the cheesy smell,*
of a festering bell,
delights those sons of bitches!'

Julius shouted a parting shot at the cavalryman's back, his voice gleeful despite the exhaustion washing over him.

'Well done, Silus, you're just the man we needed! Now lads: *The cavalry don't pay for whores when drinking 'cause of course . . .*'

The soldiers were ready this time, and most of them were singing the verse well before he'd reached the end of the first line.

'. . . *why pay for gash,*
when you can smash,
in the back doors of a horse?!'

'Well they seem to be in very good spirits for men who were fighting off cavalry only an hour or so ago!'

Leontius's first spear shook his head with an expression of doubt.

'Take a closer look, Tribune.'

'The two men stood for a moment looking down from their vantage point above the fort's gate at the approaching Tungrian cohorts before the prefect spoke again.

'I see what you mean. They may be singing, but they look all in.'

His senior centurion nodded, turning away.

'Indeed they do, sir. I'd say that's a body of men that have seen just about enough fighting for one day. If you'll excuse me?'

Leontius waved him away, and the first spear hurried down the wall's wooden steps to ground level, ducking through the small wicket gate and walking briskly down the road to greet Scaurus and Julius at the head of the First Cohort. Saluting the tribune, he thrust out a hand to Julius with a look of awed respect.

'Welcome back gentlemen! Your Decurion rode back ahead of you and briefed us as to your men's condition, so I've taken the liberty of sending men to light watch fires in your lines. There'll be a meal of stewed meat ready for you in a while, so all you have to do is get your soldiers into barracks and get them rested and ready for tomorrow morning's fun. We'll take the guard duty overnight, if that works for you?'

Julius nodded gratefully, and called his chosen man over.

'Send a runner down the column, all centuries are to parade

into camp, clean and sharpen weapons and prepare for action in the morning. Food will be provided, and guard duty will be conducted by the Britons, so there are no excuses for all men not getting a good night's sleep. Wounded men and all the bandage carriers are to report to the hospital.'

Scaurus stepped closer to the first spear.

'And what, exactly, do we believe tomorrow morning's fun will entail, First Spear?'

The First Britannica's senior centurion pursed his lips, shaking his head slightly.

'We're really not sure, Tribune. Tribune Leontius has called a command conference to be held after the evening meal's been taken, and I expect he'll share everything we know with you then . . .' He paused, eyeing the Tungrian column appraisingly. 'I was about to say what a good state your men seem to be in, sir, given you've just fought off a cavalry attack, but you took your fair share of casualties from the look of it?'

The tribune followed his gaze to the column, nodded at the sight of a stream of wounded men, some walking and nursing sword and spear wounds of varying severity to their arms and faces, while others were being supported between their comrades, their legs roughly bandaged with strips of wool obviously cut from barbarian clothing.

'Sixty-three dead in action and another seven who had to be given the mercy stroke after the battle. Of the hundred or so wounded I expect the usual ratios to apply. Our medical staff will be having a busy time of it this evening.'

'Indeed, sir. And once your medical staff have done what they can for the poor bastards I'll have them on a cart and away to the east with an escort of horsemen. There's no knowing exactly what will come up that valley tomorrow, but I'll not have your women left at risk of what will happen to them if the barbarians manage to batter their way through our defences.'

Scaurus raised a sceptical eyebrow.

'I wish you the best of luck with that. The good lady doctor is of a rather fixed attitude when it comes to care of her patients.'

The first spear opened his mouth to retort, then looked harder at the marching column.

'Are those men prisoners?'

The tribune nodded.

'Yes, and they're all yours. I think *we've* seen enough blood for one day.'

The Tungrians were still settling back into their section of the encampment when a trumpet call from the fortress's battlements announced the arrival of the first enemy scouts. Scaurus and Julius left their men to rest and recover from the day's fighting and made their way to the walls, finding Tribune Leontius watching the Sarmatae riders picking their way up the valley towards the ditch. The fort's commander spoke without taking his eyes off the riders.

'We'll let them take a while to work out that the valley's impassable without their coming through us, before we give them something more to think about.'

They waited in silence while the scouts explored the length of the fortification, and Leontius smiled grimly as they discovered the rows of fallen trees whose intertwined spiky branches made the slopes to either side impossible to traverse.

'They'll be back for a look at the bridge shortly. Bolt throwers, ready!'

The heavy-weapons crews were already waiting by their equipment, and quickly wound on the last turns of torsion into their powerful bowstrings while iron-headed bolts were ceremoniously loaded onto the weapons. Silence fell as the Sarmatae scouts made their way back across the valley, clustering together as they discussed the lay of the land around the fort.

'Wait for my command! I want to kill as many of them as possible!' He turned to the Tungrian officers with an excited grin. 'Now we'll see just how good these fellows are with live targets, eh?'

The scouts gathered around the single bridge over the ditch, and in the afternoon's pale winter sunlight Julius could see one man pointing at the crossing place, then waving his arms across the valley. Leontius turned to the weapon's commander with a boyish grin.

'I'd say that's the man to kill, given the way he's so busy telling the others his opinion. Let's see if the other crews share my feelings. Take aim!' He cupped his hands around his mouth and bellowed the command his men were waiting for. 'Bolt throwers, prepare to shoot! He waited for a moment for the crews to take aim. *'Shoot!'*

With a collective concussive thud, the four missile launchers unleashed their bolts, each one the length of a man's arm and with sufficient power to punch through any armour. One of the bolts flew over the scouts' heads by a hand's width, prompting a barrage of cursing from the weapons' crewmen, but the other three, their aim honed to near perfection by weeks of practice, placed their shots perfectly. The scouts' apparent leader was punched from his horse like a rag doll tossed aside by a child, a puff of pink spray showing the massive damage done to him by the missile's impact. Another bolt flew a fraction low, smashing clean through the neck of one of the horses and toppling it to the ground on top of its rider, while the third killed two men in succession as it blew through the first before lodging deep in the second man's body. The remaining scouts dragged their horses round and fled at the gallop trailed by the riderless horses, while the successful bolt-thrower crews laughed and slapped each other on the back in delight. The prefect called out across the walls while the fallen animal struggled in its death throes.

'Well done, gentlemen! So now the barbarians know to treat Stone Fort with a little more respect! Bolt-thrower crews, stand down! All we can do now is wait and see exactly what comes up the valley behind them.'

The answer to that particular question came soon enough, with a blaring of horns clearly intended to overawe the defenders as they watched the Sarmatae host's approach. Leontius took one look and ordered the defensive wall behind the long ditch to be manned by both cohorts of the Britons while the Thracians took up positions fifty paces behind them, ready to shower any potential attack with arrows. The infantrymen watched in impassive silence from behind the four-foot-high wall as the enemy force approached up the valley towards them. In the lead came a body of horsemen fully ten thousand men in strength, and behind them marched several rough columns of foot soldiers whose numbers darkened the valley's floor.

'Twenty thousand?'

Julius shook his head in response to Scaurus's question as the two men watched from the wall above the fort's gate.

'More like thirty. Which is a good deal more than was expected, according to your friend the Legatus. I wonder . . .' His eyes narrowed as he stared out across the oncoming mass of the enemy, and his words took on a note of disgust. 'Look at the *flags*, Tribune, and the answer becomes apparent.'

Scaurus stared across the valley's width uncomprehendingly for a moment, unsure of what it was he should be seeing, then put a hand to his head in sudden realisation.

'*Galatas?* It can't be . . .'

Julius shook his head grimly.

'It shouldn't be, but it bloody well is. I'd know that banner anywhere.'

A blood-red banner bearing the familiar white sword was floating proudly over a contingent of foot soldiers at the formation's heart, and the tribune watched in bitter silence for a moment before speaking, spitting out the words in an angry torrent.

'Well now, indeed that is King Galatas's banner. Ten thousand in gold doesn't seem to buy the sort of loyalty it used to, does it? There's a part of me that wishes our departed colleague Domitius Belletor was here to see just how long the peace he thought he was purchasing lasted. A *small* part, mind you.'

They watched as the barbarian host halted its march five hundred paces down the valley from the fort's defences and pitched camp with impressive speed. Leontius walked down the wall to join them, one corner of his mouth turned up in a sardonic smile.

'I've set my first spear to doing something creative with the prisoners you brought in this morning. We'll give this collection of uncouth tent dwellers something to think about when the time comes.' He pointed out from the walls. 'And now here comes the bit where they exhort us to leave with our skins intact . . .'

A party of twenty or so men was advancing towards the ditch-bridge beneath a flag of truce, half of them richly dressed and with gold flashing at their throats, the remainder hard-faced warriors marching before them with heavy shields. A single decapitated head was hoisted over their heads on a long spear, but another dozen lances were raised alongside it in a clear signal of intent. They stopped at the far end of the bridge and stood staring at the ranks of soldiers arrayed along the ditch to either side, and Leontius grinned at their hesitancy to advance any further.

'Shall we go and see what it is that our enemies have to say for themselves? Although I suspect they've only really come forward to have a look at our defences, rather than with any real intention of any meaningful discussion.'

The cohorts' tribunes and first spears walked out of the fort's main gate behind a half-circle of soldiers chosen for their size and sheer ugliness, every man's face having been scarred in battle over the years. They faced the Sarmatae nobles across the bridge's thirty-pace length, and Tribune Leontius called out across the gap between the two parties.

'Well now, I presume that one of you gentlemen is King Purta?' A fur-clad noble stepped forward, a golden crown atop his head, a pair of shield men moving to provide him with protection. The tribune grinned across the bridge, barking out a terse laugh before calling out to his opponent. 'I respect your men's desire to shield you Purta, but if I were minded to kill you now then a single gesture to my bolt-thrower crews would send you to meet your ancestors rather sooner than you might have expected. I am however a man of honour, and so just this once I will hold back from having you executed, despite your obvious intention to do your very best to kill me, and sooner rather than later from the look of it. The next time you approach this bridge the story will be somewhat different, unless you do so under a flag of surrender.'

He took a deep breath, then waved a hand at the defences arrayed behind him. 'And in any case, it seems to me that you've come a long way only to be faced with disappointment, wouldn't you say?'

The Sarmatae leader stepped forward once more, raising his voice in reply.

'Far from it, Roman, I see an open road with only a small obstruction to be brushed aside. Whether you attempt to hinder me or run before me the result will be much the same. While your legions tremble with fear behind the mountains I will smash my way through you and into this 'province' of yours by simple weight of numbers. And as you well know, once I am behind the line of your defences I can unleash my horsemen, and force the rest of your army to retreat simply by threatening your settlement at Napoca. We will see just how brave your legionaries are when they are forced to come out from behind their walls and face a host of this size on an open battlefield.'

Leontius nodded, muttering an aside to his colleagues.

'He's got a point there, wouldn't you say?'

He turned back to the Sarmatae, spreading his arms in an eloquent shrug.

'Your point is indeed most clearly made. And since I've never considered myself a particularly talkative man, I thought I'd demonstrate my resolve to you in a more practical way, just to be sure that you don't mistake my honouring your flag of truce for weakness.'

He turned back to the fortress and waved an arm, then swung back to watch the Sarmatae chieftains' faces as a cross was raised on the fort's battlements, the naked body of a battered warrior nailed to its timbers.

'The horsemen who played such a cruel trick on our legion cohort this morning were commanded by a man who, while he was suitably devious in waiting for the right time to reveal his hand, was less discerning in whom he chose for his victims. I expect you will have discovered the remains of his band on a frozen lake back down the valley? They made the mistake of picking a fight for which they were somewhat ill-prepared.'

He waited for a moment, allowing the sight of one of their own crucified on the fort's battlements to sink in, smiling as a second nobleman wearing a golden crown stepped out from behind the shield men. Scaurus's eyes narrowed in recognition, and he raised an eyebrow at Julius.

The Sarmatae stared back at him for a moment before calling out across the bridge.

'Well met once more, Tribune Scaurus.'

Scaurus nodded.

'Balodi. *King* Balodi now, I presume, given that you seem to be wearing a good deal more gold than the last time we met?' The Sarmatae nodded impassively, and Scaurus stared at him for a long moment before continuing. 'Well then, *King* Balodi, you will be unsurprised to hear that I find myself unable to express any pleasure at our meeting, given the extra weight you're carrying around on your head.'

The Sarmatae laughed out loud, using a forefinger to tap the crown with which he had proclaimed his nephew as king only a week before.

'This? It seemed wasted on a stripling like my brother's son. And besides, he felt obliged by his promise to you that he would withdraw his men from the war' – he held his hands up in apparent amazement – 'Whereas I, being both older and somewhat wiser in the ways of the world, obviously felt no such compunction.'

Scaurus regarded him with a level stare for a moment.

'You have no idea how dispiriting it is to discover that a man who initially seemed so reasonable is just another bastard. Although you're not *just* a bastard, are you Balodi, you're a clever, scheming, ruthless, murdering bastard, I'll give you that. Once your brother was dead you knew that Inarmaz would contest with you for the throne, so you took the opportunity we offered and convinced us to do most of your dirty work for you.'

The Sarmatae nodded.

'Indeed. Although in truth all I really expected from your man Corvus was a distraction, and enough time to reach my men and strike while Inarmaz's attention was elsewhere, instead of which he did most of the job for me. And of course disposing of my nephew was child's play. He was such a trusting fool, as, it appears, was your colleague Belletor. Did I do you a favour in making him the first of our collection of Roman heads? I'll warn you, my brother in arms, Purta here, has designs to put all of your heads alongside his.'

Leontius stepped closer, raising a hand to point at the fort again.

'It seems there's little left to be said then. Here's a small demonstration of what awaits you if you're rash enough to cross this bridge in hopes of smashing your way into Dacia.'

He waved a hand in the air, and a flame flared brightly in the late winter afternoon's gloom on the wall behind him, a torch wielded by one of the hard-faced centurions supervising the bolt-thrower crews. After a moment's silence the light brightened as it found the fuel placed around the cross's base in preparation for the demonstration. Within a few heartbeats the cross was ablaze, and the previously semi-conscious figure nailed to it was screaming at the top of his voice as the fire seared his flesh. While the expressionless Sarmatae leaders watched, he writhed horribly for a moment before sagging motionless down into the flames, lost in their twisting brilliance. The tribune turned back to them without emotion.

'Crude, I know, but to the point. He purported to serve the empire but was clearly only waiting for the right moment to savage his new master's hand. And so he pays the price by dying in screaming agony. As will you all, when you fail in this doomed attempt to break Rome's hold over Dacia. It isn't too late to turn away and forswear this rash assault on our borders.'

Purta smiled and shook his head.

'I think not, Roman. And since we're delivering public justice . . .'

He made a signal to the men behind him, who wrestled forward a struggling figure and forced him to his knees before the Sarmatae king, who raised a long knife for the Romans to see and put his hand in the captive's hair to pull his head back. His bodyguard set their shields firmly in anticipation of any attempt to rescue the prisoner.

'A head for a head, although sadly I don't have the time to make this infiltrator suffer the way you thoughtfully arranged for our brother to spend his last moments screaming in agony.' He looked up at the Romans, smiling at their lack of recognition. 'You don't know him, do you? Perhaps this will help.'

He sheathed the knife, reaching into a pocket and pulling out something that glinted in the winter afternoon's thin light, throwing it across the bridge to land at the tribunes' feet. Scaurus reached down and picked up the trinket, a gold ring with a large garnet set in its claws. He raised it for Leontius to see.

'So now we know just how secret the legatis' information was. This ring was the means by which he enabled his messengers to prove they came from him, and not from some cat's paw.'

Purta laughed at his expression.

'I see you recognise the ring. We've been using it to feed whatever information we want your leaders to have across the border for almost a year now, while this poor fool sweated and strained under my torturer's attentions and told us absolutely everything he knew. You wouldn't believe a man could have his limbs broken so many times without simply going insane.'

Marcus stared hard across the bridge, and realised that the prisoner's arms and legs were obscenely twisted, his fingers pointing in different directions. Purta shrugged, drawing the knife from his belt again.

'All good things must come to an end, I suppose.'

He cut the helpless spy's throat, dropping his writhing body onto the bridge's timbers with a dismissive shove.

'That's just a start, of course. We'll take revenge for that slow death a thousand times over, once your ditch is filled and your walls broken. If I were you I would pray to every god you hold dear to die in battle, for I will be offering a rich reward from the gold brought to our cause by Balodi for any man who captures any of you men in a fit state to receive the attentions of my flaying knives. Roman gold for a Roman officer's skin . . . I suppose it's only fitting.'

Once he was happy that his men were fed and bedded down, and with Quintus given explicit instructions to make sure that they stayed in their tents and were given no chance to wander off in search of alcohol, Marcus walked the short distance across the fort and into the hospital. The scene inside the building was much as he had come to expect, with the least seriously wounded soldiers sitting in small groups as they waited for the medical staff to work through the more seriously hurt men. Their wounds were superficial for the most part, in need only of stitching by the bandage carriers who were working their way through them with tired eyes and numb fingers, although to Marcus more than a few of them would be permanently disfigured by deep cuts to their faces. Some of them were sleeping, and one man, a long cut through one eyebrow and down his cheek already stitched, was whimpering in his sleep much to the quiet amusement of his comrades.

'He always does it after a fight, sir, like an old dog dreaming about running about an' barking, only he's killing barbarians rather than chasing sheep.'

Marcus smiled sadly and went in search of his wife, but before he found her a familiar voice called him from a side room whose floor was given over to men with more serious wounds.

'Centurion!'

He turned to find Scarface beckoning him with a respectful salute, and entered the room to find half a dozen men lying on straw mattresses, most with their eyes closed against their pain. One of them, his chest wrapped in bandages, was groaning quietly to himself but showing no other sign of life other than fast, shallow breathing, his skin pale and waxy in the lamplight. Scarface's friend Sanga was wide awake though, and seemed animated enough despite his obvious discomfort. He smiled wanly up at Marcus and went to raise his arm in salute, his eyes widening at the involuntary movement's effect on his wound.

'Relax, Sanga. Have you been seen by the doctor?'

Scarface answered for his friend, who rolled his eyes before closing them and leaving his comrade to it.

'Yes, Centurion. She took a look at him and said he'd live. I had a look in through the door of her room earlier and she was up to her elbows in blood and swearing like a six-badge centurion, so I made a quick retreat before she saw me.'

'No you didn't, soldier. I was just too busy trying to stop a man bleeding to death to turn my ire on you rather than his wound.'

Felicia walked into the room with eyes that were glazed with weariness, looking about her and weighing up the condition of the men waiting for treatment while a pair of orderlies waited behind her.

'That one, please.' She pointed to the man next to Sanga who was holding a thick wad of linen to a long gash in his thigh. 'And make sure the table's washed down before you put him on it.' She leant over the groaning man and shook her head. 'Then you can put this poor man in the quiet room. I think he's beyond helping, so we might as well allow him to pass in peace. And you, Centurion, can come with me.'

She led him down the corridor to a tiny office in which Annia was dozing with little Appius cradled in her lap, gurgling quietly.

'Thank the gods for a docile baby. Here . . .' She took the infant from her assistant and handed him to Marcus. 'Have you come for a report for your Tribune?'

He smiled at her, popping a finger into the baby's mouth and provoking a prompt and hungry sucking.

'In truth I was more interested in seeing how you're coping, but since you mention it . . .'

'We've lost five more of them, which is a fact of which I'm prouder than I probably should be. None of the men in the room you were in when I found you will die of their wounds, with the exception of that chest perforation, although I can't promise that infection won't be a problem despite the honey I'm using to pack the holes before I close them. We'll probably have to keep twenty or so of them for a while, the rest you can have back none the worse for their experiences other than some rather fetching scars.'

She reached out for the child, then remembered something else, raising a finger to Marcus in the gesture he had come to know indicated her unwillingness to compromise on a point of discussion.

'Oh, and you can tell your tribune what I told the Briton's first spear when he came calling earlier. I will *not* be evacuating from this fort, *not* now and *not* in the morning. As long as I have patients here, here I will remain.'

Marcus raised an eyebrow.

'He's probably a little nervous about the fact that an unknown number of Sarmatae warriors are camped out in the valley to our west, and will doubtless have our road to the east blocked all too soon.'

She shook her head, taking Appius from his arms.

'Not my problem, husband. You'd all better start working out how to keep them out, hadn't you, unless there's a plan to take all of these casualties away with us. And now, if you'll excuse me, I'll be feeding this little man, since you seem to have got him properly excited at the prospect of getting his lips around something more satisfying then your finger. Which, from the look of it, could do with a wash. Away with you!'

'I see. So there's no chance of persuading your doctor to leave the fortress, Rutilius Scaurus?'

Scaurus shook his head with a sardonic grin.

'None at all, I'm afraid Leontius. We've more chance of persuading the Sarmatae that it's a bit inconvenient at the moment, and perhaps they could come back next week?'

The other man grimaced.

'Very well. In which case we should probably turn our thoughts to that rather more pressing subject. It seems that every blasted barbarian from the length and breadth of the great plain is camped down there in the valley, rather than being further to the north, and champing at the bit to get their teeth into the legions as I expect we'd all prefer. There must be more than twenty-five thousand men out there, more than a third of them cavalry, including some tribesmen we believed had been sent packing from the field with their tails between their legs.'

Scaurus shook his head ruefully.

'It's clear that the legati have been misled by whoever it was that they had in the enemy camp. There's no use in wasting time on that disappointment though, since it isn't going to help us deal with those barbarians.'

Leontius nodded.

'Indeed not. So, to our situation. Despite the very welcome escape of your two cohorts yesterday, Tribune Scaurus, we still number little more than three thousand men in the face of ten times as many warriors. It looks like our defence of this pass tomorrow morning will be a brief and, if glorious, ultimately doomed affair.' He raised a sardonic eyebrow at the assembled officers to indicate his apparent amusement at the situation. 'However, I must say I cannot countenance any talk of retreat. For one thing my orders are to hold this place against any and all threats to the province from the north, and we all know what happens to officers who fail to keep faith with their orders. And quite apart from that I have every intention of continuing with the sequence of offices, once my spell with the army is complete, and there's no way I'll be granted the position of magistrate if I allow these barbarians free passage into the province without having a decent try at stopping them. So' – he looked around him with a look of challenge – 'we fight. After all, it's not as if we've been sitting on our hands these last few weeks, as this Purta will discover tomorrow if he sends his men into the teeth of our defences. And now, gentlemen, let us turn our thoughts to night patrolling. The enemy may be of a mind to send men forward to probe our defences tonight, or given his record of turning a feint into the main attack he may even try to take us unaware and storm the ditch. Either way, I'm of a mind to make him pay heavily for the pleasure of the attempt.'

'This takes me back. Do you remember the last time I took you out on a scouting mission after dark?'

Marcus paused from his careful application of mud paste to

his forehead, raising an eyebrow at his friend and replying with a sardonic tone.

'How could I forget, Dubnus? As I recall it you managed to get my helmet stove in and put me in the hospital with double vision.'

The big Briton snorted disbelievingly.

'And as *I* recall it' – he waited a moment to see if Marcus would attempt any defence against what he knew was coming next – '*you* managed to alert a bluenose scouting party by falling over a tree. And then when we carried you back down to Cauldron Fort, all you could think of was how quickly you could get your leg over your doctor! And in the name of Cocidius, would you stop smearing that stuff on your face? Why can't you just grow a decent beard?'

Marcus ignored him, spreading another handful of the paste across his cheeks.

'That should do it. Shall we go and see who Julius has mustered for us to take hunting tonight?'

A dozen men were standing to attention outside the command tent under their first spear's scrutiny. He finished his close inspection of the last of them, acknowledging his brother officers' arrival with a curt nod before turning back to the line of soldiers.

'Now jump up and down.'

The Tungrians jumped on the spot while he listened critically, eventually nodding reluctant satisfaction.

'Nothing jingling, no coins, no belt fittings, no amulets, everyone's scabbard loops are muffled with wool . . . It'll do, I suppose, although I don't think I've seen as revolting a collection of men in all my years of service.' He turned to the stores officer standing a little way back. 'Let's kit them up then.'

The storeman stepped forward and handed each man a folded piece of material, and in the torchlight Marcus realised that the material was white.

'I've been saving this for a while.'

The storeman's voice was doleful, and Julius snorted derisively.

'Then isn't it a good thing you've found a worthy use for it, and cleared some space in your store.' He watched as the soldiers wrapped themselves in the white sheets, nodding judiciously. 'Once you're out in the snow you'll be all but invisible.' Tipping his head to the centurions he stepped back. 'All yours, brothers, and the best of luck.'

Dubnus examined the scouting party with an equally expert eye, eventually signalling his own satisfaction, the cue for Marcus to brief the party.

'This is a simple enough task, gentlemen. Just after dark this evening Tribune Leontius withdrew his cohort from the ditch defences, and brought them back inside the fort. It's probably just as well, since leaving them out in this cold all night would be a good way to end up with half of them frozen to death by the morning, and the remainder exhausted from lack of sleep. What they *were* defending before he pulled them back is a walled ditch just like the one we crossed marching in this morning. There is only one easy crossing point, a wooden bridge which will doubtless be the enemy's main objective when they attack. The Sarmatae are going to want to capture it, to stop us from burning it out, and use it to bring their warriors over the ditch and into a position from which they can attack the fort. Our job is twofold, firstly to listen for any signs of enemy activity under the cover of darkness, and secondly to make sure they don't get any clever ideas about scouting or even capturing the bridge itself. There are a dozen of you, and three centurions, so we'll take four men apiece. Dubnus and his men will watch and listen for any activity to the left of the bridge, Qadir will do the same on the right, and I'm going to take my party across the bridge itself for a very careful scout forward to see what we can find out.'

He looked across the line of men, unsurprised to find that several of Qadir's Hamians had been selected for the task. Skilled hunters, their ability to move silently and without trace had already been proven the previous year in Britannia. His gaze alighted on the expected face, stolid and unapologetic at one end of the line.

'Scarface. Have you not had enough excitement for one day?

Wouldn't you rather be sleeping? Tomorrow promises to be a busy day, I'd imagine.'

The soldier shrugged, ignoring Dubnus's pitying smile.

'Plenty of time for sleep later, young sir. We can't have you on your own in the dark with only this bunch of bed-wetting faggots between you and the barbarians.'

Shaking his head, Marcus turned back to the other soldiers and performed the ritual check that none of them would make any unwanted noise, before submitting to the same inspection from Dubnus. That complete, he wrapped the white camouflage around himself, grateful for the warmth of an extra layer in the night's bitter cold. Saluting Julius he led the party away from the Tungrians' camp, out into the white expanse of the ground between the fort's walls and the forested hills two hundred paces to its south. After only fifty paces of slow, silent progress they were alone in the darkness of the wide open space. Above them the night sky was cloudless, and despite the lack of a moon the blaze of stars provided sufficient illumination for the young centurion to be able to pick his way forward over the slightly uneven ground, with only the crunching sound of his companions' footfalls through the snow's frozen crust to disturb the silence. Reaching the treeline he waited for a moment to allow the rest of the party to catch up, their breath steaming in the night's pale light, then led them on along the forest's edge at a steady pace until he reached the four-foot-high turf wall that bounded the ditch's western side. Peering over the rampart he could see the dark mass of the Sarmatae tents five hundred paces away, the bright pinpricks of their torches twinkling in the darkness. As he watched, a muffled thump sounded from the closest of the fort's four west-facing towers, as a bolt thrower spat a missile out into the night on an arching trajectory that would bring it to earth somewhere in the enemy encampment. Dubnus pushed forward to join him at the wall, listening intently for any reaction from the Sarmatae, but the shot had clearly fallen to earth un-noticed by the barbarians. He shrugged, gesturing to the wall and whispering into his friend's ear.

'Waste of a good bolt, since I don't suppose those legion pricks could hit a cow's arse with a lute in the dark, but it lets the barbarians know we've not forgotten them, I suppose. I don't understand this though, where's the sense in having a wall without men behind it? An obstacle only works when it's manned, surely this tribune in command must know that?'

Marcus returned the shrug.

'He must be quite sure they won't attack tonight . . .' He turned his head suddenly, tilting it slightly to listen better. 'Did you hear that?'

The Briton shook his head.

'Hear what?'

The Roman listened intently for a moment longer before casting a long, hard look across the white expanse between ditch and wall. He whispered again, still staring out across the open ground.

'Nothing, obviously. I thought I heard a footfall. This snow deadens noises, but it makes every step sound like a creaking floorboard. Come on.'

Turning right, he led the party along the wall, keeping low to stay in its shadow, until the bridge was in sight, then turned and signalled to Dubnus, who nodded and pulled at his men's sleeves to indicate that they had reached their listening post. Carrying on down the wall's line the Roman stopped at the very end of the turf rampart, gesturing for Qadir to take his men forward and into the cover of the defence's renewed run on the far side. Waiting until the Hamians had slid noiselessly across the open ground, he gestured to his own men to hold their positions, easing around the wall's corner and out onto the bridge with slow, stealthy footsteps.

Stopping halfway across the span he crouched and listened again, still hearing nothing more than the gentle moan of the wind through the bridge's timbers, a faint smell of pitch wrinkling his nose despite the freezing air's bite. After a moment's waiting he heard a sound from behind him, so faint as to be almost imperceptible, but nothing more reached his ears and he assumed that it was one of his own men changing position. Edging forward again he reached the bridge's far end and paused once more to listen for a long moment. Still convinced that the patrol was alone in the night, he turned to look back down the bridge and found Scarface five paces behind him, a determined look on his face as he stared out across the snow-covered landscape and avoiding Marcus's eye. Shaking his head in bemused irritation the Roman pointed to the bridge's planks at his soldier's feet and held out a hand with the palm forward in an unmistakeable command for the soldier to stay put before turning back to the open ground before them. He paced slowly forward, his booted feet sinking into the snow's crisp surface in a succession of crunches that he was convinced could be heard from a hundred paces. Pausing a dozen steps from the bridge, he squatted down under the sheet's camouflage and looked out across the landscape, the fallen snow dappled by faint shadows cast by the stars' dim light shining through the scattered trees.

In that moment of absolute silence something went click to his left, a tiny noise followed immediately by a scurry of movement that made Marcus crouch lower against the snow, pulling the white sheet over his head until only his eyes were left uncovered, waiting in absolute immobility. A wolf loped across his field of view from left to right, the animal's grey coat merging almost perfectly with the snow across which it was scurrying, clearly disturbed by something. The animal hurried away into the shadows, leaving Marcus waiting beneath the shroud in patient immobility, conscious of the hoarse breathing of Scarface close behind him who had clearly disobeyed his instruction to remain on the bridge. At the end of a count to fifty, throughout which he willed himself to remain absolutely still despite the cold seeping up into his legs and threatening to set off a convulsive shiver, he eased the sheet down from his face, allowing a mist of steam to slide from his nostrils in a long, slow exhalation of relief. Tensing his reluctant calves to start moving again he froze anew as a flicker of motion caught the corner of his eye. A man had risen out of the snow's white carpet to pace slowly but purposefully towards him, another following in his wake, and as Marcus watched, a third and fourth figure got to their feet and fell in behind.

'*Enemy scouts!*'

Incapable of remaining silent in the face of the enemy, Scarface was already on his feet and striding past Marcus with his sword drawn, ignoring the first arrow as it whipped by him with a whirr, while a chorus of answering shouts rang out. Before the Roman had any time to react a second arrow flicked out of the darkness and struck the soldier in the chest, rocking Scarface back on his heels. While Marcus was still struggling to realise what it was they faced, another arrow transfixed the reeling soldier's throat with a wet impact, and the stricken Tungrian fell backwards into the snow. A shout went up, and the ground before Marcus was suddenly alive with men running awkwardly towards him through the snow, all camouflaged in the same way that the Roman patrol had sought to merge with the icy landscape. Turning, Marcus floundered back towards the bridge, bitterly calling to mind Tribune Leontius's words when he had been briefed for the patrol. 'And in the event that you discover the blighters trying to capture that bridge under the cover of darkness, then make it look real, eh Centurion? We need you to draw in as many of them as possible before we show our hand.'

He sprinted for the bridge as best he could in several inches of snow, hearing an arrow hiss past his head and another thud into the timbers beside him as he reached the wooden surface, running faster on the firmer footing. Looking back he could see dozens of Sarmatae foot soldiers, waving swords and spears, slogging through the snow behind him, and behind them what appeared to be a solid wall of men charging out of the darkness. Raising a hand to point at the enemy he shouted to Dubnus and Qadir.

'*These aren't scouts, it's a full-scale attack! Run for the gate!*'

Pulling his whistle from its place hanging round his neck beneath his tunic, Marcus blew three short blasts, gratefully realising that his brother officers and their men were closing on him from either side. Arminius and Martos were running with them, and the Roman realised what it was that he had heard behind them earlier.

'They've got the bloody bridge!'

Glancing back, Marcus could see the truth in Dubnus's words, as the first of the Sarmatae warriors stormed across the span in pursuit of the fleeing scouts.

In front of them the fort's western gates opened ponderously, a solid column of soldiers pouring out to face the barbarian attack with spears and shields. Dubnus shook his head as they ran towards the Britons, his voice bitter with disgust at the scale of the disaster.

'Too little and too late. By the time we've got a cohort out here and ready there'll be five thousand men facing them. This is fucked . . .'

Shouting the watchword, the small group straggled to a halt behind the advancing soldiers as they formed up into a disciplined line, each century starting the ritualised hammering of spears on shields as soon as they were set in place, while fresh troops were pouring through the gate's twin openings with a speed that seemed to belie Dubnus's words. As the Tungrians watched, a column of soldiers appeared around the fort's north-western corner, and Dubnus spun to see the same thing happening at the other end of the fort's western wall. He stared at the onrushing troops for a moment before turning to Marcus with a strange expression.

'This is a trap, isn't it? Every man in the fort must have been waiting behind those gates, kitted up and ready to fight for this lot to be deploying that quickly. Did you know about this?'

Marcus shook his head.

'Not as such. My orders were to go looking for trouble, and if I found it then to give the signal and run for the gate. Why would the tribunes tell us what they had in mind, when one captured man might reveal the plan? But I don't think this can be all there is . . .'

Arminius nodded in agreement.

'The Sarmatae will send ten thousand warriors across that ditch if they are given enough time. There must be some way to stop them, or why allow them to capture the means of crossing?'

Craning his neck to look between the soldiers in front of them, Marcus realised that there were already a thousand men and more across the ditch, mostly holding their ground while their strength built with every man that crossed the bridge, while a few skirmishers ventured forward to send arrows thudding into the auxiliaries' shields. Martos stepped to his side, making the same calculation.

'Two infantry cohorts and the Thracians are all this prefect has to fight with, unless he brings our men into action. I would expect that if he has a trap to close on these men, then the time—'

With a bellowed command from the walls above them, the bolt throwers on either corner of the wall flung their missiles at the bridge in unison, blazing fire bolts which flew to impact directly beneath the structure. The timbers took light in an instant, and a moment later the bridge's length was a mass of flames, the fire's greedy roar overlain by the harsh shouts and screams of the mass of men who had been fighting to cross the span and get to their enemies. Marcus looked at his comrades, nodding slowly.

'I see. Pitch, probably painted all over the bridge timbers. I thought I could smell something odd when I was crossing. But that can't be all there is to this, or what stops them from simply jumping down into the ditch and making a run for it?'

As if to answer Martos's musing, and as the warriors who had already crossed dithered in the face of the Roman line that was still strengthening with every moment, the fire raced away from the bridge and up the ditch in both directions, following a trail of pitch which had clearly been laid with this desired outcome in mind. The roaring flames quickly set light to the pine trees that had been felled and laid along the bottom of the trench, their branches already primed with more of the sticky sap. In a dozen heartbeats the length of the defence was ablaze, denying the Sarmatae who had already crossed any means of escaping to their own side of the ditch's line. With a blare of horns the waiting lines of soldiers advanced to fight, their enemies silhouetted by the fire raging behind, and looking at his companions' fire-lit faces Marcus realised that the advancing Romans would appear to be little less than the servants of a vengeful god, their armour flashing gold in the fire's light. Panic swiftly overcame the last vestiges of discipline possessed by the Sarmatae trapped between the blazing ditch and the implacable soldiers, some men throwing themselves at the Romans in blind, mindless fury, whilst others hurled themselves at the flames, sprinting to leap into the teeth of the blaze in the hope of reaching the far side unscathed. A few men who had flung away their weapons and armour succeeded in the attempt, but many more fell short and dropped, screaming with terror, onto the burning trees. Their hair and clothing ignited instantly to leave them rolling in shrieking agony before oblivion took them. The remainder fought like wild men, caught between the two implacable threats of fire and foe, but to little avail; the Britons' spears harvested them with the efficiency of corn threshers as the desperate barbarians flung themselves at the advancing line of shields.

'It's a small enough victory, given the force still arrayed on the other side of that ditch, but perhaps still enough to give Purta pause to wonder what other tricks we have up our sleeves. I see you've collected somewhat more men than you left our camp with?'

Tribune Scaurus had walked through the gates behind the last of the Britons, raising an eyebrow at Arminius and Martos who both shrugged in response. Marcus saluted wearily, turning to make his way back to the Tungrian camp with a crestfallen expression.

'Indeed Tribune, a victory. But bought at a cost I would have been loath to pay, had I known in advance what the nature of the bargain would be.'

The Sarmatae attacked again at first light, their rage stoked by the sight of fifteen crosses raised behind the line of the now heavily defended ditch. Upon each cross writhed one of the small number of enemy horsemen captured on the ice the previous day. Tribune

Leontius nodded grimly at the doomed prisoners, speaking in conversational tones to his colleagues.

'This will provide the bolt-thrower crews with some target practice, I suspect.'

As he predicted, enemy archers quickly ran forward into bowshot of the crucified men, each man braving the artillery's long reach in the hope of putting an arrow into their helpless brothers and ending their torture. When half a dozen of the captives were slumped down lifelessly on their crosses for the death of a single incautious archer, who had chosen to string another arrow rather than move from the spot from which he had loosed his first shot only to have his spine torn out by a swiftly aimed bolt, Leontius ordered the crosses to be set alight. Greasy plumes of smoke rose into the air as the flames swiftly consumed their human offerings, and the archers withdrew in the same zigzag runs that had brought them close enough to shoot at the captives, earning a grudging note of respect in Scaurus's voice as he spoke to Julius.

'Worthy of our admiration, I'd say. I wouldn't want to run at four of those monsters whether I had the freedom to dance about and put their aim off or not. And with that done, I'd expect Purta to land his next punch quickly now. He knows every moment he's stuck on the wrong side of these walls brings the arrival of our legions that much closer.' He rubbed the amulet tied to his right wrist reflexively. 'Always presuming that Our Lord sees fit to ensure that Tribune Leontius's message reaches them, of course . . .'

Purta's response to the previous night's disaster came soon enough and to the dismay of Scaurus in particular. A ragged flood of slaves poured forward towards the ditch, goaded on by whips and spears and sheltered behind an arc of raised shields, staggering under the load of their buckets of soil and rocks. Their first task was to fill the stake-studded pits that waited to cripple the unwary, and as they laboured to follow their masters' shouted commands the enemy archers came forward again in strength, showering arrows at any of the defenders who showed themselves above the ditch or fort walls. Forced to take shelter from the hail of missiles, the soldiers hid behind their defensive wall while the barbarians' slaves completed their initial task of making the approach to the ditch safe before being driven to attack the defensive line itself. Pouring the contents of their buckets into the ditch, each of the slaves turned away to retrace their steps under the goading of their Sarmatae masters. With the Thracian bowmen unable to shoot at the Sarmatae workforce in the teeth of the overwhelming enemy archery it was left to the bolt throwers to deplete the toiling slaves, and the officers watched grimly as the pitiless bolts ploughed into their labouring ranks.

'This day would seem to have been a long time in the planning, given that our enemy clearly came prepared for a siege, although I doubt he expected to face quite such a stubborn resistance. There will, of course, be Romans among those labourers . . .'

In truth Leontius was only confirming what most men had already realised, recognising scraps of Roman garb amidst the mass of humanity toiling to build a now discernible ramp across the ditch and realising that there were captured men, women and even children among the slaves.

'We can only console ourselves that each one we kill has been freed from a grim existence that will already have visited misery and degradation upon them, and which can only end badly one way or another. You there!' he called out to the commander of the nearest bolt thrower in an admonishing tone. 'Don't shoot at the men around the ditch, aim further away to allow your bolts to spear two or three of them with one shot, rather than just pinning single men to the ground!'

The centurion saluted briskly, bellowing fresh orders at the men labouring to wind the massive weapon back to its maximum power, and Marcus turned away, sick at heart at the scale of the slaughter being necessarily visited upon the helpless slaves. He spun back as a loud bang and a scream of agony told of some unexpected disaster, finding the bolt thrower's crew in chaos and one of their number staggering drunkenly with a chunk of wood protruding from his shattered forehead. The soldier fell full length to the tower's wooden floor and lay still, one foot twitching spasmodically.

'One of the torsion bars broke. That poor sod is as good as dead.'

Leontius nodded grimly at Julius's words, pointing at the wrecked weapon.

'So is my bloody bolt thrower, and I've no means of mending the damned thing unless I take a bar off one of the weapons on the rear wall to keep this one shooting.'

He conferred briefly with Scaurus before ordering the repair, the two men agreeing that there was little option but to keep all four weapons on the western side in action. The Sarmatae slaves laboured on without rest, their loads of mud and rocks combining with the bodies of those of them that fell to the defenders' missiles to slowly but surely send the ramp's tongue poking forward into the ditch. Julius cast an expert eye across the scene soon after midday before pronouncing an opinion.

'Clever stuff. See how they're making it higher than the defences on the other side, even though that takes longer? That way when they come to launch an attack off it they'll have the high ground.' He shook his head with a worried frown. 'They've made a good start, although every pace they advance gets harder as the ditch gets deeper beneath them. And they'll slowly but surely grind the life out of those slaves if they keep working them at that rate.' He looked down at the ramp again, wincing as a bolt thrower's missile ploughed through the labouring workers in a chorus of tired screams from those around the bolt's point of impact. 'I'd give it a day, perhaps less, and then the barbarians will be at spear point with the men behind that wall, while archers on either side shoot arrows at them from close enough to make their shields useless. And there's nothing to break or burn with an earth ramp. They'll be over the wall and behind the ditch in strength soon enough after that, if they've the willpower to spend a few hundred warriors smashing their way over the wall.'

Scaurus nodded his agreement.

'Which goes without saying they do. And once they're behind

the ditch they'll have free run of the walls, and built from stone or not, that means they'll have the gates smashed in soon enough after that. For all Leontius's bravado, I'd say that the defence of this place won't last long thereafter, not with the sheer mass of men they can bring to the fight. We'll make them pay, but we won't stop them.'

Late in the afternoon another bolt thrower's torsion bar failed, with equally dire results for the crew who lost two men badly injured to the flailing bowstring. Leontius pondered taking a replacement part from the sole remaining weapon on the eastern wall, but decided against the idea after a moment of thought.

'Better to keep some means of lighting up the bridge on your side of the defence, eh Tribune? It surely can't be long now before your friend Balodi arrives on the scene?'

As darkness fell he shook his head at a request from his first spear to withdraw the Britons from the defences and pull them back into the fort.

'The blighters are within a dozen feet of the rampart, close enough that a good stout wooden plank might just be enough to get them across and over the wall. You can withdraw half the cohort at a time, but I want five centuries on duty and ready to fight them off if they try to jump the gap without finishing the ramp.'

The slaves laboured on into the night by the light of torches carried by the warriors whose sticks and whips continued to goad them on through their obvious exhaustion. Scaurus accompanied the fort's officers back up onto the walls after they had taken a quiet dinner, throughout which he had brooded on their situation with the look of a man wrestling with a personal dilemma. The torches illuminating the ramp had clearly edged perceptibly closer in the hour or so that they had been at their meal, and Julius's prediction looked likely to be fulfilled sooner rather than later. With a decisive nod he turned to Leontius, pointing down at the activity below them.

'Purta has made an error in continuing to drive the ramp's construction after dark. I think that the time has come to put a stop to this activity, at least for the time being?'

Scaurus explained his idea, and Leontius's approval was as enthusiastic as ever, though tempered by the unavoidable impact on the slaves labouring below them. Once all sources of light that might betray their new tactic had been removed from the fort's walls, the Thracian archers were marched up onto the fighting platform one century at a time, until the side of the fort which faced the attackers was thronged with men, standing as instructed in perfect silence. Leontius muttered an instruction to his runner, chopping his hand forcefully down into an open palm.

'Pass the signal to illuminate the enemy, and then to evacuate the forward positions.'

After a moment for the order to reach the forward troops, a handful of lights appeared in the darkness below them, thin shelled pots filled with pitch and topped with burning rags. The men holding the improvised missiles promptly threw them over the ditch's defensive wall and into the toiling workers where they broke, their sticky contents ignited by the flaming linen to spill across soil and workers alike. Screams rose out of the darkness as several bodies writhed in incandescent agony, their clothing aflame, and Marcus watched as Scaurus put a hand over his eyes in horror. Looking down from the wall he saw dark shapes hurrying away from the ditch, and a moment later the Thracian's prefect barked an order to his archers.

'Archers, at one hundred paces, ready!'

With a rustle of arrows being drawn from their quivers the Thracians prepared to shoot, their bows creaking in the night's calm. If the Sarmatae realised what was about to happen, the screams of the burning slaves hindered any attempt to order a withdrawal.

'Archers . . . *shoot!*'

The Thracians loosed their missiles at the lights dancing below them, hundreds of arrows arching down into the compact mass of slaves trapped under their bows. A renewed chorus of agonised screams rent the night air as dozens of men, women and children staggered and died under the storm of arrows.

'Ready . . . *shoot!*'

Another volley flashed down from the walls to riddle slaves and warriors alike, the sounds of their pain and distress redoubling in volume. Men were shouting from behind the mass of slaves, although whether their commands were to retreat or stand fast under the hail of iron was unclear.

'Ready . . . *shoot!*'

The third volley broke the slaves as completely as an infantry charge might have done, and the sounds reaching the wall became those of a desperate mob stampeding for perceived safety. The night was filled by both the desperate shouts of men as yet unhurt but in fear of their lives, and the pitiful cries of those pierced by arrows or simply trampled underfoot in the mob's panic.

The Thracian prefect looked to Leontius, but the fort's commander shook his head and raised his hand to order another volley.

'Archers, at two hundred paces, ready!' The bowmen raised their weapons to give the arrows greater range, stretching the bowstrings back to their ears in readiness to send them high into the air. *'Shoot!'*

The fourth volley whistled away, leaving a moment's silence before the arrows rained down amid the fleeing slaves and warriors, eliciting yet more screams and further panic, and Marcus knew that Leontius would repeat his hand signal before the gesture was made.

'At three hundred paces, ready!' The bows were now pointed up at the stars, their wielders forcing every possible ounce of effort into their weapons to send them high into the night sky for maximum reach. *'Shoot!'*

The cries of distress were distant now, and sounded oddly tired to Marcus's ears, as if those men struck by this final volley were so exhausted from their flight that they could muster no more energy to protest against their cruel fortune than a groan of dismay. Leontius nodded to the Thracian prefect, who turned back to his men with an unreadable expression.

'Archers, stand down. First Spear, take them back to quarters.'

The officers watched as the Thracians filed off the walls with blank faces, their minds closed to the havoc they had inflicted on the defenceless slaves. From the ditch below them the cries of the wounded were the only sound remaining in what was otherwise a sudden silence, incongruous after the long day's chaotic din.

Leontius congratulated Scaurus sombrely, although there was no mistaking the relief in his voice.

'Well that ought to be the end of their work for the rest of the night. An inspired tactic, Tribune, given that the enemy archers clearly had no means of retaliating in the darkness.'

Scaurus nodded, his face drawn at the brief action's hidden horror.

'Thank you, Leontius. And I have a further suggestion to make. My cohort will assume responsibility for the ditch for the rest of the night. Why not give your Britons a short period of rest? They will face a renewed onslaught in the morning, I expect.'

The tribune nodded gratefully, and Marcus realised that he was missing what was painfully obvious to the young Roman. Julius glanced at him, the look in his eyes making plain that Scaurus's purpose in taking the night watch was equally clear to the first spear.

'Thank you, Tribune. Perhaps our first spears might organise the handover?'

Scaurus nodded blankly, turning away and staring down into the darkness, his face set as hard as stone. Marcus stepped up behind him, speaking quietly into his plea.

'Tribune, forgive me if I speak plainly with you, but you *must not* do this thing. I realise you feel a responsibility for the men lying wounded down there, but . . .'

Scaurus's voice was hollow and emotionless, his interjection less interruption than simply deaf to his centurion's plea.

'Until you have actually ordered such a thing, Centurion, you have no idea how it tears at a man's soul to hear innocent men, women and children cry out in fear and pain as their lives are taken for a crime that was not of their doing. I heard a child cry out for her mother, Marcus. I heard a man call in despair to his wife . . .' He took a deep breath. 'I heard a man call out to Our Lord Mithras in the depths of his despair, but there was no answer, only another volley of our bloody arrows. I might have saved some of those people had I been more insistent with Belletor during the negotiations, but I allowed the self-interested fool to choose political expediency over simple humanity. So now I cannot simply stand up here with clean hands while innocents I condemned to slavery though my inaction lie helpless in the mud, torn and bleeding so that we might live a little longer. Julius, get the cohorts ready to relieve the Britons at the ditch. And find some *fucking* rope, will you?'

8

The fortification along the ditch was different to the last time Marcus had seen it, studded with arrows sunk deep into the mud wall and the ground behind it where the Thracian's shots had landed short and failed to find targets. Julius set a party of men to collecting the undamaged missiles.

'We'll be needing these before the siege ends, I'd guess,' said Julius. 'They'll provide a useful back-up supply to Qadir's boys.' He suddenly found himself off balance, having stepped into a depression in the ground, and looked down to make the unwelcome discovery of a shallow latrine pit dug to provide the Britons with some relief during their long day guarding the ditch. Grimacing in disgust he lifted his boot, the sole dark with excrement. 'Well, doesn't that just sum up this whole bloody campaign? We just can't stop treading in the fucking *shit*! Get those bloody ropes over here!'

Marcus looked over the wall at the enemy ramp, whose tongue was now less than ten paces from the ditch's steep western face.

'They'll be back in strength at first light, once their archers can see to shoot back at anyone brave enough to take potshots at them from the walls.' Martos had stepped up alongside him, his one good eye shining in the moonlight as he spoke softly in his friend's ear. 'The ramp's close enough already, I'd say. If it were me I'd flog my slaves to one last effort and make the end twice as wide as it is now, with enough space for three or four heavy planks. That way they can come at us in numbers, with their wild men up front, burning mad and with the promise of enough gold to live on for the rest of their days if they breach the wall. Ninety-nine men out of the first hundred across will die, of course, but they'll carve a foothold out on this side by sheer weight of numbers, and all the time their archers will be showering us with arrows from either side . . .' The Votadini nobleman stopped talking, looking at Marcus knowingly. 'What is it? What's crossed your mind now?'

'Something you just said. Wait here, and gather a score of your men ready for a fight, if you're ready for a little excitement.'

The Votadini prince tapped his eyepatch as he turned away to his men.

'I was born ready, Centurion.'

Marcus walked across to Julius, pulling a face at the revolting smell emanating from his friend's dirty boot. The first spear turned to meet him, his face hardening at the Roman's expression.

'And *you* can fuck right off too. I've already had Dubnus enquiring whether I'm looking for a job as a legion bathhouse cleaner.'

Marcus shook his head with a smile, and quickly laid out his idea. He'd not finished explaining the potential to undo the Sarmatae plans when Julius nodded vigorously.

'It works for me. You, Soldier Lumpyface, or whatever your name is, go and find the tribune and ask him to come and join us here. And we haven't got all fucking night, so *move!*'

The man in question scurried away with a muttered comment to his mates that the first spear's smell had finally caught up with his nickname, which Julius half heard and completely ignored mainly because he was sending other soldiers along the line to gather the cohorts' officers. Scaurus appeared out of the darkness a moment later, his gloomy expression momentarily lightened when he caught wind of Julius's distinctive new odour.

'My word, First Spear, but that really is a *most* aromatic perfume you're using these days. At least it'll make finding you in the dark easy enough.'

His subordinate smiled thinly, and laid out Marcus's proposal.

'But we'll need some gear out of the fort, and quickly too, before the chance is gone. If I send a man in to ask for what we'll need he'll just get told to piss off by the duty centurion on the grounds it all sounds like too much trouble, whereas you, Tribune . . .'

'Whereas I'm somewhat less likely to find myself holding the dirty end of the vine stick? Very well . . .' He turned away for the fort, shooting a parting comment over his shoulder. 'And that said, perhaps you could use *your* vine stick to scrape off some of the offensive material that's clinging to your boots?'

He was back within a few minutes, accompanied by two soldiers carrying the materials required. In his absence the centurions had watched as Martos and a dozen of his men roped down the ditch's steep western slope to the bottom of the trench, still strewn with ash and the remains of the burned bodies left there from the previous night's conflagration. They had climbed swiftly up the ramp's steep sides until they stood atop the earthwork, squatting low to avoid revealing their presence to any enemy scouts left to watch the deserted battlefield. The Tungrians manhandled the first of the heavy wooden planks that Scaurus had fetched from the fort across the gap, watching anxiously as the Votadini pulled it into place against the ramp's brow. Martos walked carefully down the bridge's gentle slope until he was standing three feet from the turf wall, experimentally testing the plank with his weight as he came across. He called out to Julius in a soft voice, holding up a single finger.

'One man at a time, I suggest, and definitely none of those monsters in your Tenth Century!'

Julius moved to step onto the bridge, but the tribune put a hand on his shoulder.

'Not you. I need you here to take command if anything happens to *me* over there.'

The first spear frowned in disapproval, gesturing Marcus to join them.

'I'm not allowed across, so you're going to have to take responsibility for keeping the tribune here alive. Have Martos set up a perimeter. If any of those bodies are still breathing then I want them killed, quickly and quietly, be they Sarmatae, slave or even Roman.' He turned a challenging look on his superior. 'I assume you can live with that, Tribune?'

Scaurus nodded slowly, turning back to the plank bridge, and behind his back Julius shot a meaningful glance at Marcus, muttering in his brother officer's ear.

'The *first* sign of any move by the enemy and I want him back across that plank and behind the wall, you hear me? I won't go down in this cohort's history as the man who allowed his tribune to get himself killed just because the man felt a bit guilty about some dead slaves.'

He signalled for the soldiers he had picked to carry out their orders, and the nimblest of them went across the bridge quickly and quietly, carrying the end of another plank to double the width of the crossing. Marcus stepped out onto the impromptu bridge, pacing tentatively forward as the plank beneath his feet sagged gently under his weight, but reached the far side of the gap safely enough. The ground before him was dark in the absence of any moonlight, and he was forced to call for the barbarian prince in a loud whisper.

'*Martos!*'

A darkly amused voice in his ear made him jump.

'There's no need for you to shout, Centurion. It seems I see better with one eye than you do with two?'

Resisting the urge to make an acerbic reply, Marcus pointed out into the darkness.

'We need to guard the soldiers while they do as much damage to the ramp as they can before the Sarmatae realise what we're doing. Have your men spread out and form a perimeter thirty paces around us. Anyone they find still alive as they move forward is to be killed, without any noise. And Martos, if I fall out here, your *only* priority is to get the tribune back across the bridge, you understand?'

The prince nodded and gathered his men about him. With his whispered orders given, he gestured them forward with a finger ostentatiously held across his lips. Turning back to the plank bridge, Marcus saw Scaurus kneeling next to a prostrate body, and paced back to his side with his gladius drawn. Behind him the Tungrian working party were labouring frantically at the ramp sides with their borrowed spades, shovelling the soil and small rocks that had been deposited during the previous day down into the ditch to either side while leaving a slim finger of ground connected to their bridging point as they toiled to lower the earthwork round it as quickly as they could.

'This poor man never had a chance.'

Marcus followed the tribune's pointing hand to an arrow buried deeply in the slave's chest, a wound from which the only possible outcome was a slow and painful death. The dying man gazed up at him in wonder, his lips moving as he muttered something in a language neither man spoke. Raising his dagger, Scaurus slid the weapon's point into the man's chest between his ribs, thrusting it cleanly through his heart and killing him instantly. He withdrew the blade, holding it up to look at the blood's black stain on the blade.

'I swear I'll help as many of these poor souls to find peace as I can in whatever time we have. I suggest you do the same?'

Marcus turned away and stared out into the night again, still detecting no sign that their desperate venture had been discovered. He paced forward looking for Martos, crouching low to avoid silhouetting himself against any light from the fort, and was still searching the darkness before him for any sign of his friend when a hand gripped his ankle. Spinning round, he cocked his wrist to put the spatha's pale blade through whoever it was that had touched him when a harsh whisper stayed his hand, the words haltingly slow as the man on the ground before him fought for every breath.

'*Help me . . .*'

The prostrate Roman's eyes snapped wide with the pain as he rolled onto his back. The smell of his perforated intestines was strong in the night air, and Marcus looked down at him with pity, knowing that without the mercy of a sword stroke he could live for days in agony. The man croaked out a single word, his voice raw with pain.

'*We . . . are all . . . dead.*'

The young centurion shook his head in despair.

'We?'

'*Wife . . . dead. Killed . . . yesterday. Daughter . . . raped.*' The veteran soldier sobbed, lost in his pain and sorrow, and a tear ran down his cheek. '*Sons . . . here . . . somewhere.*' He fumbled at his neck, pulling hard on a thin cord to drag a pendant from his throat. '*Take it . . . return . . . to Our Lord.*' Marcus nodded down at him, numb with dismay, and closed his hand over the metal disc. The doomed man gripped his fist tightly, his hold strong despite the pain tearing at him. '*Centurion . . . beseech you . . . revenge . . .*' He hunched over the arrow again as a fresh spasm of pain drove through him, pulling up his sleeve to display a legion tattoo. '*For a soldier . . .*'

The Roman pulled his hand free as gently as he was able, then patted the convulsing man's shoulder.

'Go in peace, brother. I will send you across the river.'

He pushed the sword's point up into the dying man's chin, and deep into his head, watching as the veteran's eyes rolled up and death claimed him. Pulling a copper coin from his belt purse he slipped it into the man's mouth, pushing it in as far as he could against the probable theft were it discovered, then turned back to his search for Martos only to find the prince waiting patiently for him.

'I fear you lack enough coins of any denomination to cope with this.'

He gestured with a hand at the ground around them, and as the moon slid out from behind the clouds that had masked it both the soldiers and Martos's barbarians froze into immobility, knowing that any movement might betray their positions. While the scene revealed by the pale light was no worse than any battlefield the Roman had witnessed, his heart fell as he realised the sheer horrifying variety in the hundreds of dead and dying bodies strewn across the snow beyond the ramp's earth surface, their blood tracing dark, evil patterns across the white expanse in extravagant gouts and delicate sprinkles depending on their wounds. The moonlight faded as another cloud scudded into place, and Martos's men resumed the grisly task of executing Julius's orders to leave no-one alive inside their perimeter.

'There isn't the time to give all of these people the mercy of our swords. I suggest you concentrate on destroying that earthwork?'

Realising the truth in the Votadini's words Marcus paced back to the ramp, finding Scaurus on his knees beside another wounded slave. The soldiers labouring at the task of deconstructing the earthwork had carved great chunks out of its flanks but were clearly starting to tire, their movements becoming slow and arduous. Ignoring his grief-stricken superior for a moment he walked carefully over the planks, saluting Julius and pointing back out across the ditch.

'The men we sent over are exhausted. We'll need to change them for fresh workers.'

Julius nodded and gave the order for replacement soldiers to cross the gap, both men watching as the worn-out men made their weary way back across the bridge. As the new work party set about the ramp Marcus grimaced at his superior officer.

'This quiet can't hold much longer. Once the Sarmatae have done with licking their wounds they'll be back, and it won't take them long to realise what we're up to. I'm going to send the tribune back now, whether he likes it or not.'

Julius tilted his head in question, his lips pursed.

'And what if he won't come with you? You can't just carry him back over.'

Marcus nodded grimly.

'I think he'll see sense. I'm going to give him something to care about more than his despair at what he's done here. But just in case more desperate measures are called for, where's Arminius?'

He stepped across the bridge with the tribune's bodyguard following behind him to find Martos waiting impatiently for him among the toiling soldiers.

'The time has come for a little haste, Centurion. The enemy are coming to reclaim their battlefield from the sound of it.'

Marcus pointed to the perimeter.

'Get all your men but one back across the bridge. Make sure the man you leave has a good pair of legs and balls the size of a horse's between them. Tell him to run for the bridge and give us the warning when they come within fifty paces of him. No sooner!' The barbarian turned away, and Marcus whispered encouragement to the digging soldiers before crouching down beside Scaurus who was still kneeling alongside the fallen slave.

'He's dead, Tribune.'

The senior officer gently placed the corpse's hand back on its chest.

'I need to seek their forgiveness, Centurion. Tell Julius he's in comm—'

'No.'

Scaurus turned his head to look at his subordinate blankly.

'You might not understand *your* position in this matter, Centurion.'

Marcus shook his head bluntly, allowing the same note of patrician aloofness he'd heard his father use on occasion to enter his voice.

'I said *no*, Tribune, and I meant it.' Scaurus opened his mouth to object, but the young centurion overrode his protest before he had the chance to speak. 'You have a greater responsibility than seeking atonement by sacrificing yourself here, however noble that death might be. You have this . . .' He pushed the veteran's pendant into the tribune's hand. Scaurus turned it over, recognising the Mithraic scene immediately. 'The man around whose neck this hung was a retired soldier, captured with his family by the Sarmatae and forced to watch them being abused, murdered and worked to death. He gave me the pendant a moment ago, before I sent him to Our Lord, and begged me to see that it is returned to a temple, and to take some measure of revenge for him.' He bent to hiss in the tribune's ear, his voice loaded with urgency. 'Tribune, you are innocent in this matter! It was Tribune Belletor who made the decision to leave Roman citizens enslaved, not you. His judgement was perverted by his need to gain a peace that would enhance his reputation and diminish yours, and it is clear to me that he has already paid the price for that self-interest.'

He waved a hand at the dead and dying slaves littering the ground around them.

'Misery and death was always the fate of these people, and all you did by calling down the arrow storm on them was to bring forward the date of their deaths, and spare them any further degradation. The man who put these people under our arrows was not *you*, Tribune, but their captor. I have accepted the duty of bringing Balodi to justice in the eyes of our god . . .' He took the pendant from his superior's palm and clenched his fist around it. 'I invite you to join me in that duty, unless you would rather stay here and give your life away? After all, you ordered me to consider my men's needs when the death of one of them unmanned me, and *I* only command a century.'

Scaurus looked down, and for a moment Marcus was certain he would decline the challenge, but Arminius spoke up from the darkness behind the centurion, his voice strong with purpose.

'And if I must, I will take you across the bridge whether you wish it or not. You will not throw yourself away over this matter, or at least not before your duty to these men is complete. If you insist on some grand gesture to the gods once this thing is over, if we survive, then I will stand as second to you, and ensure that your end is clean, but for now you must act as the warrior we know you to be.'

Scaurus stared down at the dead captive for a moment longer, but when he looked up at the two men again his eyes had regained some of the fierceness to which they were more accustomed.

'I always saw you as more gentleman than soldier, for all of your demonic skill with a blade, Centurion *Corvus*, but it seems you're a harder man than I imagined. Will *I* join *you* in the duty of avenging a dead soldier and his family? I'd call you an insubordinate young bastard and have you demoted if I didn't know why you're goading me . . .' He sighed, looking down at the dead man again. 'And I don't suppose this man's spirit is going to thank me for doing nothing to take some form of revenge for him.'

Climbing to his feet, he looked at Marcus and Arminius with fresh determination, his teeth bared in anger.

'So what would you have me do, Centurion, to make amends for this slaughter?'

The younger man pointed at the ditch, and the indistinct figures lurking behind the wall on its far side.

'Get back to your command, Tribune. Your revenge can only be taken at their head, and with a thousand swords rather than just your own.'

The Tribune nodded and turned away, walking across the plank bridge without a backward glance, and Arminius followed behind him. Marcus looked back to the open ground to see the indistinct shapes of Martos and his men picking their way through the field of corpses.

'I left the fastest of my warriors to watch out for the enemy's approach as you requested. We can hear them mustering, too far away to be seen, but they're out there.'

The Roman put a hand on the Briton's shoulder, guiding him to the bridge.

'Take your men to safety. I'll make sure your runner crosses before we drop the planks.'

He looked about him, gauging the amount of destruction the Tungrians had wrought on the Sarmatae earthwork in the little time that had been afforded to them. One of the soldiers was struggling over his shovel, and Marcus reached out to take the implement, pointing to the flimsy bridge.

'Go.'

As the grateful soldier headed for safety Marcus addressed the man's comrades, hefting the shovel ready to dig.

'We don't have long, gentlemen, before the enemy discover us. Before they do, *if* we want to see tomorrow's sunset, then we must make this ramp unusable.'

He waved a hand at the earthwork's wreckage, so badly chewed and pitted by the frantic efforts of the soldiers that the planks were now pointing up at the Tungrians' battlement, rather than running down to meet it.

'And for that to come about, we must hack away as much of this' – he pointed to the ramp's tongue, on which they were standing – 'as we can. Now we dig, as fast as possible, and when the time comes I will send you back to safety. So *dig*!'

The Tungrians set to with fresh purpose, invigorated by the sight of an officer hacking away at the compacted earth with his shovel. Looking up for a moment, Marcus found Martos at his side again, a rope in one hand and another tied about him. Martos took the shovel and pushed the Roman aside, handing him the rope's end and then taking his place among the soldiers, plying the implement with powerful strokes, chopping into the earth and flinging the resulting clods of earth into the ditch below as fast as he could.

'Tie the rope about you, and make it tight!'

The last remaining Votadini warrior ran out of the darkness, gesturing back the way he had come, and Marcus turned to his men with the rope knotted tightly about his chest, taking a shovel from the closest of them.

'Go! Get across the bridge now!'

They bolted, shaking the planks so badly in their haste that one of the boards overturned, pitching two of the Tungrians into the filthy ash residue in the ditch's bottom. Ropes were thrown down to them, but Marcus had no time to see if their rescue would be successful. Martos turned to the other plank, pushing at it with his booted foot to sending it spinning down into the ditch's gloom. He pointed at the ramp's end.

'You and I, Centurion!'

Nodding his understanding Marcus set to with his shovel again, the two men digging out chunks of the ramp's forward edge and tossing them into the ditch with the furious energy of men possessed, bending to stay out of sight of the barbarian warriors approaching out of the gloom to the west. Sliding down onto the ramp's steep side they concentrated their efforts on the tongue itself, working frantically to cast as much of it as possible into the darkness below. Straightening his back to stretch out arms made heavy by fatigue, Marcus looked round to find familiar faces behind the turf wall, and saw bows being raised to shoot. A warrior suddenly loomed over him at the ramp's edge, his mouth open with the shock of finding the Roman beneath his feet, but as the Sarmatae opened his mouth to call out a warning he was struck by first one arrow and then two more, pitching forward into the ditch over Marcus's shoulder without making a sound.

Carving out another chunk of compacted soil, Marcus dropped it into the darkness, and another, ignoring the threat of attack in his haste to do as much damage as he could to the ramp. A hand touched his shoulder, and he looked at Martos to see that the Votadini had a finger to his lips. He pointed downwards, then slid away down the earthwork's side and into the ditch's deep shadow, and the Roman followed suit, holding onto his shovel and using it to break his descent into the darkness. He landed on the ditch's floor, feeling his boots sink into the detritus of snow, ash and the rancid smelling sticky paste left by so many burning bodies. He whispered to Martos, wrinkling his nose at the smell that permeated the air around them despite the night's frigid air.

'It's a good thing it's so cold. On a warmer day this place would smell like the entrance to Hades.'

Martos pointed upwards.

'And up there, well that may well be Hades itself.'

Above them men were shouting, more voices than Marcus could distinguish, and they could see the flickers of arrows being exchanged between the two sides. He looked at Martos with a wry smile.

'Qadir and his archers will present the Sarmatae with a nasty shock, given the tribesmen have nothing to hide behind out there.'

As they looked upwards a face peered down at them from over the wall, and an arm pointed down the ditch to the west. Untying the ropes fastened about them they quietly slipped down the trench in the direction indicated for fifty paces or so, until they came across two more hanging ropes, their ends already fashioned into loops that would fit over their heads and arms to nestle snugly under their armpits. Another face appeared, familiar bearded features under a centurion's helmet, and Marcus shared a quick glance with Martos as both men simultaneously realised what was about to happen. With a terrific jerk they were hauled bodily into the air, their bodies flying up the ditch's steep face too fast for either of them to have any hope of controlling their ascent. The Roman found himself scrabbling at the turf wall as he was hauled bodily over it, then crashed heavily onto the ground on the other side. He looked up to see Titus, the hulking centurion of the Tenth Century, looming over him. The giant was grinning down at him, and two tent parties of his men were standing behind him with the ropes lying at their feet. Julius stood next to the big man, a full head shorter than his officer despite his own hefty frame. Getting his breath back Marcus nodded his gratitude to his brother officer.

'Thank you, Titus. It was an unconventional return to the cohort, but welcome nonetheless.'

'At your service, little brother. A tiddler like you is never a problem for my lads. Mind you, you might want to go and find some water . . .' His nose wrinkled. 'The smell from your feet is worse than that being given off by our own beloved first spear, if that's possible.'

'Well it's about bloody time. I lost all contact with my feet hours ago.'

Marcus looked up at Morban's words to see that the fort's gates had opened to allow the Britons to march out into a grey dawn. He turned back and looked out over the ditch at the Sarmatae mustering outside the range of Qadir's bows. The Hamians' accurate shooting had clearly discouraged any attempt to rebuild the ramp by moonlight, but now that day was breaking he knew the enemy archers would shower missiles onto both wall and fort in order to allow the workers forward with their buckets of soil.

'They'll finish that ramp today, no matter what they have to throw at it.'

His deputy stamped down the century's line with a curse at his frozen feet.

'Shall I get the men ready to move, Centurion?'

Marcus nodded his assent, watching as the stocky chosen man made his way down the ditch's line, shouting commands to his men and readying them to pull out of the position. Tribune Leontius came forward with his men, looking out over the ditch's earth wall at the ramp and smiling happily at the state of the earthwork.

'Well done, Tungrians, that's put a knot in their cocks. It'll take them a good long time to get that rebuilt and ready for an attack. And now, if you don't mind, we'll reclaim this rather desirable property back from you. There's hot food waiting for you in your barracks.'

The soldiers formed up and marched away from the wall without a second glance. With his men back in their barracks, and for the most part asleep as soon as they had consumed the meal that had been prepared for them, Marcus made a swift visit to the hospital to see his wife, who took one look at his exhausted face and sent him away to his bed. Awakened seemingly only minutes later by a heavy knocking, he opened the door to find Julius waiting for him.

'What time is it?'

The first spear hooked a thumb over his shoulder.

'Mid-afternoon. The Sarmatae are only an hour or so from completing their ramp, so Leontius and the tribune have agreed to bring our boys forward and make a stand beside the Britons. Tell Quintus to wake your men and warm them up ready to fight, then join me on the fort wall. The tribune wants us to have a look at the field of battle from an elevated position before we take up our positions.'

When the young Roman reached the walls he found Julius and Scaurus watching the enemy in silence. The duel between the barbarian archers and the Thracians was continuing in a desultory manner, although most of the enemy's attention was now focused on keeping the Britons' heads down, as the ramp inched closer to their wall. Looking along the wall's length Marcus realised that the bolt throwers were no longer sending their heavy missiles into the mass of slaves toiling at the earthwork.

'It seems that the remaining torsion bars have broken. Leontius was here a few minutes ago muttering something about dealing with a certain legion artillery officer, not that he'll ever get the chance.' The tribune fell silent, staring pensively out at the mass of humanity being driven forward behind the enemy archers. 'All of that murder last night . . . and we might as well not have bothered. There are thousands of them.'

Julius nodded.

'This Purta must have scoured the entire plain for every slave he could buy or take. No wonder he was happy to spend his labour so cheaply yesterday if he had this lot in reserve to throw at us. Obviously he came prepared.' He turned to Scaurus, straightening his back and saluting. 'The cohorts will be ready for action soon enough, Tribune. I suggest we parade them outside the barracks and get ready to sell ourselves as expensively as we can. It's been a pleasure serving with you, sir, and . . .'

His eyes narrowed as a distant trumpet sounded from the west, beyond the barbarians, answered a moment later by another which seemed to come from the hills to the east. Scaurus leant forward over the wall's parapet, ignoring the risk of a Sarmatae arrow to stare out over the enemy host.

'That sounded like one of ours . . .'

Leontius hurried up the steps behind them, pulling on his helmet and joining Scaurus at the parapet with a look of disbelief. The horns sounded again, and as they looked out over the corpse-strewn battlefield Julius gestured at a point beyond the enemy host.

'My eyes may be deceiving me, but those *look* like ours . . .'

Staring out across the Sarmatae host, Marcus found what Julius was indicating, a line of armoured men made tiny by the distance.

'They're not advancing.'

Leontius snorted in dark amusement.

'Nor would you be, Centurion, if you came round that corner and found yourself face-to-face with that many barbarian horsemen. I'd imagine that they're working like madmen to get their stakes in the ground, while their officers frantically try to decide whether they should attack, defend or just make a run for it and pretend that they were never here.'

Julius glanced at him with an amused look, then turned to Marcus.

'Your eyes are sharper than mine, Centurion. What emblem can you see on their banners?'

The Roman stared out at the legion's rapidly forming line.

'A lion, First Spear.'

The burly senior centurion turned back to Leontius with a smirk.

'In which case, I think you can stop worrying about those lads turning tail, that's the Thirteenth Gemina out there. First Spear Secundus won't be countenancing anything of the sort.'

'Excellent work, Gaius! Young Leontius will go back to Rome with a ringing commendation, and doubtless a quick step up the ladder for stopping the Sarmatae for long enough that we could bottle them up. He was decent enough to brief me properly as to what your men did last night, and from what I've heard you clearly played a key part in this whole thing.'

Legatus Albinus had ridden into the fort from the east just before dark at the head of two cohorts of legionaries, ending any lingering risk that the Sarmatae might attempt one last all-out drive to cross the ditch and escape the trap in which they were caught. He and Scaurus were alone in the fort's headquarters while Leontius assisted the Fifth Macedonica's broad stripe tribune in bringing his men forward through the fort to hold the obstacle overnight. Scaurus shook his head disparagingly at his mentor's praise.

'We were in the right place at the right time, Legatus, that's all it was. Tribune Leontius is the man who made this fort ready to repel any attack up the valley, which is more than many of his colleagues might have done.'

Albinus smiled knowingly.

'Understood, young man. But I'll make sure your part in this is recognised, one way or another. You're too good an officer to be left running an auxiliary cohort for much longer.'

'Thank you, sir. And as for our enemy?'

The legatus smiled broadly.

'Once Leontius's dispatch alerted us to the fact that we'd been fed misleading intelligence, Pescennius Niger and I agreed that our only course of action was to advance through the mountains, and come at the enemy from the rear, using Stone Fort as the anvil for our hammer.' He paused, raising his eyebrows at the tribune. '*Tremendously* risky, of course. What if we'd got here and found that the Sarmatae had already smashed through you, and were rampaging off into the province, eh? That's the kind of outcome that has a man falling on his own sword, so I really can't imagine what can have possessed my colleague to accept such a hasty course of action, although I suspect his first spear might have played a large part in overcoming his natural caution. He is a rather fearsome individual once his temper's aroused, and since he'd been urging caution as to how much of the intelligence from within the Sarmatae camp we believed, he was practically ablaze when we discovered the truth.'

He grinned triumphantly at Scaurus, waving a hand in the air in the manner of a man accepting the plaudits of a grateful people.

'But it seems to have worked out rather well, all things considered. The only ways out of this valley other than through this fort are the two valleys that combine to the west of here, and we have them both blocked by large forces of infantry behind nice strong turf walls and with plenty of wooden stakes set up to prevent any foolishness by the enemy's horsemen. There are auxiliary cohorts dug in on the high ground on all sides with archer and bolt-thrower support, so if the enemy do try to make a run for it over the hills we'll chop them to ribbons. And if they try to renew their attack on Stone Fort then we'll just swing the hammer and smash them against your walls. We have the Sarmatae hemmed in, Gaius, and Purta's balls in the palm of our hand, which will make the agreement of terms that favour Rome's interests relatively simple if he doesn't want to find his head on a sharpened stick.'

Scaurus raised an eyebrow.

'You'll make peace with him, after what he's done here, Legatus?'

Albinus smiled beneficently back at him.

'Oh yes, I have explicit orders from the provincial governor, and more than likely from the emperor above him. It's not in Rome's interests to slaughter these people, Tribune, because if we do we'll just end up with the next generation of the little bastards champing at the bit to come and get their revenge. Whereas if we make peace and then police it strongly enough they'll just have to get on with their lives, a good part of which will consist of buying as many of our luxuries as they can afford. They'll pay with gold, and horses, and whatever crop they can spare, and I need hardly remind you that the empire stands in dire need of all three of those commodities. On top of which, they'll make an effective buffer against barbarians from further north, whereas if we liquidate them we'll have to start afresh with whoever moves in to claim their tribal lands. And Mithras knows that every bloody barbarian starts out thinking he can push his way into Rome if he kicks at the door with enough force. The governor believes it's better to deal with people who've already learned their lesson the hard way, at the hands of men like you and I, and who's to say he's wrong? So yes, we'll negotiate a peace treaty with Purta and send him on his way, with the appropriate hostages taken, of course.'

'And the gold that my idiot colleague Belletor saw fit to bestow upon Balodi? It's fairly clear that he cemented his usurped position as king by making an offering of the coin to Purta in return for his backing.'

Albinus shook his head, making the warding sign at the mention of the dead tribune's name.

'Domitius Belletor doesn't seem to have been much of a judge of men, does he? May the gods preserve us both from a misjudgement of *that* order. If what you say is true, then Purta can buy his release from the trap we have him in with gold as well as the lives of his children. A day or two watching our soldiers fortify the hills around his camp ought to provide him with a decent enough incentive.'

The two legati met Purta on the far side of a newly constructed bridge over the fort's western ditch, inside the hollow square of the Thirteenth Legion's five thousand men, whose first spear oversaw proceedings with a sharp eye and a sharper tongue. The auxiliary cohorts that had defended the fort lined the ditch that had seen so much bloodshed, their shields four ranks deep behind the earth wall in a deliberately impressive show of strength. The legion's centurions served as the senior officers' honour guard, a circle of sixty hard, forbidding faces into which Purta and his fellow nobles walked with their swords held out in both hands, as instructed. Clodius Albinus waited in silence as the king and his men presented their weapons to the legion's first spear, who subjected them to a careful inspection in order to confirm that they were of sufficient quality to count as the first peace offerings. With the enemy leaders disarmed, Albinus stepped forward to face the defeated Sarmatae ruler. He looked the king up and down with a grim stare before speaking.

'This is not a *negotiation*, King Purta, and the terms I am about to impose upon you are not a *proposal*. To put it bluntly, you have gambled and lost. You chose to chance your arm against the army of the greatest empire the world has ever seen, and you have failed. You can either have peace, on our terms, or you can return to your people and tell them to arm themselves for a short and brutal fight. Our archers and bolt throwers will rain sharp iron into you from all sides, and when we judge the time is right we will send our legionaries forward to grind out any last vestiges of resistance. Then, when we've inevitably won that fight, given we have your exits barred and men on the high ground to all sides, your people will be enslaved. Not just these men here, but your entire nation. I am ordered by the emperor either to make peace, here, now and on Rome's terms, or to empty your lands of every man, woman and child in order to enable the settlement of more *amenable* neighbours. If you make it necessary I will simply erase your tribe from history and repopulate your land.'

He raised a piece of paper.

'The terms the emperor offers you are these. Firstly, you will return the gold which was recently paid to your servant Balodi as a sign of good faith. Any of the gold which has been dispersed will be replaced from your own treasury. Any shortfall thereafter will be recompensed to the empire in the form of slaves, each of whom will be reckoned in at half the market rate to account for the likely oversupply and consequent fall in their sale price.

'Secondly, you will provide Rome with a further five thousand horsemen for service on the empire's borders. Thirdly, you will present your own children and those of your nobles to act as hostages. They will be raised in Rome, trained to be model Roman citizens, and their safety will be the reward you will earn for your compliance with the terms of this treaty. We will return them when they are ready to rule in your places, at which point you will abdicate in their favour. Fourthly, you will submit to frequent and robust policing of these terms by our legions, which will be free to march across your lands without hindrance. Any gathering of more than one hundred men will be conducted under the control of Roman officers, and any such gathering which is un-supervised will be considered as an act of war. And lastly, you will free every Roman citizen currently enslaved by your people immediately. And let me warn you, Purta, that if in the course of policing this treaty our officers discover any evidence of continued enslavement of even a single Roman citizen, they will be author-ised to burn the settlement in question to the ground, and to enslave every man, woman and child they can lay their hands on.'

He looked the Sarmatae king up and down with a look of disdain.

'You have no choice in the matter of these demands other than whether to submit to them peacefully or at the point of a spear with your own shipment to Rome for public execution a conse-quent inevitability. Decide now.'

Purta bowed his head briefly in submission.

'I will comply with these terms.'

Albinus nodded tersely, passing the paper to his clerk.

'Wise, Purta, given that you have no real choice. Be very clear though, that this peace will be policed by men like these.' Albinus waved an arm at the centurions arrayed about them. 'Rome will have peace on its own terms, with routine patrols across your lands to ensure that no further stupidity of the sort we've seen here is allowed to take root. You will be king, but your position will be underwritten and controlled by Roman arms, and you will be subject to very close scrutiny.'

Purta nodded again, his face set in impassive lines. Albinus gestured to the surviving nobles from Balodi's tribe, huddled under the Tungrians' spears on the far side of the bridge.

'These men, however, do *not* come under the terms of this agreement. Their former king made a formal agreement to remove them from the war and to return to his homeland, a pledge that was agreed by all of his nobles but then repudiated by his father's brother when he murdered Galatas. The king's murderer was then foolish enough to bring them to your side in defiance of this agreement, and he has therefore doomed them all to slavery, without exception. They will carry out whatever labour Rome sees fit for them for the rest of their lives, and will content themselves that the alternative was a slow and bloody execution. I intend to sell them into the service of Rome's mines in the valley of the Ravenstone. They can spend the rest of their miserable lives tearing gold from the mountains in the service of the empire, and providing her with the treasure she needs to remain strong in the face of threats like these. They will all march south to the mine under guard, with one exception, and none of them will ever be freed to return to their homes. This is the price that must be paid by every man who reneges on an agreement with Rome. One man, however, has committed crimes too great for me to ignore, or to punish with simple servitude. Bring him forward!'

He stared into Balodi's face with an expression of contempt as the king was forced to his knees at the edge of the circle of centurions.

'This man agreed a treaty with Rome without ever intending to honour either its terms or its spirit. He enslaved hundreds of Roman citizens, and therefore presided over their degradation and murder, and it gives me great pleasure to order his execution here and now, as a salutary lesson for you all. Tribune?'

He gestured to Scaurus, who nodded to Julius. The first spear turned to Marcus, extending a hand to point at Balodi.

'Centurion, exact the justice you promised the veteran, a slow and painful death to match his family's agony.'

Only Marcus and Balodi heard the first spear's muttered command, and the tribal leader staggered on legs suddenly gone weak as Marcus lifted him by the collar of his rough tunic and pushed him forward into the ring of men. Albinus gestured to the Sarmatae chieftain with a look of scorn.

'Let this serve as an example to you, Purta, of the treatment you can expect if you make the mistake of repaying Rome's generous lenience in this matter with anything other than the greatest respect. Centurion?'

Marcus put a boot into the back of Balodi's knees and forced him to the ground in a kneeling position. Reaching into a pouch on his belt he pulled out a small object wrapped in rags, carefully allowing the protective cloth to fall away and reveal what it was he held. Albinus was speaking again, pacing towards the kneeling king but aiming his words at an ashen-faced Purta.

'This man not only bit the empire's beneficent hand, in spite of the generous terms that he was offered to put an end to his tribe's attempts at capturing the Ravenstone valley mines, he was also responsible for a crime against the Roman people. Having promised that he would ensure the release of the Roman citizens he held as slaves, he then forced them into the forefront of the attack on this place. You are *both* responsible for the deaths of innocent men, women and children who had a right to imperial protection, and it is in their name that we now punish him. Be grateful that I don't have you share his fate, and be assured that if you ever attempt to rise against Rome in the future, the justice you are about to see delivered to this man will surely be visited upon you.' His gaze swept the men standing around the king, their eyes fixed on Balodi as he knelt before them. 'Upon all of you, and your families.'

Marcus held the small object he had taken from his pouch aloft and then put it under Balodi's nose, nodding grimly as the helpless man pulled his head away from its pungent stench. Albinus smiled at the prisoner's horrified expression, waving a dismissive hand at him.

'I would have preferred to provide the shades of this man's departed victims with the compensation of their murderer suffering a rather more protracted punishment. Scourging, crucifixion and eventual dismemberment are the empire's prescribed means of executing men such as this, but I am persuaded that this alternative means of retribution is suitably fitting in this man's case.'

He gestured to Marcus, who took out the veteran's pendant and wiped it carefully down the blade of the poisoned arrowhead he had pulled from his shield weeks before, staining the metal with its yellow-green coating of poison. Jerking Balodi's head back, he pushed the metal disc into his mouth and then wrapped a hand over the tribal leader's lips to prevent him from spitting it out. Julius stepped forward and put his boot into Balodi's stomach hard enough to double the Sarmatae over, and both men watched as he writhed with the pain of the kick. Staring up at the centurions, his eyes widened as he realised that the metal disc was no longer in his mouth, and Marcus nodded down at him with a look of grim satisfaction. Albinus walked across to the stricken nobleman, looking down impassively as Balodi's eyes opened wide with the realisation of his doom.

'My officers tell me that while even a small dose of this poison administered via a cut to the skin will kill a man quickly, ingestion is rumoured to be a good deal slower and more painful.' Albinus turned back to Purta, whose face was now even whiter than before. 'The victim, they tell me, soils himself. He struggles to breathe, and he is afflicted with severe pains in the stomach as the poison works on his organs. It will take Balodi hours to die, time during which he will be guarded by my men here in order to prevent any attempt to end his life in a more merciful manner. And if by some chance he manages to survive this dose of his own men's poison, the process will simply be repeated. Let this be a warning to you all.'

9

Legatus Albinus rose and came round his desk when Scaurus, Julius and Marcus were admitted to his office, shaking his head in apology at having summoned them so late in the evening. After the ceremonious surrender of the Sarmatae nobles, the process of disarming their men had begun, although it was expected to take two or three more days to march every one of them past the growing pile of their surrendered weapons. Cattanius was standing to one side and snapped to attention, saluting the tribune with his usual precision while his legatus launched into an explanation for his untimely summons.

'I'm sorry, Rutilius Scaurus, to have dragged you away from your tent after such a long day, but news of a most alarming nature has been delivered to me by my man Cattanius here. It seems that the mine at Alburnus Major has been taken by bandits.'

Scaurus exchanged glances with his centurions, shaking his head in disbelief.

'I find that rather hard to believe, Legatus. When we left it, the mining facility was secure and under the guard of over a thousand men. I can't see why Prefect Gerwulf would have had any problem in defending . . .'

He fell silent under Albinus's stare. The legatus gestured for Cattanius to speak, and the beneficiarius stepped forward to explain.

'The legatus sent me to Alburnus Major along with a century of legionaries to procure sufficient gold from the procurator to pay the soldiers. When I reached the valley, however, I found the gates to the earth wall you built for its defence closed, and manned by Prefect Gerwulf's soldiers. When I demanded for the gate to be opened they just laughed at me. After a while Gerwulf himself appeared on the wall above me, with Procurator Maximus and the mine owners in shackles alongside him. He told me that he'd decided that when it came to a choice between serving Rome and making off with enough gold to buy an army of his own, the decision was an easy one. It seems that he has turned against the empire, Tribune, an impression I must say was somewhat re-inforced when he cut Procurator Maximus's throat and threw him off the wall to land at my feet. I decided that this was enough of a threat to justify ordering my escort back down the road to Apulum. Once I considered it safe to do so I had their centurion wait in the shelter of the forest beside the road, while I went for a quiet scout over the hills towards the mine.'

Scaurus raised an eyebrow, sharing a glance with Albinus who nodded smugly in reply.

'What did you expect, Gaius? I didn't make the man my beneficiarius just because he had his numbers and letters you know! Tell the tribune what it was that you saw, Cattanius.'

'I went over the mountain that night, and hid on the slopes close to the miners' quarters. From what I saw the Germans are still sleeping in their own barracks, and using no more than a century of men to patrol the camp once they've got the miners locked down. They don't bring the rest of the cohort out to play until it's time for the day's labour to begin again.'

'I don't suppose they need much of a presence during the night, given that they've probably worked the labourers half to death during the day. What about Gerwulf?'

'The Wolf seems to have requisitioned the woman's house, and most likely her body too. I saw him leave the place the next morning, and he was looking about as smug as you can imagine.'

Scaurus nodded grimly.

'No wonder. He's putting one over on the empire on a monu-mental scale, isn't he? The signs were there to be seen, gentlemen, but they were lost in the enmity between myself and my colleague Belletor. If the man was willing to slaughter an entire village simply to provide his men with sport then I have no doubt he's capable of murder in support of a robbery on such an epic scale.' He turned to Albinus with a note of urgency in his voice. 'I presume you plan to send a relief force to the valley at once, Legatus? Procurator Maximus's strongroom held enough gold to mint well over a hundred thousand aureii, and every day that passes will see enough for another three thousand unearthed from the mountains. And that's before we give any thought to the mineworkers, who are probably being worked to death to wring out every last speck of gold before Gerwulf quits the valley and makes a run for the north. Every day we delay will deepen the damage that he'll do to the mine's ability to generate wealth, never mind what he makes off with.'

The legatus shook his head with a scowl, waving a hand about him.

'What I didn't tell you earlier is that we don't have quite the strength to hand that we've led King Purta to believe. Put bluntly Gaius, there's no way any of the forces whose threat is keeping the Sarmatae in their camp can be spared. Our two under-strength legions and the auxiliaries supporting them are fifteen thousand men, and we have our boot on the throat of an enemy with getting on for twice that strength. While we give every indication of being in control of the situation, and of having as much time as is necessary for a managed process of disarming and dispersing the Sarmatae host, in truth it's something of a confidence trick. We keep the barbarians subdued by perpetuating their belief that they are in the presence of overwhelming strength, but if we send even part of a legion away to the south to recapture the Ravenstone valley then there is every chance that they might realise how weak we really are. Purta might decide to take the risk of attempting to smash a way out to his own land through one of the valleys to the north, if he knew that there were only a few cohorts in his path. So, until we have them fully disarmed and dispersed I simply cannot take the risk of putting the entire frontier in jeopardy, which means that I can afford no more than your two Tungrian cohorts. And you'll have to march before daybreak, in the hope that your departure will go unnoticed.'

Scaurus straightened his weary back.

'You wish me to recapture the mine, Legatus?'

Albinus smiled indulgently.

'Ever dutiful, eh Gaius? No, Tribune, I do not expect you to pull off any such masterstroke, although Mithras knows that if you did it would be good for all of our reputations. I do expect you to keep the Germans bottled up though, and give me enough time to disperse these Sarmatae animals back to their homelands. I'll follow you down the road to Alburnus Major quickly enough, once I'm assured that they can't simply turn around and come back for another try, and in the meantime all you have to do is patrol their perimeter and keep them from escaping. Think you can manage that?'

Julius opened his mouth to make a comment, but before the words were formed Scaurus had his fist against the bronze of his chest plate and then extended in a vigorous salute.

'Yes Legatus, we'll make sure that the emperor's gold stays where it is until you reach the mine. I'll go and muster my men to march.'

The three men were silent until they were outside the command building. Scaurus turned to face his officers before either of them had a chance to speak, the breath steaming from his lips as he spoke in low, urgent tones.

'I *know*. The men are exhausted, we've over a hundred men wounded, and we've no more chance of keeping Gerwulf "bottled up" than we have of taking the mine in the teeth of any sort of determined defence. Believe me, I know all these things. And so, if truth be told, does Clodius Albinus. The problem is that he has to be seen to do *something*. He can't ignore the problem and simply allow Gerwulf to get away with several cartloads of gold. Nor can he detach enough strength to break into the mine without giving Purta the scent of a chance to turn defeat into victory. All he can do is throw someone he can trust at the problem in the hope that we can pull off the impossible.'

Julius shook his head, his face creased in disbelief.

'And if we can't? What if Gerwulf decides to run for it at

the very first sight of a Roman uniform? He'll have his patrols out, that's sure enough. I very much doubt we could stop that many angry Germans with their tails up, given that they'll be fresh and we'll be in an even worse state than we are now after four days' forced marching. What happens when Albinus finally turns up to find the cupboard empty and us holding nothing but our dicks?'

Scaurus smiled wearily at his first spear's question.

'Well in that case, First Spear, I'd imagine you'll be under the command of a new tribune soon enough. Clodius Albinus knows the realities of life as well as I do. And when he has me stripped of my command and sent home to Rome in disgrace there'll be nothing personal in it. It's just the way the empire works. Now if you'll excuse me for a moment . . .'

He ushered Cattanius out of earshot as the beneficiarius left Albinus's office.

'Tell me soldier, what state were the mine owners in when Gerwulf had them paraded before you on the earth wall?'

The beneficiarius shrugged.

'Pretty much as you'd expect, Tribune. They looked as if they'd been through a hard time over the previous few days. Both Felix and Lartius had clearly taken beatings, and Theodora didn't look very much happier even if she was relatively unmarked.'

Scaurus frowned.

'Unmarked? She'd not been beaten?'

'Not from the look of it, although I'd say that she's probably been suffering in slightly less violent ways. It's hard to put a finger on exactly what it was, but as I said earlier, Gerwulf seemed very familiar with her. I might have been mistaken . . .'

'Sexually familiar?' Cattanius hesitated to answer the question, and Scaurus smiled thinly at him. 'The woman and I shared a couple of encounters, Beneficiarius. I might have found her entertaining but I wasn't about to ask for her to marry me. Whether Gerwulf has been raping her, or even if she's just decided to surrender to the inevitable in order to get an easier time of things, either way I need to know what you think. Whatever the situation is, we may be able to gain some advantage from it once we're inside the facility.'

'If I had to bet my life on it I'd say she's decided to make it easier on herself. She didn't appear to have been beaten, and her bindings were light compared with the way he had the other two trussed up.'

Scaurus patted him on the arm.

'Thank you. Be ready to march at dawn. We'll need your detailed memory of the valley's layout should we be graced with a miracle of some nature and actually get inside.'

Marcus held his wife close, feeling her breath hot on his neck as she clung to his armoured body.

'It'll be a non-event. Gerwulf's far too clever to still be in occupation of the mine by the time we get to the gates, he'll have made a swift exit to the north with his gold long before we're close enough to present any problem.'

Felicia pushed him away and held him at arm's length.

'All I'll say to you is what I know Annia's telling Julius. You're all tired, and it'll be much worse once you've marched all the way back to that damned mine. None of you will be in any condition to fight, so just make sure you don't have to. And if that means letting that odious man escape with some gold, then so be it.' She stared up at him with a fierce expression. 'No amount of treasure reclaimed for Commodus to spend on circuses will compensate your son if he has to grow up without you!' Her face softened. 'And believe me, that was the gentle version. Annia probably has your first spear by his testicles about now, and not in a way he'd prefer.'

Marcus nodded tiredly and bent to kiss his wife goodbye, watching fondly as she ducked out through the tent's flap. Taking a moment to strap on his swords, he went to follow her, only to stop and stare in amazement at the sight that presented itself as he stepped out into the early morning's torch lit gloom.

'No!' He raised a finger to silence any protest, shaking his head vigorously. '*No!* You're not coming with us!'

He looked down at the obdurate child standing before him beside his grandfather with exasperation, while Lupus stared back up with a mixture of anger and desperation. The boy was wearing the mail coat and helmet that had been made for him in Germania, and the half-sized gladius with which he was allowed to practise on special occasions was belted to his waist. The Roman shook his head again.

'You're not coming because we've four days of forced marching in front of us, thirty miles a day when you know very well your legs won't last more than ten. We're not taking any carts, so there'll be nothing to ride on. You're not coming because at the end of that forced march we'll probably have to mount an attack on a cohort of barbarians which will turn into a bloody slaughter no matter who wins. You're not coming because I won't have the time to look after you, and because your grandfather will be too busy complaining about his feet.' Morban raised his eyebrows in protest, but kept his silence. 'And you're not coming because—'

'I carry him.'

The centurion spun on his heel to find Lugos standing close behind him with a gentle smile on his face.

'*What?*'

The Selgovae tribesman shrugged, rolling his massive shoulders and putting the head of his war hammer on the ground, leaning on its handle and bending down to speak quietly in the Roman's ear, his voice a rumble.

'You forbid, I obey. But, Centurion, you *think*. Boy got warrior spirit, we all see that. Take him with is better than leave with women. I carry him. He weigh less than you, and I carry you before, eh?'

Marcus stared up at the Briton in bemusement.

'But if we have to fight?'

'Boy safe with me.' Lugos straightened his back and folded his arms. 'Is you to decide.'

The Roman narrowed his eyes, putting his head back to stare at the Briton.

'You'll carry him? For four days, thirty miles a day?'

'I carry him.'

'Very well. We'll bring him along.'

Dubnus had joined the conversation while Marcus and Lugos were discussing the matter, and he stood with both hands on his hips as the ten-year-old wrapped himself around the giant Briton's leg with a squeal of delight.

'*What?* You're seriously planning to bring a child on a mission which is likely to end up with us and the Germans hammering the living shit out of each other?'

His friend nodded, his lips pursed in comment on his own decision.

'I know, it seems like madness. I should just leave him here with Felicia and Annia, but . . .'

'But?'

Marcus shrugged.

'I've got an idea that I want some more time to mull over before I open it up to general ridicule.'

Dubnus snorted derisively.

'Any idea that needs the services of a lad whose balls haven't dropped yet won't be getting past Julius any time soon. I can assure you that the first words out of his mouth are going to be "the first spear wouldn't have . . ."'

'I know.' Marcus shook his head. 'And this time he'll be right. Sextus Frontinius would have ripped me a new one just for considering it. I'll square it with Julius once we're on the move.'

The cohort mustered before dawn with a general atmosphere of disbelief that muted most of the potential complaints, although a few of the older sweats had still managed to find their voices despite their bone weariness. Centurions and chosen men were roaming the ranks of their men whose fatigued grey faces were near invisible in the pale light, counting and recounting to be sure that every man deemed fit to march was standing in the ranks. Equally as disgusted with the situation as their men, they were taking out their frustrations by ignoring, and in some cases exuberantly punishing, their men's inevitable questions as to the sanity of their orders.

'Cocidius knows I'm not a vindictive man . . .' Dubnus ignored the look of disbelief that was promptly focused on him by the half-dozen of Marcus's men within earshot, all of whom had felt the sting of both his ire and his fists when he had been Julius's chosen man. 'But I swear if one more man has the balls to ask me what we're doing freezing our tits off by breaking camp in the middle of the night, I'm going to follow Otho's example.'

Marcus nodded absently.

'In that case you'd better follow it closely enough to be sure not to provide any of them with an excuse to fall out.'

They had already witnessed their battered colleague's spectacular temper being exercised on more than one of his men, although even in the depths of his anger the pugilistic centurion was delivering his discipline with slaps and kicks rather than the level of brutality to which he was more inclined. Morban muttered a terse comment from the side of his mouth.

'In that case just give me one good dig now and spare yourself the trouble of having to bury me by the roadside later on.'

Both men ignored him, watching as Scaurus walked past with a nod, his face hard with determination as he spoke to them.

'We'll be on the move in a moment. It's time to go and motivate your men.'

Dubnus sighed and turned away, leaving Marcus at the mercy of his standard bearer's incredulity. Before the older man could wind himself up to speak again, the Roman shook his head with a look that warned of the danger in failing to obey his unspoken command. Looking up and down the ranks of weary, sagging soldiers arrayed before him, he smiled in the face of their collective disgust.

'Well now soldiers, here's a brutal thing to do to a man.' He waited a moment for the words to sink in, and saw their faces fall further as the realisation that they would indeed be expected to march out into the dawn sank in. 'You've marched, and fought, and marched again, and fought again, in wind, and rain, and snow. And here you are once more, faced with another march and more than likely another fight at the end of it. And you'll do it, just as you always do. And if you want to know why?'

The soldiers stared back at him with blank faces, some verging on the outright hostility he knew was only to be expected, and which he would tolerate unless and until it spilled over into action.

'You'll do it because there's an imperial gold mine being stripped bare, although I doubt any of you care too much about that. You'll do it because there are several thousand miners being worked to death, although again, I don't expect that to be troubling you overmuch, given all this . . .' He raised his hands into the cold night air, watching as a fine powder of snow fell around him. 'But mainly you'll do it because that's what we do, gentlemen. We follow orders, we march, and we fight. Anyone that has a problem with that can take it up with me, *after* we've retaken the mine. It's time to earn your corn again!'

The long column ground away into the dawn, the lead century initially setting an easy pace at Julius's command to preserve his men's remaining energy for the long march before them. By the meagre light of the sunless sky the sullen Tungrians marched away from Stone Fort in silence, and headed south for the Ravenstone valley.

The Tungrians broke their first day's march at the Fifth Legion's headquarters in Napoca, a hard day's forced march from their starting point. The arrival of a strange infantry cohort in a garrison town where the resident troops were absent was usually a cause for both excitement and nervousness among the inhabitants of the fort's vicus, but on this rare occasion neither would have been justified. The small town's whorehouses and drinking establishments found themselves somewhat disappointed by the Tungrians' lack of interest in their attractions, the soldiers swiftly succumbing to an exhausted sleep once the stoves in the empty barrack blocks were hot and their rations distributed and eaten, many of them still fully dressed to ease the pain of an early start the next day.

'Can you give me another three days at the same pace, First Spear?'

Julius nodded less than enthusiastically at his tribune's question.

'Yes, sir. But they'll be beaten men by the end of it, Tribune, good for nothing much more than leaning on their spears to hold themselves up. It's a relief that we'll not have to carve out any marching camps, or they probably wouldn't even make it as far as the Ravenstone.'

Scaurus scowled despite himself.

'I know. And if I could take it any easier on them I would.'

Julius stood in silence for a moment, judging his next words carefully.

'Tribune, what are we going to do when we get there? It's all very well burning through what's left of these men's candles charging back to the mine, but what happens then? Surely all we can do is camp at the front door, and send Silus out to watch the obvious exit routes. And besides that, once Gerwulf gets even a sniff that we're in the area I'd expect him to make a swift exit over the border and off across the plains with all the gold his men can carry. These lads will be in no state to stop him, even if he does wait for us to get there before making a run for it.'

The tribune shrugged, staring exhaustedly at the floor of his temporary quarter.

'What will we do, once we're standing in front of the valley's earth wall? That's a work in progress I'm afraid. All I can think about for the time being is getting the cohorts up to the mine and working it out from there. In truth First Spear, no matter how much we might both hate the idea, I'm trusting to luck to provide us with some way to prevent Gerwulf's escape.'

Julius nodded wearily, saluted, and left his superior officer to his rumination. The barracks in which the Tungrians were housed for the night were for the most part silent, and after making a swift round of the yawning sentries, he headed for the Fifth Century's barrack to resume his earlier discussion with Marcus. His disbelief on discovering that Lupus had accompanied the cohorts on their desperate mission had swiftly turned to anger, and only his desire to avoid a public argument in front of the soldiery had restrained his temper. But when he stamped into the officers' quarter at the far end of the Fifth Century's barrack, he found the room occupied by rather more men than he had expected. Dubnus and Silus were leaning against the wall facing Marcus, who was sitting on the bed explaining something to them. Lupus himself was squatting in a corner alongside his grandfather, listlessly essaying an attempt at cleaning Marcus's boot with a look on his face that the senior centurion struggled to construe at first glance. Dubnus stepped forward and held a hand up to Julius with a knowing look.

'*Before* you rip our colleague's balls off and offer them to him on a plate, you might want to hear what he has to say.'

Julius looked at Dubnus for a moment and then shrugged, shaking his head.

'You've gone mad as well, have you, Dubnus? Well I don't suppose my temper's going to cool much for being restrained for a little while longer, so have your say, Centurion Corvus, before I reach for the rusty spoon and relieve your wife of the risk of having to carry any more of your brats.' He looked at the drinks in the men's hands. 'Is that wine I see?'

Silus passed him a cup with a weary grin.

'Quite acceptable too, I have to say. Our colleague offered Morban a way out of his rather foolish wager on the subject of ice fighting, if he could procure us a couple of jars of the good stuff. It's funny how fast the standard bearer can move for an old man when he has to.'

Julius sat down on the wooden floor and took a sip, grimacing at the wine's rough bite.

'This is the good stuff, is it? It needs more water. Go on then, what path to insanity has our brother in arms convinced you all we should be skipping down? I presume it has something to do with the boy here, or was that just soft-headed stupidity as opposed to the carefully thought through kind?'

Marcus looked at him from the bed.

'Our problem's obvious. If we march fast enough to get to the Ravenstone valley before Gerwulf decamps with the gold, then we'll arrive with two cohorts of exhausted men fit only for a week's light duties and sleep. And in any case, the Germans will probably see us coming and march out to the north before we even get to the valley, which means that we'll never catch them. Whereas if we march at a pace which will leave the men fit to fight, we risk getting there too late to do anything other than bury the bodies. Mithras only knows how many of the miners he'll have murdered in order to encourage the rest of them to screw every possible ounce of gold out of the place. Either way *we* lose, the tribune loses his position and we end up at the mercy of whoever gets appointed in his place. We'll end up being sent who knows where to deal with the next border dispute to arise, and never see Britannia again.'

Julius nodded and raised his cup to drink again.

'Right enough, I've already made just the same point to the tribune. We know it, he knows it, and all he can think to do is throw us down the road in an attempt to catch that German bastard napping. Do you have a better idea? Because he doesn't, and neither do I.'

Silus spoke up.

'I do. My horsemen could be in Apulum by tomorrow night, and knocking on the door of the Ravenstone by the middle of the day after.'

Julius shrugged wearily, taking another mouthful of wine before replying.

'And then what? Ride up to the gates and demand that the Wolf drops his linen and parts his buttocks for you? What can thirty horsemen do that two cohorts of foot can't?' He held out his cup. 'Fill that up, will you?'

'They can cover ground faster. Much faster. And if they leave the road north from Apulum at the right time, they can work their way around any scouts Gerwulf puts on the road into the mountains.'

The first spear sniffed indifferently, and sipped thoughtfully at his wine.

'So you can ride around their scouts and if you're lucky you'll be able to get eyes on whatever's happening in the valley without being spotted yourselves. So *what*? It doesn't help us to get there any earlier with enough strength to do anything more than watch, does it?'

Marcus smiled tightly at him.

'That rather depends on how many men we think we need to liberate the valley.'

Julius shook his head in exasperation.

'Spit it out will you, whatever it is that's bouncing around between your ears?'

The Roman's voice took on a note of urgency.

'There's a body of men far stronger than our two cohorts, and who'll be filled with enough anger to rip the Germans to pieces, *if* we could just unleash them in numbers.' Julius looked up from the floorboards with a gleam of interest in his eyes. 'The miners. We can be sure that Gerwulf showed his hand the night after we left, and ever since then he'll have been riding them as hard as he can, partly to get the most gold out of the ground in the time he has, but mainly just because he can. It won't have escaped your notice that he's not only capable of just about anything, but that he takes considerable pleasure in his men's depravity. He'll have had them beating and executing the miners at the slightest excuse, and more than likely making free with their women, so if we could just release those angry men at the right time they would do the hard work for us. And do you remember what Cattanius told us? The miners are locked up and lightly guarded at night . . .'

He looked into Julius's eyes for a moment to gauge his superior's reaction before continuing. The first spear nodded reluctantly, gesturing for him to continue.

'And here's the key to making that happen, not that I particularly like it. Rather than try to force our way in through the front door we could send a few picked men into the valley overnight. All we have to do is kill the men set to guard the miners. Once they're roused and armed it would take more than the strength that Gerwulf has to stop them, especially when his soldiers will be staggering out of their beds still half asleep when the wave washes over them, if we get it right.'

Julius nodded slowly.

'It makes sense as far as it goes, even if the whole idea feels little better than rolling the dice and praying for sixes. But how would you propose to get into the valley unnoticed, even at night? They'll have men on the heights watching out for exactly the sort of sneaking about you've described.'

Marcus pursed his lips.

'There's one person in this room who knows a way into the valley that doesn't depend on us having to smash the gate in, or climb over the wall, or climb over the mountains for that matter. Don't you Lupus?'

The men's eyes turned to the child, who had long since stopped any pretence of cleaning Marcus's boots. Julius looked at Marcus in amazement.

'This whole idea depends on a child? And I thought *I* was a ruthless bastard . . .'

'Yes. He's the only one of us who's been *inside* the mountain. And as it happens, the boy Mus showed him something that might be the answer to our dilemma.' He ushered the boy forward. 'Tell the first spear your story, Lupus.'

The child's voice was small in the room's silence, and his face was pale.

'My friend Mus took me into the mine. He showed me a tunnel they don't use any more, one that opens on the mountain beneath the Raven's Head. The opening is hidden from above by the rock.'

Marcus patted him on the arm.

'Well done, Lupus. Julius, the tunnel opening that the boy Mus showed Lupus is on the *south* side of the mountain, the highest level of the mine that was worked out years ago as the miners were forced to dig deeper to find the gold. Nobody works in it anymore, and it would appear to have been forgotten. A party of men could enter the mine from the south, make their way through the mountain and down into the active levels. From there they could infiltrate the valley without being seen, if they were careful . . .'

Julius waved Marcus to silence, turning to Lupus.

'And if they were lucky. Very lucky. So this would all depend on you, Lupus, wouldn't it? We'd need you to show us where the tunnel entrance is. Can you remember?'

The child nodded silently, his face white.

'You can't ask the boy to—'

Julius flicked his hand at Morban impatiently.

'Be quiet, Standard Bearer. The boy wanted to come along with us, and he seems to be the hinge on which this entire dubious plan swings, so you can let him speak for himself. Now, Lupus, you're *sure* you can find this secret entrance to the valley, bearing in mind it'll have to be a nighttime approach?'

'I think so.'

'You think so . . .' The senior centurion put his head in his hands for a moment before standing up, draining his cup. 'Come along then, all of you. We'd better lay this whole idea out for the tribune. Although whether he'll see it as the answer to his dilemma or a good way to warn the Wolf that we're on our way *and* get thirty men killed, is beyond me. And bring what's left of that wine with you. He's going to need a drink when he hears this one.'

'*If* the Gods take pity on you and actually allow you to find the way into the valley, then you are under no circumstances to take on the Germans once you've freed the miners. For a start there are far too many of them, and if you do manage to release enough of the prisoners to start a fight, they won't be able to see the difference between you and the men that have been abusing them. Understood? The best thing that you can do will be to head back for the mine and make your escape. And those are *orders*, Centurion.'

Julius looked up at Marcus until the Roman nodded his understanding, then switched his attention to the tribune mounted alongside the young centurion's mare.

'As for you, Tribune, I strongly suggest that you restrict your part in this scheme to getting into the woman's house. Once you have the mine owners freed you can step back and let them organise their people, *if* they have the balls for it.' He sighed and ran a hand through his hair. 'I still can't believe we're actually doing this . . .'

A snort of grim laughter from behind him made the first spear turn to find a big cavalry horse close enough that the animal was nibbling his helmet's crest.

'*You* can't fucking believe it? You haven't got to lead this bunch of amateurs halfway across Dacia hoping that none of them falls off or puts his spear up the arse of the beast in front of him. Just when I've got one collection of idiots properly trained to handle horses, you make half of them go back to hoofing it and give me a fresh set of virgins to break in.'

Silus had walked his horse back down the line of mounted men, expertly assessing their readiness to ride with his usual mix of jaundiced disappointment and rough humour. Julius cracked a smile for the first time that morning.

'Every dark cloud conceals a little gold, Decurion! In this case at least the prospect of my having to thrash my poor lads south at the double march will be tempered by the thought of your happy face every time one of these trainee donkey wallopers does something to upset you.' He turned back to his superior with an expression of renewed concern. 'And speaking of breaking in virgins, Tribune, I'd be most grateful if you could manage not to get yourself killed? I don't want to end up being told what to do by some other weak-chinned aristo when I've just got used to being told what to do by you.'

He watched with pursed lips as the squadron clattered out of the fort's gates and into the grey light of dawn, waiting until the riders were out of sight before turning back to his officers.

'Well then, now that this morning's excitement is over I think we'd best get back to the challenge of putting another thirty miles under our belts before the sun hits the horizon on the far side. You'd better take Silus's dismounts under your wing, Otho, I expect the poor lambs will be needing some serious encouragement before we've made the lunch stop. Right then, let's put some hobnails on the cobbles!'

The mounted detachment made better progress than Silus had feared might be the case, although their arrival at Mountain Fort soon after midday was accompanied by postures that spoke of considerable discomfort from some of the less experienced riders. The decurion ranged alongside their short column with a look of disdain for those men grimacing at their saddle sores.

'We've another thirty miles to cover before we reach Apulum, so you can have a short break to water your horses and get some fodder down their necks, and your own if there's time. Men with sore arses, report to me!'

He was amused to see the tribune join the small group of men brave enough to risk his acerbic humour.

'Well now, Tribune Scaurus queuing up for the rider's remedy with his men, that is a sight I never thought I'd see. Here you go, sir.'

He passed Scaurus a jar which the tribune uncorked, gingerly sniffing at the contents. 'It's not for sticking under your nose, Tribune; it's for rubbing on the sore skin. Best quality rabbit fat that is, nothing better for saddle sores.'

He winked at the senior officer as Scaurus dipped a finger into the jar with a look of distaste.

'No, nothing better unless you can get a skinful of a good rough red. The headache you'll have in the morning takes your mind right off your sore flaps!'

Arminius dismounted stiffly from his massive beast, reaching up to help Lupus down from the animal's back where he had ridden in front of the German.

'Does your backside hurt?'

The boy shook his head, his eyes wide at the sight of his tribune with one hand inside his leggings and a smile of relief as the fat he was rubbing between his legs eased the soreness caused by the saddle's hard surface. Arminius grinned, ignoring the tribune's narrowed eyes.

'That's the sheepskin for you. I'm just glad I had a spare piece of it in my kit.' Silus walked across and pointed to the fleece he had given Arminius to fashion a makeshift saddle for the boy before their departure from Napoca. 'If only we had a few more then we might have been spared the sight of this lot greasing themselves up for the afternoon, eh?'

The raiding party gathered in an empty barrack in the legionary fortress of Apulum that night, once the mounted detachment's horses had been fed and watered, and those of the squadron's original riders who had not dismounted and were left to march with the infantry had been provided with food and beds. Scaurus looked around the room at the men he had chosen to make the attempt to infiltrate the valley, meeting each man's eyes in turn.

'So once we're through the mine and into the Ravenstone, I'll go to Theodora's villa with Arminius and two of our Hamians, and free the mine owners from whatever duress Gerwulf has them under. At the same time, Cattanius will lead Centurions Corvus, Qadir and Dubnus plus Arabus and the other two Hamians to the miners' camp along with Martos. Our main objective is to release those labourers, and to protect them for long enough that they can get to their tools and gather enough strength to break out. Once that's achieved we'll all meet back at the mine entrance, which will be guarded by Lugos and Lupus. If Arminius and I don't make it back to the mine at the appointed time then I'll remind you all again that I expect you to continue as planned and make your way back through the mine to the southern side. There will be no heroic attempts to find or rescue me, since it will be highly likely that we will both already be dead.'

The German pulled a face, but made no comment.

'Is everyone clear as to their part? We have to get the timing right if this is going to work.'

Silus stood up and saluted.

'Yes Tribune, we know our part. I'm going to supervise the loading of the cart, and make sure the load's rainproof. You wouldn't want all of that shouting at the fortress's stores officer to have been wasted.'

Scaurus nodded his approval and the decurion went on his way with a smile at the memory of his tribune's incandescent anger when the Apulum fortress's storeman had robustly denied being in possession of any of the equipment the party needed. Having reduced the soldier to terrified silence with a violent outburst that questioned both his parentage and his desire to see the next dawn, the tribune had waved his men forward into the stores in search of their requirements. Marcus had walked back down the stores' length a few moments later with a satisfied smile.

'It's all there. Rope, rations, torches – lots of torches – and more than enough lambskin for our boots.'

The storeman had been aghast as the equipment was carried past him, but Scaurus's rebuttal of his argument had left him floundering for a response.

'But that won't leave enough torches to light the fortress!'

'In which case you'd better spend some of that gold you've been creaming off the top all these years and buy some more, hadn't you, because I'm taking these. And I'll need a cart to carry it all. Quickly now!'

Satisfied that everyone knew what was expected of them, the tribune dismissed his men, calling to Marcus to stay behind with him for a moment. The younger man turned his back to the iron stove's glowing metal, enjoying the warmth after a day in the cold winter's air, and waited for the tribune to speak. Scaurus rubbed wearily at his face with a hand before speaking.

'Earlier today I suddenly remembered a question that I've been meaning to ask you for several days, but which I keep forgetting given everything else that's been going on. After the battle on the frozen lake, you went across the ice to gather shields from Belletor's cohort, to replace the ones that had been trampled to pieces on the ice. You had to walk through the men who had made a run for it across the lake, and were ridden down by the Sarmatae.'

Marcus nodded slowly, recalling the lake's bitter cold through his fur-wrapped feet as he had walked reluctantly towards the scatter of bodies littering the ice.

'Julius sent me across the lake for shields so that I could look for Carius Sigilis. He knew that the tribune and I had established a friendship of sorts, as much as a man of that seniority ever can with a common centurion.'

'And?'

'There's little enough to tell. The men on the lake were all dead, either killed instantly or taken by blood loss and the cold quickly enough that I doubt any of them suffered for very long.'

'And Sigilis?'

'He had a spear wound in his side, deep into his stomach, and another in his neck. He bled to death.'

Scaurus got up, standing alongside his centurion and extending his hands to the stove's warmth.

'I watched you, Marcus. You went from body to body looking for him, and then when you found him you were crouched over his corpse for a good deal more time than it takes to ascertain that he was dead.'

Marcus nodded.

'True. He'd written a last message on the ice with his own blood, the words barely readable but clear enough if a man knew what he was looking at.'

'Was it *"The Emperor's Knives"* by any chance?'

'He told you, didn't he?'

The tribune gave him a slow, sad smile, his admonishment no more than gentle amusement.

'Well of course he did, you fool. When you refused to listen to what he was trying to tell you, he decided that letting me in on the secret was the best way to ensure that you learned the truth about your father's death, even if he were to die in battle. He respected you, Centurion, he saw qualities in you that he yearned to find in himself, and while he very much wanted to be part of whatever revenge you take for Senator Aquila's death, he knew there was a risk he wouldn't survive the campaign. So he told me the story of the men who killed your father.'

'I'm going to kill them all, if I ever get to Rome.'

Scaurus pursed his lips.

'Taking on men with that sort of power will be insanely dangerous. You might catch one of them unprepared, but after that the others will know you're coming, and they'll be the most dangerous prey you'll ever hunt. You'll need the support of someone powerful, *if* you ever manage to get to Rome, more powerful than I'll ever be, even if we do manage to pull off a miracle and stop Gerwulf running away with enough gold to buy a provincial city.'

Marcus reached into his purse, pulling out a heavy gold pendant.

'This was on the ice beside his last words. The Sarmatae didn't have time to dismount and rob them of their possessions.'

'And he left it there for you? It carries a heavy burden, Centurion, the responsibility of telling his father how he died. A man like that won't want to hear that his son was killed as he ran from the enemy, which leaves you with a difficult decision to make. Do you tell him the truth and risk his anger, or would it be better to sweeten the pill with a lie in order to gain his support? I don't envy you the choice.'

IO

Silus led the squadron away from Apulum at dawn the next morning, their route forking away from the road that ran on southwest towards the Danubius and climbing northwest into the mountains, the same road the Tungrians had used to reach the Ravenstone valley weeks before. After a dozen miles he conferred briefly with Scaurus before leading the horsemen off the road, and into the mountains that rose to their right-hand side. They rode slowly and cautiously up into one of the high valleys, eventually dismounting and leaving their horses with Silus's men as the sun dipped to a finger's width above the peaks to the west.

The decurion watched as the men who would be carrying out the infiltration gathered their equipment from the cart's flat, wooden bed, and prepared to march the last mile or so to the foot of the mountain that was their objective.

'Remember Silus, wait until the hunter's knee touches the mountains.'

The cavalryman saluted his tribune, then clapped Marcus on the shoulder.

'Good luck, gentlemen. I'll be back here as soon as I can.'

The raiding party went forward, behind the half-dozen Hamian scouts that Qadir had selected from among his best men, and by the time the sun was touching the mountains in the west they were squatting in the cover of the treeline below the valley's southern rim. Marcus and Qadir eased forward to the forest's edge, looking up at the forbidding beaked profile of the massive stone on the mountain's crest that gave the valley beyond the peak its name.

'There's one of them. See, up on the ridgeline.'

Qadir nodded at the steep hill before them, and after a moment Marcus found the tiny figure silhouetted against the orange skyline.

'Careless.'

Scaurus slid in alongside him to squint up at the mountain above them.

'They're bored. They've done nothing but stare at an empty landscape and push miners around for the last ten days, and they want to be away. Every one of Gerwulf's men is busy wondering what he's going to spend his share of the gold on. And let's face it, if he gives them half of the stockpile to split between themselves then even the common soldiers are going to walk out of that valley with at least half a pound of gold apiece.'

Qadir smiled knowingly.

'Think of your own men under such circumstances, Tribune. Half of them will be penniless before they're even halfway back to Germania, the other half considerably richer than when the gold was shared out. It will divide them as nothing else could, and their discipline will fall to pieces in weeks.'

Scaurus shrugged.

'Indeed. But look at it from Gerwulf's perspective. He can't run in any direction other than north, and he needs to get across the great plain without having a Sarmatae arrow land between his shoulder blades. Being the proud owner of enough gold to buy a tribe is useless if you're not alive long enough to enjoy it. All he has to do is keep them together for less than a month, until he's on safer ground, and then he can slip away with a few trusted men who he'll make rich beyond anything they could ever have imagined in return for their loyalty. Now, let's see if the boy can pick out where this mine entrance is, shall we?'

To the tribune's great relief, Lupus pointed to a section of the mountainside beneath the Raven Head peak without any hesitation, and after a moment the sharpest-eyed of the scouts opined that he could see the dark hole of a tunnel entrance among the lengthening shadows. They waited until the sun was down, and the ground around them was dark, before slowly and silently making their way to the foot of the mountain. Scaurus gathered them around him, pointing up at the peak's dark bulk looming over them and speaking softly in the night's quiet.

'The slope will be littered with rocks, so you must tread carefully and slowly as you climb. Lift your feet high, and bring them down gently, feeling for solid ground. This will make our ascent slower, but that will be better than one of us suffering a broken leg, or the guards above us being alerted. And if any of us does disturb a stone, then we must all simply stand still until any noise has died away, and anyone left on watch above us has lost interest.'

They set off up the slope behind him at a measured pace, but within a hundred paces it was clear that ascending the hillside in silence was going to be impossible, as every other footstep dislodged small stones which clicked and clattered their way down the slope in tiny cascades of sound. After a moment's climb the tribune raised a hand, whispering a command back down the column.

'Stop.'

Marcus moved forward to join Qadir at the column's head, and both men listened intently for a moment before the Roman voiced an opinion.

'Nothing. They're either sounding the alarm very quietly or the idle buggers have given up for the night. Either way we have no choice but to push on.'

As they climbed higher up the mountainside the Raven Head loomed over them, its cruel profile outlined by the stars wheeling slowly across the night sky, and Scaurus called for Lupus to be sent up the column.

'Take a careful look my lad, and tell me whether that picture looks right to you.'

The boy stared up at the distinctive rock for a moment before replying.

'We should be up there.'

'You're sure?'

Lupus nodded at Arminius's question.

'Yes. The bird's head is too far away.'

The German looked at Scaurus, his teeth a white slash in the darkness as he grinned.

'Bright boy, isn't he? Up we go then, and you tell me when it looks right to you, eh?'

The small party climbed on up the mountain until Lupus decided that they were in the right place. Qadir sent men out to left and right to broaden their search for the mine's entrance, and the rest of the party huddled down into the protection of their cloaks from the wind blowing across the open mountainside.

'Here!'

The whispered signal came from their left, and Scaurus led the party across the slope to where the man in question was squatting alongside a hole in the mountain barely large enough for a man to enter.

'Is this it?'

Lupus nodded in reply to the tribune's question.

'Yes. See?'

He pointed to the grey outline of a bird's head carved roughly into the stone by the entrance, barely visible in the moonlight, and Scaurus nodded.

'The Raven's Head. You've done well, young man.'

He gestured for the men carrying the bundles of torches they had liberated from the Apulum fortress stores to come forward.

'Now we need fire. Martos?'

The Briton stepped a few paces into the tunnel's pitch-black, taking out his flint and iron from the bag in which he carried them and arranging dry vegetation on the floor before him by touch. A few swift strokes of the flint were enough to spit sparks into the tinder, which flared briefly under the warrior prince's gentle blowing. He suspended a torch over the flames, smiling happily as the pitch-soaked head took fire. Scaurus took the torch and pushed past him, advancing further into the tunnel to avoid the sudden flare of light being visible on the mountainside.

'One torch for every three men, and the archers ready to shoot if we encounter any resistance. Centurion Corvus, lead off with Lupus if you will, but be ready to get down and leave the tunnel clear for the archers.'

Marcus advanced up the tunnel's gentle slope with a torch held up to illuminate the rough-hewn rock walls, feeling the child's hand holding on to his belt as he counted out the paces they were taking in his head. The torch's light reached out fifty paces or so before them, but beyond that was only a circle of darkness which the Roman knew might harbour an enemy preparing to attack. The party's muffled hobnails scraped roughly at the tunnel's uneven floor through their lambskin covers, the faint noise multiplied by the bare walls to a faint, eerie rattle that preceded them into the mountain.

'How far did you come down this way from the ladder before you reached open air?'

His whisper sounded hoarse, and the boy's response was equally strained.

'I don't know, Centurion.'

They walked on, Marcus straining his eyes to the limits of the torch's ruddy light, until when they had covered just less than three hundred paces he saw something poking up out of the rock floor. Squatting down, he turned and gestured to Arabus, who ghosted noiselessly to his side in the soft deerskin slippers he had donned at the tunnel's entrance.

'Scout forward and tell me what that is.'

The tracker was back quickly enough, his eyes glinting in the torchlight.

'It is a ladder. It descends to a lower level, which is lit by small lamps. Better to leave the torches here, or risk being seen before we see?'

Marcus nodded. A swift discussion with Scaurus settled the matter – a pair of men would wait in the passage with the lit torches while the remainder of the party went forward to the ladder, each man holding an unlit brand. They found it just as the scout had described, the ladder apparently well maintained despite that level of the mine having fallen into disuse. Intriguingly, two long ropes were neatly coiled on the rock floor to either side of the ladder's top-most rung, each with one end fed through a block and tackle. Both were tied to iron rings sunk into the passage wall. The tribune examined them closely by the light of a torch.

'I'm no expert, but this looks like lifting gear to me. Lupus, were those ropes there the last time you came this way?' The boy shook his head, and Scaurus exchanged meaningful glances with his officers. 'Perhaps this way into the mine isn't as disused as we might have imagined. Let's continue onwards, shall we?'

Marcus was quick to be the first man to venture down the ladder, tucking an unlit torch into his belt and swinging his legs down onto the top most rungs. He climbed down with Lupus following, and found himself standing on another rock floor in the dim light of a pair of oil lamps.

'Where now, lad?'

The child pondered for a moment, then pointed in the direction which by Marcus's reckoning would take them deeper into the mountain.

'I think that's the way to the entrance.'

Waiting until the remaining eight men had reached the ladder's bottom, Marcus led them off again, but had only covered thirty paces when the top of another ladder came into view.

'What's down there?'

Lupus stared down into the shaft.

'At the bottom of that ladder there's a big wheel that lifts water up to this level, to stop the mine filling up. There are men that turn it.'

The Roman turned back to Scaurus.

'They may have information as to what's happening in the valley. I'll go down there and speak with them.'

He eased his body silently down the long climb, taking each rung slowly and patiently to avoid making any noise. At the bottom he paused for a moment before following a line of oil lamps towards the distant sound of running water, until he found himself at the corner of the passage where Lupus had told him that he and Mus had stopped to listen. Peering round the rock wall and into the cavern, he found a scene exactly as the boy had described it. A pair of men were rotating the waterwheel while two others rested off to one side, with no sign of anyone set to guard them. Marcus drew his gladius and stepped into the open space, standing still to avoid scaring the men into flight down one of the half-dozen passages that opened off the cavern. One of the resting men got to his feet and paced forward until he was close enough to see the Roman properly. He grunted and cast a meaningful stare at the sword, the look on his face telling Marcus very clearly that without its presence the situation would be very different.

'Another soldier. But not it seems a German. Who are you, soldier?'

His voice lacked any edge of fear, and his stare was direct.

'I am a centurion of the auxiliary cohorts that defended your valley from the Sarmatae.'

The miner nodded, his expression unchanged.

'One of the men who left us to the tender mercies of these animals.'

Marcus tapped the blade of his gladius.

'We have returned to deal with them.'

The other man raised a sceptical eyebrow.

'You don't have enough strength to retake the valley, or why sneak back into the Ravenstone this way, rather than smashing through the gate and putting this Wolf and his men to the sword?'

Marcus nodded, conceding the point.

'We are the point of the spear, sent forward to seek a victory by stealth where a more forceful approach might fail. We hope to liberate the miners, and turn them upon the Germans.'

The man shook his head emphatically.

'A week ago, perhaps, but now the men of the valley are penned in at night, crowded into a single mine's barracks, which has been surrounded by a wooden wall to keep them contained while the soldiers entertain themselves with the valley's women. Every barrack's door and window is barred from the outside, and you will not free them without fighting your way through the Wolf's entire strength. You have done well even to come this far without the aid of a man that knows the mine's passages.'

Marcus shrugged.

'We have a child with us who came this way once before, in the company of another boy who used to tend the mine's lamps.'

'Mus?' The labourer stepped forward with a hopeful expression. 'You have word of the child?'

Marcus tipped his head in question.

'Surely you know his fate? He was hidden by your mistress Theodora, but he was discovered and killed by Gerwulf's men.'

The muscles in the labourer's arms corded as his fists clenched, the scarred knuckles white with the force of his anger.

'If I had known that the child was dead then I would have left this infernal place of toil and gone to take my revenge on his murderer . . .' His fists opened and clenched again, and he stared up at the cavern's roof, invisible in the gloom. 'I am Karsas, from the same village as the boy. He was all I had left . . .' He mastered his emotions, shaking his head in frustration. 'You saw the body?'

Marcus nodded sadly.

'The woman carried his corpse to the parade ground on which we were preparing to depart.'

Karsas stood in silence for a moment, and then stepped closer, ignoring the Roman's sword.

'Take me with you. I will have revenge for the child before I die.'

The Roman stared at him for a moment before shaking his head.

'We cannot take you down into the valley. This is work for men who have been trained to use the shadows, not for one man seeking revenge. But you *can* assist us.'

The two men reclimbed the ladder to where the raiding party were awaiting Marcus's return, and after a brief discussion the miner led them confidently down the passage with a torch in his hand. After walking for several hundred paces down the tunnel's gentle slope he stopped, squatting down on his haunches and pointing down the rock tunnel.

'We have come four hundred and fifty paces. Another fifty will put you within sight of the mine's entrance. There are men posted to guard the tunnel, but they usually doze for the most part, and leave one man to watch. I have considered killing them to make our escape – if only there was somewhere to run to in these barren mountains.'

Scaurus patted him on the shoulder.

'Thank you, Karsas. And if there is revenge to be taken when this is done, I swear that you will have your part of it, if I can find a way. Will you care for the boy here until we return, and keep him from harm? Whether we succeed or fail in this venture, the valley will be no place for him this night.'

Leaving Lupus with the miners, the party tiptoed the last short distance to the tunnel's exit into the valley's fresh air. Qadir nocked an arrow to his bow and slid forward to the front of the column, waiting until his eyes had adjusted to the moonlight before stepping out into the open with the slow, exaggerated steps of a hunting cat. Spotting a target, he raised the bow and pulled the arrow back until the string was nearly tight, jerking his head for Marcus to come forward past him. Pacing silently past his friend, the Roman saw a single figure sitting beside the embers of a small fire, his head nodding as he dozed, while two more men were rolled up in blankets at his feet. Raising his gladius ready to strike at the sleepers, he nodded briskly to his friend, and then stabbed the blade down into the sleeper furthest from him, opening the man's throat with a flick of his wrist. As the Roman's victim struggled in his tight wrappings, gargling blood from the horrendous wound, Qadir let his broad-bladed arrow fly into the dozing sentry's chest with a crack of breaking bone. The sentry flopped bonelessly to the ground with the missile buried in his heart, his sightless eyes opened wide with the impact's shock, and Marcus knelt to put the bloodied blade of his gladius to the other sleeper's throat, reaching down to clamp a hand over his mouth.

'If you make a sound without being told to speak I'll cut your wind and leave you to gasp out your last. Do you hear me?'

The prostrate figure nodded, lying unnaturally still as he felt the sword's fierce edge at his throat.

'How many of you were standing guard here?'

The Roman removed his hand, tensing his sword arm to strike, but the terrified German's voice was no more than a whisper.

'Three.'

'Are there any other men standing guard between here and the mining camp?'

The captive's head shook.

'How many men stand guard on the woman's house?'

'Four.'

'And how many on the miner's camp?'

'I don't know . . .' The German wriggled desperately as Marcus slipped the sword's point under his chin, his words a gabbled rush. 'Too many to count, at least a century!'

The Roman nodded, killing the man with a single efficient thrust of the gladius up under his jaw. He turned to find Scaurus nodding approval.

'It's no night for half measures.' The tribune looked up at the cloudless nights' blaze of stars. 'As we agreed it then, you go to the miners' camp and wait for the right moment, and I'll lead my party to the villa. And who knows, if we get lucky enough, perhaps I'll find Gerwulf unguarded, and take the head from this particular wolf.'

He led Arminius and two of the Hamians away down the valley's steep slope, keeping to the shadows until Theodora's villa appeared out of the gloom below them. The party watched the building from the cover of a stand of trees with a view over the courtyard's wall, as a single sentry paced up and down the length of the house's frontage.

'One man at the front and presumably one man at the back. Which means there will be two more inside, if that German was telling us the truth.' He turned to the Hamians. 'Can you put that sentry down from here?'

The archers put a pair of arrows into the pacing guard, who slumped against the house's wall without a sound, following up their first shots with two more that slapped into the wounded man, leaving a dark smear of blood on the wall as he slid down its rough plastered surface. The tribune led his party slowly and carefully out of the trees' shadows, through the courtyard's open gates and quietly up to the building's front door.

'There may be a guard in the entrance hall.'

Arminius drew a hunting knife from his belt and pushed lightly at the door, grinning as it eased open with a gentle creak from the hinges. He slipped through the narrow gap and was inside for less than a dozen heartbeats before he reappeared, shaking his head.

'No guards.'

They followed him through the half-open door, both Hamians nocking arrows to their bowstrings and moving to either side of the wide hall with the weapons ready to shoot. Scaurus paused for a moment to get his bearings, listening to the sleeping household. He gestured to the other men, sending Arminius forward with a pointed finger at the door that led to Theodora's private quarters. The German vanished inside for a moment and then reappeared, beckoning the others to join him. In the darkness of the dining room her erotic murals took on a sinister quality, half-visible couplings that made the Hamians' eyes widen whilst Arminius wrinkled his nose and ignored them, cocking his head to listen.

'You hear something?'

The German shook his head dourly in response to Scaurus's whispered question.

'Thought I heard a floorboard creak. I hear nothing now.'

He shrugged, and Scaurus moved slowly across the tiled floor to the door that led to Theodora's bedroom. Putting a finger to his lips he lifted the latch with delicate care, stepping round the half-open door to find the bed chamber bathed in moonlight from a high window. The woman was asleep on her bed beneath a sheet, and the tribune smiled gently as he stepped silently to her side, kneeling alongside her and reaching forward to put a hand over her mouth.

She started under the touch, her eyes wide with the shock of his presence, and for a moment she made to struggle. Scaurus shook his head, leaning close to whisper in her ear.

'You're safe now, madam, we've come to take you out of here. Can I remove my hand without you making any noise?'

Still startled, she nodded mutely, and the tribune removed his hand with an encouraging smile.

'There, that's better. Are Felix and Lartius imprisoned here?'

Theodora shook her head, her whispered reply confirming Scaurus's expectations.

'That monster Gerwulf had them both killed yesterday, as a lesson for their workers.'

Scaurus shook his head grimly.

'Much as I expected, sadly for them. In that case, I think our best course would be for you to put some clothes on and accompany us to safety. It's all about to get rather noisy and dangerous round here.'

'What do you mean?'

He smiled again, shaking his head and gesturing to her wardrobe.

'We've no time for a long story now – let's just say that the arrival of a full legion in the valley tonight is going to put the cat among the pigeons, shall we?'

Cattanius led the larger of the two parties down the hill to the west, heading for the lights of the miners' camp. Reaching the road the soldiers flattened themselves to the ground at Marcus's silent command, waiting for him to order them across the pale ribbon. Raising his body off the ground in readiness to jump to his feet and make the dash, the Roman stiffened as he heard the sound of boots approaching from the direction of the camps further down the valley. He shuffled backwards on his elbows and knees, whispering a command to the men behind him.

'Get back into the shadows!'

Following his example the raiders swiftly backed away from the road and into the cover of a patch of scrub, throwing themselves to the ground and pulling their cloaks over their helmeted heads. Peering through a gap between cloak and ground, Marcus saw a party of soldiers march into view, and at their heart he was dismayed to see Gerwulf himself. Qadir had slipped into the shadow of a tree trunk, raising his bow with a hunting arrow nocked and ready to fly, but after a moment he lowered the weapon.

'There are too many of them for us to deal with. And I have no clear shot with all those men packed around him.'

Marcus nodded slowly at the Hamian's muttered comment. Waiting until the Germans were out of sight before turning back to his comrades, he whispered a quiet instruction.

'They must be heading for the woman's villa. We can only hope that the tribune has already found her and headed back to the mine, and in any case it's nearly time for the show to begin. We stay here, and when Gerwulf comes galloping back down the hill from Theodora's villa we'll make our move.'

Silus and his remaining horsemen had followed their instructions to the letter since parting company from the raiders that afternoon, making a careful approach to the Ravenstone's lower reaches along forest game paths in order to avoid the risk of being spotted by Gerwulf's scouts. They waited in the trees that lined the road down through the valley's lower section until Silus judged the right time to be upon them, then crept out across the open ground in silence, labouring under their heavy burdens until they reached the road that ran up the valley's floor. Dividing his twenty men equally to either side of the road's cobbled ribbon with whispered instructions, the decurion led both parties down the track away from the mine, telling off a pair of them with every count of sixty paces and hissing the same command.

'One torch for every three steps!'

Once halted, each man quickly untied his bundle of twenty torches and set about pushing their sharpened ends deeply enough into the turf's soft soil for the brands to stand upright without support. Once he had a six-hundred-pace-long double line of torches established along the road's verges, Silus hurried back to the front of the line, gathering his men about him as he climbed the slope and shooting another glance at the sky. The lowest star in the constellation of Orion was only fractionally clear of the horizon, and the decurion nodded decisively.

'Close enough. Never mind his knee touching the mountains,

he'll have a tree up his arse by the time we get them all lit if we don't get on with it. Get your cloaks up.'

The cavalrymen did as he instructed, each of them raising his cloak to overlap with that of the man next to him to form a thick barrier of the dark, heavy wool between the decurion and the distant sentries standing guard on the earth wall. Silus took out flint and iron, quickly setting fire to a pile of tinder that he had gathered that afternoon. He put his own torch into the small blaze, waiting as the stave's pitch-soaked head took fire, still hopefully invisible to the Germans.

'Right my lads, it's time to find out if the tribune's plan is going to work. Drop your cloaks and get those torches lit!'

Scaurus led the small party back into the villa's entrance hall, pausing at the door to be sure that everyone was ready. Arminius nodded to him from the small group's rear, and the tribune opened the door as slowly as he could, smiling as the hinges groaned almost inaudibly. He stepped out into the darkness, opening his eyes wide to help them to adapt to the lack of illumination, then stepped cautiously forward with the Hamians following him and Theodora huddled into her cloak between them. Halfway across the villa's courtyard he heard a minute sound, the scrape of booted feet on stone, and in the time it took him to realise that the noise had come from in front of him rather than from the party following him it was already too late to do anything. A familiar voice was raised in a shout of command, and the raiders froze as men emerged from the shadows around them, more men than the four of them could hope to fight off. The villa's door flew open behind them, and Arminius spun to find himself facing three swords as the guards spread out behind the party to add their threat to that arraigned before them. As the circle of blades closed about them a voice spoke from the darkness.

'Well now, Tribune, I'd like to say that this is an unexpected pleasure, but in all honesty your coming here was so predictable that I'd be lying. Once that bright young beneficiarius had come and gone I knew it wouldn't be long before you made your appearance, although I hardly thought you'd go about it quite *this* naively. Put down your swords or my men will have no option but to butcher you where you stand.'

Scaurus bent and placed his weapon on the courtyard's flag-stones, hearing the sounds of blades being lowered to the stones behind him. Gerwulf's men moved in with their blades held ready to kill, and the tribune watched with the point of a soldier's sword inches from his face as the prefect stepped forward and sized up the party's strength with a triumphant smirk.

'So, what have we here? The bold tribune, come to rescue his lover, his faithful bodyguard, two rather disposable-looking soldiers, and my own dear girl.'

Theodora walked out of the small group, the Germans lifting their blades to allow her to pass, and she put an affectionate arm around Gerwulf's waist, kissing him on the cheek.

'Well done my love. I was actually afraid that they were going to make off with me, but you seem to have arrived just in time.'

'Indeed.' The prefect looked at Scaurus and his men with a calculating expression for a moment, then flicked a hand at the watch officer commanding his escort. 'I'll keep the officer and his servant; you can kill the other two.'

'Yes, my lord Wolf!'

The Hamians were dragged away to the other side of the courtyard by a pair of men apiece, their scuffles of resistance swiftly silenced by the watch officer's stabbing sword blows. Scaurus stared at Gerwulf with a sad expression, shaking his head in disgust.

'You can't help yourself, can you, Gerwulf? That urge to see men die never gets any weaker, does it?'

The German laughed in his face.

'In life Scaurus, as you well know, there are killers and there are victims. And I have no intention of becoming the latter through demonstrating any weakness of the kind that has brought you here to me. We'll go back into the villa now, shall we, and get a fire burning? I'm curious to see just how quickly you feel like telling me how you ever expected to evict me from this tidy little fortress you built for me, once you've felt the kiss of red-hot iron a few times.'

Theodora waved a hand dismissively.

'There's no need to torture him, he's already told me what's happening. Apparently there's a legion marching on the valley, and it will arrive tonight.'

Gerwulf shook his head with a bark of derision.

'Bullshit! Legions don't march in the dark, and even if such an attack was possible there's no way that infantry could have got here from Porolissum that quickly. He was feeding you false information' – a thoughtful tone entered the German's voice – 'which makes me wonder just how much the tribune here knew about our relationship before now? Perhaps we'll do without the hot iron and get straight to the point here and now, with nothing more sophisticated than the point of my dagger for an incentive to talk.'

He slid the weapon from its sheath and stepped forward, raising the knife's point to Scaurus's eye. The Roman ignored the imminent threat, shaking his head at Gerwulf once more with a pitying note in his voice.

'You've miscalculated, Gerwulf. The Sarmatae came to battle before we even reached the border, and they got their barbarian arses kicked in for their trouble. It seems *some* savages just can't be educated, doesn't it? We were already marching south as the advance guard for Clodius Albinus and his legion's return to Apulum when the news of this rather spectacular piece of larceny arrived, and the legatus has had his men at the double pace ever since. He's given orders for you to be taken alive at all costs, since he wants to make an example of you that won't be forgotten for a while. Your future holds nothing more than torture and protracted death, and Theodora's too, I'd imagine. You're about to find out what happens when you piss off a Roman aristocrat by biting the hand that's been feeding you.'

The German shook his head again with a mocking smile on his face.

'It's just not quite ringing true I'm afraid. Nice try, Rutilius

Scaurus, but I think we'll just get on with finding out the truth, shall we?' He raised the knife, putting the point against Scaurus's lower eyelid. 'This should be a novel experience for you, using one eye to look into the other.'

A centurion burst into the courtyard panting for breath, gasping out his message as the prefect spun to face him with any thought of torture momentarily forgotten.

'Lord Wolf! There are lights on the road in the valley!'

Gerwulf strode across to him.

'What lights? What are you talking about?'

Still gasping for air, the officer pointed back down the road to the wall as he panted out his news.

'Centurion Hadro sent me to find you, sir. We have torches coming up the road, hundreds of them. He said to tell you it looks like a cohort on the march!'

The German turned away from him, putting his face so close to Scaurus that the Roman could smell the spiced meat on his breath.

'What kind of fucking trick is this?'

The tribune shrugged.

'I did try to tell you. That's my lads closing the front door as the advance guard for the Thirteenth Gemina. Legatus Albinus resolved that we should all march through the night by torchlight, so by morning I expect you'll be knee-deep in legionaries, and not just in front of the wall either. He'll seal this place up tighter than an Egyptian tomb and wait until you surrender for lack of food. Of course, the miners will starve to death before it gets to that point, but the legatus doesn't really care very much about those sorts of incidentals. As we used to say when I served under him in the German Wars, there's hard, there's downright ruthless, and then there's Decimus Clodius Albinus.'

For a moment he was sure that his captor was going to slam the dagger still held in one hand into his belly, but the German turned away and dropped the weapon back into its sheath.

'You four, take these two prisoners back into the villa and keep a close eye on them. I'll be back when we know the truth of this apparent attack. The rest of you come with me!'

Marcus and the men huddled in the grass around him had watched in silence as the star that formed Orion's knee nudged down onto the horizon and disappeared, and the Roman had fingered his amulet and muttered a prayer to Mithras that Silus had managed to achieve his part of the plan as required. After a short while a centurion had run up the hill towards the villa, gasping for breath as he'd struggled against the weight of his armour. In the valley below them they could hear the sounds of soldiers being called to arms, the shouts and curses of their officers and the clatter of equipment. Dubnus had stared at the runner's back, muttering what they were all thinking.

'It seems as if Silus has managed to get their attention.'

Marcus's whispered reply had been a low growl.

'Indeed. All we need now is for Gerwulf to put his head into the noose.'

The sound of boots on the road that reached them a moment later made the raiding party tense in anticipation, every man straining his eyes up the road into the town. A body of men came running down the hill from the villa, Gerwulf once again in their midst, and Qadir raised his bow in the shadow of the tree once more, only to lower it with a disgusted shake of his head as the pack of men raced past them and on down the valley.

'There were nineteen of them before, including Gerwulf, but now there are four less. Either our tribune fought and died, but managed to kill four men, or those soldiers have been left behind to guard captives.'

Marcus pulled a face at Qadir's conclusion.

'How many men would your two archers have taken down before they were killed, do you think?'

The answer was immediate.

'Two apiece. Possibly three if they were fortunate.'

'Exactly. And the tribune and Arminius would have done at least as well. There are too many men left standing for there to have been a fight, and none of them are wounded, or even blooded. I think they've been captured.' He looked at his friend with a grimace of frustration. 'Mithras, but I'm tempted to kick the doors on that place and pull him out now, but his orders were very clear. Follow me.'

They stood, and Marcus, Dubnus and Martos put on the iron caps they had taken from the men at the mine's entrance, hefting their captured shields. Marcus led them down the road at a purposeful trot in the wake of Gerwulf's men, whose hobnails could still be heard clattering down the road towards the wall in the darkness ahead of them. Rounding a corner they came into sight of the Raven Head mine's camp, now visibly different with the erection of a high palisade around the barracks buildings. A quartet of soldiers was standing guard on the gate, and another four stood on the palisade above them with bows, the latter staring to the west from their elevated position at the lights in the valley beyond the wall. Marcus quickened his pace, running towards the guards with his swords still sheathed and trusting that the three men's disguises would hold for long enough.

'So, here we are again?'

Theodora shot a caustic look across the villa's dining room at Scaurus as he settled back into his chair and ignored the two soldiers whose swords waited only inches from his back, shaking her head at him with a disdainful expression.

'Don't go getting any ideas, Tribune. Our couplings were purely professional. You're *really* not my type.'

He smiled up at her, patting his crotch.

'Nor you mine, if truth be told. I've never really been all that attracted to maneaters, although I can only salute your abilities beneath the sheets. You were good enough value in bed, but I think you'd soon get a little monotonous as a life companion.' He returned her cold stare with an unruffled shrug. 'I'm sorry Theodora, but you must realise that your apparent nymphomania makes you somewhat more demanding than most men could manage.' He laughed at her piqued expression. 'And do please spare me the indignant glare, madam, because we both know that your main value to your partnership with your *brother* is your skill as a seductress, don't we?'

Marcus called out the night's watchword again, shouting a command as he closed with the gate guards.

'They'll be sounding the horns any moment now. Close the gates!'

Responding without thought to the note of command in his voice, the four men ran to the gates, starting to heave them closed as the Roman and his companions unexpectedly drew their swords and tore into them. Before the man on the fighting platform above them had a chance to respond to the sudden onslaught, they found themselves under attack by Qadir and his Hamians, two of the enemy falling to the first volley while the men below died on their attacker's swords without ever really comprehending what was happening. One of the men on the elevated platform drew breath to shout for help, then somersaulted over the railing as an arrow hit him in the head, the air hissing out of him in a scream that was cut off by his crunching impact with the ground.

After a moment's silence a door opened in the wooden hut that had been tacked onto the side of the palisade, an angry voice calling from just inside. The second wave of Marcus's party hurried through the arch as Martos and Dubnus put their shoulders to the heavy gates, and the young Roman slapped Lugos on the shoulder, pointing at the open door.

'What the fuck are you lot pissing about at now? I'll have your fucking—'

The guard commander stepped through the door and died without ever knowing what had hit him, his corpse bouncing off the door frame with its head smashed by Lugos's hammer. Bellowing his joy at a chance to fight, the giant Briton raised his leg and kicked the next man in line behind the guard commander back into the hut, then squeezed his bulk though the door frame and punched the hammer's head into the fallen soldier as he struggled back to his feet. A chorus of screams sounded as he waded into the remaining occupants, the flimsy structure shaking as the warrior unleashed the full fury of his monstrous strength.

'Shut those gates!'

Qadir and his archers hurried into the palisade as the entrance was secured.

'There are more soldiers coming.'

Marcus lifted a wry eyebrow, raising his voice to be heard over the bestial roars that Lugos was uttering as he ripped through the helpless guards.

'It's hardly surprising, is it? He's making enough noise to wake the dead.'

Theodora put her head on one side and looked down at him with a different, more calculating expression.

'And just how long have you known *that*?'

'How long have I known for certain that you're the "Wolf's" sister? Oh, about a week, although I was starting to wonder about you a good while before that. While we were intimate I noticed that you had the faintest hint of fair hair in your scalp, almost unnoticeable unless a man got close to you from behind and you put your head back. I put your dying your hair down to a cosmetic choice, although I've always preferred blondes myself, and so I thought no more of it for a while.But when I reached Porolissum I asked a few questions about Gerwulf of an old friend of mine, a man who moved in the same aristocratic circles that you and your brother flirted with during your time in Rome. When he reminded me that the prince had a younger sister – and told me what a swathe she cut through the youth of the senatorial class for a short time – it set me to thinking again, and my thoughts came back to those blonde hair roots. Clodius Albinus told me that Gerwulf's sister was a blonde, a particularly vivacious young woman who broke several young men's hearts when she vanished overnight, apparently following her brother when he went to serve on the frontier, and prompting all those scandalous and bitter stories about the two of you being incestuous lovers. Of course, everyone thought you'd be back in no time. The expectation was that life on the frontier would simply be too dull for you after the pleasures of the capital, but now that I've met you I know that wasn't the case, was it?'

She smiled at him, her confidence returning after the shock of his revelation.

'Far from it, Tribune. It was Rome that was tedious, compared to all the fun we had once my brother was serving. There was always a senior officer willing to look after Gerwulf's career in return for my favours, and to protect me from being sent back to Rome. It was *much* more fun after he took command of these Germans though. An independent command provides so many more opportunities for mischief.'

'Not to mention profit. And murder. And when the two of you got skilled at putting profit and murder together, you had the idea to rob the Ravenstone? It was *your* idea?'

Theodora laughed, her tone when she answered dripping with sarcasm.

'Oh, *aren't* you clever? Of *course* it was. Gerwulf's such a boy at heart, only happy when he's hacking his way through his enemies. Whereas I . . .'

She pirouetted before him, and Scaurus applauded softly.

'Yes, you're the real brains. So, having heard about this place you came here and found yourself a mine owner who was single, wormed your way into his affections and persuaded him to marry you.'

She nodded.

'I made him happier than you can imagine, Tribune. If only for a short time.'

'Until you had him killed and took over his business.'

She shrugged.

'Mining's *such* a dangerous way to earn a living. And he had no family you see, so there was no-one to dispute my claim to the mine. Besides, by that point I was already gracing Procurator Maximus's bed with my decorous presence, so all that tedious nonsense about the laws of inheritance could safely be ignored.

After all, how else do you think I could arrange for my husband to die in such unexpected circumstances?'

'We have to free the miners, before the men outside build up sufficient strength to break in. That gate's not strong enough to withstand a serious attack.'

'And yet if we do set them free, they're likely to tear us to pieces.'

Marcus grimaced at the truth in Cattanius's words.

'So we either find a way to get out without being battered to death by the men we're here to free, or we have to turn them loose and take the consequences.'

Marcus looked about him, seeing a row of a dozen barracks buildings enclosed by the palisade's twelve-foot-high circle of half-logs, the split tree trunks presenting their flat surfaces to the raiding party.

'There's no way to climb that.' Shaking his head, he turned back to his comrades in time to see a bloodied Lugos push his way out of the guard house's doorway. 'Cattanius, it's on you whether we get away with this or not. Get searching for a way out. The rest of you, with me. We've got to leave them enough weaponry out for them to fight off the men at the gate, and that means opening the tool stores. Lugos, smash open everything I point at.'

The beneficiarius hurried to the far side of the camp, looking for any sign of another exit from the trap into which they had forced themselves, muttering under his breath at the lack of any obvious answer.

'Nothing, no handy little gates to slip through, no need for the builders to leave a hidden exit route in a prison wall . . .' He pushed at one of the split tree trunks that composed the curved wall that enclosed the camp, shaking his head at its solidity. Running his hand down the wood as far as the ground, he found the thin space between wood and turf where the builders had dug a deep hole in which to anchor the log, and hadn't bothered to completely fill the resulting gap. Pulling out his dagger he ran the blade along the fingertip-wide space until he reached the next log, encountering sudden resistance from the soil packed around it. Looking up, he realised that the split tree trunk was secured on either side by wooden battens that were nailed across the joins between them.

'Got you!'

He hurried over to Marcus.

'I've found the back door, but I'll need *him* to open it.'

The Roman looked at Lugos, hooking a thumb at the Briton.

'Lugos, help Cattanius. How long will you need?'

The beneficiarius shook his head.

'That depends on him. Perhaps fifty heartbeats. But if I open the hole too quickly the boys outside will realise what's going on and be there to meet us.'

Marcus thought for a moment, looking at the heavy tools which his comrades had scattered across the ground before the barracks, having used Lugos's immense strength to smash open the stores in which they were secured. The miners had realised that something was happening, and the noise from inside their barracks was growing as men hurled themselves fruitlessly at the barred doors and windows.

'We'll open one barrack once you're ready to do whatever it is you're planning, and they can do the rest of the work on their own. Just make sure you can get this fence open quickly enough, or we'll be the first men they lay hands on. And from the sound of it they're not in the best of moods.'

Cattanius led the rest of the party back to the wall, explaining what it was he had in mind.

'This log's not been sunk into the ground, just stood on the earth and nailed to the trunks to either side. So, all we have to do—'

Lugos stepped forward and swung his hammer, turning it to present the hooked blade that opposed the heavy iron beak, already black with blood. The first of the two battens that held the log in place nine feet above the ground splintered under the blow, and a second swing of the hammer tore away its companion to leave only the two at knee level intact.

'Wait.'

Running for the corner of the barracks the beneficiarius sprinted to Marcus, who was watching calmly as the palisade's main gate rocked under a succession of blows from the other side.

'I hope you're ready. That gate isn't going to hold for much longer.'

Cattanius nodded at the barrack's lock.

'Do it!'

As he ran back to the palisade, Marcus and Dubnus lifted the second of the three thick wooden bars that secured the barrack's entrance out of its brackets, throwing it aside as the men inside heaved against the doors and provoked a creaking tear in the sole remaining bar. With a crash of splintering wood one of the palisade gates was smashed open, a stream of infuriated Germans storming through the gap and goggling at the corpses of their fellows scattered around the archway. Sighting the two men outside the last barrack in the row of buildings, they charged down the line, and Dubnus pointed at the remaining door bar as the miners inside heaved at the rapidly failing barricade.

'It's about to break! Run!'

They turned tail and followed Cattanius, rounding the barrack's corner just in time to watch as Lugos swung his hammer to smash the remaining battens holding the log in place. A sudden roar of voices told them that the miners were free, and an instant later, as the log toppled away from the palisade to leave a gap large enough for the raiders to escape through, the screams and howls of a pitched battle began.

Gerwulf panted up the wall's steps at the head of his bodyguard, standing on the rampart's fighting platform with his chest heaving from his run down the valley.

'Where's this damned cohort then, eh Hadro?'

His deputy pointed out into the darkness at a line of flickering lights.

'There, Prefect!'

The German followed the pointing hand and stared out across

the valley's darkness, feeling his sense of unease growing as he stared at distant flames, his voice suddenly acerbic as he realised what it was he was seeing.

'They don't seem to be moving, *do* they Centurion?'

'No Wolf, they marched up the road and then stopped . . .'

To his credit, he stood his ground as the prefect turned on him, his snarling face made bestial by the torchlight's shadows.

'Whoever it is down there has laid out two lines of torches and lit them one at a time from front to back, to make it look as if they were coming over a rise! You've been deceived, Hadro, this is no more than a ruse to distract our attention from something else! You' – he turned to the officer who had run to fetch him from the villa – 'take a century and reinforce the guard on the miners' camp!'

He watched as the centurion led his century off the wall and away up the road towards the palisaded barracks, then looked out at the torches again, shaking his head at the growing number of gaps as individual lights toppled to the ground. Turning back to Hadro he looked down his nose at the man for a moment, and when he spoke again his voice was contemptuous.

'That's you and I done. You've made one mistake too many. You're relieved of duty; go back to your tent. I'll come and see you in the morning when this distraction has blown over, and give you enough gold to see you right.'

He watched as Hadro shrugged tiredly and turned away for the wall's steps, waiting for the centurion to be out of earshot so that he could quietly order two men from his bodyguard to follow the man and kill him. Given any longer he knew that his former friend would make a run for it over the mountain, with the risk that he might survive to bear witness against him for their crimes over the previous few months. It would be no more than an inconvenience, given that he intended to be far away from Dacia by the time any such accusation could surface, but he wasn't a man given to leaving loose ends dangling when swift action could remove such a threat before it had a chance to become reality. He frowned, as the centurion stopped unexpectedly at the head of the stone stairs and cocked his head as if to listen. He was on the verge of losing his patience with the man, and ordering his killers to deal with him then and there, when an unexpected noise reached his ears, a wave of sound like the cheering of a body of men.

'What was that?'

For once his question went unanswered as the noise came again, the roar of voices closer this time, and its volume increased once more as the first torches appeared over the ripple in the ground between the miners' camp and the wall. He stared aghast as a flood of men spilled down the slope, sweeping down towards the century he had sent to reinforce the guards they had presumably already slaughtered.

Scaurus raised an appreciative eyebrow at the woman before him.

'I must admit that I'm impressed. With one simple act of infidelity you persuaded your lover to deal with your husband and support your claim on his assets. Although it wasn't just a share in the profits from the mine you were promising him, was it? Presumably Maximus expected to be sharing in the fortune to be made from the robbery of the mine's gold?'

Theodora nodded.

'You men are *so* suggestible as a sex. All I had to do was tell him how much I wanted to be with him, and all the good things that the proceeds from robbing the mine could bring us. He actually thought we were going to find a man that looked like him, kill him and use the corpse to fool the authorities into believing that he was dead.'

The tribune shrugged again, leaning back in the chair.

'I ought to have suspected him when he refused to move the gold out of his strongroom, nicely collected and ready for Gerwulf's arrival. After all, he really wasn't that good an actor, was he? I met him on the way up here that first night, and if looks could kill I would have been face down and six feet under. He knew that I was being brought up here to be seduced and turned into a source of information for you and your brother, and he didn't like it. What did you tell him, that you were both going to live happily together for the rest of your days, and that you were only taking me into your bed to ensure that I was under your control? The truth of just how badly you'd duped him must have been a shock for the poor man, when Gerwulf showed his hand and had him chained up like an ox ready for the slaughter. I'll bet he was desperate to get the chance to try to rescue his reputation once he realised what a fool you'd made of him. Presumably that's why Gerwulf cut the poor man's throat and tossed him off the wall, not so much to make a point to Cattanius but mainly to silence him, before he got a chance to blurt out that you were the architect of the whole thing, rather than being the poor innocent victim.'

He raised a questioning eyebrow at her.

'So once you had Maximus wrapped round one finger, you sent a messenger to Gerwulf, telling him to be ready for your call when the strongroom was full. Presumably at that point he abandoned whatever mission he'd invented to keep his men close at hand?'

'Yes, officially he's on detachment from the Seventh Claudius at Viminacium, a detachment I persuaded their legatus to grant to my brother in the usual way, but I'd imagine even that fool must be starting to wonder just where he's got to. The "Wolf's" been raiding up and down the frontier zone for months now to keep his men fed.'

Scaurus nodded, the look of amusement fading from his face.

'Which explains the destruction of the boy Mus's village, and all the other raids that had the Sarmatae so fired up for revenge. You must have thought the fates were smiling on you the day that legion cohort pulled out to go to war. You sent the call out to your brother that the time to get rich had come, only to have my men march up the valley a few days later, too late for you to stop Gerwulf coming to pull off the greatest robbery in the history of the empire.'

Theodora bent close to him, and Scaurus felt the point of a sword prick the back of his neck as the guard behind him tensed.

'You should be a little more grateful to my brother, Tribune.

If he'd not spotted the tracks left by that Sarmatae warband and followed them up into the battle, you and your men would have been torn to pieces, wouldn't you?'

He nodded equably.

'You won't catch me complaining on that score. I'll still be grateful to Gerwulf for pulling our chestnuts out of the fire even when I'm having him executed for treason.'

She bent closer, her reply soft in the room's silence.

'You're very confident for a man whose life hangs on a thread, Tribune.'

Scaurus shrugged, staring at her breasts appreciatively.

'Circumstances alter cases, my dear. Can you hear those horns blowing?' She tipped her head to listen. Barely audible through the villa's thick stone walls, a trumpet was braying in the valley below, joined by a second. 'They're sounding the command to form line and prepare for battle, not an action that would be required by a single cohort in the valley, or not yet at least. I'd hazard a guess that the men who accompanied me tonight have freed the mine workers from their barracks, and given them access to their tools. And while your brother commands a powerful unit, I really wouldn't relish having to fight off five thousand angry miners in the darkness. Oh yes, Gerwulf's men will kill a few hundred of them, but the rest will wash over his line like a pack of dogs overwhelming a wolf. Which is apt, wouldn't you say? And when they've done for the soldiers, enough of them will come here for you that you'll never want another man as long as you live.'

Theodora's mouth had tightened to an angry slash, and for a moment he wondered if he'd pushed her too hard. She spoke to the soldiers behind him.

'You, get the men ready to move and tell them to bring my chest! If the mine workers really have been released then we'll either meet my brother at the mine entrance or leave without him!'

Gerwulf instinctively knew that his command was doomed, watching in silence as the oncoming mob of miners swiftly overwhelmed those of his men who were too slow on their feet to

reach the turf wall before them. While the rampart was fifteen feet
high on the side that faced down into the valley it was necessarily
lower on the reverse, and the miners gathered in a howling sea of
men around the steps that, were they allowed to swarm up them,
would allow them to get at the soldiers who had made their lives
a misery over the previous ten days. A determined group of them
stormed up a stairway one hundred paces to his left, trading a
dozen men's lives to gain a foothold on the rampart and then railing
at the defenders with iron bars, heavy shovels and pickaxes.

'How long do you think they'll hold?'

He turned to find Hadro beside him, the grizzled veteran's face
as stolid as ever.

'Not very long. There are too many of the bastards, and
they're mad with the lust for blood. There's still time to be away
though, as long as the wall to the south remains in our hands.
Are you coming?'

The older man shot him a look of pity.

'No, Gerwulf, and not just because you were about to have me
killed to ensure my silence. This is over. These animals are going
to kill every soldier in the valley, and how long do you think
anyone that escapes will be able to run, with the legions on this
side of the mountains and the Sarmatae on the other? I think I'll
stay here and face my fate. Better to die quickly at their hands
than to end up on a cross alongside you.'

Gerwulf nodded, dismissing the man from his mind.

'Suit yourself.'

Gerwulf whistled to his bodyguard, turning away to stride
down the wall to the south behind their shields, shouting encouragement to his men as they stabbed and cut at the mob baying
for blood below them. He winced as an unwary soldier was
dragged bodily from the wall into the crowd, his leg hooked by
the blade of a pickaxe. The doomed man surfaced in the sea of
blood-crazed men that lapped against the wall, stabbing out once
with his sword before a vengeful miner buried an axe in his back
and dropped him to his knees to be kicked to death. He shouted
to his men to speed up their pace, watching in horror from the

corner of his eye as dozens of enraged miners crowded in to stamp the dying man's body to a pulp. Once they were clear of the fighting he pulled his crested helmet from his head and tossed it aside, speaking to his men as the small party hurried on down the wall's length.

'From here on, gentlemen, we are soldiers of Rome no more. We only have to escape from this fucking valley to be the richest men in the whole of free Germania.'

'I guessed that you'd have a plan to escape, if your scheme went wrong.'

Theodora looked back over her shoulder with an expression of hatred as she climbed the steep path.

'I'm rapidly growing bored of your smug satisfaction, Tribune. You're not so valuable to us that I might not just lose my failing grip on my temper and have the sword that's waiting behind you rammed through your spine. Would a period of silence be preferable to your untimely death?'

He smiled back at her and kept his mouth closed, glancing over her shoulder at the rock face looming before them. Of the four soldiers that her brother had left behind to guard him, only two were armed, one close behind and the other bringing up the rear, while the other two were struggling to haul a heavy wooden chest up the slope. After another hundred paces the path flattened out, and the light of a guard fire twinkled against the stones that surrounded the Raven Head mine's entrance. Theodora stopped ten paces from the blazing pile of wood, looking about her with suddenly aroused suspicion. Scaurus watched the realisation of the guards' absence dawning upon her, but said nothing. Theodora swung back to face him, her eyes narrowed.

'Where are they?'

He frowned at the woman in apparent indifference.

'Where are who? Your men set to guard the mine? Perhaps they're underground, looking for gold.' He raised his voice. 'Or perhaps they're still here and it's just that you can't see them.'

With a sudden start she realised that there were men all around them, rising from the cover of the bushes and trees around the mine's entrance. A bow twanged, and the man behind Scaurus yelped and fell, dropping his sword and shield. The soldier at the rear of the column turned and ran, shouting for help, but managed no more than three paces before an arrow took him in the back. A giant figure strode out of the darkness, swinging his heavy war hammer in an arc that ended against the helmeted head of one of the men carrying the chest, smearing his features across his grossly distended skull. He swept the hammer up again, slamming it down onto the last of the soldiers with a sickening crunch of bone as the man scrabbled in terror at his sword's hilt. Scaurus held up his bound wrists, grimacing in discomfort as one of the soldiers surrounding them stepped in and cut him free, while Theodora glowered at them both. Shaking his hands to restore their circulation he nodded his thanks to the soldier before turning back to Theodora.

'Thank you, Centurion Corvus. And now, madam, if you thought my smug satisfaction was becoming a little tedious before, you'll be positively disgusted with what you're about to witness.'

She drew breath to scream for help, but Dubnus stepped out of the shadows behind her and put a big hand over her mouth while the tribune smiled warmly at her blazing eyes.

'No, I think I'd prefer it if you didn't warn your brother off. We've got a little surprise for him, something of a reunion. It'll be touching, I promise you.'

Halfway up the mountainside Gerwulf called a brief halt, looking down into the valley as he sucked air into his lungs. Below him the buildings of Alburnus Major were aflame as the mob of miners ran amok, while what little he could see of the wall in the light of the remaining torches was a mass of angry humanity gathered around a dwindling remnant of his cohort. He chuckled quietly.

'They'll ransack the entire valley hoping to find the gold, tearing the place to pieces and then doing the same to each other. Thank the gods for *foresight*, eh?'

A sudden agonised grunt from behind him made the prefect

turn to find one of his men reeling with a sword buried deep in his guts, while one half of his bodyguard tore into their unprepared colleagues with murderous intent. A brief one-sided fight reduced his escort from eight men to four, and he watched dispassionately as the last mewling survivor of the short struggle was finished off.

'Well done, gentlemen, you've just doubled your money. And don't worry, there are no more coded words. If you're still breathing now it's because you're all men that I would trust with my life. Shall we go?'

He smiled to himself as they resumed their path along the valley wall towards the Raven Head mine, knowing that two of the men following him would be doing the same, waiting for the command to complete the reduction of their party to a size that would excite no interest as they rode south for the Danubius and a new life in the land beyond the river. Another five hundred paces brought them to the mine's entrance and the unattended watch fire.

'The cowards must have made a run for it when they heard the commotion in the valley. Probably wise, since I suppose those scum down there will eventually come up here, once they get bored of destroying everything else. Come on . . .'

Gerwulf led them into the mine, taking a torch from beside the fire, lighting it in the embers and holding it up to illuminate the narrow passageway. Two hundred paces up the dimly lit passage he frowned as a barely visible figure appeared before them, seemingly conjured out of the tunnel's wall. He walked on cautiously, drawing his sword with his bodyguards' footsteps close behind him.

'It's that fucking tribune.'

He nodded at the comment, pacing forward until there could be no doubt that it was indeed Scaurus waiting for them, leaning against the tunnel's side with his sword still sheathed.

'Wondering what I'm doing here, are you Gerwulf? The answer's simple enough, I've come for *you*. Much as it pains me to be the bearer of bad news, I'm afraid that I won't be allowing you to leave this mine tonight.'

Gerwulf waved his men forward.

'With you as a hostage I'm sure some agreement can be—'

The leading soldier's head snapped back, and he fell to the ground with an arrow protruding from his forehead.

'My man's arm must be tired after his evening's exertion. He usually puts his shots into the eye socket at this range. Would anyone else like a demonstration? He's not in a very good mood, I'm afraid, owing to the unexpected death of two of his comrades.' The remaining four men kept very still. 'I thought not. And now allow me to introduce, I'm sorry, *re*-introduce you to my new friend Karsas.'

A hard-faced man dressed in the rough, dirty clothing of a miner stepped out of the same side tunnel from which the tribune had emerged, his muscular arms crossed and his face set firm.

'He is unknown to you Gerwulf, and yet you two *have* met before. In a valley much like this one, and not too far from here, you set your wolf pack on his people one night, without warning and without mercy. You butchered the men and raped their women before murdering them, you showed no mercy to any of them, and you left their corpses to rot.'

Gerwulf shrugged.

'You're going to have to be more specific. There was more than one village.'

The miner scowled, and Scaurus shook his head in disgust.

'Nobody knows this better than the men who labour to keep this mine operational. They are the dispossessed, Gerwulf, men who ran from your swords and left their families to die. They have had a long time to wallow in their self-hatred, my new friend here and his comrades . . .' More men crowded out of the tunnel behind him, and hearing a scrape on the rock floor behind them the Germans turned to find another half-dozen filling the corridor to their rear. 'And they yearn for the chance of revenge. They tell me that they come from five villages, places of happiness and contentment which you had your men tear to pieces in order to satisfy your need to destroy. The boy you murdered was from this man's village, forced to witness the death of his father and brothers, and the rape of his mother and sisters. He was a boy, Gerwulf, but inside he was already an old man, his spirit shrivelled by what you did to his family. And to *his* . . .'

A miner stepped forward with a pickaxe in his hands, scowling with murderous intent.

'And to *theirs*.'

Scaurus pointed at the men behind the soldiers, who were slowly but purposefully advancing with their axes and shovels ready to fight. Holding up a hand, he showed the Germans a nugget of gold the size of a man's eye, turning it in the air before his face to examine its rough surface as he continued speaking.

'Strange stuff, isn't it? It's just a yellow metal with no obvious benefit other than a certain cosmetic value and the fact that it's quite rare, and yet it seems that once a person possesses enough it changes them. Take your sister, for example. Even with the miners released and on the rampage she still insisted that two of the men you set to guard us carry a chest full of small nuggets and dust all the way up here. It's the last sweepings of the Alburnus Major strongroom, apparently, and just *too* precious to be left behind, even if you have got several cartloads of the stuff waiting for you on the other side of the mountain.'

He hefted a tightly woven bag the size of a grapefruit, licking his finger and dipping it into the bag through a slit cut in the top. Holding the digit up, he admired the glittering sparkle for a moment before rubbing the powder off with his other fingers and causing a cascade of flashing motes to drift to the tunnel's stone floor.

'This, apparently, is gold dust. I had a look at it earlier, and I have to say I was quite impressed. Imagine, a powder almost as fine as flour, and yet so very heavy. You know I saw this, and I thought of *you*. You, and my new friend Karsas here.'

He handed the bag to the silent miner, who nodded to the men around him and behind the Germans. The trap closed on Gerwulf and his men with sudden speed, the labourers to either side of them charging in with their tools raised for battle, over-whelming the bodyguards without regard for their swords. The

German saw his men fall under their frenzied attack, then reeled
as an axe handle hammered into his helmeted head. Staggering
against the passage's coarsely chiselled rock wall, he felt rough
hands tear the sword from his grip and pinion him tightly, forcing
him to his knees. A hand grabbed his hair and dragged his head
back, and another wrapped itself around his nose and mouth,
abruptly closing off his windpipe from the mine's cold air. Scaurus
strolled into his blurred vision, gesturing to the hard-faced
labourer beside him.

'So, as I was saying, the moment I clapped eyes on that bag
of precious dust, my thoughts immediately turned to the two of
you. You see, earlier this evening I promised Karsas here a chance
at taking revenge for Mus, and for his wife and family, and for all
of the innocents you murdered to keep your men fed and amused
while you were killing time waiting for your sister to call you in
to rob the Ravenstone. So I promised to help him if I could,
although I wasn't sure if the chance would ever even become a
reality, much less how he might go about it. Then, after we'd
taken your sister prisoner and while we were waiting for you, I
naturally mentioned the usual methods of which the empire is so
very fond, but that all seemed a little tedious for Karsas.'

Gerwulf was already feeling the need to breathe, a dull nagging
insistence in his chest for air.

'And, of course, I reflected that my good friend Clodius Albinus,
when he gets here in a week or so, might not really be all that
keen on a public execution. I have a feeling that this unpleasant-
ness will be brushed under the rug, you see, and crucifixions tend
to be a bit high profile for that sort of discreet house cleaning.
So I asked Karsas what he had in mind. He told me that he wasn't
really bothered, just as long as he got to look into your eyes as
you die. Yes, I've warned him that it's not half as satisfying as a
man imagines before the deed is done, but he does seem somewhat set on the idea – and who am I to refuse the request of a
man who's suffered so badly at your hands?'

The imperative to breathe was pounding in Gerwulf's chest
now, a rending ache that felt as if he were being turned inside

out. Scaurus's words were becoming more distant, seeming to echo down a long tunnel.

'And then I remembered to open the chest which Theodora had thought so important, and it provided instant inspiration. Why not make the punishment a fitting one? Why not take your life with the one thing you seem to have craved the most? Of course, we've both heard of men being killed with gold before, molten gold poured down the neck, stabbing with a golden blade – although Mithras knows how you could ever get the stuff to hold an edge – but I've never heard of this particular method before. I think you're going to be impressed. So . . .'

He gestured to the man behind the German, and as Gerwulf was on the very brink of passing out, his eyes rolling upwards and his body starting to go limp, the hand that was clamped over his mouth and nose was removed. Staring up into the remorseless eyes of the man who was about to kill him, and with no more control over the reaction than he had over his bowels, which had already voided themselves into his leggings, he sucked in a huge, gulping gasp of air that seemed to last a lifetime, filling his lungs with an involuntary groaning whoop. And as he breathed in, sucking the mine's frigid air deep into his body, the stone-faced miner upended the bag of gold dust onto his face and poured a torrent of the glittering powder down his gaping throat.

'I have to say it all sounds rather poetic, as justice goes. Did it take him long to die after that?'

Scaurus shook his head, taking a sip from the cup of wine Clodius Albinus had poured for him. The two men were alone in the legatus's office in the Apulum fortress, the door firmly closed and both clerk and guards dismissed to prevent the conversation being overheard.

'Not really, Legatus. He flopped about on the floor for a short time and then just stopped moving. It was all rather less dramatic than the whole scourge, crucify and dismember thing we'd have carried out under normal circumstances, but it seemed to work well enough for the men whose lives he'd ruined.'

The legatus sat back in his chair, steepling his fingers and considering the outcome.

'So to summarise, you freed the miners who then proceeded to tear first the German cohort and then everything else in the valley to pieces. How many of them died in the process?'

Scaurus took out his tablet, reading the small characters he had inscribed in the wax over the preceding days, as the extent of the mayhem wrought on the town of Alburnus Major by the liberated miners had become clear.

'From what we can gather about four hundred of them died overrunning the Germans, to judge from the bodies we found around their camp and the wall where Gerwulf had his men make their stand. I was expecting more men to have died there, but it seems that the mob was just too strong for them. Another three or four hundred men seem to have died in the fighting that broke out once they had their hands on the Germans' weapons, at which point most of them did the sensible thing and took to their heels. They came back soon enough though, once they got hungry. By the time my first spear marched up with the Tungrians, the miners were a sad, dispirited collection of men scratching for food in the ruins. It was just as well that I'd thought to tell him to bring a few cartloads of rations up the road from Apulum, or we'd have been fighting off starving men with our spears. We put them back to work repairing the damage, of course, and making sure that the mines didn't fall so far into disuse that they might become useless.'

Albinus took another sip of his wine.

'Excellent! I'm delighted to say that you've quite surpassed my expectations, Gaius. I was sorely afraid that I would have to send you home in disgrace in order to cover my own backside, and yet here you are having saved the situation, and what's even better, done so in an utterly deniable manner.' He looked up at the ceiling in thought for a moment. 'So let's see if I have a convincing narrative for my dispatch to the governor on the subject. After all, he won't want to be admitting the facts to Rome any more than I do. So, the sequence of events here was clearly that Procurator

Maximus mismanaged the mine owners, they in turn mistreated their workers, and the workers eventually rioted and killed both their masters and the procurator, tore the place to pieces and then realised the error of their ways. I sent you in to restore the peace, you conducted a vigorous process of pacification, during which you were forced to kill several hundred of the blighters in order to disarm them, and then several hundred more to emphasise the heavy hand of imperial justice. I think that will suffice to get the right heads nodding in reluctant approval. All the bodies were burned, I assume?'

Scaurus nodded.

'For reasons of public health. I felt it would be cleaner than a mass burial.'

'And, of course, leaves no evidence into which an imperial investigator might pry. Excellent!'

Scaurus raised an eyebrow.

'And the Germans, Legatus?'

'Were never here. I'll make sure that the mines' new owners are very clear that any resurfacing of this matter will only end badly for everyone involved, including them. The "Wolf" and his men will be written off as having fallen victim to one of the Sarmatae warbands during their brief but ill-favoured border disputes. I'll send Gerwulf's legatus a message to the effect that King Balodi confessed to their having overrun the Germans' camp in the early stages of the revolt. That should close the book on him once and for all, which is just as well. The last thing Rome needs is another blasted Varus legend to inspire the tribes on the other side of the Rhenus, wouldn't you say? And none of us wants to be associated with the loss of control over the emperor's most valuable asset, not when we can safely drop the blame on that idiot procurator. Which only leaves one last subject for discussion before we turn to thoughts of where you might take your men from here.'

'The gold, Legatus?'

'Indeed, Tribune. The gold.'

He sat back and waited for Scaurus to speak.

'We found enough of the stuff to load four heavy carts buried in the forest on the southern side of the Raven Head mountain, Legatus, and a stack of corpses nearby. Gerwulf had clearly worked out that there was an alternative entrance to the mine, and he used it to move the gold through the mountain to a place where it could be hidden by a few trusted men. According to the miners the transfer was carried out at night, when most of Gerwulf's cohort were asleep or guarding the miners. They used mine labour to do the hard work, promising the men their freedom in return for good behaviour, and simply killed them once the night's lifting and carrying was done.'

Albinus nodded his understanding through another sip of wine.

'He really was a crafty bugger, wasn't he? I'll bet his plan was to make a discreet exit one dark night, after killing every man who might bear witness to either his departure or the gold having come through the mine, and taking just enough men and gold with him to enable a quiet escape from justice. And then, when the excitement had died down in a year or two, he'd have quietly brought his men back and dug it up at his leisure.'

A thought occurred to the legatus.

'How did you find the stuff, if it was buried? Presumably there weren't any obvious giveaways?'

Scaurus smiled, as much to himself as to the man across the desk.

'Indeed, and Gerwulf's sister wasn't about to tell us, no matter what I threatened her with. It happens that I have an enterprising young centurion who seems to attract useful men, and he has a native tracker from Germania Inferior in his service, a man who can read ground as easily as you or I could read a scroll. He ran the hiding place to earth in a matter of hours simply by following their tracks, or so he told us. I suspect that his worship of a barbarian forest goddess may be some part of his secret, but I'm willing to tolerate it as long as he provides results like that.'

Albinus nodded sagely.

'Quite so. Pragmatism in all things, Gaius, we both know the value of that adage. So do you think we recovered *all* of the gold?'

He fixed the tribune with a steady gaze.

'I think so, Legatus, with the exception of the dust that was poured down Gerwulf's throat. And, of course, the relatively small amounts that I managed to slip into my cohorts' burial clubs.'

Albinus nodded beneficently.

'Well I won't begrudge you that, Tribune. Your men have paid in blood to take this valley, and in defence of the province for that matter, so the least we can do is ensure they have a decent send off. Let's just not have a rash of ostentatious altars springing up across the province though, or difficult questions may be asked. Who did you make responsible for counting the gold?'

'We're back to my centurion again. He has the most amazingly meticulous standard bearer who has counted every last coin and weighed every last nugget. Under the supervision of several of my officers, of course.'

He smiled inwardly, recalling the hawk-eyed attention with which Marcus and Dubnus had watched an increasingly frustrated Morban's every move while he counted the dead German's booty. The legatus nodded briskly.

'Excellent! I'll have the gold shipped down here as soon as I can, and in the meanwhile I'll have this standard bearer's records of the count, if you please. *All* of the records, Gaius. We don't want any contradictory numbers coming to light at a later date saying that there was more gold recovered than actually made its way to Rome.'

Scaurus looked at his mentor for a moment before nodding slowly.

'Yes, sir. *Pragmatism* in all things.'

Albinus raised an eyebrow at him.

'As I said before, quite so. I'll remind you that these are troubled days. We have an emperor on the throne who is little more than a puppet for the Praetorian Prefect, and the distinct possibility of a good deal more terror of the type that led to the murder of the Aquila brothers. You're familiar with the atrocity, I presume, a pair of trusted senators murdered on false charges of plotting against the throne simply to allow the *throne* to confiscate their wealth?'

Scaurus nodded.

More familiar than you'd imagine, Legatus.

'Well then, you'll understand that everyone with any public profile in Rome needs something tucked up their sleeve. And a box or two of that gold hidden away for a day when the wind blows hard is a precautionary opportunity I won't be passing up. And don't worry man; you'll be well looked after in the fullness of time.'

Realising that this would not be the wisest of moments in which to refuse his mentor's implicit offer, Scaurus nodded with a carefully blank face.

'Thank you, Legatus.'

'A wise choice, Gaius. And in that case, I'm very happy to inform you that I've had my clerk write a set of orders directing you to return to your home province as soon as you've been relieved from your duties at Alburnus Major. I've sent an order to the commander of the Danubius fleet that you're to be shipped as far upstream as the river is navigable and I'm sure your natural powers of persuasion, combined with orders from the governor, will get you some transport thereafter. You might be wise not to stop at Fortress Bonna though.'

Scaurus stood and saluted briskly.

'Thank you, Legatus. My men will be delighted, and I am forever in your de—'

Albinus raised his eyebrows in reproach, wrapping his protégée in a hug and slapping him firmly on the back before stepping back to regard him at arm's length.

'*Legatus?* To you, Gaius, I am simply Decimus, once your mentor and now simply your friend. Your *grateful* friend. And as to your men's delight at being sent home, just get them to make a modest offering at the temple in my name and I will be happy to bask in the favour of their gods.'

Scaurus bowed, his face set in a grateful expression.

'Thank you . . . Decimus. The temples of Alburnus Major will be littered with offerings to your name.'

He emptied his cup of the last dregs of wine, saluted again and was turning for the door when he remembered that he had one last question to ask the legatus. Turning back, he found the man waiting for his question with a knowing look, and he realised that he knew the answer without even having to ask.

'To be frank, Tribune, I couldn't care less what he does with the woman. You said yourself that she's the type a man can swiftly grow tired of, so perhaps he'll have her dealt with in a manner that befits her crime once she's greased his candle a few times? And besides, I can't bring myself to speak against the man who's just told you to take us all home.'

Scaurus sank wearily into his camp chair, taking the cup of wine that Julius was holding out to him.

'It seems that I'm surrounded by pragmatists today.' He raised the cup in salute, smiling gently at Julius's look of mystification. 'I mean realists, First Spear. And here's to realism. Since it seems I have little choice in the matter, I shall now put it from my mind. Now that I think about it, I seem to recall that Legatus Albinus, or Decimus, as I am instructed to call him now that I've played a key part in both enhancing his career and making him somewhat richer, never could keep his sausage tucked up safely beneath his tunic when there was a finely turned ankle in sight. And speaking of man's uncontrollable urges, I take it all these rumours I'm hearing about your woman being with child are true?'

The first spear nodded, a stupid smile creeping onto his face.

'Indeed they are, Tribune.'

'And will you be following your colleague's example in making an honest woman of the lady?'

Julius looked at Scaurus over the rim of his cup, watching as conflicting emotions played on his face.

'Not at this point, Tribune. We don't feel that it's necessary, and since it's still legally forbidden there seems to be little benefit to the child.'

The tribune took another sip.

'Very wise, First Spear. A sensible decision, given how hard some women find pregnancy . . .'

'His decision?' Felicia laughed out loud, a sound Marcus quickly decided he could do with hearing more. 'The way I heard it, she told him that given they're never having intimate relations again as long as she lives, marriage would be both superfluous and a waste of money.'

Marcus raised an eyebrow at his wife, whose cart had arrived in the Alburnus Major camp only an hour before.

'So she's not taking to pregnancy that well then?'

Felicia smiled at him, happy to see Appius clinging to the neck of his father's tunic and working his gums vigorously on a heavy gold pendant that hung around her husband's neck.

'Vomiting every morning, bilious for the rest of the day, and overcome with an inexplicable desire to eat raw onion. And if that's how she is after three months, then life's certainly going to be interesting for your colleague for the next six. What's that the baby's chewing on?'

Marcus looked down.

'It belonged to Carius Sigilis. I took it from his body out on the lake, after that battle on the ice. I promised Tribune Scaurus that I would return it to his father, if I ever get the chance.'

Felicia took the baby from him, gently easing the pendant from between his jaws.

'He likes the cold metal on his gums, I suppose. Watch out, by the way, he doesn't have any teeth yet but he can still nip hard enough to raise a bruise.' She looked at her husband with a gently raised eyebrow. 'Another dead friend, Marcus? How are you sleeping?'

His reply was unruffled, despite the unnerving accuracy of her question.

'Well enough, my love.'

Apart from the hour before dawn, when his father still haunted him with demands for retribution, frequently accompanied of late by the ghost of Lucius Carius Sigilis. While the senator simply berated his son to take revenge, the tribune's ghost was at the same time both silent and yet gorily persistent in his demands, simply scrawling the same words across whatever surface was to hand in the dream's context, writing with his fingers with the blood that ran from his wounds.

Felicia took his arm, pulling him close so that the baby was sandwiched between them.

'You do seem happier. Perhaps you just needed a few good fights to get whatever it was that was troubling you off your mind?'

He smiled back at her, musing on the havoc he intended to wreak if he ever got the opportunity to return to the city of his birth. Praetorian Prefect Perennis and the four men known to him only as 'The Emperor's Knives' were enough of a list for the time being, although he was sure that other names would come to light once he started working his way through the first five. His hand tensed on the dagger at his belt, the scarred skin over his knuckles tightening until the marks disappeared into the white flesh.

'Yes my love. Perhaps I did.'

HISTORICAL NOTE

As a historical people the Sarmatians are easily the equal of the Romans, with whom they interacted and frequently fought. Entering known history in the seventh century BC, they occupied the land to the east of the Don River and south of the Ural Mountains. Having lived in peace with their western neighbours the Scythians for several centuries, it was in the third century BC that this pattern abruptly changed. The Sarmatian tribes came across the Don and took on the Scythians, driving them off their pastures and establishing a new reign over this fertile land that was to last for centuries.

A nomadic people who largely lived off their herds, the several Sarmatian tribes – Roxolani, Iazyge, Aorsi, Siraces and Sauromatae – were tent dwellers whose young women, trained to fight along-side the men, are thought to have given rise to the legend of the Amazons. Hippocrates described how female Sarmatian babies were deliberately mutilated by the cauterisation of the right nipple, to inhibit growth of the breast so as to make the resulting adult female's right arm as strong as possible. The bulk of the Sarmatian forces tended to be light cavalry armed predominantly with bows, but just as the main battle tank tends to get most of the media attention on the modern battlefield, it was the more heavily armoured lancer, named by the Romans as the *contarius* for the three- to four-metre-long *contus* lance with which the rider was armed, that was the focus for the writers of the age. Manoeuvring in massed squadrons, Sarmatian heavy cavalry used the classic tactics of mounted shock to overcome their enemies, tactics which could only be matched by either superbly disciplined and trained heavy infantry, preferably armed with long spears and sheltered behind sharpened wooden stakes, or by highly mobile horse archers who could outpace their charge whilst peppering them with heavy-headed armour-piercing arrows.

By the first century AD the Iazyge were frequently engaging with the Roman Empire in the form of regular border incursions, often crossing the Danube in winter when the river's ice was sufficiently thick to support the weight of their horses and wagons. As the Sarmatian tribes leapt into the pages of history in a series of devastating attacks on their neighbours the Parthians, the Armenians and the Medians, the Iazyges laid waste to the Roman provinces of Pannonia and Moesia (the provinces that lay on the southern side of the Danube river) as they pushed up the Danube to occupy the Hungarian plain between the Dacian kingdom and Pannonia Inferior. In AD 92 they provided a portent of the danger that they were to present to the empire for centuries to come, combining with the German Quadi and Marcomanni tribes to destroy an entire Roman legion – Twenty-First Rapax (a name which meant 'Predator' and proved sadly unapt for this last action in their long history). During the same period the Roxolani made repeated raids into Moesia, and came to side with the Dacians in their wars with Rome, while the Iazyge were more closely aligned with the empire as its expansionary impulse led to a series of assaults on the powerful Dacian kingdom. When Dacia was eventually conquered by Trajan, placing a well-defended piece of imperial territory between the two tribes, the Romans astutely allowed them to maintain contact through the province, and paid generous subsidies to ensure peace. Nevertheless, the time was bound to come when this would no longer be sufficient.

So it was that the Iazyges once again joined forces with the German tribes in the Marcomannic wars of the 160s, taking the fight to a disease-weakened Roman army afresh in an alliance that was to last until a seemingly unmatched battle fought out on the frozen Danube. A dazzling Roman victory resulted – I did mention the efficacy of superbly disciplined and trained heavy infantry against the *contarius* – with 8,000 Iazyge horsemen being sent to serve in Britain as the price of failure. The uneasy peace that followed is the context for the fictional events described in *The Wolf's Gold*, based on Cassius Dio's report that two future contenders for the throne, Niger and Albinus, were instrumental in dealing with an Iazyge revolt early in Commodus's reign, ten years after the battle on the Danube. After this heavy defeat the Sarmatians were not to trouble Rome sufficiently for it to enter the surviving historical record for another fifty years, but they continued to harass the empire throughout the third century until increasingly pragmatic imperial policy made a virtue out of a necessity, and allowed several mass Sarmatian resettlements inside the empire's frontiers as a means of building a bulwark against the encroaching Goths. By the time of the *Notitia Dignitatum* (a documentary 'snapshot' of the Roman state's geography and organisation at the end of the fourth century), Sarmatian settlement throughout the northern empire was apparently commonplace, and Sarmatians rose to positions of power and influence as the western empire began to succumb to the pressures building upon its borders from the east. But that, as more than one of my historical fiction colleagues would tell you, is another story altogether.

One last (but important) point. As the regular reader will know, I present my stories against the background of documented history and set them in the authentic context of the empire's topography as much as is possible. When it comes to the names of the places I use, I do try to present an understandable version of the Latin place name wherever possible – where it can be translated straight into English and make sense. Hence – my usual example – Brocolitia on Hadrian's Wall becomes the wonderfully evocative Badger Holes. This isn't always possible, of course, since the Romans were great adopters of other people's ideas, weapons, tactics and yes, place names. Alburnus Major, Apulum, Porolissum and Napoca are all good examples of this, with their roots believed to lie in the names given to them by the tribes that founded the original settlements on which the Romans built their cities and fortresses. Just as the conquerors knew that allowing the locals to worship their own gods made for a happier subject population (as long as they recognised the emperor as the supreme deity), so it made sense to use the place name that was already in common usage. With this in mind, and where prudent to do so, I have stayed on the safe side and retained the Roman name by which we know these fortress settlements. On the other hand, where Roman forts are known to have existed but whose original names are unknown, I have felt free to come up with my own name for what would otherwise be an anonymous fort, and something of a blot on the narrative. As ever, in the event that my research is proven to be at fault, I will be eternally grateful for any clarification that any reader can offer.

THE ROMAN ARMY IN 182 AD

By the late second century, the point at which the *Empire* series begins, the Imperial Roman Army had long since evolved into a stable organization with a stable *modus operandi*. Thirty or so **legions** (there's still some debate about the 9th Legion's fate), each with an official strength of 5,500 legionaries, formed the army's 165,000-man heavy infantry backbone, while 360 or so **auxiliary cohorts** (each of them the equivalent of a 600-man infantry battalion) provided another 217,000 soldiers for the empire's defence.

Positioned mainly in the empire's border provinces, these forces performed two main tasks. Whilst ostensibly providing a strong means of defence against external attack, their role was just as much about maintaining Roman rule in the most challenging of the empire's subject territories. It was no coincidence that the troublesome provinces of Britain and Dacia were deemed to require 60 and 44 auxiliary cohorts respectively, almost a quarter of the total available. It should be noted, however, that whilst their overall strategic task was the same, the terms under the two halves of the army served were quite different.

The legions, the primary Roman military unit for conducting warfare at the operational or theatre level, had been in existence since early in the Republic, hundreds of years before. They were composed mainly of close-order heavy infantry, well-drilled and highly motivated, recruited on a professional basis and, critically to an understanding of their place in Roman society, manned by soldiers who were Roman citizens. The jobless poor were thus provided with a route to both citizenship and a valuable trade, since service with the legions was as much about construction – fortresses, roads, and even major defensive works such as Hadrian's

THE CHAIN OF COMMAND
LEGION

LEGATUS — LEGION
CAVALRY
(120 HORSEMEN)

BROAD STRIPE
TRIBUNE

5 'MILITARY'
NARROW
STRIPE
TRIBUNES

CAMP PREFECT

SENIOR CENTURION

10 COHORTS
(ONE OF 5 CENTURIES OF 160 MEN EACH)
(NINE OF 6 CENTURIES OF 80 MEN EACH)

CENTURION

CHOSEN MAN

WATCH OFFICER   STANDARD BEARER

10 TENT PARTIES OF
8 MEN APIECE

The Chain of Command
Auxilary Infantry Cohort

Legatus

Prefect

(or a Tribune for a larger cohort such as
the First Tungrian)

Senior Centurion

6-10 Centuries

Centurion

Chosen Man

Watch Officer   Standard Bearer

10 tent parties of
8 men apiece

Wall – as destruction. Vitally for the maintenance of the empire's borders, this attractiveness of service made a large standing field army a possibility, and allowed for both the control and defence of the conquered territories.

By this point in Britannia's history three legions were positioned to control the restive peoples both beyond and behind the province's borders. These were the 2nd, based in South Wales, the 20th, watching North Wales, and the 6th, positioned to the east of the Pennine range and ready to respond to any trouble on the northern frontier. Each of these legions was commanded by a **legatus**, an experienced man of senatorial rank deemed worthy of the responsibility and appointed by the emperor. The command structure beneath the legatus was a delicate balance, combining the requirement for training and advancing Rome's young aristocrats for their future roles with the necessity for the legion to be led into battle by experienced and hardened officers.

Directly beneath the legatus were a half-dozen or so **military tribunes**, one of them a young man of the senatorial class called the **broad stripe tribune** after the broad senatorial stripe on his tunic. This relatively inexperienced man – it would have been his first official position – acted as the legion's second-in-command, despite being a relatively tender age when compared with the men around him. The remainder of the military tribunes were **narrow stripes**, men of the equestrian class who usually already had some command experience under their belts from leading an auxiliary cohort. Intriguingly, since the more experienced narrow-stripe tribunes effectively reported to the broad stripe, such a reversal of the usual military conventions around fitness for command must have made for some interesting man-management situations. The legion's third in command was the camp **prefect**, an older and more experienced soldier, usually a former centurion deemed worthy of one last role in the legion's service before retirement, usually for one year. He would by necessity have been a steady hand, operating as the voice of experience in advising the legion's senior officers as to the realities of warfare and the management of the legion's soldiers.

Reporting into this command structure were ten **cohorts** of soldiers, each one composed of a number of eighty-man **centuries**. Each century was a collection of ten **tent parties** – eight men who literally shared a tent when out in the field. Nine of the cohorts had six centuries, and an establishment strength of 480 men, whilst the prestigious **first cohort**, commanded by the legion's **senior centurion**, was composed of five double-strength centuries and therefore fielded 800 soldiers when fully manned. This organization provided the legion with its cutting edge: 5,000 or so well-trained heavy infantrymen operating in regiment and company sized units, and led by battle-hardened officers, the legion's centurions, men whose position was usually achieved by dint of their demonstrated leadership skills.

The rank of **centurion** was pretty much the peak of achievement for an ambitious soldier, commanding an eighty-man century and paid ten times as much as the men each officer commanded. Whilst the majority of centurions were promoted from the ranks, some were appointed from above as a result of patronage, or as a result of having completed their service in the **Praetorian Guard**, which had a shorter period of service than the legions. That these externally imposed centurions would have undergone their very own 'sink or swim' moment in dealing with their new colleagues is an unavoidable conclusion, for the role was one that by necessity led from the front, and as a result suffered disproportionate casualties. This makes it highly likely that any such appointee felt unlikely to make the grade in action would have received very short shrift from his brother officers.

A small but necessarily effective team reported to the centurion. The **optio**, literally 'best' or **chosen man**, was his second-in-command, and stood behind the century in action with a long brass-knobbed stick, literally pushing the soldiers into the fight should the need arise. This seems to have been a remarkably efficient way of managing a large body of men, given the centurion's place alongside rather than behind his soldiers, and the optio would have been a cool head, paid twice the usual soldier's wage and a candidate for promotion to centurion if he performed well. The century's third-in-command was the **tesserarius** or **watch officer**, ostensibly charged with ensuring that sentries were posted and that everyone know the watch word for the day, but also likely to have been responsible for the profusion of tasks such as checking the soldiers' weapons and equipment, ensuring the maintenance of discipline and so on, that have occupied the lives of junior non-commissioned officers throughout history in delivering a combat-effective unit to their officer. The last member of the centurion's team was the century's **signifer**, the **standard bearer**, who both provided a rallying point for the soldiers and helped the centurion by transmitting marching orders to them through movements of his standard. Interestingly, he also functioned as the century's banker, dealing with the soldiers' financial affairs. While a soldier caught in the horror of battle might have thought twice about defending his unit's standard, he might well also have felt a stronger attachment to the man who managed his money for him!

At the shop-floor level were the eight soldiers of the tent party who shared a leather tent and messed together, their tent and cooking gear carried on a mule when the legion was on the march. Each tent party would inevitably have established its own pecking order based upon the time-honoured factors of strength, aggression, intelligence – and the rough humour required to survive in such a harsh world. The men that came to dominate their tent parties would have been the century's unofficial backbone, candidates for promotion to watch officer. They would also have been vital to their tent mates' cohesion under battlefield conditions, when the relatively thin leadership team could not always exert sufficient presence to inspire the individual soldier to stand and fight amid the horrific chaos of combat.

The other element of the legion was a small 120-man detachment of **cavalry**, used for scouting and the carrying of messages between units. The regular army depended on auxiliary **cavalry wings**, drawn from those parts of the empire where horsemanship was a way of life, for their mounted combat arm. Which leads us to consider the other side of the army's two-tier system.

The **auxiliary cohorts**, unlike the legions alongside which they fought, were not Roman citizens, although the completion of a twenty-five-year term of service did grant both the soldier and his children citizenship. The original auxiliary cohorts had often served in their homelands, as a means of controlling the threat of large numbers of freshly conquered barbarian warriors, but this changed after the events of the first century AD. The Batavian revolt in particular – when the 5,000-strong Batavian cohorts rebelled and destroyed two Roman legions after suffering intolerable provocation during a recruiting campaign gone wrong – was the spur for the Flavian policy for these cohorts to be posted away from their home provinces. The last thing any Roman general wanted was to find his legions facing an army equipped and trained to fight in the same way. This is why the reader will find the auxiliary cohorts described in the *Empire* series, true to the historical record, representing a variety of other parts of the empire, including Tungria, which is now part of modern-day Belgium.

Auxiliary infantry was equipped and organized in so close a manner to the legions that the casual observer would have been hard put to spot the differences. Often their armour would be mail, rather than plate, sometimes weapons would have minor differences, but in most respects an auxiliary cohort would be the same proposition to an enemy as a legion cohort. Indeed there are hints from history that the auxiliaries may have presented a greater challenge on the battlefield. At the battle of Mons Graupius in Scotland, Tacitus records that four cohorts of Batavians and two of Tungrians were sent in ahead of the legions and managed to defeat the enemy without requiring any significant assistance. Auxiliary cohorts were also often used on the flanks of the battle line, where reliable and well drilled troops are essential to handle attempts to outflank the army. And while the legions contained soldiers who were as much tradesmen as fighting men, the auxiliary cohorts were primarily focused on their fighting skills. By the end of the second century there were significantly more auxiliary troops serving the empire than were available from the legions, and it is clear that Hadrian's Wall would have been invalid as a concept without the mass of infantry and mixed infantry/ cavalry cohorts that were stationed along its length.

As for horsemen, the importance of the empire's 75,000 or so **auxiliary cavalrymen**, capable of much faster deployment and manoeuvre than the infantry, and essential for successful scouting, fast communications and the denial of reconnaissance information to the enemy cannot be overstated. Rome simply did not produce anything like the strength in mounted troops needed to avoid being at a serious disadvantage against those nations which by their nature were cavalry-rich. As a result, as each such nation was conquered their mounted forces were swiftly incorporated into the army until, by the early first century BC, the decision was made to disband what native Roman cavalry as there was altogether, in favour of the auxiliary cavalry wings.

Named for their usual place on the battlefield, on the flanks or 'wings' of the line of battle, the cavalry cohorts were commanded by men of the equestrian class with prior experience as legion military tribunes, and were organized around the basic 32-man **turma**, or squadron. Each squadron was commanded by a **decurion**, a position analogous with that of the infantry centurion. This officer was assisted by a pair of junior officers: the **duplicarius** or **double-pay**, equivalent to the role of optio, and the **sesquipilarius** or **pay-and-a-half**, equal in stature to the infantry watch officer. As befitted the cavalry's more important military role, each of these ranks was paid about 40 per cent more than the infantry equivalent.

Taken together, the legions and their auxiliary support presented a standing army of over 400,000 men by the time of the events described in the *Empire* series. Whilst this was sufficient to both hold down and defend the empire's 6.5 million square kilometres for a long period of history, the strains of defending a 5,000-kilometre-long frontier, beset on all sides by hostile tribes, were also beginning to manifest themselves. The prompt move to raise three new legions undertaken by the new emperor Septimius Severus in 197 AD, in readiness for over a decade spent shoring up the empire's crumbling borders, provides clear evidence that there were never enough legions and cohorts for such a monumental task. This is the backdrop for the *Empire* series, which will run from 182 AD well into the early third century, following both the empire's and Marcus Valerius Aquila's travails throughout this fascinatingly brutal period of history.